CW00661656

BLOODSTONE'S FURY

Jake Jacobs

HIGH
WOOD

This book is a work of fiction and, except in case of historical fact, any resemblance to actual persons, living or dead, is purely coincidental.

First published in Great Britain in 2023 by High Wood Books

Copyright © Jake Jacobs 2023

Jake Jacobs asserts the moral right to be identified as the author of this work

A catalogue record for this book is available from the British Library

ISBN: 978 1 7393068 0 9

All rights reserved. No part of this publication may be reproduced, stored in a retrieval system, or transmitted, in any form or by any means, electronic, mechanical, photocopying, recording or otherwise, without the prior written permission of both the copyright owner and the above publisher of the book.

enquiries@highwoodbooks.com

For Avelaina and Horatio. May you never see such things.
And in loving memory of Bill, Ray and Ron, who did.

CHAPTER ONE

It was a typical dockside pub; smoky, stinking and no different to thousands of others that peppered the coastal towns and cities of wartime Britain. And, just like most of them, it was a dump.

The once-white ceiling was stained a filthy yellow from fifty years of pipe smoke and the paint on the walls was cracked and peeling. A thick fog of tobacco filled the room, making it barely possible to see further than a few yards, and the stench of sweat, cigarettes and stale beer wafted through the fetid air.

An enormous crack, large enough to give any structural engineer a heart attack, snaked its way up one wall from floor to ceiling and was a grim reminder of a Luftwaffe bomb that had annihilated a nearby row of terraces houses just a few days before. On the opposite side of the room hung a painting of a three-masted sailing ship, which, thanks to the blast of the Heinkel's thousand-pounder, now sat dangerously skewwhiff.

Scattered across the space between the crack and the painting were a dozen tables, each surrounded by a motley assortment of chairs and stools, while a brass-topped bar took pride of place against one wall. Upon one end of the bar stood an ancient bust of Admiral Lord Nelson, minus the nose, and the great man himself would undoubtedly have been appalled at the collection of drunkards and degenerates that were shouting to make themselves heard over the wail of a crackling gramophone record.

At one table sat a hunchbacked old woman, whose thick make-up was unable to hide her wrinkled skin or the sprouting whiskers of her top lip. Blind to the woman's ugliness and about to make the biggest mistake of his life, an inebriated infantryman, not more than nineteen years old, caressed her bony thigh with his hand.

A gaggle of bell-bottomed sailors watched on in amusement from a nearby table, their hands clutched around half-drunk pints of ale and cigarettes protruding from the corners of their mouths. Their white collars were stained with the remnants of beer, rum and, in the case of one, what appeared to be vomit.

Seated at the head of the table and holding court over the seamen was an enormous petty officer, with sleeves rolled up above bulging forearms that bore an inked tapestry of anchors, swallows and sea creatures. His long-ago broken nose was squashed almost flat and his thick lips were fixed in a cruel smirk that told the world exactly what he was; a bully of the finest ilk.

The smirk widened as he took a last suck on a cigarette, plucked it from his mouth and, with thumb and forefinger, flicked it in the direction of the young solider. The butt catapulted through the air but missed its target by a hair's breadth, bouncing instead off the greasy head of the old woman and coming to rest on the floor. The infantryman, still stroking her thigh, was oblivious to the incoming missile, while the woman glanced briefly in her assailant's direction before returning her gaze to the boy at her side.

Encouraged by the guffaws of his cronies, the big man tried again.

"Oi, nipper," he bellowed in the direction of the mismatched couple, "You makes me sick."

Another titter of laughter from his crewmates.

"I said you makes me sick, pawing a pox-ridden creature like that, you should be fuckin' embarrassed, son."

Still the pair ignored him, one drunkenly oblivious to the goings-on around him and the other simply wise enough to stay quiet.

Enraged by the lack of reaction, the petty officer shoved back his chair and pulled himself to his full towering height, dwarfing his comrades as he glowered in the direction of his victims with a face like thunder.

"I said," he repeated, taking a step across the pub, "You makes me..."

"I say, sailor, show some respect," slurred a plummy voice from behind, stopping the giant in his tracks.

He twisted his meaty neck around, his face almost purple as he glowered through the smoky air in search of the fool that had dared to interrupt him. He found him in seconds, sitting on a barstool next to the noseless bust of Lord Nelson and swaying slightly. A half-drunk glass of whisky was in one hand and the other clutched the bar as if he'd tumble from his perch if he lost his grip.

One look was enough to see that the man didn't fit in among the rogues, criminals and assorted dregs of society that were boozing away their Saturday night just a stone's throw from the dockyard gates. Because this was no place for a gentleman, and a gentleman he most certainly was. And handsome too, infuriatingly so, almost as if he'd wandered straight out of a film set and plonked himself down in this grubby Portsmouth pub.

His hair was a mane of neat black locks, perfectly parted on one side, and his young suntanned face possessed a chiselled jawline and a pair of dimples that hinted at some sort of devilment deep within. A fashionable and flawlessly trimmed moustache sat astride a mouth containing two rows of the pearliest of pearly whites, while a pair of eyes the colour of sapphire twinkled through the tobacco-laden fog.

It was the sort of face that the girls went wild for, so it was an undeniable shame when the sailor's well-aimed and monstrous fist landed plum in the centre of the handsome head. It squished the nose like a ripe tomato and dislodged one of the perfect teeth so that it tumbled to the floor to rest amid a scattering of weeks-old cigarette butts, spilt beer and broken glass.

It was to the same floor that, moments later, the tooth's owner followed, dead to the world and with his head coming to rest in the filth. Blood seeped from the freshly broken nose and the tiniest trail of whisky-sodden saliva dribbled onto the still impeccably manicured moustache.

The petty officer flexed his giant fingers, flicked a speck of blood from the back of his hand and looked down at the figure slumped on the ground.

"*You* show some respect, sonny."

CHAPTER TWO

He awoke with a shudder, his head thumping like a freight train and an ominous taste of blood and snot in his mouth. His nose throbbed hellishly and his throat felt like it hadn't seen a drop of moisture in a lifetime, which, ironically, couldn't have been further from the truth. He opened one eye, the daylight instantly burning through his iris and into the very core of his brain, and quickly thought better of it, instead choosing the ever so slight peace of darkness.

Flailing his arm out to his left, he found a bedside chest of drawers and scrabbled his fingers across the top, locating a mercifully full glass of liquid, which he proceeded to tip down his parched throat in one swift movement. The foul and unexpected taste of still-warm urine hit the back of his gullet like fire, causing him to sit bolt upright in bed and vomit a rancid cocktail of last night's booze and his own bodily fluids across the entirety of his naked self.

"BARNABY!" he yelled, "Why in God's name is there a pint of piss in here? What's wrong with you, man? Trying to poison me?"

"I think you nearly managed that yourself last night, sir, if you don't mind me saying so," the elderly gentleman in a perfectly tailored butler's suit said as he appeared at the bedroom door with a glass of water in one hand and a towel in the other.

"What the devil are you blathering about?" the vomit-covered man demanded with a pathetic flap of his hand. "Quickly now, towel. And eggs, bloody big ones like we used to have before that blabbering fool Adolf escaped from the funny farm."

With a nod to acknowledge the naked man's breakfast order, Barnaby handed his master the towel and glass and stooped to pick up the remnants of clothing that were strewn across the floor. Khaki pantaloons, silk underpants and a crumpled beret all found their way into his arms before being rolled expertly into a ball and disappearing from sight. Next, he stooped to recover a bloodstained army issue shirt, straightening an epaulette that displayed the twin pips of a major, before he brushed at the row of medal ribbons that would have been a dazzling display of colour had they not been stained with beer, blood and God alone knew what else.

The sight of those ribbons brought a rueful smile to the old man's face as he wondered at whatever madcap escapade had resulted in one of the finest chestfuls of medals in the entire Allied forces lying soiled on the floor, while the owner of said decorations sprawled butt naked and stinking like a latrine just a few feet away.

Major Albert Beaumont Fortescue Bloodstone, DSO, DSC and MC with bar, forced his eyes open, groaned deeply and attempted to raise himself from the remnants of his soiled bed.

"It must have been a rare night," he mused through swollen lips.

"The last thing I remember was gallivanting down Queen's Street with Jones. We were on the prowl for that gorgeous creature that used to pull pints at the Trafalgar, you know the one, redhead, bumps in all the right places. Damned fine filly."

"Can't say I do, sir," the laundry-laden Barnaby replied, searching in vain for a lost sock.

"We thought we spied her inside the Admiral so popped in for a snifter. Turned out it wasn't her at all, just a gaggle of bloody Jack Tars and an old hag flogging cockles. Damned bad luck."

"So it seems, sir," the white-haired man mumbled, the lost sock now retrieved from a particularly putrid pool of vomit and carefully deposited with the rest of the laundry.

"That reprobate Captain Jones carried you in here at midnight, face looking like you'd been ten rounds with John Shaw and babbling all sorts of drivel. Apparently you'd been ticking off a boatload of sailors who didn't take too kindly to you interfering in their fun and games. It sounds to me like a miracle he got you out of there alive. You really shouldn't be frequenting the likes of the Admiral, sir, war hero or no war hero."

Another groan was all that came in response to the thinly veiled ticking-off as Bloodstone dragged his naked self across to the nightstand and squinted into the mirror to assess the swollen mess that only eight hours before had been a fine example of a nose.

"Bloody shambles those matelots made of this honk, eh Barnaby?" he growled, tenderly prodding the offending protrusion that now pointed towards the left side of his face, with a kink of almighty proportions betraying the broken bone.

"Indeed, sir," the manservant responded, "We'll have to get you off to the MO before it sets like that for good. I doubt your strawberry-haired lady would look twice at you with a crooked face piece like that."

"Balderdash!" the still-naked Bloodstone scoffed, "No bloody maniac surgeon's going to get his filthy paws on me. A spot of DIY is what's needed, no time for faffing about, breakfast can wait. Find me two chopsticks, a pair of pliers and a slug of whisky. Scotch, strong, this is going to hurt like the devil."

Resigned to the fact that there was little point trying to talk sense into his charge, Barnaby shuffled off to source the necessary equipment and returned fully laden a few minutes later to find the Major propped in a chair with a towel finally covering his nether regions.

"A Chinese trick I saw in the Orient back in '38," Bloodstone offered in explanation as he took the chopsticks.

7

"Jock artillery chap had got his snout into all sorts of mess in a particularly fruity game of mess rugger. Buggered the chandeliers up something rotten too. The Adj nearly had our guts for garters. Good times, eh?"

"It sounds splendid, sir," Barnaby half-heartedly agreed, before the chopstick-holding major continued with his tale.

"Anyway, local mess fellow says he's got the solution, shoves two sticks up the gunner's nose, quick crunch of the pincers and hey presto, damned thing was straighter than Cupid's arrow. Poor chap snuffed it the next day, mind you, although apparently entirely unrelated. Shard of chandelier in his ear, the doc reckoned, poked its way into his brain when he was trying to scale the barracks roof after too much grog. Damned unlucky way to go."

Barnaby shook his head in consternation while his towel-clad master laid out his plans for the forthcoming operation.

"I'll do the sticks and you can do the pincers. When I give the nod just grab that broken bugger of a bone and yank it into place. And be ready with a rag, this is going to bleed like a stuck pig."

With that, Bloodstone took a giant swig from the bottle of Scotch, grasped the first chopstick and shoved it pointy end first into his left nostril. The second followed into his right a second later, gouging its way through blood, snot and gristle as he forced it a full two inches up his protesting nasal cavity. The broken bone grated horribly as he grasped the protruding end of both chopsticks and gave them a swift twist to the right, bringing the shattered bone into some semblance of shape.

"Now!" he rasped through clenched teeth and Barnaby obediently gripped the point where the two ends of broken bone met and squished once with the pliers.

The cartilage and bone were crunched together into perfect unison and resulted in an almighty torrent of blood that cascaded from the tortured nose and flowed into the moustache and down onto the major's chest. With slippery hands, Bloodstone gently withdrew the Chinese eating implements from his newly straightened nose, took another gulp from the bottle and slumped back in the chair with satisfied grunt.

"That's how you fix a hangover, eh Barnaby?" he laughed, the delight that the homemade surgery had returned his face to something close to its normal symmetry making him ambivalent to the pain that throbbed through his head.

"And what about the missing tooth, sir?"

"Even Chinese nosh sticks and a rusty pair of pliers can't fix that," Bloodstone responded, eyeing the gap in his teeth in the mirror.

"Gives me a roguish look, don't you think? No doubt it'll help snare a piece of crumpet or two. Can't be a war hero and not have a few scars is what I say. And anyway, Uncle Willy's sister's latest fancy is one of the finest toothsmiths in all of London from what I hear. I'll pay him a visit sometime."

"Probably sensible," Barnaby agreed, "I wouldn't want to see you trying to fix your own teeth, which I wouldn't put past you, sir."

"Ha, you're a damn scoundrel," the major scalded with a laugh, "But what would I do without you, eh Barnaby? Now how about that breakfast? And remember, bloody big eggs. I think I'm going to need them; I've a feeling that the fun is well and truly about to come to an end."

CHAPTER THREE

Four hours later, soaped, bathed and fed, Albert Bloodstone bounded up the steps of Whitehall's War Office, dressed to the nines in the crisply laundered uniform of an army major, the badge of the Parachute Regiment adorning his maroon beret and two purpling eyes and a swollen nose the only evidence of the previous night's miscreancy.

His paratrooper's boots, buffed to perfection, clip-clopped on the marble floor as he strode through the entrance hallway and presented himself to a harassed-looking clerk, pausing on the way only to return the hasty salute of a gaggle of junior naval officers who looked barely old enough to tie their own bootlaces, let alone don His Majesty's uniform.

"Bloodstone, to see General Wilkins," he announced to the clerk, noticing an inordinate and precarious pile of papers at the man's elbow, the very height of which defied all rules of physics.

"Very good, sir," the clerk replied, glancing at yet another piece of paper and running his ink-stained finger down a neatly typed list.

"General Wilkins, ah yes, down the corridor on your right, take the stairs, follow the left-hand corridor and then it'll be the fifth door on the right, opposite the WAAF Activities Office. May I suggest you knock loudly, sir."

Thanking the clerk, Bloodstone set about navigating the myriad of stairways and corridors of one of London's most famous buildings, amusing himself by wondering exactly what activities the Women's Auxiliary Air Force were engaged in across the hallway from the general's office. His meandering mind came to an abrupt halt, however, as he arrived at his destination at exactly the same time as a severe-looking middle aged woman emerged from the door opposite, her blue uniform stretched violently across her ample bosoms and large belly.

Brought back to his senses with a bang, Bloodstone rapped on a door displaying a bronze plate with the general's name and waited to be summoned inside. After a half-minute and no answer, he tried again, this time with enough force to shake the solid oak door from its hinges.

"Enter," boomed a voice from within and Bloodstone pushed the handle and stepped inside, closing the door behind him and coming to attention in front of the General's desk with a crisp salute and a back as straight as a ramrod.

The officer who rose from behind the desk to return the salute was the thing of a child's nightmare. An absolute beast of a man, standing over six and a half feet tall, well into his sixties and sporting a balding crop of snow-white hair below his army cap; to look at General Wilkins was to see war personified in all its true horror. One ear was missing, as was an eye, a leg, one arm and two fingers on the remaining hand. A vicious scar ran horizontally from hairline to top lip, dissecting the empty eye socket that was now a puckered mass of scar tissue, while the left side of the head was a morass of long-healed burns punctuated by a single hole that was all that remained of the missing ear.

Wilkins gestured to a chair in front of his desk and Bloodstone sat, as always feeling dwarfed by the sheer size of the elderly general.

"Good to see you again, Bloodstone," the old man greeted, "Although it looks like you've been in the wars again, what?"

Bloodstone thought that a little rich, especially coming from a man whose mangled appearance was known to be the result of a howitzer shell that had left his shattered body abandoned in a Passchendaele shell hole for five excruciatingly long rat-infested days.

"Yes, sir, walked into a door on leave," he agreed, choosing not to notice the amused look on the General's face and the accusing rise of the man's one good eyebrow.

"No doubt," the superior officer continued, "Although I wouldn't blame you for blowing off a little steam on leave after that last show you put on. Jerry's going to be picking up the pieces for a long time to come thanks to the hiding you gave him.

"Bloody Bertie I hear they're calling you now, is that right? Mugshot on the front page of the Times, nice promotion, shiny new gong from His Maj, price on your head from old Adolf himself. Jolly good show is what I say. Nothing like a good war and a spot of maniac bloodletting to raise one's share price."

"I just happened to be there, sir, it was the chaps that did the real hard work," Bloodstone responded, trying and failing not to picture the familiar faces of his fellow Red Devils who now lay six feet under the Italian soil.

"Gibberish!" Wilkins exclaimed, "Although nothing wrong with a little modesty if used sparingly now and then. Good quality, yes. But it doesn't hurt to blow one's own trumpet occasionally, too. The older you get the less likely you are to find others willing to blow it for you. You remember that, young man."

Bloodstone agreed that he would, silently musing to himself that, for him, the war had provided an unexpected number of people more than willing to put a spot of puff into his trumpet. In fact, his trumpet had never been more blown in his life than it had in the three and a half years since the war had broken out, which, he reasoned, probably had something to do with why he'd been ordered to see the General today.

"You're probably wondering why you've been ordered to see me today," the General continued. "No doubt you're jolly keen to get back to the regiment and crack on with this godforsaken shambles of a war?"

"Yes, sir. A week of leave, some sea air and I'm ready to get back to it. It'll be good to see the boys again. No doubt they've got slack while I've been away. I'll soon thrash that out of the blighters, sir."

"No doubt, no doubt," the elderly general agreed with a smile, tapping his three remaining fingers on the desktop, before continuing, "So it sounds like I'm about to do your fellows something of a favour, Bloodstone, although I'm sure you're going to disagree. You see, we've got some quite special orders for you here.

"Not your usual cup of tea this one, less blood and thunder than you're used to and slightly more spit and polish. But there's a war on and we must all do our bit, especially when it's come from the top as this one has. And when I say top, Bloodstone, I mean top. Winston himself has had his fingers in this particular pie."

Images of monotonous guard duty and endless hours of driving a desk flashed through the major's brain, a far cry from the dangerous action he was used to and had discovered that, not only did he enjoy, but seemingly had a rare talent for. None of that showed on his face, of course, the years of military discipline deeply ingrained. Orders were orders and he'd have to lump it, like it or not and no matter how dull or depressing the task turned out to be.

"Operation Bumblebee," the General announced, "And don't ask me why it's called that. In my day they had proper names. Operation Spartacus, Operation Flaming Sword, Operation Smash the Hun. Anyway, I digress.

"Now, the aim of this one is to give the good old hard-working British populace a damned fine bit of fire in their belly and a reason to keep buggering on despite the lack of proper tea and the bloody miserable casualty lists. One can publish as much good news in the newspapers as one wants but the days of the common man believing the tosh that their betters are feeding them are long gone. They need to see it for themselves, they need to believe it. Damn it, Bloodstone, they need to taste it with their own parched tongues, hear it with their own Blitz-battered ears. Which is where you come in."

"Me, sir?"

"Yes, you. A good old-fashioned war hero. A dashing knight returning from battle with the severed heads of the murderous Boche bouncing from your saddle. Golden haired maidens throwing themselves at your feet for saving them from being rogered senseless by a panzer full of black shirts. You're just what we need to keep those spirits up and show them that this filthy war is ours for the winning."

"I'm not sure what I can do, sir, apart from keep giving Jerry a bloody nose with the regiment."

"Nonsense man!" Wilkins exclaimed, jumping to his foot and slamming his hand on the table with a speed and agility that belied the fact that he was a man missing fifty percent of his full complement of arms and legs.

"War's become clever," he continued. "It's no longer just about being able to poke your spear into the other poor fellow before he can poke his into you. The boffins are taking over, whether it's bouncing bombs or code machines or psychobabble, things are changing, Bloodstone. It's a damned shame for good old warriors like us but you evolve or you die. Luckily a busted up old chap like me doesn't have to change, but a sprightly young thing like you has no choice."

"But what does all that have to do with me, sir?" Bloodstone asked, remaining in his chair as the monstrous general towered over him.

"Simple," he replied, "You're to become the face of the Allied victory. Thanks to that stunt you pulled off in Italy there's not a man, woman or child in the entire civilised world who doesn't know the face of Albert Bloodstone. The newspapers plastering you across the front pages and that idiotic footage of the Fuhrer tearing up your photograph are to thank for that.

"So, the powers that be have decided to make you a film star."

"A film star?"

"That's what I said and stop staring at me like I'm a lunatic. For the next three months you'll be appearing in every picture house from here to Timbuktu, once a week, regular as clockwork, that glorious face of yours telling every Tom, Dick and Harry how we're winning the war bit by bit. How we're giving the Hun a taste of his own medicine and how we're slowly but surely battering him back to the fetid hovel from whence he came.

"Nobody believes a crusty old civvy but, by Jove, they'll get their knickers in a twist for you, Bloodstone."

"But I've never even seen a film camera, sir," the confused Bloodstone remonstrated.

"Details, details," the old man scoffed, sitting back behind his desk. "You don't need to worry about that. They've got you the very best in the business apparently. Camera chap with top-notch kit, producer fellow recently back from Hollywood and even a make-up girl to make you look remotely palatable. No expense spared on this one.

"All you need to do is stand in front of the camera every week and tell Joe Public how fabulously we're doing. Your little crew will do the rest and, hey presto, it'll be whizzing its way across our theatre screens a few days later just as our brave boys and girls settle down to watch whatever the latest soppy drivel is that's on the evening's schedule."

"Roger, sir, understood," nodded Blackstone, not sure that he really did understand.

"Like you say, sir, not my usual cup of tea but be assured I'll give it my best shot," he continued as he gave his tender nose a gentle once over with the fingers of his right hand.

"One question though, sir, where am I to be based for this one? Here in London or back at regimental HQ?"

"Ah, good question," the General said, peering closely at a piece of paper in his maimed hand before continuing, "RAF Scapton, according to these orders. Or is it Scampton? Or Scumpton? Some such place anyhow. Bloody illiterate clerks need to learn their letters I say."

"RAF, sir?" Blackstone asked with a quizzical look, "Is it some sort of special ops base we're borrowing from the Crabs?"

"Not quite," Wilkins replied. "It's home to our esteemed friends of 513 Squadron, part of Five Group, Bomber Command. A Lancaster set-up run by a rogue called Wingco Grubb; quite a reputation apparently. He and his poor fellows are dragging themselves out three miles high over Germany every night and unleashing hell on the Hun from the heavens. Sounds damned dangerous to me and I'd rather fight with mud on my boots any time, but it's giving old Jerry a serious headache so it must be working."

Noticing that Bloodstone's swollen face was looking a little confused, the general cleared his throat and continued.

"You're probably wondering why a good old one hundred percent through-and-through Army chap like yourself is off to shack up with the Brylcreem Boys," he said, fixing Bloodstone with his one eye. "Well, I'll tell you."

"You see, despite all the good news about what we've been doing down in Italy these last few months and of course your humdinger of a show out there, the truth is that things aren't going too well elsewhere. The invasion looks like it's still a good year or so away and we've not really got much else to bang the drum about.

"The sad reality is that one of the only ways we can keep the pressure up on Adolf and his nest of dimwits is through smashing the buggery out of him with bombs. Big fat heavy ones, not the girly little things the Yanks are dropping. We do the proper stuff at night and they tickle him during the day and, hey presto, Jerry gets no rest at all.

"So, every night we've got fellows heading out over Europe in their hundreds, dodging the ack-ack guns, getting it in the neck from Mr Messerschmitt and laying waste to their factories and railway lines and submarine pens. That's the stuff that the good old chap on the home front needs to know about. And who better to tell him about it than you, Bloodstone?"

16

"Wouldn't it be better coming from one of their own, sir? Another RAF type?" the major queried, once again involuntarily prodding his tender nose.

"Not such a foolish question," Wilkins agreed as he lowered his enormous frame back into his chair with a creak, "After all, us and the fly boys and the sailor chaps usually keep ourselves to ourselves. Which is why, for this little operation, it's been decided that a spot of cross-service cooperation is the name of the game.

"Winston's been keen on it for a while, you see, so this is the perfect opportunity for him to give it a go. Good for the esprit de corps and all that; show the masses that we're all in it together; air, sea and land. Damned lucky that you're not doing it from the frozen deck of a corvette up in the Ruski seas if you ask me."

"Indeed, sir," Bloodstone agreed with a shudder, "I never was too clever on water. Give me some land or a piece of sky anytime. Although I'm still not sure I'm entirely cut out for larking about in front of a camera, sir."

"Look here, Bloodstone," the General said as he once again raised himself up to his full six and a half feet, this time with a reassuring and fatherly look on his face.

"There's a war on and we've all got to do our bit, even if we'd rather be out running amok and bashing Jerry over the head. And believe me when I say that I know that you've got more reason than most to be wanting to give him a damned good bashing. But think of this one as adding another string to your bow and doing your bit for King and country while you're at it. A few months of this and you'll be right back up to your ankles in the mud and the blood and the gore, which I know is where you want to be, you damned maniac."

Realising that resistance was futile, Bloodstone pulled himself to his feet and stood at ease, his head level with the elderly general's shoulders.

"Absolutely, consider it done, you can count on me, sir,"

"Good man," replied the general, handing him a brown envelope containing his orders, before picking up an enormous cane that was resting against the corner of his desk.

"Now then young Bloodstone, let's get out of here. There's a screaming she-devil of a WAAF across the corridor that even a crippled old war hero can't dislodge. We'll go for a brandy and you can tell me all about that old man of yours. Is he still as much of a deviant as when I shared a dugout with him back in '15? Talking of deviancy, did he ever tell you about the time he...."

Wilkins trailed off mid-sentence, a mischievous grin spreading across his scarred face, before he continued, "Actually, probably not, I can't imagine it's the sort of things fathers tell their little boys. And, on the subject of your father, please do pass on my condolences regarding your mother, damned wicked business that. Truly wicked."

CHAPTER FOUR

For a man missing so many limbs and appendages, General Wilkins certainly had an extraordinary capacity for liqueur, so much so that even a hardened drinker like Bloodstone found himself unable to keep up. After what seemed like the thousandth generous measure of cognac and with the enormous elderly warrior still fully compos mentis, Bloodstone could feel his world starting to spin.

Despite the warm fuzz that was starting to appear in the corners of his periphery, he was in no mood to wake up a broken man for the second day running and was fully aware that the morrow was destined to be a day of much ado as he got his house in order ready for his new assignment. So, making his excuses to the general, he extracted himself from the smoke-filled lounge of the fashionable gentleman's club that they had occupied for the afternoon and headed out into the early London evening.

Pre-war London had never held any sort of attraction for the major, who had considered it far too busy, dirty and noisy for his liking, with a distinct lack of fresh air to breathe and certainly not enough muddy puddles to splash about in. The war, however, had given him a new appreciation of the city and he became more and more intrigued by it every time he found himself in the capital.

It was the contrasts that fascinated him, he thought as he stretched his legs and headed for the closest Tube station, ignoring the attentions of a passing cab in an effort to walk off the afternoon's brandy. And the London of autumn 1943 was a place of wild contrasts indeed.

On the surface it was like any other city that had suffered the ravages of four long hard years of war; ruined buildings, endless queues and a multitude of faces hiding all manner of misery, worries and fears. But scratch that surface, he knew, and the picture was something else entirely; a cacophony of joy, opportunity and unlimited decadence. From Woolwich in the east to Chiswick in the west, he was in no doubt that London on that October day was packed with souls living as if today was the last day on earth, which for too many was probably the reality.

Not too far away, he thought, there was probably an airman on his last day of leave, sipping a pint in blissful ignorance of the fact that tomorrow he would be plummeting from the sky to his death, his body a bubbling, burning, melting agony. And equally close was probably a sailor, hand-in-hand with his fiancée and oblivious to the torpedo that would see his body blown into a thousand pieces the next night.

But he'd long ago discovered that one couldn't dawdle on such things, or madness and a sense of impending doom were sure to set in and suck the life out of a man. So, the only option was to keep buggering on, as the Prime Minister was reputed to have so delicately put it. And Albert Bloodstone was certainly happy to keep buggering on, making the most of the opportunities that the war threw his way and getting as much enjoyment out of the chaos as possible before an armistice or, more likely, a Nazi bullet, put an end to it all.

While his mind had been wandering, he had made his way down the steps at Oxford Circus station and hopped aboard the next underground train heading to Waterloo, where a short walk would see him at his usual London hotel.

His hangover was still nibbling at the back of his skull as he chose a seat in the half-empty carriage, looking forward to a soft bed and a decent slap-up meal courtesy of the establishment's French chef who had a questionable but useful habit of sourcing tasty ingredients that certainly weren't on the ration book. The thought of a juicy steak, combined with the gentle jolting of the train and a bellyful of brandy, started to lull him into a cozy sense of drowsiness and he closed his eyes as his backside nestled into the worn cushion of the seat. In a matter of heartbeats he was fast asleep, his woozy head finally free from the vestiges of booze as his brain filled with the blissful peace of dreamery.

Within seconds he was a small boy again, running through the Hampshire countryside of his childhood, his little legs making easy work of the soft grassy hills as his favourite companion, Bess the sheepdog, loped at his heels. Through forests and across streams they roamed, passing flint villages with their square Norman church towers and smelling the distant sea in the air. He stooped to pick up a stick from the undergrowth and hefted it in his hand as the raggedy dog barked excitedly and jumped up, desperate to play with the knobbly piece of wood.

He laughed with childlike delight as he held the stick aloft, daring the dog to jump higher and higher. On its hind legs it stood, almost as tall as himself, its paws scrabbling on his chest and its mouth open in a joyful bark as it tried to grab the stick between its teeth.

But suddenly the face transformed, the playful eyes turning evil and the bark becoming a vicious, snarling roar. Where there had been a yapping mouth there was now a mass of ferocious, angry teeth, gnashing at his face as the beast tried to rip the flesh from his skull. Desperate, he pushed the stick against the creature's throat, his left hand grabbing the fur that seconds ago had been soft and fluffy but was now a writhing mass of festering maggots.

As he pushed, he felt his child's strength growing, forcing the snapping beast backwards, rolling it onto its back as he clambered on

21

top of it, the stick still at its throat and his left fist firmly entangled in the mangy fur.

He woke with a jolt and the image of the terrifying creature vanished as he snapped back into consciousness. To his horror, it was replaced with the petrified face of a young teenager, whose bumfluff-topped mouth was open in a silent scream as Bloodstone sat astride him, his wickedly sharp combat knife at the boy's throat and his other hand grabbing a fistful of the youngster's grubby jumper.

Appalled, and not just a little conscious of the shocked silence emanating from the handful of wide-eyed passengers in the carriage, he quickly sheathed the ten inches of razor-sharp steel and jumped to his feet, clapping the white-faced boy on the shoulder.

"Sorry about that young man, are you alright?"

The boy, who Bloodstone guessed to be about 13 years old and was sporting a skew-whiff cap, baggy shorts and knee-high socks, stared at him from the seat with a look of pure fear.

"I only tapped you on the leg, Mister," he stammered with an East End accent, "I didn't mean nuffin by it. I'm sorry, honest I am."

Bloodstone shooed away the apology with a friendly wave of his hand and took his place on the seat next to the boy.

"A word of advice, my little friend," he said as he fixed the still-shaking teen with a wide grin, "Never wake a sleeping soldier. Or if you do, make sure you do it from behind, otherwise you might end up with a sword in your gullet. An old Gurkha trick that; clever fellows eh?"

The boy didn't respond but the fear slowly drained from his face, replaced instead with something akin to wonderment as he took in Bloodstone's uniform and the impressive row of medal ribbons perched proudly on his chest.

"You're a Para, ain't you?" he asked as the other passengers in the rattling carriage returned to their newspapers and hushed conversations, the excitement now over, although a few barely disguised glances still came the major's way.

"Jolly good observation, young man," Bloodstone responded, "You know your stuff, don't you? I'm impressed."

"My Pa was a Para," the boy said with a hard face, his jaw tight. "Killed in Tunisia on Christmas Day just gone he was. Corporal Potter, did you know him?"

If it was the Potter that Bloodstone was thinking of, he remembered him well; a small, wiry man in his old platoon with the strength of a lion and a particular habit of brawling and excessive whoring when he wasn't on duty. So much so that he would have made an excellent Sergeant had he not been involved in one too many punch-ups with the Red Caps.

"Corporal Alf Potter?" he asked.

"That's him," the boy nodded, a look of sadness spreading across his face. "Do you know what happened, you know, when he was killed and that? They never told us."

Bloodstone looked at the boy sitting next to him, the face full of expectation and the grubby hands grasped tightly together. How could he tell him the truth? No son wanted to hear that his father had taken six long hours to die, howling in agony as his bullet-riddled organs failed one by one. He remembered it like it was yesterday; the cruel lack of morphine, the blood in the sand and the stench of shit as the dying man's bowels opened in his final horrible scream-filled moments.

"It was quick," Bloodstone said, looking the boy in the eye. "A Hun sniper got him. He didn't know anything about it, dead before he hit the floor. Your father was a damned good soldier, son, you should be proud of him."

The boy glanced away, cuffing a tear from his eye, before turning back to face the major with his teeth gritted and a look of pride on his face.

"One day I'm gonna join your lot and I'm gonna kill every one of those dirty German bastards," he said, causing a tut of disapproval to come from an elderly woman a few seats away.

"Good for you, young man," Bloodstone laughed as he gave the boy another clap on the shoulder, "Make sure you do."

"I will," replied the youngster with a grin that bordered on psychotic, before he looked up at Bloodstone once more with a quizzical look in his eye.

"By the way, Mister, what happened to your nose?"

CHAPTER FIVE

T he dew was still wet on the ground and the starlings had barely risen when Bloodstone pulled up to the main gate of RAF Scampton, deep in the Lincolnshire countryside with not a hill for miles around. Announcing himself to the sleepy-looking air force sergeant on guard duty, he received a crisp salute and a bemused glance at his uniform before the man retreated into his guard box to use the telephone. Returning, the guard inspected Bloodstone's papers and took another look at the parachute wings on his maroon beret before remarking in distinctly Brummie drawl,

"We don't sees many of yow lot here, sir."

"I don't doubt it, Sergeant, I don't doubt it. Long way from home. Now where should I report? Wing Commander Grubb if you'd be so kind."

"Head across to the mess, sir, straight up this road here, you can't miss it. The boss will meet yow there. Leave your kit here with us, sir, we'll make sure it's all squared away proper like."

Thanking the sergeant, Bloodstone took his kitbag from the boot of his MG convertible, handed it to the man and climbed back into his seat. Gunning the engine, he steered under the red and white barrier being held aloft by the cheery guard and headed into the aerodrome.

As he drove along the perimeter road in the direction that the guard had pointed, he noticed the unmistakable and all-too-familiar wafting smell of aviation fuel mixed with the subtler stink of paint. Every airfield he'd ever been on had that same smell, he mused, be it China, Africa or occupied Europe. It seemed familiar, somehow comforting, and it made him feel slightly more at home in this damp corner of eastern England.

In the distance he spotted numerous black shapes sitting on their haunches, like oversized and muscle-bound dragonflies, with tiny ant-like figures buzzing about the ground beneath them. Several of the beasts had steam rising from their engines and Bloodstone realised with a little surprise that, despite his long, bloody and illustrious career, he had never actually set eyes on a Lancaster before. He was several hundred yards from where they sat at their various dispersal spots but, even from that distance, he was impressed with their graceful yet malevolent-looking beauty. Thanking his lucky stars that he wasn't a Jerry, he continued on his way towards a mass of buildings in the distance, putting his foot down and giving the MG some welly along the empty perimeter road.

A quarter-mile further on he entered the bustling business centre of the airfield, where blue uniforms scuttled between the cluster of drab-colour buildings and small bands of grubby airmen huddled in groups, cups of tea in hand as they chatted in muted tones. His destination wasn't difficult to spot, an oversized hut with *Officers' Mess* daubed above the door in flaking white paint, and he pulled up outside, switched off the engine and made his way inside.

The interior of the building was like most wartime messes that Bloodstone had frequented, with armchairs and tables strewn throughout and a well-stocked bar occupying pride of place. Pinned to the wall were an array of photographs showing grinning airmen, four-engined bombers and long-legged film stars, while a worn snooker table stood in one corner, ready for action minus a missing yellow ball. Nailed above the bar was the obligatory wartime trophy, which in Bloodstone's battalion mess was a red and black swastika-emblazoned flag, but here at RAF Scampton was a fire-damaged and bullet-ridden tail fin complete with Luftwaffe insignia.

The mess was empty except for a middle-aged man in overalls who was busy sweeping a multitude of cigarette butts into a pile in the corner, so Bloodstone selected a battered-looking Chesterfield sofa, plucked yesterday's Daily Express from a stained coffee table and settled down to wait for the station commander to make his entrance.

He was halfway through an article about fears of a jam jar shortage when the shrill noise of a siren and a series of muffled shouts reached his ears from outside the mess. Throwing down the paper, he jumped to his feet, rushed to the door and went back outside, just in time to see the rear end of a fire truck disappear behind a nearby building in the direction of the main runway, which stretched off into the distance from just a hundred yards away.

A group of seven airmen were standing in a huddle nearby, flying kit still on and cigarettes dangling from their mouths as they peered and pointed at the sky to the east where an incoming four-engined bomber disappeared behind a low cloud a mile away.

"I say, what's going on?" Bloodstone asked one of the men, a blonde-haired youngster with a thin moustache, red-rimmed eyes and pilots' wings stitched above his left breast pocket.

"That's the last ship coming in," the pilot replied with a tired smile, "We thought we'd lost her last night over Bremen, but it seems she's made it back after all. Shot to bits apparently but better late than never, hey boys?"

"Aye, aboot bloody time too," a small sergeant wearing a leather flying jacket chipped in with a Scottish accent so thick that Bloodstone could barely decipher the words, "Keepin' wee Bill from his bed, so they are."

"Belt up Jock, you'll get your kip soon enough," another of the group offered with a friendly ruffle of the sergeant's dark hair, before turning to Bloodstone and continuing, "This'll be the first time we've all made it home. A nice change that'll be and no doubt the boss will treat us all to a snifter or two tonight to celebrate."

A thin cheer went up from the small huddle of airmen at the thought of the evening's festivities but was quickly stifled as the incoming plane emerged from behind the cloud, swaying drunkenly and with a trail of thick black smoke pouring from one engine.

"Jesus," the blonde pilot muttered through clenched teeth, "Look at the state of that."

And a state the Lancaster was, Bloodstone realised with a shiver. Three propellers stood stationary while the fourth spewed a mixture of flame and smoke out into the morning sky. One wing was missing a third of its length and even from this distance he could see holes the size of rugby balls peppered throughout the fuselage. The nose was a flak-riddled mangled mess, the upper turret was shot away and one tail fin seemed to be dangling by a thread, bouncing and bumping in the slipstream as the crippled plane lurched through the air towards the nearby runway.

"The poor bastard's only got one wheel down," one of the group whispered out loud and the small knot of airmen held their breath as the battered Lancaster neared the ground, choking and coughing as it came and swinging wildly from side to side. The entire airfield seemed to be in a trance, unable to move, the silence broken only by the distant wailing of the fire truck and the spluttering plane that was now only feet from the earth.

The Lancaster hit the ground with a gruesome crunch, its one wheel buckling under its monstrous weight and a shower of sparks spinning skywards as it gouged its way across the tarmac. Sheering off the runway, it careered in the direction of Bloodstone and the gathered airfield personnel, tearing up grass and mud as it went and shedding the remains of its broken wing, leaving in its wake a trail of torn metal, shattered struts and leaking aviation fuel.

An abandoned Jeep, just fifty yards from the horrified spectators, was in the path of the stricken plane and it was crushed as nearly 40,000 pounds of heavy bomber ploughed into it, ripping off another wing and throwing yet more bits of broken aeroplane into the ether. The vehicle acted as an anchor, however, bringing the mangled

Lancaster to an ungraceful halt on the grass, now almost silent after the last few seconds of carnage and destruction. The only sound was a hissing of steam and an ominous drip-drip-drip as the shattered fuel pipes leaked their contents onto the grass.

As the crippled plane came to a rest, a leather helmet-clad head appeared where the Perspex mid-upper turret should have been, eyes wild and blood sheeted across one side of the pale and panic-stricken face.

"My God, that's Johnny," the man next to Bloodstone gasped as the blood-soaked airman clawed at the remnants of the broken turret, desperately trying to climb out of the jagged hole, "Get out of there man!"

As if hearing, the wretched man looked directly at Bloodstone's group with a face contorted with fear and sheer desperation, eyes pleading for help as he struggled to pull himself from the Lancaster, which continued to spew fuel and smoke from its broken body.

"HELP ME!" he screamed, his voice screeching with panic as he clawed at the ragged hole with his bare hands, the sharp Perspex ripping his skin and leaving smears of blood across the tattered canvas of the fuselage.

Bloodstone looked beyond the pitiful scene to see that the fire engine was still three hundred yards away and tearing across the airfield as it frantically returned from where it had expected the Lancaster to land. Two men clung to the rear as it bumped and banged its way over the grass, with its precious cargo of water the only thing that could save the trapped airman and any other crew that still lived inside the shattered wreckage of the bomber from the fire that was sure to rip through it in a matter of seconds.

"Bugger this," he said to nobody in particular, damned if he was going to stand by and watch as a man roasted to death in front of him. And with that he set off, head down and arms pumping as he sprinted for the smoking wreck that lay just fifty yards away.

"Get back ye loonie, she's gonna blow," a Scottish voice yelled after him but it was too late; instinct had taken over and not for the first time in his life Bloodstone found himself heading into unnecessary danger without first having put a great deal of thought into the consequences.

It took seconds to cover the first twenty yards as the years of extreme physical fitness paid dividends and he ate up the distance like an Olympic athlete. Ten more yards passed in the blink of an eye and Bloodstone looked up to see that the stricken airman was now halfway out of the ruined turret, wriggling like a hooked fish as he tried desperately to extricate the lower half of his body.

Seeing his saviour nearing, the writhing man locked eyes with Bloodstone, who saw the panic and fear give way to something akin to relief. All of a sudden realisation had hit the flyer that life was now to live; it was no longer going to end in fiery agony.

Five more yards and the stench of petrol was almost unbearable, burning the back of Bloodstone's throat as he took in a lungful of air to get him through the last bit of the sprint. His eyes stayed locked on the blood-soaked airman who had now finally freed one leg and was about to swing the other out of the broken turret, a smile spreading across his battered yet youthful face as a did so.

The explosion was instant and enormous. The Lancaster simply disintegrated in an apocalyptic ball of flame and Bloodstone was blown from his feet as his world became an airless vacuum of heat, smoke and flying metal. The last thing he saw before he was blasted to the ground was the leather-helmeted youngster, his eyes staring into his own and his face turning from joyous relief to hideous realisation as the explosion engulfed him and vaporised his body in an instant.

Bloodstone, deafened by the explosion, covered his head with his hands as debris rained down all around him. He willed his body into the ground and it was a miracle that he wasn't crushed by the falling wreckage that had been sent streaming into the sky by the dying Lancaster. It was over almost as quickly as it had begun and the noise rumbled away into the distance to be replaced by the smell of burning petrol and roasted meat, which, despite his dazed state, he knew was the cooking flesh of the seven crew members who had been entombed in their aircraft.

Pulling himself to his feet and shaking his head to clear the fuzz, Bloodstone looked around him. The Lancaster was spread across half of the airfield and burning, broken bits of bomber stretched as far as the eye could see. The fire truck had finally reached the scene and was spraying water at was left of the aeroplane, while the small groups of RAF personnel were still huddled together outside the mess. He noticed that the right sleeve of his tunic had been burnt away, exposing the skin beneath, and the left leg of his uniform trousers was smouldering slightly above his boot. He slapped out the singed breeches and realised that his maroon beret was no longer sitting askew on his head.

Searching the wreckage-strewn floor around him and wondering at the miracle that had left him untouched by the deadly rain of fire and metal, he spotted his beret a few feet away. Next to it lay a uniformed arm, perfectly preserved but torn off halfway between shoulder and elbow, bone and bloodied muscle protruding from the ragged, ruptured and burnt wound. The carefully sewn triple stripes of a sergeant were visible on the blue material, while a wristwatch displayed two hands that had stopped at exactly eight forty-seven. The little finger at the end of the arm was missing, a cauterised nub in its place, while a gold wedding ring occupied pride of place on the finger next to it.

"Major Bloodstone, I presume," a gruff Australian voice barked suddenly from behind, bringing Bloodstone back to his senses. He brought his gaze up from the mangled limb on the ground and turned to see an RAF officer striding towards him across the grass, his uniform decorated with the rank of a wing commander.

"Get yourself cleaned up and report to my office in thirty minutes, not a minute more," the stern-face Aussie ordered with a glare, before turning on his heel and marching back towards the buildings, leaving Bloodstone to scoop up his crumpled beret from beside the severed arm and cram it miserably onto his head.

CHAPTER SIX

Exactly half an hour later, dressed in a hastily pressed shirt, new breeches and with the grime of the explosion scrubbed from his face, Bloodstone presented himself at the office of Wing Commander Aubrey Grubb, commanding officer of 513 Squadron and known throughout the aerodrome, he had discovered in the last thirty minutes, simply as The Boss.

With his ears still ringing from the blast and the smell of petrol and burnt manflesh strong in his swollen nostrils, he knocked at the door and was curtly summoned inside. Looking around, he saw that the room was small and bare, with whitewashed walls and a tiny window that looked out towards the control tower and the runway beyond. A functional wooden desk, complete with a tidy pile of papers, stood in the centre of the office and the only concession to indulgence were two photo frames on the windowsill. One displayed a faded image of two small children with their arms around a vicious-looking mongrel of a dog, while the other contained a photograph of three beautiful young women huddled around a microphone.

The man sitting behind the desk acknowledged Bloodstone's salute with a swift touch of his forelock and, with barely a glance up, continued reading from a paper file in his left hand. Not invited to sit, Bloodstone stood at ease in front of the desk and studied the man who had spoken to him so bluntly amid the wreckage of the burning Lancaster.

A good few inches shorter than Bloodstone's own six foot and in his mid-forties, the Wing Commander appeared lean and lightly muscled beneath his tight-fitting blue uniform. He had a head of tightly curled fair hair and his face seemed to have slightly too little skin, almost as if someone had unstitched the back of his head and pulled his flesh as tight as a drum. The result was an exceptionally hard face, not quite cruel, Bloodstone thought to himself, but certainly ruthless. A neatly groomed blonde beard sat upon a razor-sharp jaw and two dark eyes, edged by spidery crows' feet, pierced the face and it was those eyes that finally looked up from the file to fix Bloodstone with a deathly stare.

"Don't you ever let me see you trying to play the fucking hero on my airfield again, do you understand me?" he snapped in a sharp Australian twang, taking Bloodstone aback by its ferocity.

Before he had chance to respond, Grubb continued, not taking his eyes from the surprised Major, "This isn't Fighter Command, this isn't the Eighth Airforce and this certainly isn't the fucking Parachute Regiment. This is five-one-three, the best Goddamned bomber squadron in the whole RAF and do you know why, Major?"

Bloodstone thought it apt not to respond, instead allowing the angry Wing Commander to continue his unexpected rant.

"We're the best because we get our heads down and do our job. We don't fuck about trying to win medals or get our faces in the newspapers or prance around with our cocks out. There's no place for any of that nonsense here; a bomber crew needs to be calm, methodical and follow their orders to the letter. As soon as they get a taste for hero shit then it's fancy flying, missed targets and telegram boys knocking on Mummy's door. And I can promise you that won't be happening on my watch, do you hear me, Major?"

"Absolutely, sir."

"Glad to hear it. Now sit the fuck down."

As so delicately instructed, Bloodstone pulled out the lone chair facing the desk and sat down opposite the bearded Wing Commander who, strangely for a senior officer, he thought, seemed to possess a mouth filthier than his own Sergeant Major back at barracks.

"I'll make no secret of the fact that I don't want you here, Major," Grubb said, dropping the file and pointing a finger in Bloodstone's direction.

"I've got a hard enough job as it is with keeping planes in the air and the boys focused on their jobs and I certainly don't want them distracted by all this Hollywood gash. But I'll follow my orders like the next man, just as long as you keep out of the way and do what you need to do. And if you paint this squadron in anything other than the fucking glorious rainbow of colour that they deserve then I can tell you right now that me and you will be having words. And you don't want to be having words with me, MC or no MC."

Bloodstone wasn't so sure about that, he thought to himself, musing that he'd probably quite enjoy using some of his vast array of state-trained violence on the tight-faced and unnecessarily angry Australian. Before he could decide whether he'd prefer to go with a forefinger through the left eyeball or a chop to the windpipe, however, Grubb grasped the file again and looked up.

"Talking of Military Crosses, let's take a look at your record shall we, Major? If a man's serving on my station then I like to know what makes him tick, and you're no exception."

With that, Grubb opened the file in his hand and scanned the top sheet of paper, his eyes darting quickly along the type-written lines and his mouth moving silently as he absorbed the information on the thin yellow paper.

"Born 1919 in Cologne, eh? That sounds distinctly Kraut to me. Not a Kraut are you, Major?"

"No, sir," Bloodstone replied. "Father was stationed there after the last war. My mother was Austrian. I came back here to Blighty when I was six months old."

"*Was* Austrian?" Grubb interrupted, looking up from the file.

"Correct, sir, *was*. Killed by the Nazis in '41," Bloodstone replied with no trace of emotion, his eyes locked firmly on the Wing Commander's dark pupils.

"I see," the senior officer responded, quickly looking back to the file before continuing his interrogation of the neatly typed paper.

"Schooled at Eton, I see. Although not very successfully from the look of these grades. Although it says here you've got a knack for languages. Fluent in French, German and Mandarin apparently. What the hell is Mandarin?"

"Chinese, sir," Bloodstone responded and received what could only be a withering look of contempt, before Grubb looked back at the file.

"So, you enrolled at the Royal Military College at 16 and joined the Grenadier Guards as a second lieutenant in '36. Eton and the Guards, not exactly slummed it have we, Major. Blue blood or something?"

"Not exactly, sir. I guess I've just been fortunate."

"Fortunate, ha. I was born on a piss poor sheep farm in the Australian Outback, Bloodstone, did you know that? Joined the army as a fresh-faced Digger in '15, found my way into the RFC, ended the war with a commission and here I am, me on this side of the table and you on that side. Funny how things turn out, isn't it?"

"Hilarious, sir."

Grubb greeted the response with a disapproving scowl before turning to the second page of yellow paper and continuing with his scrutiny of the text, the fingers of his left hand drumming on the desk as he did so.

"Served nine months in the East in '38 and '39, I see; training capacity it says here, attached to the Chinese National Revolutionary Army. Poor bastard," the Wing Commander continued with a throaty chuckle and a smirk at Bloodstone, "Explains the lingo I guess, although I wonder whose boots you pissed on to be given that particular posting."

The humour left Grubb's face as quickly as it had arrived and he returned to his probing examination of the major's career, his dark eyes flicking from word to word as he drank in the details. Bloodstone was beginning to feel a little like an errant schoolboy sitting before a particularly vicious house master, which he thought was rather uncalled for considering that his only crime had been attempting to save a helpless man from a fiery tomb.

He was more than used to military discipline and the unnecessary bunkum that it often spewed forth from those who enjoyed the privilege of their rank a little too much, but the Wing Commander was quickly making him wonder if the RAF was on another level entirely. Or maybe it was just this particular creature, he thought to himself. His previous experience of fliers had always been positive; granted, a little too much flash sometimes, even for his dashing tastes, but generally good chaps. The blonde-haired pilot that he'd briefly spoken to before the exploding bomber had ruined his morning had certainly seemed like a decent sort. So maybe it was just this tight-faced Antipodean that was giving the rest an unfair tarring with his angry brush.

Before Bloodstone could continue his disgruntled musing further, Grubb started to read aloud from the file once again.

"Back to the Guards in April '39 as a first lieutenant, I see, and off to Norway a year later. Awarded an MC there and then a DSC in the Dunkirk shambles a few weeks later. Quite the hero aren't we, Major," he scoffed with a piercing look, before continuing in his Australian drawl, "DSC, that's a naval gong isn't it?"

"Yes, sir. Well you've got to be at sea to get it. It was during the evacuation. I must've been in the right place at the right time."

"Don't try that humble bullshit with me, Major," Grubb said with a shake of his bearded head as he turned to the third and final page of the file in his right hand.

"Promoted to captain at Christmas 1940, then transferred to the Parachute Regiment the following summer. North Africa in

November '42 with Operation Torch, a second MC and no doubt that's where you got this ridiculous tan you're sporting, eh?"

Again, Bloodstone chose not to reply, remembering the deserts of Tunisia and Egypt as anything but a holiday, and instead let the Wing Commander continue with his scathing probing.

"Sicily this summer for Primosole Bridge, which was a bloody fiasco from what I've heard. Then across to the Italian mainland where it seems that you excelled yourself. A DSO for what it says here was suicidal bravery in the face of the enemy and a bump up to major to go with it. That must be where you picked up this idiotic nickname I've been hearing; Italian Butcher is it?"

The ridiculous moniker was something that the German press had seemingly created after his recent shenanigans in Italy and, despite it sounding too much like some sort of war criminal for his own liking, the British newspapers had adopted it too, albeit it with a sense of pride.

"Anyway, now here you are," Grubb summarised, closing the file with theatrical aplomb and looking Bloodstone in the eye.

"Either you're a bloody maniac or you've got someone at the top of the tree throwing you gongs like confetti. I've got my suspicions which it is, but I'm going to give you the benefit of the doubt, Bloodstone. Just remember what I said, none of that hero shit on my airfield. Get your head down, do your job and don't you dare distract my boys from the task at hand. Do you understand me?"

"Completely, sir," Bloodstone agreed, pleased that his morning grilling seemed to be nearing its end.

"One more thing," the Wing Commander said as he rose to his feet, straightening his tunic as he did so. "Get control of your film crew or they're gone. They arrived on Saturday and rumour has it that your make-up girl has already been shagged silly by two of my mechanics. I've put her in the Waafery, but you need to get a rope on that.

"Your cameraman also appears to be a raging homosexual. I'll have none of that filthy business on this base. It's your job to manage, I'll be leaving it with you."

Bloodstone scowled as he stood up, thinking that it was none of his business what a man did with his own private parts, while wondering at the bizarre turn of fate that had transported him from his usual gun-toting world into this unfamiliar land of angry airmen, randy make-up girls and camp cameramen.

His thoughts were distracted by a half-arsed salute, which he returned with parade ground efficiency, before the Wing Commander offered Bloodstone a hand.

"Welcome to 513 Squadron, Major," he said, shaking hands with a vice-like grip. "That'll be all."

CHAPTER SEVEN

Just before three o'clock that afternoon, Bloodstone drove back out of the airfield gates and made the half-mile journey to the local pub, where he'd sent for his film crew to meet him. He navigated the leafy country lanes with ease and pulled into the gravel car park of the Fox and Hounds, finding himself in front of a traditional white-fronted building complete with thatched roof and a peeling sign that swung gently in the breeze.

Removing his beret, he made his way into the dark interior, nodded to two ancient tweed-clad farmers who were huddled together at the end of the bar sipping murky brown pints, and ordered a whisky from the rotund middle-aged landlord. With glass in hand, he selected a table by the window and settled down to wait for his three guests, once again mulling the morning's conversation with the vociferous Wing Commander Grubb over in his mind.

He was snapped out of his disgruntled musings by a high-pitched feminine giggle and a raucous guffaw as a couple entered the pub, arm in arm and faces split with enormous grins. The girl must have been no more than eighteen with a lithe body and dark hair pulled into two pigtails, under which sat a pair of enormous brown eyes and lips bright with rouge. The man, old enough to be her father, sported a gold watch chain tight across his waistcoat-clad paunch, while a flowery cravat was tied at his neck. His rosy pink cheeks shone brightly and short black oiled hair stuck up wildly in all directions, almost as if the man had just got out of bed. Which he probably had, lucky blighter, Bloodstone thought to himself, noticing how closely the two clung to each other.

The couple sauntered giddily across the room, still arm in arm, and propped themselves against the bar, their gossipy whispering punctuated only by regular outbursts of raucous hilarity. The barman approached with a smile and, instead of serving them a drink, he pointed a chubby finger in Bloodstone's direction.

They turned, suddenly silent, and looked at the major, the girl turning a bright shade of red and a barely disguised smirk on the man's face. Grabbing the brunette's hand, he led her across the room to the table, where he offered an elaborate bow and a bizarre salute that certainly hadn't come from any drill manual Bloodstone had ever seen.

"Huckleberry James at your service, sir," he announced in a bizarre accent that mangled English aristocrat with American cowboy.

"Discarded movie star, lover of all things fantabulous and now, it seems, the man destined to make you a superstar of galactic proportions. And my golly, what a finely proportioned fellow you are, if I may be so brash."

Slightly taken aback by the flamboyant introduction and a little surprised that this strange character was a man assigned directly by the Prime Minister, Bloodstone rose to his feet and offered his hand.

"Bloodstone, Albert Bloodstone. You're my director?"

"Director, cameraman, dogsbody extraordinaire, that's me," he confirmed and shook hands before offering another bow, this time almost low enough to scrape the floor with his brow.

"But where are my manners, I do apologise," Huckleberry James continued as he rose back to his full height, placing his hand gently on the girl's bottom and manoeuvring her in the general direction of the major.

"Allow me to introduce the delectable, wonderful, bombshellian little rose that is Miss Kitty Blythe, finest make-up artist in all the world."

Kitty let out a stifled giggle and blushed even redder as she curtsied, before rising to shake Bloodstone's outstretched hand that dwarfed her tiny fingers.

"Pleasure to meet you, sir," she whispered in a barely audible voice, sweet with the lilting tones of the Welsh valleys.

"Likewise, Miss Blythe," Bloodstone offered, catching her eye for only a millisecond before she looked away with another mouse-like giggle.

"Now please, sit down," he invited, lowering his backside into his chair and summoning the barman with a wave of his hand.

As the man took the newcomers' drinks order, Bloodstone reached into his pocket for a gold case and popped it open, offering his guests a cigarette. James declined, instead pulling an enormous pipe from his own pocket and clamping it firmly in the corner of his mouth. Kitty, however, shyly accepted and allowed Bloodstone to light the cigarette with a matching gold lighter. He selected one for himself and leaned back in the chair, sucking the smoke satisfyingly into his lungs while the dark-haired girl sitting opposite coughed politely as she drew tentatively on her own cigarette.

"I thought there was supposed to be three of you?" Bloodstone asked, aiming his question at the pipe smoking James.

"Indeed there were, Major, indeed there were," he responded, removing the pipe from his mouth and holding it theatrically in mid-air by the stem.

"Poor fellow named Butler was supposed to be here too. Something of a wizard with a camera, destined for great things, so he was. Unfortunately, the gods have a funny way of playing the game it seems. Killed stone dead by a German bomb just three days ago in London. While visiting his invalid mother, too. Did you ever hear of anything so ghastly?"

Bloodstone, who had lost count of the number of men he had personally seen killed by bombs, bullets and worse, scowled slightly and tapped the ash from his cigarette into a battered ashtray on the table.

Seeing the expression, James waved his pipe reassuringly before continuing.

"Worry not my brave soldier, I can handle a film camera with my eyes shut. We'll be just fine, the three of us. I'll do my magic, Kitty here," he paused to give her a gentle nudge with his elbow, "Will make you look even more handsome than you already are and together we'll be bamboozling theatregoers across the Empire with your dashing tales of heroism."

"We can't fail, Major; they'll be showering us with rose petals and we'll be sucking heavenly milk from the teats of the angels before you can say bugger me with a broomstick," he continued, eliciting yet another giggle from Kitty and a look of shock on the face of the landlord who had chosen that moment to arrive with a tray of drinks.

Bloodstone waited for the man to unload a gin and tonic along with a garish looking pink concoction complete with miniature umbrella and a slice of apple, which he half hoped was for Kitty but already knew that was unlikely, before resting his half-smoked cigarette against the ashtray and clearing his throat.

"Look here, I'll be the first to admit that this isn't my usual cup of tea, but orders are orders and we've got a serious job to do here. So, I'll be making damned sure that this is done properly, no faffing about and no tomfoolery. Do I make myself clear?"

Suddenly conscious that he was starting to sound a little like the angry wing commander who had given him such a rollicking a few hours before, Bloodstone gave his guests no time to reply, instead breaking out one of his finest smiles and adding, "I have no doubt that you both know exactly what you're doing, so let's make a splendid job of this, agreed?"

With that he raised his whisky and the three clinked their glasses together, knocking the precariously perched slice of apple from the top of James' pink monstrosity, sending it tumbling into the ashtray.

Returning his glass, minus the apple, to the table, James took a deep suck on his pipe and blew out an enormous fog of smoke before looking Bloodstone in the eye with his most serious expression yet.

"Major, when I said I was going to make you a star, that's exactly what I meant. I am the very best at what I do, which is why the powers-that-be have seen fit to pluck me from the delicious delights of Hollywood and deposit me here in this frightful northern backwater. The great Huckleberry James doesn't come cheap, I'll have you know, but there's a reason for that. So, let me run this show and we'll have you back in the trenches drinking the blood of the goose-stepping heathens before you know it."

With that, he pulled a small pocketbook from his waistcoat and flicked through it until he found the page he was looking for. One more puff on the pipe followed before he announced, "We'll be shooting our first news report on Wednesday, that's tomorrow.

"I've already written the lines, so I'll give you those this evening and you'll need to practise until you know it by heart. The delightful Kitty here can be your muse, if you so desire," he said with a wink that resulted in yet another giggle from the blushing girl.

"Dress rehearsal will be at half past three tomorrow afternoon, which I understand is fifteen thirty hours for you warrior chaps, so Kitty will need to have given you a full going over with her brushes by then. We'll then be shooting the thing for real at sixteen hundred, which is when the sun should be just right in the sky and, equally importantly, gives me just enough time to get to York for a spot of dinner with a distinctly dashing cavalryman called Philip.

"You see, all under control. Don't you just love the war?" he finished with a beaming grin and final suck of his pipe, giving the brown eyed girl a playful slap on the leg.

Bloodstone, knocking back the remnants of his whisky, wasn't so sure anymore.

CHAPTER EIGHT

The sun had just slipped beyond the horizon as Bloodstone
walked the short distance from his quarters to the mess hall
with the script for the next day's shoot tucked neatly into the
trouser pocket of his undress uniform. He'd spent the last hour
practising the words in front of a large mirror that Huckleberry James
had delivered to his room and, despite initially feeling somewhat
ridiculous doing so, he was starting to look forward to his first foray
into the world of the movie star. But only ever so slightly, he allowed
himself to admit.

After a dinner of egg and chips, which he was delighted to
discover were real eggs and not the powdered monstrosities that his
battalion usually served, he strolled across to the officers' mess.
Opening the door, he found the room to be a very different place to
that which he had occupied prior to the unfortunate incident of the
burning Lancaster. A thick fog of tobacco smoke hung throughout
the interior and the previously empty stools and chairs were now
packed with young airman, animated in conversation and their hands
clutching half-drunk pints of beer.

Bloodstone made his way to the bar and ordered his usual tipple,
a generous measure of Glenfiddich's finest, and was about to hand

over the requested pennies to the barman when a voice chipped in from behind.

"Let me get that one, sir."

Looking over his shoulder, Bloodstone was pleasantly surprised to see the blonde pilot he'd met earlier that morning, although now the tired eyes were sparkling with life and the previously tousled hair was combed into a perfect side parting.

"I say, thank you very much. Jolly kind of you," Bloodstone said, offering his hand to the other man.

"Bloodstone, Albert Bloodstone."

"Ronald Ashton," the pilot responded, shaking Bloodstone's hand warmly, before ordering himself a beer and passing a handful of coins to the barman.

"That was damned brave of you this morning," he continued, "Damned brave, although no doubt the Boss tore you off a strip or two for it."

"You could say that," Bloodstone responded with a smile, remembering Grubb's potty-mouthed tirade with a sense of amusement mingled with a fair dose of dented pride.

"I wouldn't worry about it if I were you, sir," Ashton said, wiping a foam of beer from his thin moustache, "His bark is a lot worse than his bite."

"In fact, the boys love him," he continued as he took another sip of his drink. "He's fiercely protective of us and he makes sure we get the best kites and the best grub. But he expects the best from us too and woe betide any chap who doesn't toe the line.

"He's also got a bee in his bonnet about heroes, although I think you found that one out for yourself," he said with a grin.

"Indeed," Bloodstone agreed, "Not my favourite way to spend a Tuesday morning."

"Well, the boys were damned impressed," Ashton said, his face suddenly serious. "Johnny Jackson, the fellow you nearly pulled out of that wreck, used to be in our crew on G for George, so I'd say they all owe you a drink. In fact, Chalky, our navigator, was his best man just a few weeks ago."

Ashton nodded in the direction of the snooker table, where a lone airman, not yet twenty years old and a face like thunder, potted balls with a battered cue. "That's him, poor chap. Although, I'll wager that you've seen your fair share of horror too. Anyway, enough of all that, let me introduce you; it looks like he could do with a spot of cheering up."

With that, Ashton led Bloodstone through the cigarette smoke to the corner of the mess and waited for the navigator to smash a pink ball into the corner pocket before speaking.

"Hey up Chalky, how are you doing, old chap?" Ashton asked as he put a friendly hand on his crew mate's shoulder.

"Not so bad, Ronnie, you know how it is," he replied, straightening up from the table with a sad smile, "I just can't get that poor bastard's face out of my head."

"I know, just give it some time. Today had Johnny's name on it, nothing any of us could've done," Ashton said, giving the shoulder a squeeze.

"Well, this fellow certainly tried his best," Chalky responded, looking at Bloodstone with eyes that had quite clearly spent much of the day crying.

"I owe you my thanks, sir," he continued, shaking Bloodstone's hand.

"Not necessary," Bloodstone replied kindly as he took in the youngster's red-rimmed eyes and the blue uniform that hung from his bony teenage body like a scarecrow, "I wish I could've been quicker."

"Well I reckon the boys owe you one for trying," Chalky said and bent back to the table to pummel the black into a pocket, "If there's anything we can do for you, sir, anything at all, just say the word."

As a tiny seed of an idea planted itself in Bloodstone's brain, he promised the navigator that he would, before he turned back to Ashton and asked, "Where are the rest of your crew this evening?"

"Chalky and I are the only officers in our mob, sir, the other five are enlisted chaps. With no raid tonight they're probably tearing it up in the sergeants' mess or, more likely, terrorising that poor landlord at the Fox and Hounds."

"Cheers to that," Bloodstone laughed, knocking his glass against the pilot's.

"Now, who fancies a round of the old snooker? A shilling a frame, what do you say?"

Two hours later and a nearly a week's wages poorer, Bloodstone made his way back to his quarters, the idea growing from a seed to fill his brain entirely. Tomorrow, he thought, tomorrow.

CHAPTER NINE

Bloodstone slept like a baby with a long dreamless sleep that saw him wake with the rise of the sun and the chatter of birds in his ears. Looking down at his belly he noticed that his stomach was starting to lose its usual rock-hard and sculpted form and realised that it was almost a week since he had done any proper exercise. He knew that such slovenliness would see him in a world of pain when he finally returned to the regiment, so he pulled on his PT kit, tied his boots and filled his bergen with sand from the fire point outside his quarters.

With the bag firmly strapped to his back and his rifle in his hands, he set off, jogging down the aerodrome perimeter road and out of the main gate, noticing that yesterday's sergeant was on duty again and gave him a friendly nod as he passed. A half-mile further on he started to get into his stride and his mind no longer noticed the weight on his back and the muscles in his legs felt loose and strong as he pounded along the country lanes, his brain mulling over the idea that had come to him in the mess the previous evening. Past the Fox and Hounds he went, narrowly avoiding a dehydrating pile of vomit that lay ominously in the centre of the road, before he turned off onto a narrow footpath that wound away into the fields.

Several miles later he came across a small copse and, selecting a tree, he dropped the bergen from his back and grasped hold of a branch. He pulled himself up until his chest was level with the branch and, enjoying the burn in his arms, lowered himself back down again. Repeating the exercise again and again and again, he heard the words of his first Army training instructor, a wily old veteran of the Boer War, hammering through his head.

"Never give in, never stop. Pain is nothing, pain is weakness leaving the body. Never give in, never stop..."

At one hundred, Bloodstone did one more for luck, then another, dropped to the floor and took a mouthful of water from his canteen before he re-strapped the Bergen, hefted the rifle and set off again at a run. The pain in his biceps and chest reduced as he ate up the miles and he practised his script for the afternoon's shoot in his head as he pounded through the fields and back onto the road. As he neared what he reckoned to be the ten mile mark, he looped back in the direction of the airfield and, as his legs began to feel heavier and heavier, he was thankful that the countryside had a distinct lack of hills. He forced himself into a sprint as he arrived back at the main gate, offered a sweat-filled wave to the Brummie sergeant before a full-pelt run back up the perimeter road saw him arrive at his quarters, gasping for breath but with the familiar sense of achievement coursing through his veins.

He stripped off his kit in his room and dumped it on the floor, then wrapped a towel around his waist and padded down the corridor to the communal showers, where he washed away the morning's sweat and grime under a torrent of blissfully hot water. Feeling fresh and smelling of Imperial Leather soap, he strolled back to his room, where he glanced at his naked self in the full-length mirror, smiling at the ridiculous soldiers' sun tan that had left his arms and face the colour of deep oak, while the rest of his body was whiter than snow.

As he gave himself another once over in the mirror, a familiar giggle squeaked out from behind him. He whipped around, his hands clamped over his crown jewels, and was shocked to see the diminutive figure of Kitty Blythe sitting on his bed, a mischievous grin on her flushed face and a wanton look in her eyes.

"What the..." Bloodstone exclaimed, shocked at the sight of the girl, who was clad in a summer dress entirely unsuitable for this time of year.

"Jesus, Kitty, what are you doing? Hold on, how the devil did you get in here?"

"I thought I could help you with your lines, but I must be a little early," she said in her Welsh lilt, a look of wide-eyed innocence on her face, before nodding at Bloodstone's hands and continuing, "And you don't need to worry about covering that up, I've already seen it. All of it."

Before Bloodstone could respond, she fixed him with a distinctly sultry look and muttered, "So I guess it's my turn now."

With that she reached behind her neck, unclasped her dress and pulled it down to her waist in one swift movement, revealing a distinct lack of underwear and a pair of small but perfectly formed breasts. Bloodstone was shocked into silence by the unexpected sight and his manhood involuntarily started to swell beneath his hands as he stared at the nipples that pointed accusingly in his direction.

He had never been one overly blessed with self-control, especially as far as topless teenage girls were concerned, and his brain was fighting a losing battle with his undercarriage, which was now fully ready for action and quite obviously so, despite the hands that tried to cover it. Summoning every last vestige of willpower, however, he retrieved his towel from the floor and knotted it firmly around his waist, inadvertently creating something of a penile tent-like structure in the process.

"Cover yourself up, Kitty," he ordered gently and reached forward to pull up her dress. As he did so he got a waft of perfume, which did nothing to help his troublesome erectile situation.

With the deliciously tempting bosoms now covered again, Bloodstone stepped back, secretly proud of his show of restraint, albeit tinged with a slight sense of regret and a decent dose of what if.

"Don't you want me, Mr Albert?" the pretty girl on the bed asked with a childlike voice as her face once again returned to its wide-eyed innocence.

"One mustn't mix work and pleasure, Kitty," he replied confidently, sounding a lot more certain than he felt.

"Now I won't tell a soul about this, but it mustn't happen again. And no more sneaking into the mens' quarters or the Wingco will have you off the station as quick as a flash. Do you understand?"

Kitty gave a nod and re-tied her dress with a crestfallen look on her face. Concerned that she might burst into tears at any moment, Bloodstone changed tack.

"Did you say you wanted to help me with my lines?" he asked softly and received another nod in response.

"Excellent, well let's crack on then," he said, pulling on his uniform as Kitty's eyes followed his every move, just as a hawk does its prey.

Finally dressed and with Kitty perched expectantly on the corner of the bed, Bloodstone cleared his throat and began, the words firmly engrained in his head, but the paper script clasped behind his back in case of emergency.

"Greetings fellow subjects, wherever in the Empire you may be..."

Twice through the piece he went, with barely a stumble, as Kitty bounced up and down on the bed with childlike glee and regular claps of delight.

"Bravo, bravo," she exclaimed as he completed the second attempt, "Perfect Mr Albert, just perfect.

"Now let's get you made up for the camera, shall we?"

"Is that really necessary, Kitty?" Bloodstone asked, not especially enamoured with the idea of wearing make-up, "Surely I don't really need lipstick and all that sort of gumph, do I?"

"You'd be surprised," she responded with a giggle, opening a leather bag containing a multitude of potions, pastes and brushes, "The camera can do some strange things to a face, even one as handsome as yours."

"Now, sit here please," she said and pulled out a chair from the under the room's small writing desk.

"The first thing we're going to need to do is sort these out," she ordered with a newfound professionalism as she pointed at the bruises around Bloodstone's eyes that had now faded from their original angry purple to a dirty shade of yellowy brown.

Bloodstone groaned as Kitty squeezed a generous dollop of something pink onto his cheek and started attacking it with a small brush. She sung to herself as she worked, the soft and unintelligible words of a Welsh lullaby emanating from her lips as Bloodstone's face become her canvas. After a few minutes she paused, standing back to admire her handiwork with a look of satisfaction in her eyes.

"There we go, all finished."

She held out a hand mirror and Bloodstone recoiled in horror at the make-up clad face that stared back at him. My God, he thought, if only his father could see him now. Kitty busied herself with her collection of pots and tools while Bloodstone took another glance at his reflection and shuddered.

"Oh, and by the way, Mr Albert," she said, her face colouring slightly as she darted a glance in the direction of the Major's nether regions, "Your, er, thing, I've never seen one so, um, big."

Bloodstone, somewhat taken aback by the unexpected comment, sighed in despair and felt his tackle start to grow again, pushing not so subtly against the confines of his uniform trousers.

"Indeed, my dear Kitty, indeed," he said, trying but failing to change the subject, "Unnaturally large genitals. It's the Bloodstone curse. You should've seen the size of my poor Grandpa."

"I'd rather see yours again," she replied with a wanton look in her eyes and, stepping forwards, unbuttoned Bloodstone's breeches with one swift movement and grasped his manhood in both hands.

As she dropped to her knees, his resolve crumbled completely and he simply closed his eyes as Kitty set to work, realising with a mixture of delight and disgust that her mouth was far too advanced for her eighteen years. Too late to stop now, though, he thought, as he watched the top of Kitty's head bob up and down, while an enormous grin spread across his face.

CHAPTER TEN

At twenty-five past three and with Kitty in tow, Bloodstone arrived at the allotted meeting place, which was a dispersal point in a quiet corner of the aerodrome that had an undisturbed view across the runway to the control tower.

A film camera was already set up on a tripod, while a Lancaster sat magnificently at ease twenty yards away with its great wings flexing gently in the afternoon breeze and its four engines huge and brooding. Fifteen black swastikas were painted beneath the pilot's window alongside a cartoon of a scantily clad beauty astride a bomb, next to which were scrawled the words Salty Suzy.

Looking up at the splendid beast, Bloodstone was more determined than ever to pursue the idea that had come to him the previous evening so, when Huckleberry James appeared from behind one of the bomber's enormous wheels with his hair once again wildly unkempt and a fresh cravat at his neck, he explained his proposal.

"I think you may be slightly addled in the brain, Major," James said after he had heard him out, "But I love it, it's simply glorious. There's only one problem, though."

"Grubb?" Bloodstone asked.

"Absolutely, I can't see that jolly old fellow going for it," James said with a mock grimace.

"Ha," Bloodstone exclaimed, "Leave that with me. I'm not just a pretty face you know."

"No doubt, Major, no doubt," James responded with a wink. "Now let's get this show on the road, shall we?"

He manoeuvred Bloodstone onto a white cross that had been chalked on the tarmac, five feet from the camera and directly in front of the Lancaster, and handed Kitty a microphone.

"You hold that just out of shot, my darling," he instructed, before turning to Bloodstone and continuing, "When I say the word just start speaking. Remember to look at the camera and, if you foul up, all you need to do it start the sentence again. I'll do any slicing and dicing afterwards. We'll run through it once to make sure all the kit is working tickety-boo, then we'll do it for real. Ready?"

"Ready," they both confirmed.

"In that case, action!" shouted James from behind the camera, a flamboyant wave of a handkerchief thrown in for good measure.

"Greetings fellow subjects, wherever in the Empire you may be. I'm Major Albert Bloodstone DSO, DSC and MC with bar..."

Several minutes later and with his spiel complete, Bloodstone took a breath and stepped off the chalk cross.

"Spiffing, Major, absolutely spiffing," Huckleberry James announced, "You, sir, are a natural.

"Now, Kitty, love, make sure you keep that microphone nice and high and, Major, please remember to keep looking at the camera, not at me. Although I know I'm damned hard to resist."

With a smile he handed Bloodstone a small silver flask from which the major took a large gulp of something fiery, swilled the liquid around his mouth, swallowed painfully and handed the container back to the waiting fleshy hand of James.

The cravat-clad cameraman deposited the flask in a waistcoat pocket, twiddled a knob on his camera and looked back up at his quarry.

"Ready? Right, let's go in three, two, one, action!"

Another wave of the handkerchief and Bloodstone was off again, the words now rolling off his tongue without thought.

"Greetings fellow subjects, wherever in the Empire you may be. I'm Major Albert Bloodstone DSO, DSC and MC with bar and I'm here on an RAF airfield in eastern England, home of our brave bomber boys, to bring you all the latest news of the week.

"From this very base alone, Lancasters have flown nearly one hundred sorties in the last week, dropping an unprecedented number of bombs on the industrial heartland of the Nazi Reich, severely damaging Germany's infrastructure and crippling her twisted ability to wage war.

"They were joined by their brave comrades from other squadrons throughout Bomber Command and, together, they've rained close to a quarter of a million pounds of bombs upon the factories, railroads and military establishments of the enemy during the last seven days. We lost just a handful of our aircraft in these attacks, while twenty-three Luftwaffe night fighters have been confirmed as destroyed.

"The Fuhrer himself, that warped purveyor of malfeasance and evil, has publicly expressed his fear of our brave RAF boys and has ordered his generals to prepare plans in case of a full breakdown of German infrastructure. But we will not rest until that day comes and our brave bomber crews, supported by their heroic brothers in arms from Fighter Command, as well as our Eighth Air Force cousins from across the Atlantic, will continue to pound Hitler's Reich into submission.

"On the ground the fight continues too, with our Army pushing the German and Italian forces back across southern Europe. Just a few days ago our troops seized the city of Naples and it's surely not long now until all of Italy collapses completely, hammering yet another nail into the fetid coffin of the Hun.

"In the East, Stalin's Red Army continue their relentless bleeding of the German forces, where the Nazi invader's Dnieper Line is about to collapse. With the bitter Russian winter just around the corner, it's only a matter of time before Hitler's troops are forced back into their battered homeland, where be assured that we'll be waiting to finish them off once and for all.

"But until that day, which is now tantalisingly closer than it's been at any point during the last four years, we must keep fighting, both at home and on the front line. The Empire expects that every man, every woman and every child will do their duty, be it in the munitions factories that supply our gallant warriors, on the farms that keep our bellies full, on the ships that guard our seas or here with our fliers in the skies above.

"As our tireless behemoth of a Prime Minister famously said not so long ago, we will never surrender; never. So, hear this, Adolf, we're coming for you. Be afraid, be very afraid. Or, if you prefer, in your own heathen tongue, Wir finden Dich. Furchte Dich, furchte Dich sehr!

"So, until next week my brave boys and girls, keep up the good fight, wherever you may be, and God bless you one and all."

Completing his speech with a punctilious salute and his most dazzling of smiles, Bloodstone exhaled deeply and stepped off his chalk cross.

"And cut! That's a wrap, as we thespians say," Huckleberry James announced from behind his camera before he emerged with a huge grin plastered across his face to shake Bloodstone's hand and plant an enormous kiss on Kitty's cheek.

"That was just the ticket, my dear Major, just the ticket. Maybe we should whisk you off to Hollywood to join the red-carpet gang as soon as this beastly war is over. I must say I'm mightily impressed; you really are a natural."

Blushing slightly beneath his powdered cheeks, Bloodstone thanked the man, thinking to himself that this current gig was certainly a damned sight easier than killing Germans, yet for him it lacked some of the action that helped to keep the blood pumping through his veins.

"I'll go back to my pokey little cell of a room and get this film edited up right now," James explained.

"I'll add in some footage of aeroplanes and bombs and all sorts of other willy-raising stuff and we'll have the finished product on the overnight train to London. Those miserable bumsniffs at the Ministry of Information will have put their grubby little approval stamp on it by midday tomorrow, so you better get yourself a date for the cinema on Friday night, Major, because you'll never need to ask for one again after this hits the screens. You'll be fighting them off with a stick, isn't that right Kitty?"

Kitty giggled her usual giggle and looked at Bloodstone with her big brown eyes and the now familiar wanton look plastered across her face. Knowing what delights were hidden beneath her skimpy summer outfit and unable to stop himself undressing her in his mind, he pulled himself together and set off in the direction of Wing Commander Grubb's office. He had business to attend to.

CHAPTER ELEVEN

"Enter," growled the familiar Australian accent and Bloodstone took a deep breath, opened the door and let himself in.

"Ah, Major, what can I do for you?" Grubb asked, returning a salute without bothering to get out of his chair, before continuing, "I've got a raid on tonight, this better be quick."

"Absolutely, sir, I'll take just two minutes of your time, if you'd be so kind," he replied with a smile, earning a scowl from the bearded Wing Commander.

"I thought you'd be interested to know that we've just shot our first news piece, sir. It'll be sent to London tonight and should be showing in the theatres on Friday. I wondered, seeing as this is your command, if you'd like to take a look at the film before we ship it? You know, just to give the proverbial thumbs up."

Grubb put down a pen that he was holding in his hand and looked at Bloodstone for several seconds before replying.

"I think I would, thank you, Major."

He picked up his pen again, before looking up once more and demanding, "Will that be all?"

"Not quite, sir," Bloodstone said, pointing at the empty chair facing the desk and asking, "May I?"

"If you must," Grubb replied impatiently, waiting for Bloodstone to sit down before he asked, "So, what is it?"

"Well, as I mentioned, sir, we've just shot our first newsreel and I think it's splendid, really I do. It paints the squadron in a wonderful light and I'm sure the boys, and you, will be incredibly pleased with it. But I'm not sure it really shows how brave the chaps are and what a fantastically tough job they do, day in, day out.

"I think the British public, and the Australian, of course, need to know that, sir. In fact, I think they need to see it for themselves."

"Get to the point, Bloodstone."

Bloodstone took a breath before he continued. "I want to film a mission, sir. From aboard a Lanc."

Down went the pen again. "Absolutely no fucking way. Anything else?"

"I'm serious, sir. I'm confident that this can really help with the morale of the chaps and it'll be the perfect way to write the squadron into the history books. When this is all over, generations to come will know what a crucial part five-one-three played."

"Are you arguing with me, Major?" Grubb asked, picking up the pen again.

"Certainly not, sir. It's just that I heard that the squadron should be completing its thousandth sortie within the next few weeks and I figured that footage like this would complement that story wonderfully. I presume there'll be some sort of party for the boys, sir, when they hit that milestone?"

"You seem very well informed, Major," the Wing Commander commented, "And yes, I'm sure they'll deserve a bevvy or two. Now, this meeting is over, I've got things to do."

"Of course, sir," Bloodstone said, rose to his feet and made his way towards the door, where he paused with his hand on the knob.

"By the way, sir, is that the Appleford Sisters?" he asked innocently, pointing at the photo frame on the windowsill that displayed a picture of three glamorous singers behind a microphone.

"Yes, it is, good looking Sheilas," Grubb acknowledged as he glanced behind him at the photograph, "For a bunch of Pommie girls, that is."

"Indeed, sir," Bloodstone agreed, "Perhaps you could get them to perform at the thousandth raid party? I hear that they do their fair share of shows for the troops."

"Not a chance, those little beauties are booked up for months to come. Fucking Yanks are snapping up every bit of skirt in this miserable country."

"Really, sir? Well, it just so happens that I may be able to help there," Bloodstone offered as he paused by the door. Down went the pen again.

"You see, the tall one in the middle, Jane I believe her name is, is a particular, how do we say, friend of mine. I'm sure I'd have no trouble at all in persuading her to bring her sisters along to Scampton for a singsong. In fact, I'm sure they'd be positively enamoured with the idea, sir."

"Is that so?" the Wing Commander said as he leaned back in his chair and fixed Bloodstone with a withering look. "Clever little bastard aren't you, Major?

"Alright, you win. I see how this works. You get your flight, I get my Sheilas. In which case, I presume you already have a crew lined up to take you up on this little jaunt of yours?"

"I do, sir," Bloodstone replied, hardly able to believe that his ruse had worked. "I'm sure that Pilot Officer Ashton would be more than willing to let me hitch a lift."

"Ronnie Ashton, eh? Best bloody pilot in the squadron. Only two more missions left for him and his crew if I'm not wrong. Well, I guess there's no time like the present is there," Grubb said with a sardonic smile, picking up a telephone receiver on his desk and barking an order into it.

Two minutes later Ronald Ashton arrived with cheeks flushed, hat askew and a half-eaten bacon sandwich in his hand.

"Good evening Pilot Officer," Grubb said, waving away Ashton's attempt to straighten his hat while simultaneously hiding his sandwich behind his back, before continuing, "Major Bloodstone here will be flying with you tonight in a strictly observational capacity."

"Tonight?" Bloodstone blurted, shocked.

"Tonight. Any problems with that, Ashton?"

"None, sir."

"Good stuff. That'll teach you to play silly bastards with me, eh, Bloodstone?" Grubb said with a grin.

"Now, scram. Ashton here will tell you everything you need to know. And don't forget, we've got a deal," he finished with a nod towards the windowsill.

"By the way, are you wearing make-up?"

"Long story, sir," Bloodstone replied, noticing a befuddled glance from Ashton.

"Jesus Christ," Grubb despaired. "Now get going, and good luck to both of you."

The two men saluted the Wing Commander and left the office together, Ashton taking a bite from his sandwich as soon as the door was shut behind them.

"That's jolly decent of you, Ashton," Bloodstone said, "I must say I'm most grateful."

"No problem at all, Major, it's the least I can do," Ashton replied through a mouthful of bread. "Now, we're scheduled for take-off at twenty hundred hours, so you've already missed the test flight and the briefing, but it's a quick one to Wilhelmshaven with a light load, which is why the Boss must be letting you join the party.

"I suggest you get yourself across to the stores and find some kit. The QM will give you what you need. Then meet me back outside the mess at eighteen hundred and I'll introduce you to the rest of the crew before we head across to George."

Nodding in agreement, Bloodstone glanced at his watch and, seeing that it was already half past four, set off at a run towards the small building that housed Huckleberry James' billet. Finding the man's room, he rapped once on the door and burst in without waiting for an answer.

James was sitting at a desk, surrounded by a multitude of film reel, scissors in hand and wearing nothing but an enormous pair of silk underpants. He turned with a scowl to see who the intruder was and his face softened as he saw Bloodstone.

"Sorry to disturb you, Huckleberry," Bloodstone gasped between breaths, "But I need you to show me how to use a camera."

CHAPTER TWELVE

At six o'clock on the dot Bloodstone arrived outside the officers' mess, sweating in his recently acquired fur-lined leather flying suit and laden down like a packhorse. Over one shoulder was slung a parachute pack, over the other was a flight bag containing gloves, hats, scarves and a multitude of other paraphernalia deemed vital by the chirpy quartermaster running the stores, while in his hand he carried an obscenely heavy solid leather case that contained, according to Huckleberry James, the very latest in handheld film camera technology. Completing the load was an oxygen mask slung around his neck, while his chunky service revolver and twelve-inch combat knife were each tucked into the top of one of his second-hand flying boots.

Ashton, Chalky and the five enlisted men were already gathered in a huddle, half-smoked cigarettes in hand and all similarly attired save for a gaudy selection of scarves at their respective necks. Bloodstone staggered across to them, lugging his cumbersome load with him, and the group turned to cast their eyes on the new arrival.

"Fits all this, like? Well if it isn't our bonnie soldier," said the dark-haired Scot that he remembered from the previous morning, shaking Bloodstone's hand with a huge grin plastered across his face, "Foos yer doos a day min? Bill's the name, bomb aimer's the business and, och aye, it's a pleasure to have ye aboard, sir."

"Likewise, Bill, likewise," Bloodstone replied as he put the camera case gently on the floor to shake the sergeant's hand, not having the foggiest what the small Scotsman had just said to him.

"You've already met Chalky, sir," Ashton said as he stubbed out his cigarette with his boot, before he pointed at another man in the group, "And this is Buster, our tail-end Charlie."

Buster reached out to shake Bloodstone's hand, a toothless smile on his face, a cigarette drooping from the corner of his mouth and a puckered scar across his wrinkled forehead.

"Don't be alarmed by his frightful looks," Ashton said with a laugh, "The poor blighter went down with a Whitley in thirty-nine. Knocked out all his teeth and mashed his swede up something rotten."

"Yeah, while you was still in your short pants, Capt'n," the grinning Buster replied in a tuneful Cockney accent, winking at the pilot.

Ashton winked back and introduced the next man, a good-looking boy in his late teens with mop of dark hair and a suspicious looking purple bruise on his neck.

"Jimmy," the youngster shyly announced in a boyish voice with a hint of West Country and self-consciously shifted his scarf as he saw Bloodstone glance at the bruise, "Mid-upper gunner. Good to meet you, sir."

"And you too, Jimmy," Bloodstone said, noticing a slight twitch in the boy's left eye and a right hand that visibly trembled, albeit minutely. Poor blighter, just like my Uncle Cecil, he thought to himself as he remembered the twitching gentleman who had been a regular at family Christmases of his youth. Too many shell bursts in the fourteen-eighteen war, his father had discretely told the inquisitive young Albert one evening; the body just wasn't designed for the mechanics of modern warfare. Which, he thought as he looked at Jimmy, was a phenomenon that he had witnessed for himself far too many times to count over the last four years.

Before he could brood on the depressing subject any longer, the next flier stepped forward to shake his hand with a vice like grip.

"My name Przybylowski," the man grunted in a thick Polish accent, his hand still gripping Bloodstone's as the Major studied his face, noticing hard eyes, a long-ago broken nose and a square jaw. Not a man to be trifled with, Bloodstone thought to himself as he was finally freed from the iron handshake.

"Bloodstone. It's a pleasure to meet you, Przybylowski," he replied, stumbling over the tongue-twisting name and earning a titter from the rest of the crew.

"We just call him the Count," Ashton laughed, "I haven't met a man yet who can pronounce our Polski friend's name properly. And how he's managed to stick around with the RAF this long, God only knows. But a better engineer you won't find, in Poland, here in Blighty or anywhere else for that matter."

"Amen to that," the final member of the crew announced and reached out a long gangly arm to shake Bloodstone's hand. "Nobby Ball at your service, sir, wireless op and the only remotely normal one in this crew of freaks and misfits."

"Normal? Don't make me laugh," Buster the rear gunner cackled, sending flecks of spit flying from his toothless mouth, "Look at the size of this creature, have you ever seen anyfink so fuckin' giraffe-like?"

Studying the man at the end of the gangly arm, Bloodstone had to admit to himself that Ball did have an uncanny resemblance to a giraffe, with an abnormally long body and a neck that looked as if it might have been stretched by some sort of medieval torture device. Atop the neck was a bulbous head and giant eyes ringed with excessively long lashes, while the mouth was fixed in a permanent impish grin that Bloodstone couldn't help but warm to.

Releasing Ball's thin fingers and with a nod to acknowledge his welcome, Bloodstone shrugged the parachute from his shoulder, took out his gold cigarette tin and offered it around to the crew. He lit one for himself and sucked in a delicious lungful of smoke before looking around at the small huddle of men.

"It's damned good of you to have me aboard, really it is. And by the way, call me Bertie when we're upstairs."

He paused to release a mouthful of smoke into the chilly evening air before continuing.

"I hear that you're the best bloody crew in the squadron, so I'll be sure to keep out of your way and let you get on with your jobs. Ashton's the boss up there, so just forget that I'm even here.

"And by the way, I've done a hell of a lot more take-offs than I have landings, so I'm hoping that tonight's going to be a little different."

"It fuckin' better be," Buster replied with a grin as a fresh fag hung from his mouth, "I don't fancy floating my ass down to earth on a piece of string, no fank you."

"Don't worry, my brave darlings, I'll take good care of you all as always. We'll have you home in time for breakfast, not a Hun scratch on you," Ashton said as a battered green Jeep pulled up alongside the gaggle of aircrew, "Now, here's our cab, look lively chaps."

The eight men, festooned with kit, clambered onto the Jeep and clung to each other for dear life as a pretty WAAF driver gunned the engine, ground the gears and staccatoed the vehicle away from the mess, picking up speed as she sped away towards the far side of the aerodrome.

Balanced precariously on the bonnet of the Jeep, Bloodstone looked out across the airfield to see a multitude of vehicles, all similarly piled high with aircrew and bouncing across the grass as they made their way to their dispersal points. Waiting for them, loaded, armed and ready to rain hell from the skies, were nineteen Lancasters, parked, silent and beautiful, beneath the setting sun.

How many of those Jeepfuls of young men would be coming home tomorrow morning, Bloodstone thought to himself as the driver pulled up beneath an enormous and brooding wing of G for George. Would he be returning here with the dawn, he wondered as he jumped down from the bonnet, or would this be the last time that he'd feel the ground beneath his boots?

No going back now, he said to himself as he pushed the niggling thought out of his head. No going back now.

CHAPTER THIRTEEN

"Right chaps, here's the gen," Pilot Officer Ashton said to the seven men of his crew who had gathered in a tight knot close to one of the Lancaster's enormous wheels.

With the whiff of aviation fuel strong in the early evening air, there was not a cigarette to be seen and all eyes were fixed firmly on the blonde-haired youngster, the joking and banter now replaced with serious faces.

"You've all been briefed already but we'll run through it one more time," he continued as he glanced down at a series of handwritten scribbles in a battered leather notebook in his hand.

"The target tonight is the docks at Wilhelmshaven. We've all been there before and you know how fiery those damned AA guns can be, so we'll be dropping our load at 14,000 feet. There'll be nineteen of us tonight and we'll be joined by fifteen of our Aussie friends from 460 over at Binbrook. 626 from Wickenby and 290 from Skellingthorpe will also be in on the show, although they'll be splitting off to give Hamburg a pounding.

"We'll all be heading off out over the North Sea in the direction of Denmark to try and give Jerry the slip, then we'll be doing a sharp turn to starboard towards the German coast, before another turn to target. Chalky, you're happy with the bearings?"

"Yes, Skipper, all under control," the skinny youth replied with a confident nod, "We should be over target two hours and fifty-five minutes after takeover if the wind stays as expected."

"Splendid," Ashton acknowledged before glancing at his notebook once more and addressing the group again.

"The Pathfinders will be dumping green TIs as the primary marker tonight so, Jock, keep your eyes peeled for that. As you can see, it's a pretty murky night but the Boss is expecting the cloud cover to be fairly sparse by the time we get to the German coast, so you should get a good view of those docks."

The small Scotsman gave a swift thumbs up and Ashton continued with his briefing, inadvertently stroking the hairs of his thin moustache as he did so.

"Gunners, the weather and our route should help to keep those night fighters at bay, but you never can be too sure, so keep your eyes peeled and shout out anything you see. As always, don't go blasting away at shadows, remember your deflection and don't waste your ammo."

Turning to Bloodstone, Ashton continued, "There won't be much moon tonight so I'm not sure what you're going to get on that camera of yours, sir. But base yourself on the rest bed for this show, just astern of Nobby, and you might catch a bit of the action. That's Jock's usual spot for take-off but I'm sure the two of you can cosy up until we're off the deck.

"Like I said, we're not expecting this to one to be too rough, but you never know with Jerry, so it might be useful to have an extra pair of hands aboard. Jimmy will get you settled in and show you the ropes, and then just keep your ears open in case we need you to be Johnny-on-the-spot when we're on route.

"By the way, have you checked your pockets, sir?"

"Pockets?" Bloodstone asked with a cocked eyebrow.

"Apparently it's amazing what the Hun can gather from a bus ticket or last night's cinema stub if you get shot down, so nothing personal in your pockets is the rule," the pilot replied.

"Absolutely, skipper, it's the same with us brown jobs too before we go into action," Bloodstone nodded and padded down his bulky suit despite the fact that it contained nothing more exciting than his personalised cigarette case and his ever-present lucky charm, a dented Mauser bullet that had been agonisingly dug out of his chest three years before.

"Excellent," Ashton acknowledged and tucked his notebook inside his jacket before looking around his crew with a grin.

"Right chaps, shall we?"

A series of enthusiastic nods followed from the assembled men and Bloodstone watched with some consternation as the small group sidled closer to the Lancaster's wheel, unzipped their respective flies, flopped out their manhoods and proceeded to urinate as one onto the rubber tyre.

"Come on Bertie, sir," Nobby the lanky wireless operator ordered with a smirk as he looked back over his shoulder, "It's good luck."

With a mock shrug of despair and not wanting to tempt fate on his first mission, Bloodstone waddled across to his seven crewmates, lowered his zip and added his stream to the stinking torrent that was soaking the poor wheel.

A shout came from above as an overall-clad member of G for George's ground crew poked his rotund and grease-streaked face over the front edge of the Lancaster's wing, "Oi, will you filthy bastards stop pissing on my ship."

Buster gave a friendly hoot of derision and used his free hand to aim two fingers in the general direction of the oil stained mechanic, who responded with a similar salute before continuing his profanity-ridden ticking off.

"Twenty-eight times you scabby creatures have taken a slash on that tyre, and twenty-eight times I've had to make sure that piss-soaked rubber is still in one piece when you're back on the ground. King George don't pay me enough to be manhandling your syphilis-ridden wazz, let me tell you that."

"Don't worry Chiefie," Ashton called up to the wing, ducking as a flying spanner cartwheeled overhead to land on the tarmac fifteen feet away, "Only one more to go after tonight, then we'll be out of your hair for good."

"And about time too, sir," the face replied with a gap-toothed smile before it retreated over the wing with a final muffled shout of, "Good luck boys, give those dirty Krauts one for me."

With their ritual complete, the eight men zipped themselves back into their clothing, picked up their kit that was piled nearby and made their way towards the rear of the Lancaster, where a three-rung ladder gave them access to a small door on the aircraft's starboard side.

The pilot, Ronald Ashton, hauled himself up the ladder first, ungainly and awkward in his thick leather suit, followed by Chalky who, Bloodstone was pleased to see, appeared far less miserable than in the mess the previous evening. Next to clamber up the ladder was Przybylowski who had a tool bag slung over his shoulder and a faded red and white Polish eagle stitched to the back of his jacket. Bill the Scottish bomb aimer was next through the door, his diminutive figure given a slap on the backside from a hooting Nobby Ball, who proceeded to contort his gangly body almost double as he bent himself into the aircraft.

Buster, his scarred head and toothless gums giving him a positively vicious look in the early evening light, hawked a stringy globule of phlegm onto the tarmac and clambered up the ladder, turned left towards the tail and squeezed his squat shoulders through the doorway.

"After you, Jimmy," Bloodstone gestured to the only other man still standing beside the aircraft. The youngster seemed not to hear as he stared back across the grass in the direction of the small cluster of distant buildings that made up the operational heart of the airfield, his hands clasped together in front of him, his left eyelid still twitching and his lips moving as if in silent prayer.

"Jimmy," Bloodstone repeated gently as he touched the gunner on the arm, causing him to snap out of his trance, "Are you okay, chap?"

"Yes, sir, I'm fine," the teenager responded quietly, his face pale and beads of sweat visible on his forehead despite the chilly evening air.

"Fine, sir, absolutely fine," he repeated, almost to himself, as he started up the ladder, the fingers of his right hand inadvertently stroking the purple bruise on his neck. He paused as he reached the doorway, turned to take one last mournful look back across the airfield, before he took a deep breath and ducked through the opening.

Jimmy certainly wasn't fine, Bloodstone thought to himself as he lumped his bags up into the Lancaster and climbed up behind them. Not fine at all.

CHAPTER FOURTEEN

The interior of G for George had the familiar whiff of aircraft the world over, Bloodstone thought as he hauled himself through the small door. The odour of oil, mixed with the tang of metal and the musk of sweat-dried leather, attacked his nostrils and, taking a deep snort of the comforting aroma, he looked around as his eyes adjusted to the dim lighting inside the Lancaster. To his left, the leather-clad backside of Buster was squeezing itself into the rear turret, while to his right the fuselage sloped away uphill, a dark narrow corridor punctuated by the raised floor of the bomb bay and the dangling seat of Jimmy's gun turret ten feet away.

He hefted his various bags over his shoulders, picked up the camera case and made his way up the slope, squeezing past Jimmy and his two vicious looking Browning machine guns as he searched for his allocated spot.

"The rest bed's ahead on the port side, sir," Jimmy said, glancing down from his turret as he fiddled with his guns, "I'll be along in a second to get you sorted."

Nodding his thanks to the youngster, Bloodstone continued his journey into the belly of the Lancaster and found himself astonished by the tight confines in which the crew had to operate. The transport aircraft he was used to, the Dakotas and Yorks, were veritable buses compared to this sleek war machine, he mused as he clambered over the waist-high barrier of the aft wing spar, bouncing his helmeted head off the low roof as he did so.

Finally arriving at his destination, he dropped his kit onto the small rest bed and noticed an ominous dark stain on the cracked and worn green leather. Some poor bugger's copped one here, he thought grimly as he pictured some long-gone airman bleeding out three miles up in the sky and wondering what he was letting himself in for.

Ahead of him, over another wing spar, he could see Nobby setting up station by his wireless dials, while further on Chalky, the Count and Ashton were busy settling into their positions and preparing for the mission ahead, just as they had twenty-eight times before. Bloodstone couldn't see Bill, deep in the nose in his bomb aimer's station, but a series of barely decipherable oaths and curses echoed their way back up through the fuselage, confirming the man's presence.

Jimmy appeared from behind and climbed over the rear spar with his scarf now wound tightly around his neck and tucked into his thick leather jacket.

"Settling in alright, sir?" he asked in his seesawing West Country accent.

"Absolutely, just wizard," Bloodstone replied as he unclipped the latches of the camera case, took out the fancy device and laid it gently on the green leather.

"Stow your chute here, sir," Jimmy instructed as he motioned to a net on the starboard wall and then pointed to the opposite side of the fuselage, "Here's your oxygen supply and above it's your intercom connection.

"Not much else to know really, sir. If the skipper orders abandon ship then get yourself back out the door you've just come in or down into the nose. There's a trapdoor down where Jock lives that you can drop out off. Whatever you do, don't use the emergency exit above you unless we're on the deck."

"True that," chipped in Nobby as he poked his bulbous head around the corner of the wireless station, "Else you'll end up splattered all over Jimmy's turret and take the poor fella with you. And what would your little bit of crumpet think about that eh, Jimmy?"

"Got yourself a lady, have you?" Bloodstone asked, straightening up and giving the youngster a wink. "Jolly good show young man."

Jimmy mumbled something incomprehensible and looked at the floor as his cheeks blushed a deep shade of red.

"Of course he has, good looking boy like that," Nobby continued, "How do you think he got that whopper of a hicky on his neck. Proper wild one she is."

"You can say that again," came a Cockney voice from behind, as Buster emerged from the depths of the tail with a forefinger burrowing deep into his left nostril. "Humping him half to death behind the Fox last night she was."

There were more mumbles and uncomfortable glances at the floor from Jimmy who, Bloodstone thought, resembled an oversized and embarrassed schoolboy.

"You wanna be careful there, son," Buster carried on, inspecting a particularly sticky lump of snot that he'd excavated from his nose, "You'll be riddled."

"He's right, Jimmy," Nobby grinned, "Rumour is Chiefie and his number two have both had a ride on her. And I wouldn't want to be anywhere that Chiefie's been poking his filthy sausage."

"Both at once, I heard," Buster laughed as he sucked the bogie from his finger with a satisfying grunt, "On the roof of the main hangar."

"While the Boss watched," Nobby added with an idiotic grin spread across his face.

Jimmy's head, now entirely purple, finally jerked up from the floor.

"Why don't you both just sod off," he snapped, his eyes wide and seemingly close to tears, before he shoved past Buster and stormed off towards the back of the plane.

"Come on Jimmy, we're only joshing," Nobby shouted after him, with little effect.

"Buster, go check he's alright," he ordered, receiving a roll of the eyes from the snot-gobbling gunner, who proceeded to shrug dismissively before turning on his heel and trudging after the youngster.

"Poor chap," Bloodstone said to Nobby, "Young love, eh?"

"Not quite, sir," the wireless operator replied with a sad look on his face, "Bloody woman's going to break his heart. He's a decent lad and this war's been tough for him, he doesn't need that too. Maybe you could have a word with her?"

"Me? What can I do? I don't know this creature from Adam."

"Of course you do, sir, it's your film star girl. Kitty I think her name is."

"Kitty?" Bloodstone repeated as his brain finally clicked into gear, "Oh bloody hell."

CHAPTER FIFTEEN

The Lancaster's four engines kicked into life one by one, each giving out a cough and a splutter before settling into a rhythmic growl that echoed throughout the plane. The hum of the engines sent vibrations through the airframe and the teeth of the eight men on board rattled and chattered as the power of the four Merlins reached every corner of the craft.

Bloodstone and Bill sat on the rest bed as the Lancaster taxied from its dispersal point and made its way towards the main runway, to which eighteen other bomb-laden aircraft were headed. Above them, through a small window in the out-of-bounds emergency hatch, they could see a succession of coloured flares lighting up the evening darkness.

"That's the signal, laddie," Bill shouted over the hum of the engines as one of his gloved hands tapped an impatient rhythm on his knee, "We'll be on our way in a minute."

The small Scotsman noticed Bloodstone looking at the drumming fingers and flashed a forced smile.

"The waiting's the worst bit, always gets my belly a-shuggling. Twenty-eight times I've done this the now and, I don't mind telling ye, twenty-eight times I've nearly wet ma breeks. But when we're off the deck I'll be fine as a fiddle; always was an impatient jobbie."

Bloodstone smiled back, albeit with a slight effort, as he thought that only a fool wouldn't be nervous at what was ahead. Eight men, strapped into a flimsy conglomeration of fabric, metal and plastic and sitting astride thousands of pounds of high explosives, were about to launch themselves into the darkness of the most heavily defended skies in the world. He felt entirely naked, his only weapon the useless revolver tucked into his boot, and realised for the first time that whether or not he came home for breakfast tomorrow morning was completely out of his hands.

It was a strange feeling, especially for a man so used to controlling his own destiny with a rifle, a handful of grenades and, if things got really sticky, twelve inches of razor-sharp steel. A spot of mud and a shell scrape seemed especially attractive right now, he thought as he wondered at the strange set of orders that had brought him to this distant Lincolnshire airfield.

He was snapped out of his depressing meanderings by a slap on the leg from the bomb aimer, who had no doubt seen the concern creeping across his face.

"Och, don't worry, sir, you'll be just fine," he offered with another friendly slap, "The skipper's a lucky laddie, we'll be home before you know it.

"Now, how about making me famous with that camera of yours? There's a bonnie wee WAAF I've got my eye on and nae doubt she'll look at me a little finer if ma coupon's all over the silver screen."

Not entirely sure what coupons had to do with it but getting the gist of the sergeant's request, Bloodstone nodded, plucked the camera from where it lay by his feet and hefted it onto his shoulder. With the twist of a few knobs and the flick of a switch, just like Huckleberry James had shown him, the expensive piece of machinery whirred into life.

"Give us a smile, Jock," he instructed, aiming the lens at the dark-haired Scotsman who gave a grin that was barely distinguishable in the dark confines of the fuselage, followed by a good natured two fingers up in the Major's direction.

"Well that's buggered up your chance of fame, hasn't it," Bloodstone said with a chuckle and turned his lens towards the rear of the plane where Jimmy's booted feet protruded beneath his turret, swinging gently as the Lancaster made its way across the tarmac.

Reaching its allotted place at number two in the queue of aircraft waiting for their signal to take off, G for George paused for barely a minute at the end of the runway, her engines idling, before the light of a green flare flooded through Bloodstone's small Perspex window and lit up the gloomy interior.

"That's us, Skipper," Nobby announced over the intercom, "Chocks away."

In the cockpit, Ashton and the Count pushed the four throttle levers to maximum, causing the engines to growl and the Lancaster to buck slightly, as if suddenly released from an invisible rubber band. Finally off the leash, she accelerated down the runway, her four Rolls Royce Merlins pumping out vicious amounts of power as she picked up speed. On the rest bed, Bloodstone attempted to keep his camera steady as the plane bumped and jolted along the runway, the roar of the engines increasing and the vibrations threatening to tear the aircraft to pieces.

Just as he thought she was going to shake herself apart, the Lancaster's two huge wheels came unstuck from the tarmac and the nose rose towards the clouds, ever so slightly at first and then increasingly steeply as physics started to do its thing. Finally off the ground and in the air where she belonged, G for George's shaking reduced considerably as more than six thousand galloping horses of engine power drove her onwards and upwards, defying gravity and eating up the chilly October sky.

As the Lancaster climbed, Bill abandoned his spot on the rest bed and made his way down into the nose, leaving Bloodstone to switch off his camera and stow it against the fuselage wall. He leaned back against a strut, enjoying the sensation of the rhythmic vibrations that echoed through his spine, and wondered what the next few hours would bring. The light was so poor that his camera was pretty much useless, he realised, secretly admitting that he had known all along that was likely to be the case. Once again, he thought, he had put himself in harm's way for no good reason other than to get in on a bit of the action. To scratch at the itch that only living on a cliff edge and knocking on the reaper's door could satisfy.

But what else was there to do on a chilly Lincolnshire night, he mused, and instantly remembered Kitty's perky bosom and skillful tongue and realised that there most certainly was something else he could have been doing tonight. But, if Nobby and Buster had been right with their sordid tales of the nymphomaniac teen, any more than this afternoon's shenanigans would undoubtedly result in a spot of the clap, which, he admitted, wasn't overly appealing. He'd been there before and the idea of an evening of being shot at by Jerry flak guns and night fighters was infinitely more attractive than the thought of a disapproving nurse shoving sharp implements down his todger.

Wincing at the memory, he was snapped back to the present by the crackle of the intercom in his ear.

"Keep your eyes peeled for friendlies, chaps," said Ashton's voice from the pilot's seat, "It's cloudy as hell tonight and I don't want us coming a cropper because some green crew isn't looking where they're going.

"Major, an extra set of eyes would be useful up here, if you'd be so kind."

Pleased to have something to distract him from his thoughts of VD, teenage breasts and scathing nurses, Bloodstone clambered to his feet and squeezed his way past Nobby, feeling as if he was walking uphill as the Lancaster continued its climb into the night sky. The next obstacle was Chalky who was hunched over his small navigator's desk and scribbling calculations on a piece of paper, beyond who were Ashton and the Count. Przybylowski was sitting in a fold-down jump seat on the starboard side of the cockpit with his eyes flicking constantly across the seemingly endless array of dials and gauges, while Ashton was strapped into the pilot's seat, his gloved hands gently nursing the control column.

The pilot cocked his head slightly towards Bloodstone while his eyes remained fixed on the cloudy horizon as he spoke.

"Welcome to where the magic happens, Bertie. The best view in the house."

The Count snorted sarcastically into his mask while Ashton continued, "Get your noggin up into the astrodome if you would and shout out as soon as you see anything. There's more than sixty of us up here tonight and we'll all be milling around like a bunch of lunatics."

The astrodome was a Perspex blister at the rear of the canopy, located above and behind the wireless operator's seat, and Bloodstone shuffled his way back down the sloping floor of the Lancaster until he reached the lookout spot. He climbed onto the raised platform of the wings' forward spa, grasped a handhold on the roof and pulled himself up until his head poked out into the transparent blob.

CHAPTER SIXTEEN

A fter the claustrophobic confines of the plane's interior, Bloodstone was delighted to find that the astrodome gave him a full three-hundred-and-sixty-degree view from the top of the aircraft. The Lancaster's enormous wings stretched out powerfully either side of him, while to the fore he could see out over the top of the pilot's head and off into the night beyond. Twisting his body round to face the aircraft's stern, he had a view along fifty-six feet of fuselage, the end of which was tipped with the Lancaster's beefy twin tail units. Halfway between his viewpoint and the tail, the bubble of Jimmy's turret bristled with dual Browning machine guns and he could just make out the silhouette of the youngster's helmeted head inside.

As G for George ploughed on into the night sky, still climbing gradually, Bloodstone scanned the darkness for any sign of nearby aircraft, amazed that sixty-something Lancasters could simply vanish into thin air. He'd heard tales of deadly collisions as bombers left their bases throughout eastern England and climbed up to their assembly points in preparation for their journey to target and, now seeing for himself the darkness of the cloud-filled sky, he realised just how easy it could be.

He felt the aircraft level out under his boots and relaxed slightly as the intercom crackled in his ears once more.

"We're crossing the coast right now, Skipper," Chalky announced matter-of-factly, which was followed by Ashton's calm voice as he addressed the crew.

"We're on our way now boys. You all know your jobs so let's get it done. Keep the intercom clear and call out those night fighters as soon as you get a sniff. Buster, everything alright back there?"

"Aye aye, Capt'n. Freezing ma bollocks off as always but still alive, more's the pity," came the muffled response from Buster, tucked away in his wind tunnel of a turret.

"Jolly good," the pilot replied, "Now, let's do this."

Silence descended over the intercom once more and Bloodstone resumed his surveying of the night sky, which, somewhat eerily, lacked even a semblance of moonlight and was so cloudy that the tips of the Lancaster's wings regularly vanished into the murk. Somewhere, fifteen thousand feet below, he thought to himself, was the North Sea, no doubt cold, grey and a thoroughly miserable place to be on a night like this. Warm and cosy in his thick flying suit and with the rhythmic hum of the engines starting to feel almost comforting, he realised that he was starting to enjoy this unexpected nighttime soirée. Certainly one more thing to tell the grandchildren about one day, he mused, if he lived that long of course.

The thought of little Bloodstones was dashed from his mind an instant later as a deep roar, almost like the sound of a freight train, assaulted his ears from above. Snapping his head upwards, he was shocked to see the black belly of a Lancaster emerge from the gloom, its bomb bay doors not five feet from where his head protruded out into the night sky.

"Right above us, Skipper!" he screamed into his intercom, "Get out of here!"

Obeying instantly and seemingly without thought, Ashton yanked the nose downwards and G for George dropped sharply, causing Bloodstone to lose his handhold and stumble from his perch, giving

Nobby an elbow in the back of the head as came tumbling down. The last thing he saw through the astrodome was the aircraft above bank sharply to port as its pilot realised the situation and the propeller of its outer engine missed Jimmy's turret by millimeters as the Lancaster took its own evasive action. A hair's breadth closer, Bloodstone thought as he picked himself up from the floor, and Jimmy wouldn't have a head anymore.

"Everyone okay?" Ashton asked in his ever-calm voice as he levelled the aircraft out, "Check in please."

One by one, the crew responded.

"Rear gunner, fine."

"Navigator, okay."

"Wireless op, okay."

"Bomb aimer, just bonnie."

"Engineer, alright."

"Cameraman, checking in," the Major said as he clambered back up into the astrodome and looked for the offending Lancaster that had now long disappeared into the night sky.

"Mid-upper, call in please," Ashton ordered and received nothing but radio silence in response.

"Jimmy," he asked again, "Are you okay?"

A second passed, then another, before a barely decipherable whimper reached Bloodstone's ears.

"Jesus," it shuddered, and then a moment later, again, "Jesus," followed by a muted sob.

"What's going on, Jimmy?" Ashton demanded, "Are you hurt?"

Another sob emerged before Jimmy's soft West Country accent whispered over the intercom, "They nearly took my head off, I saw it coming."

A pause and then, again, "Jesus," followed by another whimper.

"I said, are you hurt?" Ashton demanded, his voice revealing a sharp edge for the first time.

"No, skipper," Jimmy replied in a whisper that was hardly audible over the sound of the engines, "But I can't do this anymore, I just can't."

As the whimpers tailed off into silence, Ashton's voice exploded into Bloodstone's ears.

"Yes you bloody well can," he barked harshly, "You've got a job to do and you'll damned well do it.

"Now get back up in that bloody turret and do what you're paid to do. You've got seven men relying on you, so get to it. Right now. And that's an order."

Another sob crackled through the intercom and a few seconds later the sound of a sniff and a throat being cleared.

"Yes, sir," Jimmy obeyed, sniffing again, "Sorry, sir."

"Well done," Ashton responded, his voice now back to its usual calm tone, "Good boy."

Bloodstone, looking back towards the rear of the aircraft from his Perspex bubble, saw Jimmy's head reappear in the turret. Poor blighter, he thought to himself, the youngster really did have it bad.

With all eight men now back in their positions and numerous eyes scanning the darkness for dangers, both friendly and foe, G for George continued on into the night and inched ever closer to the skies of the Third Reich. Inching closer to Lord alone knows what, Bloodstone mused and felt for the lump of the lucky bullet that nestled within his suit. Something told him that he was going to need every bit of luck he could muster before the night was out.

CHAPTER SEVENTEEN

The clouds thinned as the bomber stream continued eastwards across the North Sea, so much so that it wasn't long before the first twinkling of stars were visible to the men aboard George. Another few minutes and the moon emerged too, finally casting a dull light across the wings of the Lancaster.

Bloodstone balanced on his makeshift step and, with the skin of his neck starting to chafe from the constant swivelling of his head, now realised why silk scarves were such a firm favourite of aircrew the world over. One to remember for next time, he thought, before quickly reminding himself that there was unlikely to be a next time. He couldn't imagine Wing Commander Grubb giving him another opportunity to take to the skies, which, he reasoned, was rather a shame. Despite the sore neck, he was starting to enjoy himself, especially now that the flight had taken on something of a peaceful turn. Yes, the engines still howled like the devil and the whole ship still vibrated insanely, but the view from his astrodome was incredible.

There probably wasn't a better view in all the world, he reckoned, up here on top of the earth with only the moon, the stars and the blackness for company. Several other Lancasters were now visible to the fore and aft of George and their shapes formed blurry shadows in the moonlit night, a far cry from the cloudy filth that had seen Jimmy almost decapitated just an hour before. But with the moonlight came danger, Bloodstone knew. If he could see his fellow bombers, no doubt those with more malevolent intentions could see them too. And those with such intentions had the upper hand in their Messerschmitts and Junkers, bristling to the teeth with cannon and equipped with their cruelly effective Liechtenstein radars. He'd been around enough RAF types during the past couple of days to know that, all too often, the first thing a bomber crew knew of a night fighter in the vicinity was a stream of explosive shells raking their aircraft from stern to nose and marmalasing anyone unlucky enough to be in the way.

Being shot from below by a 20mm cannon ball wasn't on Bloodstone's list of preferred ways to go and, subconsciously rearranging his undercarriage through the thick leather suit with his left hand, he narrowed his eyes and swivelled his head once more in search of the enemy.

Several minutes later the intercom buzzed to life as Chalky's voice broke the silence.

"Steer to starboard, Skipper. Bearing one three five."

"One three five," Ashton repeated, adjusted the rudder and hauled his control column to the right, resulting in the Lancaster banking steeply to starboard as she yawed her way around in the direction of Nazi Germany.

"Thirty-eight minutes to target," Chalky announced as the Lancaster straightened out on her new course.

"Thanks Navigator," acknowledged Ashton, "Keep your eyes peeled boys."

Just then, as Bloodstone rotated his body to give himself a view out over the rear of the aircraft, a sudden explosion lit the night sky half a mile astern. No noise accompanied the flash, which subsided as quickly as it had appeared, and a series of flaming droplets were the only evidence that the incident had happened at all.

"Lanc gone at six o'clock," Buster's cockney voice reported matter-of-factly, almost as if seven men and sixty thousand pounds of aeroplane, fuel and bombs hadn't just been obliterated in an instant less than a thousand yards away.

"See who got her, Buster?" Ashton asked from the pilot's seat.

"Didn't see fuck all, Capt'n," came the response, "Although Jerry's definitely sneaking about up here; not seen no flak yet."

The concept of being blown out of the sky by an invisible killer was certainly a new one to Bloodstone, who was used to being able to see the enemy that was trying to slaughter him. Knowing there was a Luftwaffe fighter in amongst the bomber stream at that very moment, potentially lining up George for his next kill, didn't sit well with him at all, especially when all he had to fight them off with was a combat knife and a revolver. He might as well be stark bollock naked for all the good he could do, he thought uncomfortably.

Two seconds later the flash of another explosion ripped through the sky, this time to Bloodstone's right and considerably closer, and the sound of the blast was clearly audible over the noise of George's engines. Instead of an instant vapourisation of men and machine, however, this unlucky Lancaster spewed a gigantic sheet of flame from its belly, disgorged a wing and fell sickeningly towards the darkness below, vanishing from view several heartbeats later. As Bloodstone stared at the piece of dark sky where, only seconds before, had been a perfectly serviceable aircraft, he felt a cold shiver run down his spine. This was getting serious, he thought, touching the shape of the Mauser bullet once more, and he didn't like it one little bit.

No sooner had his fingers found the lump of the bullet than an enormous roaring noise attacked his ears like a banshee and caused him to whip around to his left just in time to see a huge black shape emerge from the darkness and roar overhead, not ten feet above his Perspex bubble. As the shadow passed above him and away into the night, he had just enough time to recognise the bulbous-headed shape of a twin-engined fighter and to notice an assortment of aerials protruding from the nose and the unmissable white outline of a cross painted on the fuselage.

"There's the bastard!" Buster's voice screamed into the intercom, battering Bloodstone's already half-deaf ears, "Jimmy, shoot the fucker!"

Jimmy didn't shoot the fucker. In fact, Jimmy's turret didn't even move.

"Jimmy!" the tail gunner yelled, enraged, "What the fuck are you doing you useless little bastard? Shoot him!"

"Tail gunner, shut up," ordered Ashton, his voice its usual calm self, "Jimmy, what's going on back there?"

No answer.

"Jimmy," the pilot repeated, "What's happening?"

Silence.

Bloodstone ducked his head down out of the astrodome and peered into the belly of the Lancaster but the light was so poor inside the fuselage that he couldn't see as far as Jimmy's turret.

"Permission to take a look, Skipper?" Bloodstone called into the intercom as he peered into dark interior once more.

"Granted, but make it quick," came the response, to which Bloodstone dropped down from his perch, clambered over the wall of the wing spa and, bent almost double, scurried towards the rear of the plane.

Before he reached the gun turret he could see by the lack of dangling legs that Jimmy wasn't there. As he got closer, the darkness faded slightly as the light of the moon flooded down through the turret and cast a triangle of light onto the fuselage floor. Protruding into the light was a single fur-topped flying boot, attached to a body that was huddled in a ball against a metal strut, with arms wrapped tightly around its knees and chin tucked down into its chest.

As Bloodstone bent down, Jimmy looked up with wide eyes, his face deathly white and his teeth chattering. There was no blood to be seen and no wound visible, but his body rocked backward and forward against the fuselage, while a high-pitched mewing noise emanated from his throat.

"Jimmy, are you hurt?" Bloodstone shouted over the noise of the engines and padded down the airman's suit in search of a wound. The gunner didn't respond but simply mewed again as his eyes stared off into space.

"Jimmy," he repeated as he grabbed the man by the collar and shook him, "Are you injured?"

The youngster's eyes, wild, staring and other worldly, finally looked in Bloodstone's direction. He shook his head slowly and mouthed something incomprehensible, a look of pure fear on his face.

"It's alright son, it's alright," Bloodstone said gently, putting his arm around the gunner's shoulder and knowing that the poor fellow had finally cracked.

Reaching out to the other man's intercom, he clicked the switch and spoke into it, "Jimmy's not in good shape, Skipper. He's out of this one."

A few seconds passed before Ashton responded, his voice as calm as always. "Understood, thanks for the update."

A couple more seconds passed before the pilot's voiced buzzed through the intercom once more.

"Jimmy, get yourself along to the rest bed. Bertie, sir, I'm going to need you up in Jimmy's turret. Jerry's in amongst us and I'll be damned if I'm going to leave us undefended up top. No time to show you the mechanics I'm afraid, you'll have to work it out for yourself."

"Roger," Bloodstone responded, giving Jimmy a reassuring clap on the shoulder before he hauled himself up into the vacant turret and wriggled his backside into the seat.

The view here was even better than from the astrodome, Bloodstone realised, although he was acutely aware of the fact that his entire head was now practically sticking out into the air, just waiting to be shot off. No wonder Jimmy had got the jitters, he thought to himself as he reached for the trigger of the twin Browning machine guns, enjoying the feeling of the metal in his gloved fingers. It was good to have a weapon in his hands again, he realised as he licked his lips and felt the familiar sense of adrenalin start to pump through his veins. Now all he needed was something to shoot at.

CHAPTER EIGHTEEN

"That's the second right, Skipper, bearing one nine five please," Chalky announced over the intercom and Ashton promptly adjusted the Lancaster's course with another turn to starboard.

The past half hour had proved uneventful after the near miss with the Luftwaffe night fighter, which seemed to have vanished into the moonlit skies to leave the bomber stream to its own devices. Bloodstone, lodged firmly in his turret, had spent the previous thirty minutes swinging his guns through 360 degrees and staring intently into the cloudless night in search of prey. His quest had thus far been fruitless, however, with nothing more interesting entering his periphery than the occasional friendly Lancaster with its wings catching the reflection of the moonlight.

"One minute to enemy coast, Skipper," Chalky declared from his navigator's table, which caused every man aboard George to subconsciously take a deep breath and sink a little deeper in his seat in readiness for what was to come.

Bloodstone peered down over the side of the fuselage and secretly hoped to see the land of his birth; a land which he hadn't set foot in since he was a scabby-kneed schoolboy over a decade before. His peering proved futile, however, with nothing to see but blackness, not even a stray twinkling light, and he abandoned his search to continue his scrutiny of the sky around him.

A second later a beam of yellowish light broke the darkness ahead of the Lancaster, with one end attached to the ground and the other probing the sky like a giant elongated finger. Another came to life, then another, searching the darkness like some sort of gaggle of phosphorescent grim reapers.

"Searchlights at seven o'clock," Bill reported from his bomb aimer's spot in the nose.

No sooner had his words crackled through the intercom than two more beams of light sprang to life, one the same yellow colour and the other an eerie blue.

"Master beam," Bill announced again, "Keep oot of the way of that wee bastard, Skip."

"Thanks, Jock," the pilot replied and dipped his port wing slightly to give Bloodstone and Buster a new field of vision, which was a tactic he had been employing regularly since crossing the Lincolnshire coast several hours before.

Using his fresh view, Bloodstone did another three-sixty of his surroundings and ended up facing out towards George's nose. The searchlights continued to prod and probe the night sky ahead of him as they hunted for invaders and Bloodstone couldn't help but be fascinated by their sinister dancing.

His fascination turned to horror a heartbeat later, however, as the blue light caught a Lancaster in its beam and locked on. As the bomber twisted and turned like a hooked fish, frantically trying to escape, the other four lights raced across the sky and latched on to the doomed bomber. The pilot threw the aircraft around in desperation but to no avail and it was only a matter of seconds before flashes of red light started to appear around the Lancaster.

The flashes looked innocent enough, but Bloodstone knew that they were anything but. He had seen flak at work on numerous occasions, albeit always from the ground, and he was depressingly aware of how lethal the anti-aircraft shells could be if they were on target. And the flak tonight, he noticed, was most definitely on target as it began to pummel the Lancaster that was desperately attempting to escape the cruel attention of the searchlights. Shell after shell tore into the writhing bomber, blasting holes in its wings and fuselage and, Bloodstone assumed, turning its crew to mincemeat. It took only a few more seconds for the doomed aircraft to cease its futile attempts at escape and it dropped from the sky in a vertical dive, with three of its four engines aflame and shedding burning chunks as it fell. Bloodstone watched the gory descent from his turret and silently prayed that the burning chunks were bits of aeroplane, but he knew that some were just as likely to be parts of mangled airmen.

With the dying Lancaster disappearing from view, an explosion burst just off George's starboard wing and rocked the aircraft with a ferocious bump. Another, red and blinding, burst fifty yards ahead, causing the ship to buck like a twig in a stormy sea.

"Christ, here we go," came Buster's cockney voice over the intercom, followed up by a "Fucking flak," through gritted teeth from someone else.

As Ashton interrupted the curses to demand radio silence, one of the probing searchlight beams, now free to hunt a new victim, momentarily caught G for George in its gaze, filling the aircraft interior with a dazzling white light that half-blinded the eight men aboard. Before Ashton could throw the Lancaster into an evasive manoeuvre, however, the light mercifully moved on to trail its evil yellow finger across the sky in search of fresh meat.

Another flak burst exploded close to the nose, jerking the Lancaster across the sky in a drunken lurch before Ashton wrestled her back on course and, seconds later, an almighty flash lit up the port wing and sent an enormous tremor through the entire aircraft. Bloodstone gripped onto his turret for dear life and, appalled by the deafening noise of the assault, peered across to survey the wing and was shocked to see a singed hole the size of a deckchair close to the outer engine. He was impressed to see that the aircraft seemed to have soaked up the damage with no great concern, however, which he thought was surely a good omen considering the amount of exploding metal that was being hurled into the air by the AA gun crews below.

His intercom buzzed to life again, snapping him back from his mechanical musings, and the voice of Chalky crackled into his ears.

"Three miles to target, Skipper."

"Thank you Chalky," Ashton acknowledged and then a few moments later, "This is it chaps, straight flying from here on in so I'm afraid you're just going to have to put up with the flak. Jock, she's all yours now."

The flak bursts continued to pepper the darkness and the searchlights persevered with their wild meanderings across the night sky, but Bloodstone was pleased to see that they were yet to combine to bring down another unfortunate bomber. Looking down from his turret in the direction of the target town of Wilhelmshaven, he could see a fiery mass of flames lighting up the area surrounding the docks. Even from fourteen thousand feet he could make out the bright green of the initial target markers, mixed with the reds and yellows of burning buildings and the flashing whites of exploding bombs. The colours intermingled to form a spectral dance on the water of the docks, around which the falling bombs unleashed carnage and destruction.

Bloodstone thanked his lucky stars that he wasn't down there underneath the torrent of death and was privately pleased when George's approach to the target blocked his view of the burning town, leaving him instead to scour the skies in search of enemy aircraft.

Bill, lying face down in the nose, was now calling out directions to the pilot to bring George immediately above the target, requiring Ashton to make the minutest changes of course amidst the buffeting of the flak.

"Left a bit. Steady. Left a bit more. Aye, that's it. Steady. Steady. Right a smidgen."

Another flak shell hit the aircraft with a deafening crash, this time just six feet from Bloodstone's turret and plum through the

96

Lancaster's Elsen toilet, smashing it to pieces and spraying a shower of metal fragments, cleaning chemicals and human excrement throughout the fuselage. Miraculously, the burning metal fragments missed him completely, but he wasn't so lucky with the other remnants of the explosion, which left his flying boots and lower legs coated with a considerable quantity of pungent greeny-brown, and particularly watery, faeces.

While Bloodstone watched the deadly flak from his turret and simultaneously wondered who in the crew had unleashed a bellyful of diarrhoea during the short journey from Scampton to Germany, Bill continued to call out his instructions as he attempted to get the docks into his bombsight.

"Left. Hold it there. Right. Right. Steady. Hold it. Hold it. Hold it."

Ashton expertly held the Lancaster on course despite the flak that assaulted her from all sides, while the entire crew willed Bill to say the magic words.

Finally, Bill said them.

"Bombs away!"

As the bomb release switch was flicked, ten thousand pounds of ordinance fell from George's belly and the Lancaster, suddenly bereft of almost four tonnes of weight, leapt up into the sky as if jerked by an invisible wire. Bloodstone, not expecting the sudden jump, felt his stomach drop as his body went up with the aircraft, his head colliding with the roof of his turret in the process.

He shook his head to clear the stars that were hovering at the edge of his vision and was surprised to find that the Lancaster was still over the target and hadn't yet changed course. He had assumed that as soon as the bombs were gone they would be out of there as quickly as possible, racing away to escape the murderous flak that still banged and crashed and flashed around them and the searchlights that stalked the night sky in pursuit of prey.

His question was answered as Bill's Scottish tones crackled through the intercom once more.

"Wait for the camera flash, boys, nae be long now."

To Bloodstone, and to everyone else on board, it seemed like an eternity as the Lancaster continued to fly in a straight line with deadly balls of flame creeping ever closer as the gunners on the ground lined up their next victim. Before they could add another notch to their gun barrels, however, the Lancaster's camera finally snapped a photo of the target, a full twenty-eight agonising seconds after the bombs had tumbled from the aircraft.

With confirmation from the bomb aimer that the photograph had been taken, Ashton pushed his four throttle levers to maximum, banked to starboard and dived to safety, away from the deadly guns and the probing fingers of the searchlights.

"Good work chaps," he said brightly, "Now let's go home."

CHAPTER NINETEEN

Her bombs delivered and now ten thousand pounds lighter, George felt like a fighter in Ashton's hands as she struck out for home. The turn to starboard saw the aircraft heading south-west away from the maelstrom of the burning docks as the pilot attempted to put as much distance as possible between herself and the piercing searchlights, before she turned again in the direction of England.

Bloodstone, finally breathing normally again after the torment of the camera run, looked astern from his turret and gazed down upon the smashed remnants of Wilhelmshaven. Fires raged uncontrollably around the docks and spread through the town, where stray bombs had wreaked havoc on the tightly packed buildings. An enormous pillar of dirty grey smoke, illuminated by the fires below and the moonlight above, reached up to the heavens and smeared the horizon for miles around.

All around him Lancasters were turning away from the town as they started their journeys home, seeking out sanctuary from the flak and praying for clouds to swallow them up. This night, however, the weather gods were otherwise engaged and the moonlight and the raging fires combined to turn the October night into something akin to daylight. With darkness denied to them, the aircraft of Bomber

Command sought safety in numbers and inched closer together into a ragtag formation that stretched for several miles across the night sky.

As the searchlights retreated into the distance and the flak became less concentrated, so the Luftwaffe returned, eager to seek revenge for the carnage that had been heaped onto Wilhelmshaven. The first sign that enemy aircraft were once again on the prowl was a flash of tracer that jabbed out into the night from a Lancaster to Bloodstone's left side. He spun his turret around to face the fight and watched as the thin lines of gunfire arced erratically through the sky as they sought out a target somewhere in the half darkness. Tracer from other nearby Lancasters joined the deadly firework show and blasted away into the moonlight as the gunners defended themselves from the invisible foe.

Several seconds later the port outer engine of a Lancaster several hundred yards away suddenly burst into flames and coughed out a sickening torrent of burning fuel, which quickly proceeded to eat its way along the aircraft's wing, devouring everything in its path. Several more seconds and the bomber rolled onto its side and fell from the sky, a trail of smoke the only evidence of its existence. Seven more men wiped out, Bloodstone thought to himself as he fingered the trigger of his Brownings and squinted into the half-light as he searched the sky for the unseen enemy who had just brought yet another bomber crashing down to earth.

Rotating his turret from port to starboard and back again while he scanned the autumn night, his attention was caught by a faint red glow above and behind George. It wasn't flak, not bright enough, he thought as he peered at the dull light, which seemed to be shifting slowly across the sky and increasing slightly in size as it moved. What was it? Was his mind playing tricks? He didn't want to make a fool of himself by calling out a figment of his imagination, so he continued to watch, following the red glow. As he stared, it suddenly grew in size and brightness, attaching itself to a black shadow that then, like something from a nightmare, sprouted two dark wings and a fuselage and proceeded to dive down towards him, hurtling in his direction at an obscene speed.

With no time to shout into the intercom, he tore his guns around to face the intruder and squeezed the trigger, spurting bullets out into the sky. As he did so, the Junkers JU-88 unleashed its cannons and sprayed out an arc of shells that jabbed towards the Lancaster like deadly needles, peppering the fuselage and missing Bloodstone's turret by a matter of inches. As the aircraft hurtled closer, the red glow now revealed as its glowing exhaust, he followed it with his guns and held the trigger flat as he hurled bullet after bullet in its direction before it disappeared from view and vanished into the darkness below with his tracers following in its wake.

"Fuck me," came Buster's voice over the intercom, a trace of anger in his Cockney accent, "You nearly shot our bloody tail off. Watch where you're pointing them pistols will you."

Before Bloodstone could reply, a tremendous roar erupted and the black shape of the night fighter zoomed into view again, this time attacking upwards from the port side, tracer shells vomiting from its guns and, once again, smashing home into the thin metal of the Lancaster's body. Gripping his trigger with renewed vigour, he yanked his guns around to follow the flight of the twin-engined beast that had now overshot the bomber and was arching up into the sky above him, and unleashed hell, pumping bullets crazily into the night sky. As round after round left the muzzle of his Brownings and filled his vibrating turret with the stench of cordite, he bellowed in rage at the night fighter, willing its destruction, daring it to live.

"Come on!" he screamed as his fingers squeezed the trigger, wrenching his machine gun barrels around violently as he followed the trajectory of the enemy aircraft into the sky above his head, "Have it!"

To his surprise, bullet after bullet thumped into the JU-88, smashing its fuel tanks, hammering its engine into a useless lump of red-hot metal and tearing the crew to pieces. His bullets were still pouring into the doomed aircraft when it could take no more and it

101

simply blew up, exploding into a ball of flame and sending a burning mass of molten metal and mangled flesh tumbling down to the earth below.

"WOOHOO!" Buster's whoops of joy echoed through the intercom as the flaming mess fell past his rear turret, "That's how you fuckin do it, sir!"

"Jolly good show," Ashton added, his ever-calm voice cracking slightly with a hint of approval as he watched the remnants of the Junkers disappear from the sky.

Bloodstone's throat stung from the smoke that hung in his turret and his ears smarted from the racket of the Brownings, but he grinned to himself as his heartbeat returned to something close to its normal rate. With his lust for destruction now satiated, at least for the time being, and his mind replaying the annihilation of the Nazi aircraft, he slumped back in his seat and let out a satisfied grunt.

"Jolly good show," he repeated, to nobody in particular.

CHAPTER TWENTY

As the returning bomber stream left the German coast and headed out over the North Sea, so the thick clouds returned and offered a blissfully grey safety screen to the Lancasters who had sweated and suffered in the moonlight. Bloodstone remained in his turret and peered into the cloudy murk in hope of spotting another potential target, but the Luftwaffe appeared to have vanished for the night and the bombers continued unmolested.

The men aboard G for George relaxed slightly as the Lancaster neared the Lincolnshire coast and Ashton gave permission for a flask of tea and a packet of ginger biscuits to be handed out to the crew. Their distributor was Jimmy who, free from his gunner duties and now with a little colour returned to his face, clambered through the aircraft with a handful of tin mugs.

As he handed a steaming cup up into Bloodstone's turret and avoided the major's eye, Bloodstone could see that youngster was embarrassed.

"Thanks Jimmy," he said, enjoying the scolding liquid that spread a blissful sense of warmth through his chilly limbs.

"And by the way, son, don't worry about earlier; it happens to the best of us. Just forget it."

Jimmy nodded in silent thanks and headed off towards Buster's turret, taking care to step around the remnants of the smashed toilet.

"Crossing the coast now, Skipper, eight minutes to base," Chalky announced and received a cheer from the crew, although they all knew that coming into land in thick clouds still had its dangers.

Now free from the threat of the Luftwaffe, Ashton switched on the Lancaster's navigation lights, making the ship visible to other incoming friendlies, and dropped down to one thousand feet in readiness for his approach. As he emerged below the gloom of the clouds, the welcoming spire of Lincoln cathedral appeared as a dark shadow in the distance off to starboard.

"There's nae a better view in all the world," Bill commented through the intercom and took one last glance at the towering spire before he abandoned his position in the nose, clambered up into the fuselage and returned to the rest bed in readiness for touch down.

The twinkling flare path of Scampton's runway was now visible ahead in the distance and Ashton fixed the base in his sights as he awaited the go ahead to make his final approach.

"We've got permission to land, Skip," Nobby announced from his wireless station and Ashton reduced the power to his engines, dropped the nose a few more degrees and lined the bomber up with the runway.

A perfect three-point landing followed as the weary Lancaster came gracefully down to earth, sped along the runway and, with a hiss of brakes, rolled to a halt as she reached her dispersal pan. With the aircraft now stationary, Ashton turned off the engines one by one and, for the first time in nearly six hours, the Lancaster was silent.

Bloodstone let out a deep breath, closed his eyes, rested the back of his head on the Perspex of his turret and let the peace and silence envelop him, feeling the tension of the night drain from his body. Opening his eyes again, he watched for a second as a torrent of steam rose from one of the engines before he unclipped his harness and dropped down to the fuselage floor. He padded his way towards the rear of the aircraft and climbed down the ladder and onto the tarmac of the dispersal pan to join Buster, Jimmy and Chalky.

The solid ground felt strange under his feet and he was surprised at how weary his body suddenly felt. I must be getting old, he thought to himself as he stretched out the muscles of his legs and watched Nobby's lanky body contort itself out of the door and jump to the ground. The wireless operator dropped to his knees and kissed the tarmac, before he rose back up to his full six foot five and grinned at Bloodstone.

"Well that was a barrel of laughs, hey Bertie?" he said with a wild glint in his eye and clapped Bloodstone on the shoulder before wrinkling his nose at the stench of dried faeces that emanated from the stained flying suit.

Before Nobby could crack a joke, the remainder of the crew climbed down from the ladder and joined them to form a tight circle with Ashton in the centre.

"Good show boys," the blonde-haired pilot said to the men around him, his eyes tired and his young face lined from the rubber of his oxygen mask.

"You all did well up there and we're home in one piece, which is the main thing," he continued, looking around the small circle.

"All of us, Capt'n?" Buster asked, looking at Jimmy, who was staring at the floor.

"We're a crew Buster," Ashton said to the scarred man, "Which means we stick together when it's good and we stick together when it's bad too. Jimmy knows he's screwed up and I'll be speaking to him later about that."

Looking around the circle of men again, he continued. "In the meantime, I'll ask you all to keep that little incident to yourselves. We've all got one more mission until we've done our thirty, so I don't want anything distracting from that. Do I make myself clear?"

The knot of men nodded.

"Good stuff. Anyone else got anything they'd like to discuss before we get ourselves some scram?"

"Just this, Skipper," Bill said with a grin as he held up what had once been a shiny leather case. The heavy brown case had three neat punctures the size of pound coins in the front, while the back was a tattered mess of three fist-sized holes, each leaking a collection of broken glass, shattered metal and twisted rubber.

"Oh bugger," Bloodstone exclaimed with a laugh as he recognised the smashed remains of his extortionately expensive camera, "Old Huckleberry is going to get his knickers in a twist about this; he'll have my guts for garters."

"Must've been that Jerry night fighter," Nobby offered, "He fair peppered us with shells. Lucky it's not one of us full of holes."

"Aye, ye can say that again," Bill said as he placed the mangled case on the floor. "Well at least you're a better gunner than you are a cameraman, sir."

Bloodstone, nodding, could not agree more. At least now he didn't need an excuse for his feeble efforts at filming the raid, he thought, secretly pleased that his reason for joining the mission in the first place, and the laughable quantity of film that he'd produced, couldn't now be questioned by Wingco Grubb.

But, he thought, going over the last six hours in his mind, it'd been damned good fun. Frightening, yes, and exhausting, absolutely, but damned good fun all the same. Nothing like a good old fashioned scrape with death to put a bit of lead in your pencil and some fire in your belly, he thought, as he picked up the tattered case and followed the rest of the crew to a waiting jeep, the stench of shit wafting after him.

CHAPTER TWENTY-ONE

B loodstone awoke, stretched out his arms and enjoyed the feel of the crisp sheets under his skin as he blinked away the last remnants of sleep. Before he had clambered into bed in the early hours of the morning, five hours before and utterly exhausted, he had attended a debriefing session with the squadron's Intelligence Officer, during which the crew made no mention of Jimmy's breakdown and, on Ashton's insistence, Buster had begrudgingly claimed the downed Junkers. A late night plate of eggs and bacon had followed, after which Bloodstone finally stripped off his stinking flying suit and, with his belly stuffed, it wasn't long before he was sleeping like a baby, his dreams filled with the flash of gunfire and the stench of cordite.

The morning's to-do list was extensive but a distinct step down from the excitement of the night before, he thought to himself as he swung his legs out of bed and looked around for a pair of slippers that would save his bare feet from the chill of the concrete floor. For starters there was Kitty to have a stern word with, a destroyed camera to return to the no-doubt apoplectic Huckleberry James and a telephone call to be made to the Appleford Sisters.

"Ah, Jane Appleford," he said out loud as he reminisced about the long-limbed beauty that he had spent a blissful week of leave with back in '41. If Grubb could see into his head right now, he would probably have a heart attack, he thought with a smile, picturing the singer's glorious nakedness and remembering the picture book smile that hid a carnal energy that almost outstripped his own. Almost. On second thoughts, maybe the phone call should go to the top of the list, he mused as he imagined the delights that he knew the arrival of the delicious Jane would bring.

But first, a shower, he decided, and searched the room for a towel. Where was Barnaby when you needed him? That was another one for the list, he decided as he failed to find a towel, making a mental note to summon his trusty manservant up from the Hampshire estate. No doubt a spot of northern air would do the old man some good and it would certainly help with the more domestic elements of Bloodstone's time at Scampton. He had noticed that even the most junior flying officers on the base were issued with a batman to allow them full focus on their flying duties and, after Ashton and Chalky's performance last night, he thought they thoroughly deserved such a luxury.

He was distracted from his hunt for the lost towel by a knock on the door. Twisting the handle, he was greeted by a saluting RAF corporal who held a piece of paper in his hand.

"Good morning, Corporal."

"Morning, sir," the corporal replied, glancing down at the paper in his hand.

"I'm to tell you that there's a Captain Jones to see you, sir. He's waiting in the officers' mess, sir."

"Jones? Algernon Jones?"

"I'm not sure, sir," the corporal replied, looking puzzled.

"Pug-nosed fellow, ugly as sin? Wonky eyes? Face like a bulldog chewing a wasp?"

"Um, maybe a little, sir," blushed the corporal, looking down at his paper again and anxious to be away from the questioning major.

"How very strange," said Bloodstone as he dismissed the corporal and wondered why on earth his great chum had travelled all the way to deepest, darkest Lincolnshire and was now sitting in the mess just a few yards away. But, he reasoned, touching his nose that was still not completely healed after the antics of the weekend, seeing Jones could only result in all manner of good things.

Twenty minutes later, in a fresh uniform and with the grime of last night's mission finally scrubbed from his body, Bloodstone opened the door of the officers' mess and bounded inside. As he entered, a squat pint-sized man in his mid-twenties stood up from a chair with a beaming smile on his face.

"Bertie, you damned rogue," the man, who sported ginger hair, a freckled face and a flat nose, exclaimed as he shook Bloodstone's hand tightly.

"Algy," Bloodstone replied gleefully as he pumped his friend's hand, "What the devil are you doing here?"

"You know how it is, old chap, I was in the neighbourhood and thought I'd drop in to see how my old pal is getting along. I say, frightful up north isn't it? Reminds me of that time at Eton when they sent us off into the wilderness with nothing but a penknife, a piece of string and a bag of boiled sweets. Character-building they said. Bloody savage I say."

"Well it obviously didn't do you any good, you damned snob," Bloodstone laughed as he opened his cigarette case and motioned for Jones to sit down.

He helped himself to a Woodbine, sparked it to life and passed the case to Jones before he leaned back in his chair and blew a particularly impressive smoke ring towards the ceiling. As the pair watched the circle of smoke drift upwards, a mess waiter approached to take their order. When the man had retreated behind the bar to fetch their drinks, Jones took the cigarette from the corner of his mouth and fixed Bloodstone with a squinty eye.

"A little birdie tells me you've been in the sky shooting up Jerry. I thought you were here on press duties only, you damned lunatic."

"How the devil do you know that?" Bloodstone asked in a hushed voice as he looked around the half-empty room to double check that nobody had overheard the Captain.

"I'm not in the Intelligence Corps for nothing old chap," Jones grinned, tapping his nose.

"But worry not my friend," he continued with a wink, "Your dirty secrets are safe with me. Speaking of which, I see you straightened out your nose. No doubt you did it yourself with a screwdriver or some other damned fool scheme. Am I right?"

Bloodstone gave a non-committal shrug, amazed, as always, how his old school friend had an uncanny knack of knowing his every move.

"Couldn't do much about that missing tooth though could you?" the grinning Jones continued as he eyed the gap in Bloodstone's otherwise row of perfect top teeth.

"I'm beginning to quite like it," he replied, blowing a stream of smoke through the gap and barely believing that it had been only four days since his boozy night out in the pubs of Portsmouth had ended in bloodshed.

"Damned good evening, though, hey Algy?" he said wistfully as he stroked his nose, "At least until those bloody sailors ruined it."

"Ha, you can say that again, although we never did find that gorgeous redhead piece of crumpet, did we? Ah well, let's see what we can spot this evening; fancy gallivanting over to Lincoln for the night?"

"Jolly good idea," Bloodstone agreed, thinking that a night on the sauce with Jones was just the thing he needed to work off the tension of the previous night over war-torn Europe.

"So, you've come all the way up from London just for a night on the smash, have you? Come on Algy, I know you better than that. What's all this about?"

"Nothing gets past you does it, Bertie?" Jones said with a wan smile and leant forwards in his chair to look Bloodstone in the eye.

"There's something I need to talk to you about," he continued, his face suddenly serious. "I'm afraid it's about your mother."

CHAPTER TWENTY-TWO

As the mess waiter unloaded two glasses of whisky from his tray, Bloodstone allowed his mind to wander back to the final days of 1941 and the telegram that had shattered his world. Those three typed lines, informing him of his mother's death, had seemed so business-like and blunt, like a delivery notification or a summons to a meeting, that he had barely believed them. It was only in the days that followed as more details emerged that it had become reality and, with it, the realisation that it wasn't some sort of bad dream or a sick joke.

The hardest bit to bare had been discovering that it wasn't a car accident or some other twist of fate that had killed Amelia Bloodstone, but a bullet between the eyes; a bullet that he hadn't been there to stop. He had been able to do nothing about it; he had failed her when she had needed him most. He should have been there to protect her, just like she had protected him for so many years of his life. But he wasn't and now she was dead, with the muzzle of a Luger the last thing she would ever see.

He was snapped back to the present by Jones chinking the rim of his glass, "Cheers, old chap."

"Cheers, Algy," he responded, knocking back the Scotch in one and enjoying the burn in his throat that took his mind from the past. "So, come on then, what's the gen?"

Jones took a sip from his glass, sighed satisfyingly and shuffled his rear end into the worn leather of his armchair. Clearing his throat, he began.

"So, you'll know only too well that we've been giving Jerry a damned good hammering in Italy these past few weeks. Rolling their troops up like a carpet, you could say, pushing them north and taking godforsaken town after godforsaken town. It's been damned hard work, as you've seen for yourself, but good old British steel always wins in the end, hey?"

Bloodstone thought that a rather simplistic view of the bitter mountain warfare that he had played such a bloody part in less than a month before but, knowing his friend was partial to a spot of gross under-exaggeration, chose to let him continue.

"Well, our fellows took the town of Piello last week. Scabid sort of place, Piello, typical of those ramshackle hovels that seem to infest every corner of Italy. But this particular one turned out to be something of an unexpected treasure trove. For starters there was a vault stuffed full of Nazi gold. Some damned fool Wehrmacht general chose the wrong place to stash his horde by the look of it.

"For some reason this Piello hellhole also had a brothel of galactic proportions. Beauties from every corner of the world holed up in a fornication farm the likes of which you've never seen before. No wonder Jerry had no energy left to fight. The poor Sherwood Foresters who stumbled across it didn't know what to do with themselves, poor blighters. Damned shame you missed that show, hey Bertie?"

Bloodstone nodded and wondered what any of this had to do with his mother. Before he could ask, Algy continued.

"Our chaps also unearthed something else. A pot-bellied Italian baker called Gianluca Culo. Italian for bottom is culo, did you know that?"

Bloodstone didn't but thought it a particularly unfortunate name. Almost as unfortunate as the boy in his form at school who had the misfortune to be called d'Arse, he mused with a smile, remembering the youngster's podgy face.

"Reminded me of old Fatty Arse back at Eton," Jones said with a laugh, once again shocking Bloodstone with his scary ability to read his innermost thoughts.

"Anyway," Jones said, shifting his backside in the chair, this Culo chap wasn't just a baker. When he wasn't making crostinis he was hiding in plain sight for the last few years as a German plant, feeding intel back to Berlin."

"Back to Berlin?" Bloodstone asked, confused, "But Jerry and the Eyeties are on the same side."

"They might be on the same side, dear chap," Jones said with a lopsided grin, "But even allies don't always trust each other. You'd be amazed how much us, the Frogs and the Ruskis are peeking on each other. You never know when your so-called friend is about to stab you in the back.

"But I digress. So, our fellows picked up this bum fellow and had a little chat with him. Nothing like the methods of our Gestapo friends of course, no pincers or electrodes on the ballbags, that's just not cricket. A friendly conversation you understand."

Jones winked and Bloodstone could only imagine the sort of conversation that his friend's colleagues had had with the baker-turned-spy.

"So did the chap squeak?" he asked.

"Squeak? He chirped like a canary. Couldn't tell us enough. Must've been desperate to go back to baking his bread. Which I imagine isn't surprising when you're faced with the sort of rogues we've got working with the Corps out in Italy. Poor fellow.

"Lots of useful stuff about troop movements and agent networks, not to mention some particularly fruity gen about the madame of that glorious local brothel, damned filthy harlot. But there was something else too."

"Go on," Bloodstone prompted as he took a sip from a newly arrived whisky.

"Well, it seems that Culo had a particular knowledge of an especially nasty piece of work that we've been hoping to pin down for a while. An SS standartenführer, that's colonel to us..."

"I know what a standartenführer is Algy," Bloodstone interrupted, "I've polished off a few in my time."

"Of course you have old boy, of course you have," Jones said with a smile, before picking up where he'd left off.

"Well this SS fellow is one of the Nazi's crack assassins. Heidler's his name, Otto Heidler. He keeps popping up all over the Continent, bumping off our agents and sticking a bullet in anyone Adolf and his cronies want rid of, even a few of their own included. Do you remember the Krüger killing earlier this year?"

Bloodstone nodded, vaguely recalling the name of the Gestapo chief who had been killed by the Polish resistance a few months before.

"Well it wasn't the Poles that did for Krüger," Jones continued, "Even though that's the story we all heard. No, it was this Heidler devil, on direct orders of the Fuhrer himself. Lord alone knows why, no doubt another bout of his crazy paranoia.

"Anyway, our chubby Italian friend seemed to know a lot about Heidler. Apparently the Standartenführer was rather keen on Piello's seemingly legendary brothel, filthy blighter. But we also found out something else."

Jones leaned slightly forward in his chair and paused as the roar of a low flying aeroplane passed overhead. He waited for the sound of the engines to fade before he spoke again.

"In December '41 this chap was smuggled into Blighty aboard a fishing boat for a particular mission, again on the direct orders of old Adolf. He made his way from the drop off point in Cornwall and across to Hampshire, just in time for Christmas Day.

"You know what I'm going to say next, don't you Bertie?" Jones whispered as he looked his friend directly in the eye.

Bloodstone, his blood running cold and the fingers of his right hand gripping the arm of his chair, knew exactly what was coming next. He nodded slowly and motioned for Jones to continue.

"It was Heidler that shot your mother."

Bloodstone could just picture it. His mother in her bedroom, straightening her favourite Austrian dress in readiness for Christmas lunch, a family tradition for as long as he could remember. His father downstairs in the library with a cigar in one hand and a brandy in the other. The echo of a gunshot. His father rushing upstairs to find her lying on the floor, a hole between her eyes and a bloody assortment of brain, black hair and bits of skull spread over the dressing table and across the wall. And pinned to her motionless chest a single paper swastika signed by the Fuhrer; the personal calling card of Hitler himself.

"I'm sorry to have to put you through it all again, Bertie," Jones said gently, giving him a manly squeeze of the knee. "I know it's not really anything new, but I did promise that I'd let you know if ever I found out who it was that had pulled the trigger."

"I appreciate that, Algy, really I do," Bloodstone replied and pushed the nightmarish image out of his head as he took a small black and white photograph that Jones had passed him.

The photo showed a man who was Aryan to the core. Short blonde hair, piercing eyes and high cheekbones framed a hard face, which was set above the dark uniform of an SS colonel, complete with insignia on the collar and a Knight's Cross with oak leaves and swords at the man's neck.

Bloodstone instantly hated the man in the image. "So where is this Heidler bastard now?" he asked.

"Paris apparently, according to the baker. Well out of harm's way and I can't imagine he'll be back here in Blighty anytime soon, what with the way the war's going."

"Shame," Bloodstone said under his breath, a mad glint in his eye that didn't go unnoticed by Jones, "Shame."

"Damnably so," Jones agreed and tipped the remnants of his glass into his mouth, "But it just goes to show what we're fighting for doesn't it?

"I mean, we'll have our victory in the end, come hell or high water," he continued, his face serious.

"We have to Bertie, don't we? We can't let a madman like Hitler call the shots. Just look at the lengths he's prepared to go to for God's sake. I mean, having his own cousin shot in cold blood in her own home. And on Christmas Day of all days."

CHAPTER TWENTY-THREE

The old adage that a man can't choose his own family could not have been more true than for Bloodstone, who had lived with the shame of the dark deeds of his Austrian-born relative for more than a decade, like a millstone around his neck.

Fate was a strange thing, he thought as he sipped the morning's second glass of whisky, just as he had mused fruitlessly about the concept countless times over the years. The simple truth was that fate had nothing to do with it; Adolf Hitler was his mother's cousin, which meant that the Fuhrer was his own cousin once removed, and that was purely a case of unfortunate genetics.

He knew the family history only too well; it was etched into his brain. His Grandmother Theresia, his mother's mother, was the younger sister of one Klara Polzl. Klara, married to a man called Alois who was twenty-three years her senior, gave birth to a baby in a small town near the Austrian-German border in the spring of 1889. The baby was a boy and the couple christened him Adolphus, giving him their married name of Hitler. Adolf Hitler was born.

Six years later, Theresia had a child of her own, a beautiful baby girl she named Amelia; future wife to Sir Montgomery Bloodstone, future mother to Albert Bloodstone and, for the duration of the forty-six years of her short life, cousin to one of the most evil men ever to walk the earth.

In truth, young Amelia and Adolf had never been close. As children they had spent time together during family gatherings and the occasional summer holiday, but there was a distinct difference between the two, noticeable even as youngsters. Where Amelia had been giddy and playful, young Adolf had been serious and dour. Where she had been kind and loving, her cousin was distant, arrogant and aloof.

One summer she had discovered the twelve-year-old Adolf crushing an extended family of woodlouse, one by one, with a large rock and had attempted to save the helpless beasts. Her efforts had been futile and her laughing cousin had tied the six-year-old Amelia to a nearby tree, helpless and hysterical, and had forced her to watch as he added a host of other tiny woodland creatures to his miniature slaughterhouse. Since that day, their already distant relationship soured extricably and they barely spoke, except to bicker once a year around the compulsory Christmas dinner table.

The Great War put an end to their irregular and frosty meetings, with Adolf marching off to the trenches and Amelia training as a nurse and serving with the German Red Cross in the military hospitals of the Western Front. Now adults and with no requirement to ever see each other again, that would have been a fitting end to their troubled relationship. But it was not to be.

Following German defeat in 1918, the two cousins began their journeys along radically different paths. The beautiful young Amelia fell for a dashing British Army officer and the vast differences in social standing and birthplace were forgotten by the lovesick couple as they were swept away in a whirlwind of youthful romance. Marriage and a baby boy, Albert Beaumont Fortescue Bloodstone, followed shortly after, proceeded by a decampment to her new husband's Hampshire estates for a life of unbridled luxury.

For her cousin, life took a very different route. Bitter and resentful at his adopted country's defeat, Adolf fixed his blame firmly on the Jews and Marxists that he held responsible for the outcome of the war. He entered politics and showed a rare talent for his chosen profession, appealing to the masses and swiftly climbing the ranks, his policies becoming increasingly extreme as he did so.

Throughout the twenties and most of the thirties, Amelia was blissfully far removed from the goings-on on the Continent. She threw herself into the joys of married life and motherhood and adapted to the life of an English socialite with an aplomb unexpected of an Austrian nurse from peasant origins. Despite her newfound fortune, she remained fiercely proud of her homeland and ensured that her only son was able to speak the tongue of her birth like a native. She even arranged an annual pilgrimage to the mountains of her youth, taking young Albert with her as she visited her family.

But not once during her visits did she see her cousin Adolf, who was away injecting his vitriolic poison into the minds of not only the German people, but her beloved Austrians too. Over the years her visits left her increasingly disillusioned with her homeland and her fellow countrymen, who seemed to be following their leader into the abyss, so much so that she chose not to set foot again in Austria after her mother died in 1935.

Instead, she began to use her position in British society, the beautiful wife of an aristocratic war hero, to speak up against her estranged cousin and the dangerous direction in which Europe was heading. It started off small with letters to The Times and the BBC, but her passion grew as she saw the situation worsening and she became a vocal opponent of Neville Chamberlain's policy of appeasement. She began to become renowned as a vehement critic of Nazism, not just within the British Isles but on the Continent too, where Hitler started to bristle at her public and increasingly personal condemnations.

As war began, Amelia Bloodstone's criticism attracted more followers than ever before and it was rumoured that many within the borders of the Third Reich began to pay heed to the stories that they heard on the banned wireless stations and in the illegal newspapers, both of which loved nothing more than espousing the damning views of one of the Fuhrer's very own family.

In late 1941, while accompanying her husband on a business trip to the United States, she was invited by a close friend to address Congress and warn of the dangers of sitting impotent while Nazi Germany was allowed to wreak havoc across the Atlantic. Her speech, which made the front pages for its damning indictment of Hitler's ambitions, as well as a thinly veiled reference to family rumours of the teenage Adolf's warped sexual desires, proved fateful.

One week later Japan attacked Pearl Harbour and the United States found themselves at war with Germany. Just two weeks after that, Amelia Bloodstone lay dead in her bedroom with the personal calling card of the Fuhrer pinned to the lace of her Christmas dress. There were those that said that her impassioned plea to the American government had been the last straw for Adolf Hitler, who had dispatched his henchman to silence her and send a message to the world that he would not tolerate dissension, no matter from where it came.

As Bloodstone took another sip of whisky, he reflected on the fateful set of circumstances, so many years in the making, that had resulted in his mother's murder at the hands of a Nazi assassin. For nearly two years he had tried to imagine the face of the unknown killer and now, at last, he had a name and, looking again at the photograph in his hand, a face to match it.

Standartenführer Otto Heidler. One day, somewhere, somehow, I'm going to kill you, Bloodstone vowed silently as he drained his glass. And it's going to be slow, he promised, so very slow and so very painful.

CHAPTER TWENTY-FOUR

As Bloodstone gulped down the last of his whisky, the roof of the mess shook as another aircraft passed overhead, low enough to rattle the glasses stacked neatly on the bar. That was the tenth this morning and the major, now fancying himself as something of an aircraft aficionado, recognised it as the four-engined roar of a Lancaster.

"They're up early this morning, must be something afoot," he said to Jones, before he slammed his glass on the table and jumped to his feet.

"Come on Algy, let's take a look," he continued, keen for something to distract him from the mental image of his mother's bloodstained corpse.

He opened the mess door and the pair walked outside into the chilly autumn air, just as yet another Lancaster swept overhead low enough to cause them to duck, before it roared away to touch down at the far end of the distant runway. A particularly pretty WAAF, with red hair wound tightly into a bun beneath her cap and bosoms straining against the blue of her tunic, swerved from the path to step around the officers as they peered at the far-off bomber.

"Excuse me, Corporal, why are the chaps up at this time of day?" Bloodstone asked, flashing the girl one of his finest smiles and noticing the twin stripes on her arm.

The WAAF paused, smiling slightly as she took in Bloodstone's dashing looks and the impressive row of medal ribbons on his chest.

"Ops are on again, sir," she said through a smear of non-regulation lipstick with a voice touched with a soft Scottish lilt, "That'll be the last couple of air tests coming back in."

"Rather early isn't it?" Bloodstone asked.

"Take-off scheduled for twelve hundred hours, sir."

"Twelve hundred? A daytime raid? What's the target?"

"You know I can't tell you that, sir," the pretty WAAF replied with a bedazzling smile of her own, "Even though I'd love to, of course."

"Unacceptable behaviour, Corporal...?" Bloodstone asked with a wink.

"Bell, sir, Corporal Rosie Bell," the smiling red mouth responded.

"Well it's a pleasure to meet you Corporal Bell," Bloodstone beamed as he locked the WAAF's green eyes with his own, "And thank you, you've been most helpful."

The red-haired girl half-saluted, half-curtsied and let out a giggle as she turned on her heel and continued her journey towards the collection of nearby buildings, her perfectly proportioned uniform-clad bottom swaying gracefully from side to side.

"You and the bloody redheads, Bertie," Jones laughed as the WAAF disappeared from earshot, "I think you've got a problem old boy."

"Now that's a problem I'd like to have," Bloodstone replied wistfully as he watched the scrumptious sight fade into the distance and imagined the delights that were no doubt concealed beneath the blue uniform.

His debauched musings were cut short as another Lancaster thundered overhead and glided into land on the opposite side of the

123

airfield, coming to rest amid a gaggle of mechanics who busied around her like a swarm of ants.

"Bloody odd to have a daylight raid, hey Bertie?" Jones commented as the pair stared out over the huge expanse of grass that bordered Scampton's three runways.

"You can say that again," Bloodstone agreed, "Damned rare as far as I know."

"Let's pop across to the Ops Office," he continued, "Find out what's happening. I can't imagine G for George is up again after the battering she got last night, but it's worth a check. If she is then we'll need to get old Huckleberry across with his camera. Last mission and all that."

The two officers turned on their heels and headed along the path towards a squat whitewashed building adjacent to the control tower. A single pink rose was planted beside the door and a row of badly disguised bullet holes scarred the building's front wall. Either the Luftwaffe had had a pop at some point, Bloodstone mused, or a Lancaster gunner had lost the plot. Whichever it was, someone needed to do a better job with their paintbrush, he thought as he knocked once on the door and twisted the handle.

He stepped inside to find a small room complete with a paper-strewn desk, behind which sat a grey-haired RAF squadron leader, while a chalk-spattered blackboard adorned one wall and a map of mainland Europe was pinned to the opposite wall. The left side of the squadron leader's face was puckered with the scars of long ago burns and his hand was missing a finger, but his eyes twinkled with boyish good humour, despite the dark rims beneath them.

"Major," he beamed as he stood up from his desk with a broad smile and gestured around the small room with his good hand, "Welcome to my little cave."

"Good morning, Squadron Leader," Bloodstone responded while shaking the hand of the aerodrome's intelligence officer who had debriefed him in the early hours of the morning and had jotted down his excited post-Wilhelmshaven chatter in a thick leather-bound book.

"Allow me to introduce you to Captain Jones, Intelligence Corps," he continued, gesturing in the direction of his friend.

"Pleasure," the scarred man said as he offered Jones his hand, "Squadron Leader Williamson. Good to have another member of the club in town."

Sitting back down behind his desk, Williamson straightened a rogue piece of paper and looked up at Bloodstone.

"So, what brings you here?" he asked, "I thought you'd still be tucked up in bed after last night's antics."

"I heard there was another show on," Bloodstone replied, "I was just wondering if Ashton's lot are on the roster?"

"Need-to-know only, Major, you know that," Williamson smiled, "The Boss would have my guts for garters if I was telling every Tom, Dick and Harry what the good old Five-Thirteen are up to."

"I completely understand, mum's the word and all that. Can't blame a chap for trying though, hey?" Bloodstone said and turned back to open the door, "Thanks anyway, Williamson."

"Shut the door, man," Williamson ordered, a mischievous look in his eye, "The Boss isn't here right now. And when the cat's away...

He didn't finish his sentence but tapped his nose, got back to his feet and stepped across to the stained blackboard.

"And anyway," he continued, " A man with ribbons like yours deserves a bit of slack now and then, especially if the rumours about last night's show are true."

He winked at Jones and, before Bloodstone could attempt any sort of diffident fibbery, snatched up a pencil and started tapping down the barely legible scrawl of a list on the blackboard.

"Susan, Apple, Jane, Mother, Romeo, Charlie, Fox, Uncle, Mary, Lucy, Piper and, here, one more, George. That's Ronnie Ashton's kite isn't it?"

"That's the one," Bloodstone replied, somewhat surprised that G for George was in any fit state to fly.

"I'm surprised she's fit to fly," the squadron leader continued with the uncanny mind-reading ability that all intelligence officers seemed to possess, "Poor damned fitters have been up all night gluing her back together after you chaps buggered her up something rotten last night.

"But she's certainly on the schedule, the crew's final op if I'm not wrong. Flying at number two behind A for Apple. That's the Boss' kite; it seems he's decided to take her up for a rare trip."

"Grubb's flying?" Bloodstone asked, surprised as he pictured the tight faced Australian at the controls of a Lancaster. No doubt abusing his crew mercilessly, he thought to himself.

"He might be somewhat, um, unconventional, Bloodstone, but the Wingco damned well knows his way around an aeroplane. One of the finest pilots I've ever seen. Brave as a lion too; he only puts himself on for the tasty missions."

"So, today's a tasty one?"

"Any mission in the daylight is a tasty one, my friend," Williamson replied, his usual jocular look replaced with a sad smile, "But we've got to give the Yanks a hand occasionally, even if it means we take a pounding for it."

At that moment the door handle turned and the door opened inwards, bringing with it a gust of chilly morning air and a WAAF carrying a mug of steaming tea. Bloodstone was delighted to see that it was Corporal Bell, the pretty girl he had bumped into on the path not five minutes before, now with her cap slightly askew and her cheeks glowing a rosy pink.

"Ah, Bell," Williamson greeted cheerfully as the WAAF handed him the cup, "Thank you; what would I do without you?"

"You're welcome, sir," Rosie Bell said, acknowledging Bloodstone's presence with a thinly disguised smirk, before she made her way across to the blackboard, picked up a cloth and rubbed off one of the scrawled names from the list.

"Jane's Jugs is a no-go, sir," she announced, "Dynamo drive on the port outer just blew, erks won't get to it in time."

"Bugger," Williamson said with a grimace, "Well there's no reserve ships so that takes us down to eleven. Not many for a long old trip to Jerryland, hey Major?"

"Whereabouts in Jerryland?" Bloodstone enquired.

"Corporal Bell, if you'd be so kind," Williamson said, waggling his pencil at the WAAF.

Bell strode across the room, her RAF issue heels clattering on the wooden floor, and paused by the map that took up a full wall of the small office. She plucked a cane from a nearby umbrella stand, cracked it once into her open palm and thrust the tip in the vague direction of the Alps. Bloodstone, trying hard not to let his imagination run wild at the sight of the cane-wielding beauty, peered at the brightly coloured paper.

"Freiburg," she announced, tapping the map, "Five hundred and twenty-seven miles as the crow flies from Scampton, or, factoring in payload, grouping up and feints, three hours and twelve minutes to target."

Not just a pretty face, Bloodstone, thought, impressed, as the Corporal continued with her impromptu briefing.

"Eighty-four B-17s from the Eighth Airforce and thirty-five, well now thirty-four, Lancs will be hitting the railway yards in central Freiburg. There'll be a feint at Paris and one at Turin en-route and they'll pick up an escort of the new P-38 Lightnings over the Channel. Take off at midday, assembly over Northampton and home in time for supper."

Concluding her speech with another slap of the cane against her palm, Bell turned back to the two officers and looked from one to the other.

"Sirs, any questions?"

"Yes, Corporal," Jones piped up, "Why the daylight mission? And why with the Yanks?"

"Good question, Captain," Williamson offered from his desk, "A spot of, what shall we say, cross-Atlantic cooperation. The powers-that-be have deemed it politic to join forces to give the Hun a bashing. And today is the day."

"But in daylight, is that not a tad dicey for the Lancs?" Bloodstone asked.

"In theory, sir," Bell answered, "But the escort will be there to lend a hand. And you'll know that the Lancaster's weak spot is being attacked from below, so the plan is for the Forts to take the lower rung and give us as much cover as possible."

"I see, well God be with them," Bloodstone said, glad that he wasn't the one to be dragging his backside across the skies of occupied Europe in the broad daylight but, at the same time, feeling a pang of concern for Ashton and his crew.

Thinking of Ashton made him glance at his watch and he noticed that it was already half past ten. He'd have to be quick if he wanted to get some footage of G for George as she headed off for her final mission.

"Squadron Leader, are you happy for me to nip across to the dispersal and get the camera on old George? I don't want to get in the way, but it'll make some damn fine footage."

"Absolutely, Major," Williamson answered as he took a sip from his tea. "In fact, Bell here will drive you over there herself. I need her to get some signatures from Chiefie anyway."

"Splendid, much obliged to you," Bloodstone said, "Come on Jones, let's shake a leg."

He turned to Rosie who had placed the cane back in its umbrella stand and was now nonchalantly brushing a smear of chalk from the breast of her tight-fitting tunic.

"Lead the way, Corporal, if you'd be so kind."

"Of course, sir, with pleasure," she replied, as she gave her bosom one last rub, tucked a stray strand of red hair beneath her cap and opened the office door.

Bloodstone followed her out into the brisk morning air and failed miserably to avert his eyes from the tantalising backside in front of him.

"Oh dear, Bertie," he said under his breath as he watched Corporal Bell walk towards a nearby parked Jeep, "Oh dear, oh dear."

CHAPTER TWENTY-FIVE

The Jeep tore across the grass at a speed not dissimilar to a grand prix car, while Bloodstone clung to the passenger seat for dear life as the vehicle bounced and jolted over the ground. Huckleberry James, who had been hastily collected from his quarters, was wedged into the back seat alongside Jones and an assortment of camera equipment was piled between them.

Bell looked even more alluring at 40mph, Bloodstone decided as he watched her from the corner of his eye, one of her dainty hands shifting through the gears and the other gripping the wheel tightly. Certainly one to nail down for a date before the day was out, he promised himself, once again inadvertently picturing her without her blue uniform and feeling a stirring in his trousers as he did so.

Thirty seconds later his thoughts returned to business as the Jeep took a sharp right, swerved around a fuel bowser and came to a skidding halt alongside a steel Nissen hut, beyond which G for George rested proudly on her haunches. A trolley load of bombs was being loaded into her belly and a gaggle of oil-stained mechanics swarmed around and over her, prodding and poking at her various lumps and bumps.

There were still forty minutes until take-off and the seven airmen of the crew were gathered in front of the open double doors of the

Nissen hut, dressed in their flying kit and sprawled across a collection of wooden boxes and spare tyres. Cigarettes drooped from the corners of most of their mouths, with the exception of Przybylowski, who lay flat on his back, snoring loudly. As Corporal Bell went in search of Chiefie with a sheaf of forms in her hand, Bloodstone left James and Jones with the Jeep and strolled across to the crew.

"Good morning gents," he greeted cheerfully, cracking open his cigarette case and offering around a replacement fag, "Fine day for it."

"Scuse me for saying so, sir, but kiss my stinkin balls," the toothless Buster replied with a cheeky grin as he helped himself to a fresh cigarette.

"I ain't designed to fly in daylight," he continued, "Too dangerous with me guns I am, not fair on old Jerry is it?"

Nobby, his lanky body propped up against an empty crate, hooted with laughter.

"The only thing I've ever seen you close to shooting is your own load, you bald bastard," he said, flicking his cigarette butt at the Cockney rear gunner, "I think Jerry's safe for another day."

Buster stuck two fingers up and let out an enormous belch, which he blew in the direction of Nobby. "Have that you gangly prick."

Nobby blew a kiss back before looking up at Bloodstone.

"Coming along for the ride again, Bertie sir?"

"Not today, Nobby, more's the pity," Bloodstone replied as he stooped to pass his lighter to the wireless operator, "I was hoping to get some film of you chaps heading off today. If that's alright with the Skipper?"

Ronnie Ashton, who was deep in hushed conversation with Jimmy, turned his head and took a pipe from between his teeth.

"Of course, come to make us famous again, Major?" he asked with a tired smile.

"I can but try, Ashton, I can but try," he answered with a wink and looked past the blonde pilot to give Jimmy a discreet once over.

He noted that the love bite was still visible on the youngster's neck and his face was as handsome as ever, but the eyes were rimmed with circles so dark that it looked like the boy hadn't slept in a week. His black hair was lank and greasy and his left eyelid fluttered uncontrollably, while his right hand, which clutched a squashed pack of Players cigarettes, shook like a man in the final stages of Parkinson's disease.

"How are you doing today, Jimmy," Bloodstone asked, "All good?"

The gunner looked up, a distant look in his tired eyes, and nodded slowly, his fingers twisting the paper of the cigarette packet. Ashton, facing away from Jimmy and looking Bloodstone in the eye, grimaced slightly and gave the briefest shake of his head. He got the message; once again Jimmy was far from alright.

A Scottish voice distracted him from the sorry-looking youngster.

"Och, I see you've met Bombshell Bell then, Major," the small dark-haired figure of Bill chirped up from his seat on an old Lancaster tyre as he nodded in the direction of the WAAF corporal who was holding out her papers for Chiefie to sign.

"Good Scottish lass that, none of your Sassenach scrawniness he continued, "No finer creature this side of the border, let me tell ye that, sir. And apparently she's got a twin sister just as fine."

"Twin or no twin, she's way out of your league, Jock," Nobby chipped in, "She wouldn't look twice at the likes of you. Me on the other hand..."

Before he could finish his sentence, Buster interrupted, "You do talk some bollocks Nobby. You've tried your luck like every other fucker on this base and she's told you where to go.

"I reckon she drives the other bus, she does," he continued, "Rumour is she's even turned the Boss down. Ain't natural is it, cheeky mare."

"He's right," Chalky the navigator agreed, putting down a book he was reading, "You've got no chance there, sir."

Bloodstone, never one to be fazed by a challenge, blew out a perfect smoke ring and grinned at Chalky, "She won't be able to resist old Bloodstone, whatever bus she drives. She'll be chomping on Bertie's balls before you know it chaps, you just wait and see."

Hoots of derision echoed around the group, only to fall quickly silent as seven pairs of eyes watched Corporal Bell stride confidently back towards the Jeep, her papers now signed by Chiefie's grease-stained fingers. They held their breath as she reached the vehicle and climbed back into the driver's seat, exposing a brief glimpse of stocking-clad thigh in the process.

The spell was broken by Ashton who glanced at his watch, pulled himself to his feet and ordered the crew to collect their belongings.

"Look lively you deviants, time to mount up," he announced as he crammed his battered cap firmly down onto his head, "Let's go give Uncle Adolf his daily dose for one last time."

A particularly apt choice of words, Bloodstone thought as he wished the crew luck and retreated to the Jeep, from where he smiled with amusement as they huddled around the Lancaster's wheel and completed their urinary ritual. As he watched the seven men, he felt a tinge of regret that he wasn't joining them, which was quickly replaced by a sense of relief as he remembered Squadron Leader Williamson's dour look at the thought of daylight bombing.

Huckleberry James, aided by Captain Jones, was busy setting up the camera a few yards in front of the Nissen hut, where it would have a perfect view of George's taxi to the runway and lift-off towards the East, while Corporal Bell remained in her seat and leafed through the sheaf of papers. No time like the present, Bloodstone thought to himself, wandering around towards her side of the vehicle.

"Got your autographs, Corporal?"

"Yes, sir, all present and correct," she replied in her soft Scottish lilt while not taking her eyes from the oil stained forms, "Although Chiefie's made a right mess of them."

"No excuse for filthiness," Bloodstone offered lightly as he watched a strand of red hair flutter in the late morning breeze.

She tore her gaze from the papers and looked up at him with a wicked glint in her eye, "Oh I don't know, sir. There's a time and a place for everything."

The glint faded as quickly as it had appeared and Bloodstone was just about to follow up with a cheeky comment of his own when a commotion at the rear door of the Lancaster caught his attention. He couldn't see exactly what was happening, but two men seemed to be in frantic discussion with arms waving and muffled shouts echoing across the tarmac. Looking more closely, he realised that the two men were Ashton and Jimmy, both clad in their flying suits with their gloved hands gesturing wildly. Seconds later a third figure climbed down from the rear exit of the Lancaster and joined the commotion, his voice joining the incomprehensible noise that made no sense to Bloodstone's ears.

No sooner had Bloodstone recognised the third figure as Buster, than the rear gunner swung a mighty punch at Jimmy's chin and knocked him flying from his feet. As his body hit the floor, Buster leapt upon him, his hands grasping the youngster's collar and his mouth screaming unintelligible words into his face.

A friendly bit of banter was one thing, Bloodstone decided quickly, but a full-on brawl was something else and, as the most senior officer present, it was his was responsibility to get it sorted.

"Will you excuse me, Rosie, I'll be back in a jiffy," he said to the WAAF corporal as he snatched up his beret and set off at a run towards the Lancaster, quickly covering the short distance with his powerful strides.

By the time he had ducked underneath the aircraft's fuselage and reached the rear door, Ashton had pulled Buster off Jimmy, who now lay on the ground, curled into a ball with his body racked by childlike sobs.

"What the bloody hell is going on here?" he demanded of Ashton.

Before the pilot could answer, Buster butted in, his face a mask of fury, "Fuckin' coward doesn't wanna fly. I'll be fucked if I'm not finishin' my tour today because of this numpty."

Bloodstone rounded on him, the anger on his face matching that of the rear gunner but his voice as cool as ice, "I didn't ask you, Sergeant."

He turned back to Ashton, "Pilot Officer?"

"Buster's right, sir," the pilot replied sadly, his usual calm demeanour looking flustered, "Jimmy's refusing to get aboard."

"Is that so, Jimmy?"

The teenager on the floor let out a whimper but Bloodstone didn't need a response; he knew when a man had cracked. It looked like ops, and no doubt the war, were over for Jimmy.

"So, what happens now, what's the protocol?" he asked Ashton.

"It's never happened to me before to be honest, sir, but we'll radio Control, they'll find a new gunner from the stand-down crews and send him on out."

Buster piped up again, although the rage had now subsided from his scarred face to be replaced by something akin to concern, "No chance of them makin it in time though, Capt'n, the rest of the boys will be halfway to Krautville by the time the dicky gunner's aboard."

Ashton nodded, his brow creased with worry.

"He's right again, sir. They'll send us off late and we'll have catch to up with the stream, which would be damned risky in the daylight. To be honest, I wouldn't give us good odds of making it home this evening. Which is a bloody shame, what with it being the boys' final op."

"Fuckin typical," Buster spat, glaring at the pitiful sight of Jimmy, "Get through to the last op and they send us off for the chop."

"Any other options?" Bloodstone asked, looking at the pilot.

"Short of dragging him aboard and flying one man down, that's it, sir. Rules are rules I'm afraid."

"There's always a way, Ronnie," Bloodstone replied absently as an idea sprouted in his mind, "There's always a way."

With that, he turned back to Buster and handed him his hip flask.

"Sergeant, I want you to take Jimmy over to the Nissen hut and give him a tot of this. And gently now, I'm making you responsible for him."

The rear gunner nodded obediently and bent down to Jimmy, who had now pulled himself into a sitting position with his head slumped forward in despair. He lifted the younger man to his feet and guided him across the tarmac with his arm around the quivering shoulders, the almost fatherly approach in sharp contrast to the aggression of just a few moments before.

Bloodstone waited for the pair to disappear from earshot before he swivelled on his heel to look at Ashton.

"Ronnie, I have an idea."

CHAPTER TWENTY-SIX

Sometimes in life you just have to make a call and be damned with the consequences. And today, Bloodstone decided, was one of those days. A man didn't win a DSO, a DSC and two MCs by faffing about and he certainly didn't snap up a seemingly unobtainable filly like Corporal Bell without a spot of bluster.

And so it was, ten minutes later, that he found himself behind a pile of boxes in the Nissen hut, tucking his combat knife and revolver into the top of a newly borrowed flying boot, pushing his now half-empty hip flask into his battledress pocket and pulling up the zip on the front of what, five minutes before, had been Jimmy's fur-lined flying suit. As he removed his Parachute Regiment beret and manoeuvred a leather flying helmet onto his head, he smiled inwardly at the fact that his hasty plan was coming together.

Jimmy, now devoid of his flying kit, was safely secreted on a camp bed on the opposite

side of the building with Chiefie for company who, aside from having a mouth like a potty, seemed to possess a somewhat grandfatherly ability to comfort the tormented youngster. Chiefie was sworn to secrecy and had assured Bloodstone that Jimmy would stay put until George returned to Scampton in the early hours of the evening, following which nobody outside the crew or those in on the plan would be any the wiser. And if she didn't return, they had agreed, Jimmy would just have to come clean and prepare to have his logbook stamped with the three red LMF letters that indicated the cursed lack of moral fibre.

Rosie Bell had left George's dispersal and had headed back in the direction of the Ops Office with her Jeep bouncing across the grass and the pile of stained papers stashed in her holdall. She too had agreed to keep Bloodstone's scheme to herself, unless of course George failed to make it home, in which case she was to tell all to Squadron Leader Williamson. Even more importantly, Bloodstone thought, he had persuaded her to meet him at the Fox and Hounds that very evening for a post-flight snifter. He'd be the envy of the station, he grinned to himself, and no doubt Wing Commander Grubb would despise him even more. The idea made him chuckle out loud as picked up Jimmy's oxygen mask and strolled out towards the nearby Lancaster.

The thought of Grubb made him look out across the airfield to where he knew the Boss would be at the helm of A for Apple, readying for take-off and preparing to lead the ten ships of 513 Squadron out across occupied Europe. He had no doubt that Grubb would tear more than just a strip off him if he discovered what Bloodstone was planning and would probably have him banished from the airfield. However, he reasoned, that was a risk worth taking if it meant that Ashton and his crew had a decent chance of survival on their final mission. No doubt Ashton would get a rollicking too, but orders were orders and Bloodstone had given his, which meant it was he who would pay the price if the secret leaked out.

Captain Jones and Huckleberry James were standing by the camera tripod and he gave them a cheerful wave as he reached the Lancaster's rear door.

"Good luck, you damned lunatic," Jones shouted across the tarmac and Bloodstone responded with a wide grin before he clambered up the steps of the ladder and ducked inside the aircraft.

The now-familiar odour of oil, metal and leather that hit his nose like a sledgehammer smelt almost homely and he was decidedly pleased to notice that last night's stench of human faeces had now vanished. A quick glance at the Elsan revealed that the smashed toilet had been completely replaced, while the multitude of bullet and flak holes that had peppered the aircraft had been patched up overnight too. Chiefie might be able to swear like a trooper and he might have an uncanny knack for looking after tormented fliers, Bloodstone mused, but he also ran a damned efficient team of fitters.

No sooner had he boarded the Lancaster than the four Rolls Royce Merlin engines roared to life, one by one, and the noise inside the fuselage grew as each engine powered up before rising to a crescendo that sent bone shuddering vibrations through the aircraft. Bent almost double, he staggered the few steps towards Jimmy's turret, pulled himself up into the Perspex bubble and plugged his intercom into the socket.

"Mid-upper gunner in position," he announced into his microphone and received a chorus of ironic cheers in return.

"About time too, sir," came a cheeky Cockney voice, followed by Bill's thick tones.

"You just could'na keep away could ye, Bertie sir. Now yer doomed like the rest of us poor bastards."

Before Bloodstone could throw some banter back, Ashton interrupted the chatter.

"Belt up, boys, time to hit the road. One last radio check if you please."

As each crew member called in over the intercom, the Lancaster began taxiing towards the main runway, bumping and jolting over the tarmac. From his position in the turret Bloodstone had a clear view of the other ten aircraft of the squadron emerging from their dispersal points to congregate in one long line at the edge of the airfield. G for George was number two in the queue and, as she slowed to a halt, Bloodstone could clearly see the tail gunner ahead in A for Apple, his turret turned perpendicular to the aircraft so he could tumble backwards to safety in case of an emergency.

The sight brought the reality of what he was about to do back to him with a bump and the realisation that once again he was throwing himself unnecessarily into the jaws of mortal danger. He knew that casualty rates for Bomber Command were over sixty percent, which gave him a fairly decent chance of going for a Burton, but he was also fully aware that the odds of a crew reaching their full thirty sorties was five to one against. Add to that the fact that George was about to hit the skies in the full light of day, a juicy target for half of the Luftwaffe, and he didn't rate his chances of making it home for tea and crumpets. Or, more's the pity, for a drink and who knows what else with Bombshell Bell.

The thought of the curvy WAAF made him glance out towards the control tower, where a crowd of people had gathered on the grass outside to bid the bombers farewell. Sure enough she was there and, despite being little more than a red-topped blob in the distance, she still looked good enough to eat, Bloodstone thought. He wondered if she really did have a twin sister but dismissed the idea as pure fantasy; surely God wasn't that good.

His wandering mind was refocused as A for Apple received the signal for take-off and began to barrel down the runway ahead with the rear gunner still ready to fall backwards in case Grubb fouled up the take off. But the lift off was perfect and Apple soared gracefully into the sky half a mile ahead, pointing her nose southwards as she left Scampton in her wake.

As Apple's wheels left the tarmac, the noise of George's engines increased as Ashton pushed all four to full throttle. The vibrations surged through the aircraft at even greater levels, causing Bloodstone's teeth to chatter and making him wonder if the airframe was about to tear itself apart. He watched as an oversized spider struggled to maintain its foothold on the outside of his turret, just inches from his eyes, the vibrations causing the unfortunate creature to scrabble across the Perspex like a drunkard. He willed the spider to maintain its grip, but the tremors were too great and it slipped one last time, hopelessly flailed out a limb and fell from view. As it disappeared, Bloodstone realised that it had only had seven legs. Poor bugger, he thought.

The green light of a flare arced overhead and Nobby's voice crackled through the intercom.

"That's the signal, Skipper, we're good to go."

Ashton acknowledged the message and, like a runner reacting to a starting pistol, G for George bucked ferociously as the brakes were released and six thousand horsepower was let off the leash. Within seconds the Lancaster was hurtling down the runway and bumping wildly over the tarmac as she picked up speed, the needle of her speedometer passing forty, then eighty then one hundred miles per hour.

As the needle touched the one hundred and twenty mark, Ashton pulled back on the controls and the Lancaster rose gracefully into the air and left the cold tarmac in her wake. She climbed comfortably and the mind-numbing vibrations ceased as she quickly acclimatised to the autumn air, eating up the altitude with ease.

From his turret Bloodstone watched as Scampton disappeared astern and the personnel on the ground quickly turned into dots and then vanished from view completely. The remaining nine aircraft of 513 Squadron left the ground one by one and climbed to form a staggered line that stretched away into the distance behind, while Ashton swung George's nose to starboard and headed south towards central England.

The sight could not have been more perfect, Bloodstone thought, as the Lancaster continued to climb and he swung his turret through three hundred and sixty degrees to take in the view. The clouds that had laid thick and grey that very morning had now started to disperse to leave a blue expanse of sky that would have looked more at home in midsummer, not an early October day. Looking to starboard he could see Nottingham in the distance, while far off to port the waters of The Wash twinkled in the midday sun.

As the Lancasters of 513 headed south, specks of other aircraft started to appear all around as they climbed into the sky from their various bases throughout eastern England. Some were bunched together in tight knit groups and some were stretched out in elongated lines, but all were headed in the same direction. And, Bloodstone mused, all were packed to the rafters with deadly ordnance. The citizens of Freiburg would be getting something of a headache in three hours' time.

His wandering mind was interrupted as Chalky's voice crackled into his ears.

"Five minutes until the grouping point, Skipper."

"Roger, Chalky," came the response from Ashton, who then dipped his wings slightly to give the navigator a better view of the terrain that was now ten thousand feet below the slowly climbing Lancaster.

As the port wing dropped slightly, Nobby's excited voice burst through the intercom.

"That's my village down there boys, good old Mears Ashby, clear as day. Come on Skip, go down and say hello to Mummy Ball will you."

"Bullshit," scoffed Buster from the rear turret, "You's talkin rubbish again. There's sumfink wrong with your head."

"It's true," the wireless operator continued, "See that barn down at three o'clock, the one next to the forest? That's where I popped my cherry."

"With a sheep no doubt," Buster offered, "You country bumpkins make me sick. Fuckin freaks."

"Better to be a bumpkin than a smoggy street urchin, you bald-headed monkey."

Before the two could continue their joshing, Ashton interrupted.

"Give over will you boys, it's time to get ourselves lined up. Navigator, how are we looking?"

142

"Bang on schedule, Skipper," Chalky replied as he scribbled figures into his logbook and then twisted to glance out of his small window at the cluster of aircraft surrounding George.

He turned back to his desk, surveyed his notes once more and then spoke confidently into his intercom.

"Skipper, form up a hundred yards astern of Apple, same altitude. Charlie should come 100 yards to our port and Lucy the same to starboard."

As Ashton followed his navigator's instruction and manoeuvred the Lancaster directly behind Grubb's ship, Bloodstone watched with awe as Cheeky Charlie and Lady Lucy swooped into position on either side of George's wings with perfect timing. Other Lancasters were doing similar all around, creating a multitude of tight arrow-like formations across the sky.

He strained his neck to peer downwards and saw that the air below him was now filled with silver four-engined bombers who were moving in unison into neatly packed ranks. The B17s, their multitude of protruding machine guns visible from a thousand feet above, glinted in the sunlight and Bloodstone felt a wave of gratitude that hundreds of pairs of friendly eyes would be guarding the Lancaster's vulnerable belly for the next few hours.

Bill, watching the manoeuvres from his position in the nose, let out a wistful sigh. "Och, now that's a bonnie sight. Those Yanks sure would've been nice to have along for the last twenty-nine."

"Pah," replied Przybylowski in his thick Polish accent, "Give me ze night any time. And those Americans, toy soldiers. You just vait and see."

CHAPTER TWENTY-SEVEN

The bombing force continued south with one hundred and fourteen British and American aircraft bound for the depths of the Third Reich. Bloodstone, warm and cosy in his Perspex turret, basked under the heat of the early afternoon sun and watched the world go by. The fields, forests and rivers of England passed lazily by and so peaceful was the view that one could be forgiven for forgetting that mankind was trying its damnedest to tear the world to pieces.

The spires of Oxford appeared off to starboard and a few minutes later a grey smudge on the eastern horizon quickly turned into the sprawling mass of London. The burning fires of the Blitz had long ago been put out and the clouds of smoke that now lingered over the city belched from the factories that worked around the clock to feed the nation's war machine.

Bloodstone found it difficult to believe that it had only been four days since he had been down there in London, standing in front of the maimed figure of General Wilkins and receiving the orders that had led to him to where he was now, 20,000 feet high with twin Browning machine guns at his fingertips. Those four days had certainly packed in their fair share of frolics, he mused, thinking back over the last ninety-six hours. The exploding Lancaster, the rollicking from Grubb, the delightful mouth of Kitty, his first foray into the silver screen, a sortie over the Fatherland, a downed Hun, the identity of his mother's killer and now another chance to give Jerry a damned good walloping from three miles up. At least life wasn't boring, he admitted, although he wasn't sure how long life would continue if he carried on at this rate.

"Two minutes to the coast, Skipper," announced Chalky and Bloodstone glanced down once more.

Below him was the land of his youth and he watched with a fuzzy feeling as the rolling greenery of the South Downs gave way to the island city of Portsmouth. Row upon row of terraced houses were squeezed onto the small blob of land and the tiny black specks of barrage balloons could be seen floating above the city's harbour, where hundreds of ships lay at anchor.

The sight of the familiar harbour reminded him of the white-moustached ex-admiral who had been a booming presence throughout his boyhood. Bloodstone's grandfather had been the last of a long line of naval officers, stretching all the way back to the Battle of Trafalgar, and it had often been said that a Bloodstone vein contained more saltwater than haemoglobin. He could still see Grandpa Horatio's look of abhorrence when sixteen-year-old Albert had announced his wish to forsake the navy and follow his father into the army instead.

If only the old chap could see me now, he chuckled to himself as he watched the Hampshire coast fade into the distance to be replaced with the greeny-blue seas of the Channel.

"Say goodbye to Blighty, boys," instructed Ashton from the pilot's seat as the force of bombers left the English coast in its wake, "And get those game faces on."

"You know the drill," he continued, "Keep your eyes peeled and shout out anything you see. Nobby, any news from our escort?"

"Nothing yet, Skipper, although they're due any moment."

"The pricks are probably too busy prancing around tryin' to shag our birds, fuckin' Yanks," Buster offered helpfully from his rear turret, "Two to one they don't turn up."

Bloodstone thought that a little harsh, especially considering that there were 840 American airmen who had bothered to turn up, encased in their Flying Fortresses, just a thousand feet below G-George. Personally, he had never been overly fond of Americans, far too noisy and brash for his English tastes, but his experience of fighting alongside Eisenhower's infantry in Italy had softened his view slightly. Yes, still uncouthly loud and with a disgusting penchant for chewing tobacco, but they were certainly handy to have in a scrap. Nowhere near the standard of the British soldier of course, but decent fellows all the same.

The French coast became visible in the distance and still the promised escort of P38 fighters remained absent, leaving the bomber force to drone on southwards alone. Remembering his rudimentary schoolboy geography, Bloodstone realised that the coastline ahead was that of Normandy, not only the home of William the Conqueror but also the place where Jones had slurringly told him, after one too many brandies, that the invasion was likely to take place at some point the next year.

A year was a long time in this game, Bloodstone thought, but nevertheless he craned his neck to peer down at the ground where he would no doubt be plying his fighting trade in the future, if, of course, he somehow managed to stay alive until then. Nothing of note jumped out at him from his perch high in the autumn sky, except for wide sandy beaches and, as the sea gave way to land, lush green fields, small forests and a sprinkling of higgledy-piggledy villages.

A black puff of smoke out to starboard, followed half a heartbeat later by a loud crumping noise, brought him back to the present with a jerk. The dreaded flak was back and within a matter of seconds the sky was filled with hundreds of balls of dirty black smoke as the previously silent German AA guns below unleashed their hellish welcome on the invading aircraft.

"Here we go, boys," Ashton said over the intercom, "Hold on tight."

Bloodstone tried to squeeze his body into itself, mentally making his six-foot figure as small as he could, and he was acutely aware that his crown jewels were likely to be the first things turned to mincemeat if a shell decided to find its way to his vicinity. Oh for a piece of armour plating to sit on instead of a flimsy seat, he thought to himself as he desperately willed his balls to stay clear of the fiery shells.

G for George bucked and jolted as she rode the wave of incoming artillery and it wasn't long before the gunners on the ground claimed their first casualties. A Lancaster several hundred yards astern seemed to lurch in the air like a bucking bronco, before it spewed out a torrent of black smoke from one engine, dropped its nose towards the earth and proceeded to plunge from the sky, ejaculating burning fuel and bits of airframe as it fell. The three remaining aircraft in the stricken Lancaster's formation closed their ranks and seemed to huddle closer together as their compatriot tumbled from the sky, leaving a faint trail of grey smoke and a single white parachute as the only sign that it had ever existed.

A Flying Fortress was next and simply erupted into a ball of fire as a four-inch shell pierced its fuel tanks, incinerating ten men in an instant and sending burning debris spinning hundreds of yards in all directions. Bloodstone watched as the maelstrom of vaporised flesh and mangled metal vanished into the ether and he involuntarily squeezed his legs together even tighter.

As the Channel faded from view astern, so the murderous flak slackened and soon faded away altogether to leave the surviving bombers to continue south in relative peace. Several aircraft trailed black smoke from their engines, a telltale sign that the anti-aircraft fire had made its mark, and a Lancaster away to George's starboard pulled out of formation and turned back towards home with two engines stationery and a large section of wing missing.

"Lucky bugger," Buster commented as he watched the injured aircraft limp away northwards, "No doubt the Brass will chalk that down as an op."

"Aye, home in time for afternoon tea," Bill agreed in his sing-song Scottish tones, "Although I'd nae wanna be oot on my tod in this light."

Bloodstone silently agreed, glad of the gun-toting company that droned onwards around and below him, the silver B-17s sparkling in the early afternoon sun and the Lancasters dark and brooding in the camouflage paint that was far better suited to their usual nighttime flying.

As he continued to look out from his turret, he felt the ship bank to port slightly and change direction.

"That's right, Skipper, bearing oh-nine-five," Chalky announced, "Just stick like glue to the Boss, he's bang on track."

"Roger," Ashton acknowledged as he corrected his trim slightly and followed the Wing Commander's aircraft as it turned south-east and began its feint towards Paris, aimed at keeping the German radar operators guessing at the true destination of the bomber force.

Bloodstone found it surreal to think that Paris was only a short distance away and he craned his head to peer at the horizon in the hope of spotting the fabled city. He'd had more than his fair share of adventures in the years before the war broke out, tearing up the streets of the capital and overindulging in Montmartre, just like any other teenager with too much cash in his pocket and a particular thirst to slake. But now Paris contained something else too; Otto Heidler, his mother's murderer and a man he had never met but hated with every fibre of his being. One day, he promised himself for the fiftieth time that day, one day.

His thoughts of bloody revenge were interrupted as Buster's voice crackled through the intercom, "Fighters, seven o'clock high."

Bloodstone swivelled his turret to face the rear of the aircraft and peered into the distance. A smear of tiny black specks was just about visible to the naked eye, a thousand feet or so higher and, Bloodstone guessed, four or five miles distant.

148

"Are they ours, Buster?" Ashton asked.

"Don't fink so Capt'n," replied the tail gunner, "But they definitely ain't P38s if they are. Three-and-a-quarter-miles out by my reckoning, heading our way."

Bloodstone marvelled at the Cockney's eyesight, amazed that he had spotted the minuscule dots in the first place, let alone be able to recognise what type of aircraft they were.

"Make ready boys," Ashton ordered in his ever-calm voice, "You know the drill."

Bloodstone, squinting into his sights, wasn't sure that he did know the drill but figured that he had no choice but to work it out as he went along. As he stared, the specks became clearer and it wasn't long before he could tell that there were nine of them, strung out beside each other in a loose formation. What they were, though, he still had no idea.

"190s," Buster announced as if reading his mind, seemingly recognising the incoming dots as Focke Wulf's latest incarnation of flying devildom.

As the enemy aircraft continued closer, they began to take form and it wasn't long before even Bloodstone's untrained eye was able to recognise the low-slung belly and malevolent looking nose of the Nazi fighters. He felt his heart begin to pump faster as they neared and he fingered his trigger, willing them to come within range.

But this group of Luftwaffe pilots weren't going to give him an easy job and, a mile from the closest Lancaster, they split into three. One trio swept left, one swept right and the third climbed to give themselves extra altitude as they prepared to select their targets from the thirty-two Lancasters that lumbered onward over occupied Europe.

With every foot that they grew closer, Bloodstone's heart rate increased and he felt the familiar knot of fear steeped with excitement start to seep through his body. Buster, on the other hand, calmly reported in on every move that the attacking force made and, so relaxed was he, that Bloodstone thought he would have been more at home casually commenting on the progress of a family of ducks gliding across a village pond instead of nine harbingers of aerial death.

The Flying Fortresses below seemed about to be ignored by the FW190s, who probably fancied the easier pickings of the Lancaster over the heavily armed B17s. However, that didn't stop the Americans from wanting to get in on the action and several opened up with their fifty calibre machine guns, pumping lead out toward the Luftwaffe craft who were still way out of range.

"Fuckin' idiots," Buster chided as dozens of other B17s joined in the fun and added their bullets to those already arcing crazily across the sky in the vague direction of the German fighters. The Lancaster gunners, on the other hand, held their fire and waited for the attackers to make their first move.

They didn't have to wait long. A thousand yards from the British bombers and the Focke Wulfs finally committed to the attack. Each group of three split into three again and, released from the pack, the individual aircraft swept in amongst the Lancasters, ready to unleash maximum carnage.

Bloodstone attempted to fix one of the squat fighters in his sights, but they moved with such pace that his target was gone before he even had chance to squeeze the trigger. He watched helplessly as two of the black-crossed machines swept down onto Cheeky Charlie, the Lancaster immediately to George's starboard, and riddled the aircraft from nose to tail, their 20mm cannon balls causing devastation inside the plane's thin fuselage. So close was the doomed Lancaster that Bloodstone could see explosions of blood and flesh inside the cockpit as the pilot and engineer were turned to mincemeat by the ferocious attack.

Within seconds the crippled Lancaster's nose dropped and she twisted to port before she rolled onto her back and plunged headfirst towards the ground, shedding bits of wing and fuselage as she fell.

Bloodstone, his ears full of the shouts of his crewmates as they called in incoming fighters, tore his eyes away from the vanishing Lancaster and tried to make sense of the frantic situation taking place in the skies outside his turret. The fighters were dipping and rolling and looping with such speed that he found it impossible to keep up and he thought it something of a miracle that George had thus far escaped unscathed.

He forced himself to focus and ignored the rat-tat-tat and the vibrations as Buster and Bill unloaded at anything that came within range. He began to listen to the noise in his ears and started to take note of the words pouring through the intercom.

"Three o'clock high, watch out for that yellow bastard."

"Fighter coming in at five o'clock, tail gunner he's all yours."

"Two of the fuckers dropping at eleven o'clock, keep an eye on them, Jock."

The sky was filled with bullets and smoke and twisting turning aircraft, yet still G for George continued unscathed as the 190s chose other victims among the force of Lancasters. It was almost as if the Luftwaffe pilots knew that George held a veteran crew, hardened by twenty-nine missions, and were wary of testing their skill.

One fighter obviously thought differently, however, and positioned himself for the attack just behind and below Buster's tail. The bullets of the B17 gunners continued to arc upwards but were just as much of a risk to the RAF as they were to the Luftwaffe, such was the close proximity in which the aircraft duelled.

As the fighter prepared to pounce, out of view from Bloodstone's turret, Buster continued his constant stream of chatter.

"Cocksucker twelve o'clock low, he's comin' in. Capt'n, prepare to corkscrew."

A moment later a trail of shells streamed past Bloodstone's ears as the Focke Wulf committed to attack.

"NOW!" yelled Buster, almost deafening his crew mates, and Ashton reacted instantly and yanked his controls to send the Lancaster twisting down and to port in one violent manoeuvre.

Bloodstone was entirely unprepared for the corkscrew and felt as if his stomach had dispatched itself to his chest and his heart was pumping through his ears. But the evasive manoeuvre had worked

151

and the fighter was now in front and above the Lancaster and was desperately trying to pull away to avoid the bullets that spat from Bill's nose guns. His attempts were futile, however, and the tail gunner of Grubb's aircraft joined in the turkey shoot and pumped bullet after bullet into the wings and engine of the Nazi.

In a matter of seconds the twin streams of shells did their job and the aircraft exploded, sending scraps of fuselage and chunks of metal in all directions. The last thing Bloodstone saw as George passed through the fiery remnants of disintegrated aeroplane were two blackened legs, held together by a thin string of flesh, as they cartwheeled sickeningly through the air.

The furious dogfight continued for another two minutes, during which time two more Lancasters and a single Focke Wulf were blown from the sky in various grisly ways. Then, as one, the remaining seven Luftwaffe pilots disengaged from the fight, pulled into a ragged formation and zoomed away eastwards with British and American bullets snapping at their tails.

"Buggers must be running low on fuel," Ashton offered from the cockpit as he pulled the Lancaster back into formation, albeit a formation that now contained only three of its original four aircraft following Charlie's bloody destruction.

He then instructed each crew member to check in and, when all six had confirmed that they were at their posts alive and well, he requested a damage report, to which there was a muted silence.

"Nothing at all?" he asked.

"Nothing," Przybylowski confirmed, "Not a scratch, as you English say."

"Bloody hell," Nobby responded, "That's a first, it's usually us getting chunks blown off all over the place. Maybe it's our lucky day, eh boys? I can see us making it home tonight after all."

God in heaven Nobby, Bloodstone thought to himself as he reached for his lucky bullet, nothing like tempting fate. Speaking of which, he wondered, where the bloody hell had that escort of P38s got to?

CHAPTER TWENTY-EIGHT

One hour and thirty-seven minutes after take-off and with twenty-nine Lancasters still in the air, the group of British bombers prepared to change course once again. Below them the B17s, now outnumbering their RAF counterparts by nearly three to one, filled the sky like so many silver birds as they powered on above the French countryside. The force circumnavigated Paris, giving the city a wide berth, and turned eastwards in the direction of Nazi Germany.

Bloodstone thought it strange that he hadn't been to the land of his birth for years but was about to pay a visit for the second time in twenty-four hours. This time, with the Nazis' murder of his mother fresh in his mind again, he realised that he hated the place even more than he did the previous night. Actually, that wasn't strictly true, he thought; he didn't hate Germany per se, just the evil that had seeped into her every pore and had infested her people. Cousin Hitler and the masses that had blindingly followed him into the abyss had a lot to answer for. And Bloodstone was going to be asking some serious questions, he promised, as he flexed his gloved finger on the metal trigger of his Brownings.

His thoughts of vengeance were interrupted as Nobby's voice crackled to life in his earphones.

"Bad news, Skipper. I've just heard from Apple and apparently the escort isn't coming to the party. Got busted up over the Channel and thrown in the towel. We're on our tod, boys."

"Fuckin' Yankee ponces," Buster chipped in before Ashton's ever-calm voice echoed through the intercom.

"Not to worry, chaps. We've come this far on our own. We'll be just fine. Who needs the Brylcreem boys anyway?"

Remembering the blood-soaked destruction of Cheeky Charlie just a few minutes before, Bloodstone thought that the remaining Lancasters could certainly do with a spot of help from the absent American fighters. But a pilot didn't survive twenty-nine missions without knowing his stuff, so if it was good enough for Ashton then it was good enough for him.

"Two minutes until course change, Skipper," Chalky reported from his small flying desk, "The Boss should be steering to zero six nine, just stick to his tail."

"Roger," came the response from the cockpit as Ashton continued his constant glancing between dials, horizon and the dark green tailplanes of A for Apple, which stood out so clearly in the cloudless French skies.

Forty feet behind the pilot, Bloodstone wiped his forehead with the back of his leather glove for the hundredth time that day. Despite being at an altitude of eighteen thousand feet and with no heating aboard the Lancaster, he felt like he was sitting in a greenhouse. The sun was beating mercilessly down onto the small Perspex bubble that surrounded his head and the combination of vest, shirt, tie, thick wooly jumper, scarf, uniform trousers and leather flying suit, let alone two pairs of socks, boots, helmet and gloves, was causing the sweat to pour off him. What he wouldn't do for a glass of ice-cold beer, he thought, licking his lips in anticipation and remembering that the deliciously proportioned Corporal Bell would be supping with him in just a few hours' time.

After the stresses and strains of the last few days, a spot of female company was just what he needed, he thought as he recalled the tantalising bottom of the red-headed WAAF and wondered if he'd be able to talk her into a post-drink roll in the hay on the way home. He gave himself even odds, which, he realised with a pang of depressing realisation, was probably better than the odds of making it back to base in one piece.

As his mind stripped off the WAAF uniform, followed by the entirely non-regulation undergarments that he imagined she favoured, G for George swung gracefully and ever so slightly to starboard as she took to her new course and headed towards northern Italy in an attempt to keep the watching enemy on their toes.

He looked down over the side of the Lancaster's fuselage, expecting the force of B17s to be turning towards the south-east too, but was somewhat surprised to see them continuing on their way, now off to port and still heading east. Did they have a wider turning circle, he wondered? Before he could ask the question himself, Bill's broad Scottish accent echoed through the intercom.

"Fit are them bloody Yanks doing? Ya ken?"

"English, Jock. How many times?" Ashton ordered from the cockpit.

The bomb aimer tried again, "The wee bastards haven't changed course, they're still heading off to Krautville. What the hell's goin' on, Skip?"

Ashton's voice crackled into his ears once more. "Wireless Operator, find out what they're up to. The rest of you, stay on the lookout for Jerry."

A minute of radio silence followed, during which time Bloodstone watched the rearmost Flying Fortress pass under the Lancaster's tail and fade away into the distance, leaving a thin vapour trail in its wake.

Sixty seconds later Nobby was back on the intercom.

"Apple's been in touch with the Yanks, Skipper. I'm not sure what's happening but apparently they ain't coming with us. Something about the secondary target."

155

"Secondary target?" Ashton asked, the veneer of calmness cracking slightly.

"That's what Apple's wireless op said. the Boss is going berserk up there, but the Yanks won't budge. Grubb's ordered us Lancs to carry on as planned. Target remains as briefed, Skipper."

"Jesus," Ashton whispered under his breath but not quite quietly enough for the rest of the crew not to hear.

Thirty seconds passed before the pilot spoke again and it was obvious to the six men on board that he was trying to hide his nerves as he talked.

"The Boss has given his orders, boys. You all know your jobs so let's get them done. Those B17s will give Jerry a much bigger fish to fry so we should be able to sneak in, dump these bombs and get back home pronto.

"This light means Jerry won't be able to sneak up on us so just keep your eyes peeled and shout out anything you see. We'll be just dandy, boys, nothing to worry about."

The words were brave enough but, despite the heat, Bloodstone shivered. Here they were, en-route to the centre of occupied Europe in broad daylight, with no escort and with their heavily armed comrades swanning off to bomb somewhere else. The odds of a cosy drink with Bell were lengthening by the minute, he thought, sighing heavily.

Before the air had finished escaping from between his lips, a roar like thunder almost deafened him, followed milliseconds later by the rat-tat-a-tat of machine gun fire and a gut-wrenching explosion at the rear of the aircraft, which rocked the Lancaster like a ship in a storm and left a sound like a howling gale emanating from somewhere below his feet.

Bloodstone swung his guns furiously in the direction of the explosion and was met with the dark underside of a fighter not twenty feet above his turret. The black and white crosses were clearly visible on its wings before it zoomed overhead, dropped away to starboard and vanished from view.

The whole incident had lasted a matter of seconds and neither Bloodstone, nor anyone else aboard George, had had an inkling that there was a fighter in their midst. The aircraft had seemingly sneaked up on them as they were all preoccupied with the departure of their American allies, unloaded a bucketload of lead and then dropped away out of range.

Beware the Hun in the sun, Bloodstone whispered to himself, remembering the Biggles books of his youth, as he held a gloved hand above his eyes and peered into the sun, desperately searching for another intruder. As he did so, he realised that he hadn't fired off a single round all day, despite ten German fighters rearing their ugly heads in the last hour. He was beginning to conclude that he was far better suited to combat on the ground when Bill's voice buzzed into his ears.

"109 making a run for it at five o'clock low, he's outta here. Lone wolf by the looks of it."

"Roger," acknowledged Ashton as he adjusted the trim to prevent the Lancaster yawing to port, which it seemed determined to do following the sudden attack.

With his corrections working and G for George begrudgingly returned to an even keel, he spoke into the intercom once more.

"Crew, check in please."

The airmen responded one by one.

"Navigator, checking in."

"Wireless op, all fine."

"Bomb aimer."

"Engineer."

"Mid-upper gunner, checking in."

Silence.

"Rear gunner, check in please," Ashton requested.

Again, silence.

"Rear gunner, come in."

Nothing.

"Buster, do you read?"

Still nothing.

Maybe Buster's intercom wasn't working, Bloodstone thought. Or perhaps he just couldn't hear, which wouldn't be surprising considering the gale that seemed to be blowing from somewhere down near the tail.

Ashton's voice come over the intercom once more, "Bertie, you'll need to have a quick check on Buster. Make it snappy though, we need you back up in that turret sharpish."

"Roger, Skipper," acknowledged Bloodstone, who disconnected his intercom, unclipped his harness and dropped down to the fuselage floor before.

As his boots landed on the riveted metal, he slipped on something wet, tried to grab a nearby handle, failed, slipped again and landed painfully on his backside with his head coming to rest inches from the floor. He could feel the wind whipping around his face and it took a few seconds for his vision to adjust to the relative darkness of the fuselage's interior. His eyes focused in the windy murkiness and the sight that greeted him, not six inches from his face, made him scrabble back in shock as the bile instantly rose in his throat.

There on the cold metal floor was a head. Or, more precisely, half a head. Buster's head. Just like a hard-boiled egg, it had been sliced neatly down the middle, from scarred forehead to chin, with its one eye wide and staring and the remaining half a mouth fixed in a toothless grin.

A stringy globule of grey brain matter leaked from the nostril and a pool of thick congealing blood lay underneath, making the mangled head look like some sort of monstrous platter about to be served to a tableful of cannibals. A green shard of metal protruded from the remaining ear, completing the full horror of the spectacle, and Bloodstone tore his oxygen mask from his face as he gagged in disgust.

Of the rest of Buster's body there was no sight. Instead, chunks of meat and scraps of flying suit were strewn around the interior of the fuselage. Pools of blood, quickly solidifying in the freezing air,

158

were spread around the floor while large splinters of razor-sharp metal lay everywhere.

Pulling himself to his feet and trying to avoid the head, from which the single eye seemed to follow his every move, Bloodstone stepped around the lumps of mangled flesh and made his way towards the tail. As he got closer, the noise of the wind increased and he shivered at the icy chill that was blasting into the unprotected skin of his face.

Where the doors of the rear turret had been, he discovered, there was now just a jagged hole, with thin strips of manflesh impaled on the ragged metal edges. The gun turret itself had disappeared completely, leaving an array of jumbled wires, torn cables and broken metal. And, of course, a slick of frozen blood across everything.

Whatever had hit the rear turret had destroyed it entirely and had blown Buster, or the remains of him, backwards into the main fuselage of the Lancaster. Based on what little remained of the Cockney gunner, it must have been mercifully quick and painless but, Bloodstone thought grimly, some poor bugger was going to have a hell of a cleaning job to do when George returned to base.

He left the shattered turret and the buffeting wind and made his way back towards his own turret, carefully stepping around as much of Buster's torn flesh as he could. When he reached the remains of the head, he noticed that the single eye was still staring at him, so he poked the monstrosity behind a strut with the toe of his boot. As he did so, an almost entirely intact brain slid from within the broken skull and slipped across the vibrating floor of the aircraft, leaving a sticky trail of blue slime in its wake. Before Bloodstone could prod it away, the Lancaster hit a particularly vicious air pocket and the brain leapt a full foot into the air before it splodged back down onto the metal floor and slid away towards the rear of the aircraft.

Despite all the carnage that he'd seen over the last few years, there was something especially nauseating about the sight of the mangled remains of Buster, a man who was just hours from completing his fifth and final tour. He may have been foul-mouthed sod with a vicious temper, but a man who volunteered for four extra tours was undoubtably brave. Some would say stupid, he reasoned, but all that was irrelevant now because Buster was just a pile of offal and another statistic.

Back up in his turret and pleased to be away from the gruesome scene below his feet, Bloodstone plugged his intercom back in and spoke into the microphone at his neck.

"Rear turret out of action, Skipper. And Buster's gone."

"Roger. Anything you can do for him?" Ashton asked.

Bloodstone pictured the staring eye and the jelly-like brain.

"Nothing, Skipper."

"Understood, thank you," Ashton responded matter-of-factly and the intercom went quiet as the remainder of the crew silently absorbed the loss of their crewmate and tried to guess what fate had befallen Buster.

Thirty seconds later Ashton's voice crackled through the intercom once again.

"Listen in, chaps. We're going to be wide open up our back passage so I'm going to get us up above the rest of the flight to try and give us some cover. Navigator, how far to target?"

Chalky did some hasty sums before he reported back, "Forty-three minutes, Skip."

"Thank you. We're too far gone to abort so we'll stick it out with the rest of the pack, which means you're all going to have to look out for Jerry like crazy blighters. Nobby, let Apple and the rest know the situation please."

Another pause before Ashton's voice crackled to life again, "Chin up, boys. I'll have you home in no time."

It was a nice afterthought from the pilot, but Bloodstone could hear the tension in the man's voice. The chances of an evening date with Bombshell Bell seemed even slimmer than ever, he thought as he surveyed the cloudless sky for enemy aircraft, which was a damned shame indeed.

CHAPTER TWENTY-NINE

The group of Lancasters, now alone in the afternoon sky, ploughed onwards. Acutely aware of their vulnerability, they tightened their formation to give themselves as much protection as possible, none more so than the wounded G for George, who sat as close as possible above and behind Apple. Ashton had been amazed to discover that, despite whatever other havoc the lone Messerschmitt had wreaked upon Buster and his turret, all the Lancaster needed to keep her on course was a brief spot of trimming.

Across the French countryside they continued, three miles high above the fields and rivers of Burgundy, unmolested except for the occasional bout of anti-aircraft fire that puffed its dirty grey smoke among the bombers. The gun crews in this part of the country were either having a bad day or were particularly inept as the shooting was sporadic and so off-target that they may as well not have bothered wasting their shells.

As the group passed just north of the city of Dijon, a Lancaster off to Bloodstone's starboard coughed out a splutter of black smoke from one of her four Rolls Royce Merlin engines and the propeller was quickly feathered. Less than a minute later another engine followed and it wasn't long before a third lost power and hung impotent and stationary, leaving the ship struggling along on a single source of power. The strain quickly took its toll and the unfortunate aircraft started to slow and, losing height, it was soon left behind as the rest of the Lancaster force powered mercilessly onwards. The last Bloodstone saw of it, the lonely craft was turning for home and struggling to maintain altitude, making something of a pathetic sight as it vanished into the distance.

A few minutes later the seemingly incompetent AA gunners dealt an ace as one of their shells hit Lady Lucy, the aircraft immediately below and to starboard of G for George, plum in the bomb bay. The explosion that followed was immediate and ghastly as the aircraft simply disintegrated amid a fireball of apocalyptic proportions, with fifteen hundred gallons of aviation fuel and ten thousand pounds of high explosive bombs igniting in an instant. George was rocked by the blast and Bloodstone, who had been admiring Lucy's pornographic nose art at the moment of impact, was temporarily blinded by the scorching flash of the explosion. When his vision returned he was shocked, and somewhat a little disturbed, to find that his turret was not only stained black by the blast but that a rain-like mist of blood had splattered its way across the Perspex. At least it was a quick end, he thought grimly, wondering which poor airman had ended up decorating his turret with their innards.

Ten minutes later and with no further incident, the force, now numbering twenty-eight of the thirty-five British aircraft that had set out that lunchtime, changed course again. Their feinting and shimmying were now complete and they headed north east in the direction of Freiburg, with the Swiss border to their right and the towering peaks of the Alps visible in the distance.

Despite the noise of the gale that howled around his feet and the roar of the four engines that reverberated through the aircraft, Bloodstone could feel his eyelids becoming heavy. A combination of the beating sun, yesterday's late-night mission and the generous helpings of whisky that he'd shared with Jones only a couple of hours before were beginning to lull him into a delicious sense of sleepiness.

He rubbed at his eyes and chewed at the inside of his mouth but still the drowsiness dragged at his eyelids, tempting him to close them just for a brief second, daring him to give in. A flask of steaming hot coffee would be just the ticket right now, he mused longingly, but refused to be beaten and imagined the bitter taste of the beans that Great Uncle Barney grew on his Trinidad plantations and sent by the sackful to his father every Christmas.

Uncle B's special brew might not be much use right now he thought but, he remembered with a start, he had something in his pocket that would certainly come a good second best. Just before he'd pulled himself into Jimmy's leather suit, Ashton had handed him a small foil-wrapped packet of Benzedrine pills, the ingenuous little inventions that had famously kept thousands of bomber crews awake during the long dark nights of the last few years.

Bloodstone fished the packet out of his pocket, picked at the wrapping with his thick gloves and tapped three small pills into the palm of his hand. How many was he supposed to take, he wondered as he looked at the white tablets that jiggled in his gloved hand in time with the vibrations of the aircraft. One? They did look fairly small; was one enough? Two? Is that what Ashton had said? Or was it three? He racked his brains but for the life of him he couldn't remember what the pilot had suggested when he passed him the small packet as they stood on the runway just a few hours before.

"Oh bugger it," Bloodstone said out loud and put his gloved hand to his lips, hocked a ball of phlegm into his dry mouth and knocked back the three tablets with a gulp.

The metallic taste of the pills quickly disappeared and he waited for them to kick in, feeling his eyelids getting even heavier as he resumed his scanning of the skies. Seconds later the intercom crackled to life and Bill's broad Scottish voice echoed through his earphones.

"Ware fighters, twelve o'clock."

Bloodstone swung his turret to face the front of the aircraft and peered into the blue sky ahead. Sure enough a group of dark specks were visible out towards the horizon, several thousand feet higher and slowly but surely getting closer. He tried to count them, but the distance and the shimmer of the sun made it impossible; ten was his best guess.

"Sixteen of ze bastards. One oh nines," Przybylowski announced in a voice that seemed to lack any sort of concern, almost bordering on scathing.

"Bugger me," Nobby swore from the belly of the plane, "The whole bastard Luftwaffe is up today. Haven't they got anything better to do?"

"Watch the bloody chatter," Ashton scolded, before continuing confidently "And don't worry, they can't touch us if we stick together."

Remembering the bombers that had already been blown out of the sky that afternoon, Bloodstone thought that a little optimistic and tightened his grip on his trigger as he watched the enemy close in. Staring through the crosshairs of his sights, he felt his heart rate increase and the sweat begin to prickle on his brow.

"Come on," he muttered under his breath, willing the enemy to come within range, "Come on you filthy Jerry scum."

The group of fighters continued to close on the Lancasters and Bloodstone's fingers and toes began to tingle as he begged them, dared them, to fight him. His heart was now pumping like a mad thing, the blood thumping in his eardrums, and he felt as if it would tear itself from his chest, while every muscle under his heavy flying suit seemed to tense and swell.

"Come on, come on."

He found it impossible to sit still on his seat and jiggled up and down like a boy with ants in his pants, while his gloved hand fingered the trigger impatiently, desperate to unleash carnage on the enemy. He felt invincible. He wanted to fight. He wanted to take on the whole Luftwaffe on his own. And he wanted it now.

"Come on you cowards," he muttered, louder now as the sweat poured off his brow and into his eyes. But he didn't notice; his whole world had become the group of fighters that were inching ever closer, inching towards the slaughter.

When they were a thousand yards off, the fighters broke formation and dived off to pick targets of their own among the lumbering group of Lancasters. One seemed to have chosen George and swooped down from above and lined the four-engined bomber up in its sights as it careered almost vertically out of the cloudless sky.

Bloodstone, his heart now beating at an impossible rate and feeling like someone had injected ten thousand cups of coffee into his veins, closed one eye and lined the fighter up in his crosshairs. As he waited impatiently for it to come into range, he suddenly realised that his tiredness had vanished and laughed manically as he remembered the three tablets that he'd swallowed, now distinctly recalling that Ashton had told him, under no circumstances, to take more than one.

Bugger waiting, he said to himself, and squeezed the trigger gleefully, pumping bullet after bullet at the incoming Messerschmitt.

"AAAGGGHHHHHHHH! he yelled incoherently at the attacking Nazi, for whom he seemed to have developed an immediate and irrational hatred, "COME OOOOOOOOON!"

The Luftwaffe pilot appeared to be put off his stride by the hail of bullets that tore madly across the sky as if fired by a drunken maniac and he adjusted his dive and veered away from George. But the pilot's instincts were wrong and he dived nose-first into Bloodstone's random stream of shells, which punctured the engine, tore through the pilot's chest and ripped into the starboard fuel tank. Within seconds the aircraft was aflame and the bullet-riddled youngster at the controls was roasted alive as his crippled craft plummeted to the earth below.

Before Bloodstone could catch his breath, Bill's excited voice echoed through the intercom, "Jesus Christ, Bertie sir, two of the wee bastards in twenty-four hours, you're a natural!"

Bloodstone just grunted in reply, his thirst for blood not yet slaked and his body feeling like it was running on liquid adrenaline.

With the flaming Messerschmitt now out of view, he yanked his turret round in search of his next victim.

All around him, fighter planes were rolling and looping through the sky, some trailing smoke and some pumping out streams of lead as they attacked the bomber formation with merciless efficiency. The noise was constant and Bloodstone's ears felt like they were being deafened by a combination of the gale that still swirled around his feet, the roar of George's engines and the explosions and gunfire of the fierce dogfight that raged in the sky outside his turret.

Lancasters seemed to be dropping out of the sky wherever he looked, with some gliding gently towards the earth with trails of dirty smoke pouring from their engines and others falling like stones with wings or tails missing or aflame. Occasionally a Luftwaffe aircraft would join them, it's pilot dead or wounded at the controls as the squat fighter vanished from the fight.

As Bloodstone swung his turret from side to side in pursuit of new prey, his heart still thumping madly, he spotted a 109 trying to sneak in from below on the starboard side. He attempted to line his guns up on the fighter, but the attacker was too low and he couldn't get an angle on him. Instead, he was forced to watch helplessly as the Nazi pounced on A for Apple and pumped shell after shell into the aircraft, riddling the fuselage and turning her starboard engines into bullet-ridden scrap metal.

Fires instantly broke out across the wing and ate into the fuselage and, as the 109 came around for a second attack, still too low for Bloodstone to shoot at, he watched as the Lancaster's crew hurled themselves out of their burning aircraft. He saw the men fall towards the earth and counted six parachutes, their white silk mushrooms looking strangely out of place amid the fire and flame and smoke of the deadly combat.

From his turret he had a clear view of the burning Lancaster and could see the pilot still in the cockpit, wrestling with his controls to keep the damaged aircraft airborne. With a start he remembered that the man was Grubb, the angry Australian that had been so thoroughly

166

unwelcoming over the last couple of days. As he watched the Wing Commander fight to keep the undefended Lancaster on the straight and narrow, he felt an inkling of newfound respect for the man who had quite obviously ordered his crew to save themselves before him. Not such a complete bastard after all, he grudgingly admitted.

Ten seconds later the attacking Messerschmitt returned to finish off its victim, hurtling towards the flaming Lancaster and spitting out shells as it came. The bullets smashed into the nose of the bomber, tearing off pieces of metal, and the 109 followed the attack in as it wreaked untold havoc on the doomed Lancaster from as close as possible.

Still unable to aim his guns low enough, Bloodstone watched as the fighter pressed home its attack and went to pass over the top of Apple, just twenty feet above the crippled bomber. As it did so, he saw Grubb, still in his pilots' seat, glance towards the incoming enemy and yank his control yoke up and back. The Lancaster responded instantly and appeared to rear up on its hind legs as its nose searched for the stratosphere.

The Messerschmitt pilot, his finger barely off the trigger, yanked his own control column backwards into his belly as he tried desperately to get enough altitude to avoid the hulking nose of the Lancaster that was now directly in his path. He had no chance, however, and his aircraft collided sickeningly with the dying Lancaster, killing him instantly, decapitating Grubb and, milliseconds later, the entwined aircraft exploded like some sort of giant grotesque firework.

The explosion rocked George and showered her with burning fuel, lumps of torn metal and pieces of her Wing Commander, and Bloodstone, with the wakey-wakey pills still pumping through his blood, nodded to himself in silent respect.

"Fair play, Boss," he said to nobody in particular, "Fair play."

CHAPTER THIRTY

A for Apple's heroic but messy end meant that Ashton and his crew were now leading the Lancasters as they continued on their way towards Freiburg, while the 109s still buzzed in and around the weary formation like a horde of angry mosquitos. Six bombers had met their end at the hands of the latest batch of Luftwaffe attackers and another three were so badly damaged that they limped along like a trio of cripples and were slowly but surely left behind by their comrades.

Bloodstone, with the Benzedrine still coursing through his veins, ground his teeth and swung his turret frantically from port to starboard and back again as he searched for another fighter to tangle with. There was no shortage of Germans ducking and diving through the bombers as they selected their victims, but none ventured close for long enough for Bloodstone to blast them out of the sky. Instead, he had to be content with sporadically spraying bullets at anything that came into range, however fleetingly.

His headphones buzzed to life and Chalky's voice, sounding even younger than usual, crackled into his ears. "Fifteen minutes to target, Skipper."

Fifteen minutes, Bloodstone thought miserably, was that all? Was that enough time for him to shoot every last Nazi out of the sky?

He hoped so, he mused, feeling his fingers and toes tingle again as a delicious sense of invincibility coursed through his body, despite the obvious death and destruction that was unfolding in the skies around him.

A movement in the corner of his eye made him turn his head to the left, just in time to see a yellow-nosed Messerschmitt swoop down from the heavens, spitting fire at George as its guns blazed away viciously. With an incoherent yell of rage and surprise, and with no time to scream at Ashton to corkscrew, he wrenched his turret towards the incoming fighter and desperately squeezed the trigger of his Brownings, spraying out a vicious stream of lead that missed the attacker by a country mile.

The Lancaster shuddered as the German shells hit home, punched holes the size of fists in the fuselage and shredded the machinery of the port inner engine. One bullet found its way into the navigator's compartment where it hit Chalky plum in the forehead, punctured his skull and killed him instantly, before it ricocheted away towards Nobby's small desk. The bullet, now spinning after the impact with Chalky's forehead, gouged its way through the edge of a wireless set, sending a shower of metal shards into Nobby's face, before it burst a hole though the other side of the fuselage and disappeared off into the blue sky beyond.

Bloodstone, entirely unaware of the carnage that had been unleashed just twenty feet away, yanked his guns around as he tried to follow the 109, which was now looping back for a second pass. The speed of the fighter was unbelievable and he found it impossible to keep it in his crosshairs, instead choosing to blast away indiscriminately as the attacker descended on the Lancaster from several hundred feet high on the port side.

The bullets of his Browning machine guns failed to find their target and the Messerschmitt let rip with its own cannons, pumping 20mm shell after 20mm shell at George as it thundered through the air and closed the distance between the two aircraft at a frightening pace. Ashton threw the Lancaster down and to starboard in a desperate attempt to escape the attentions of the yellow-nosed Nazi, but his efforts proved fruitless and the 109 stuck to the bomber's undefended tail and smashed the port outer engine and shredded the nearby aileron with its missiles.

The Lancaster bucked horribly as the bullets struck home and Ashton wrenched at the controls as he tried in vain to shake off the fighter, yet still the shells continued coming, blowing chunks out of the bomber wherever they struck home.

Bloodstone, strapped into his turret and firing madly at the 109, felt like a twig in a whirlpool as George ducked and weaved through the sky, buffeted by the deadly hail of lead that kept coming, seemingly without end. One round crashed through the fuselage beside him, narrowly missing his leg, while another plucked at the sleeve of his flying suit and left a gash in the thick leather but missed his flesh by millimetres.

Two seconds later his world exploded in a nightmarish crescendo of shattered Perspex and twisted metal as the fighter's shells homed in on his turret, smashing his gun mechanisms, tearing the trigger from his fingers and destroying the transparent bubble that protected him from the 200mph winds and the freezing air of the autumn skies.

As his attacker passed overhead, not thirty feet away, and zoomed off into this distance, Bloodstone's first realisation was that he was still alive, which seemed to be something of a miracle considering that his entire turret had been shot away around him.

Second was the feeling that an invisible and gargantuan blacksmith had just walloped him about the head with an oversized hammer, while third was the realisation that his face was cold. Damned cold. Freezing in fact. So freezing that he felt like his eyes were turning into lumps of ice and the skin of his cheeks was being flensed by a knife. And the noise, like a thousand steam trains battering his eardrums, deafening him, turning his world into a cacophony of hurricane-like winds, freezing air and eye-watering agony.

Desperate to escape before he turned into a block of wind-battered ice, he scrambled to unclip his harness and dropped to the fuselage floor, leaving behind the wrecked turret and the now useless Brownings. His intercom was destroyed so, with no way of letting Ashton know that the aircraft was now entirely undefended except for Bill's guns in the nose, he decided to make his way forward to the cockpit. He was still unaware of the carnage that had just unfolded at the navigator's table but, nevertheless, he could tell that the Lancaster had taken a battering in the last few minutes so thought it prudent to grab his parachute from the wall rack before he set out for the cockpit.

He might as well not have bothered. Not only was the parachute pack smeared with something blue and slimy, which no doubt was some part of Buster's innards, but it had a hole the size of a cricket ball through the middle of it, from which burnt fragments of white silk were visible.

"Damn it," he muttered as he tossed the useless bundle towards the rear of the aircraft, hoping that if the worst came to the worst then he'd be able to find a spare chute elsewhere in the aircraft.

The noise inside the fuselage was deafening as the wind poured in through both the smashed tail and the missing turret and still the Lancaster vibrated madly, despite now only flying on two engines. Bloodstone couldn't see what was happening outside the aircraft but no doubt the Messerschmitt would return shortly and he didn't want to be hanging around midships with only a measly revolver to defend himself, so he set off towards the nose.

The interior was dim and shadowy after the dazzling sunlight of his turret and it took a while for his eyes to adjust as, bent almost double, he shuffled through the tight space of the fuselage. Past the ammunition boxes he went and towards the main spar, noticing the multitude of round holes that peppered the walls of the Lancaster and were testament to the accuracy of the Luftwaffe fighters that had dogged the bombers ever since the Channel.

The sight of the bullet holes reminded him of the 109 that was undoubtedly lurking about somewhere nearby and the thought hurried him on his way. He pulled himself over the waist high wall of the main spar, which brought him out by the rest bed, where he spotted the old blood stain on the cracked leather. On he continued, into the cramped workspace that housed the wireless and navigator desks and stumbled across a scene that resembled a slaughter yard.

Slumped against his desk, his face a blood-strewn mess, was Nobby. One eye dangled on a thread by his cheekbone, the socket empty and gaping, while the other was a mangled mass of metal splinters. The youngster was very much alive, although the pain was obvious, and his gloved hands gripped the table while a faint whimpering noise emanated from behind his oxygen mask.

Close to his feet was Chalky, who was most certainly not alive. The navigator lay face down on the floor and the only obvious sign of a wound was the enormous hole in the back of his head. The bullet that had killed him had blown away the back of his skull as it exited, leaving a jagged hole of bone, brain, blood and torn leather.

Chalky was clearly beyond help so Bloodstone turned his attention to Nobby and, giving him a squeeze on the shoulder, bent down to his ear and said, "I'll be right back in a jiffy, sit tight chap, you'll be just fine."

As Nobby's mangled face turned blindly in his direction, Bloodstone grimaced at the sight of the dangling eye and gave him another squeeze on the shoulder before he stepped over Chalky's prostate body and made his way up to the cockpit, where he was greeted by a scene of frantic activity.

Ashton, his face red and flustered and his eyes darting from dial to dial, was wrestling with the control column while Przybylowski, his jump seat stowed, was on his feet frantically pulling levers and pressing switches. The cockpit was filled with traces of smoke and Bloodstone noticed the windscreen was riddled with so many cracks that it was almost impossible to see through.

The pilot turned briefly to give Bloodstone a weary smile before his head snapped back to his dials.

"Good to see you, Bertie," Ashton shouted over the noise of the engines, his eyes still moving constantly across the dials, "I thought you were a goner. Tell me, what's going on back there?"

"Mid-upper turret's kaput, Skipper. Chalky's dead. Nobby's been hit," he replied.

"How bad is he?" the pilot asked without looking around.

"He'll live, but he's blind as a bat. He'll be no use for the rest of the show."

"Understood," Ashton acknowledged, leaning forward to push a red button on the control panel, "Get him comfortable and then jump on Chalky's maps will you."

He pushed another button and continued, "Those bloody Jerry fighters seem to have buggered off for now but no doubt they'll be back. We're not in good shape I'm afraid, Bertie, steering all shot to hell, two engines gone and number three is on its way out. If that goes then I'm going to have to dump these bombs and make a run for Switzerland. No chance of making it home on one engine and the rest of the fellows are already way ahead."

He waved an arm towards the cracked windscreen and Bloodstone could just about make out the shape of the surviving Lancasters, powering away into the distance and leaving George behind as they headed for the target.

"We are, as they say, royally buggered," he continued with a grim laugh, "So clip on a bloody chute will you."

At that moment and before Bloodstone could obey, a loud bang thundered out from his right and he turned just in time to see a stream of flame erupt from the starboard inner engine.

"That's number three gone," Ashton announced with a scowl of despair as Przybylowski leapt into action without a word and cut the engine, feathering the prop which quickly stopped turning and hung limp, useless and pathetic.

"We've no choice now," the blonde-haired pilot shouted over the din of the last remaining engine before he yelled into his intercom.

"Jock, are you on those nose guns? You're all we've got if Jerry comes back. I'm going to release the bombs."

"Aye aye, Skip," Bill replied and, moments later, Ashton flicked the release switch and ten thousand pounds of high explosive ordnance tumbled out of George's belly.

As the weight vanished, the Lancaster lurched upwards and Bloodstone had to grab onto Ashton's seat to stop himself falling.

"Steady, Bertie," Ashton half-laughed as he hauled on the control and slowly but surely dragged the crippled bomber in a wide arc to starboard.

"So, Switzerland it is," he continued as the aircraft settled on its new course, "It's going to be an internment camp for us I'm afraid, but it doesn't look like we've got any other option. Sorry I couldn't do any better for you, chaps, damned bad luck."

Bloodstone was just about to reply that Ashton, whom he had come to respect immensely in the past twenty-four hours, had no reason whatsoever to apologise, when an explosion several yards ahead, complete with dirty grey smoke, rocked the Lancaster. A split second later another explosion burst to starboard and then a third hit the tip of the port wing, tearing off a huge chunk of metal.

Flak, again. And this time it seemed that the crews on the ground were far from incompetent.

"For God's sake, give us a bloody chance will you," muttered Ashton at the unseen enemy gunners, just loud enough for Bloodstone to hear, before he turned back to face the major, the tension obvious on his young face.

"We're only a few minutes away from the Swiss border as far as I know, but it looks like it's going to be a dicey run in. So get Nobby to the rest bed and make sure he's got his chute on just in case."

"Will do, Skipper," Bloodstone obeyed and turned back into the navigator's cabin as yet another flak burst tore through the port wing and rocked the Lancaster from nose to tail.

Chalky's corpse was still lying on the floor, half blocking the walkway, so Bloodstone bent down and, grabbing an arm and a leg, pulled him to one side. As he did so, the wind plucked a map, complete with Chalky's scribblings, from the desk above his head and blew it into his face. He grabbed at the paper and shoved it inside the half-open zip of his flying jacket, before he plucked a parachute from a stowage rack on the fuselage wall, stepped over the navigator's body and made his way across to the wireless operator's desk.

Nobby was exactly where he'd left him, with his hands still gripping the table and the awful pain-racked whimpers still mewing from his mouth.

"The skipper's got it all under control," Bloodstone told the maimed man, "Next stop Switzerland. But we need to get your chute on."

The wireless operator turned his head, complete with dangling eye, in Bloodstone's direction and mumbled, "Switzerland? That's where Heidi's from isn't it?"

"Um, I think so."

"Good, I always did think she was a decent piece of totty," Nobby continued, as the eye bounces across his cheek as yet another piece of flak rocked the aircraft.

Bloodstone wasn't sure if Nobby was in shock or was just a loaf or two short of a full picnic, but he pulled the man to his feet and clipped the parachute onto his chest. Next, assuming they were low enough to come off oxygen, he detached Nobby's mask and turned the man around in the direction of the stern. Guiding him from behind, he steered Nobby towards the rest bed when, all of a sudden, the world exploded in a tumultuous crash of blinding light and deafening noise.

The blast blew him from his feet and sent him sprawling back on to Chalky's body, half deafening him and turning his vision into white nothingness. It took a couple of seconds for him to realise that the aircraft had been hit by another piece of flak, and this time seemingly just feet from where he been standing. He tapped at his limbs to check they were all still in place, which he was slightly shocked to discover that they were.

Nobby, on the other hand, hadn't been so lucky. As Bloodstone's vision returned, he discovered that the shell had come up through the open bomb bay, blowing not only a manhole-sized hole in the metal flooring, but had also taken Nobby's hands with it. The gangly youngster now stood upright with a look of pure horror on his mangled face, a silent scream emanating from his open mouth and two bloody stumps where his hands had been.

A second later the youngster let out a bloodcurdling howl as the pain hit him, driving him wild with fear and causing him to flail out with his newly severed arms. Searching for help but unable to see, he stepped forward and, before Bloodstone could reach him, he put one boot then another through the hole that had just been blasted into the floor of the Lancaster. His leather clad feet stepped on nothing but fresh air and he tumbled through the hole and out into space, the look of abject fear on his blind face the last thing Bloodstone saw as he disappeared through the jagged hole.

For Bloodstone, the next five seconds passed as if in a single heartbeat. He didn't make a conscious choice, he didn't think, he didn't consider the consequences. He simply leapt to his feet, stepped towards the hole in the floor and launched himself through it and out into the ether beyond. As his body left the aircraft and began to tumble through the air, the wind whipping his face and the noise hammering his ears, his mind was filled with only two thoughts. One, Nobby couldn't pull his own ripcord with no hands and, two, he had just leapt out of an aircraft at fifteen thousand feet with one vital thing missing, a parachute.

CHAPTER THIRTY-ONE

It was only as Bloodstone saw the black belly of the Lancaster disappearing above him that the reality of what he had just done finally registered in his drug-fuelled brain. He had made hundreds of jumps in his short career, yet never had he done so without a parachute. In fact, he'd never heard of anyone even attempting it and, if he had, he'd have thought them a damned fool.

Which, he considered, as the deafening wind buffeted his face, was a pretty fair assessment. But, he thought, one had to make his bed and lie in it, and he had most definitely made his, albeit a bed of monumental stupidity.

There was only one way to avoid being turned into strawberry jam in the next minute and that was to catch up with Nobby, open the poor fellow's parachute and cling on for dear life. Easy in theory, he thought, but nigh on impossible in reality. But what choice did he have? There was no option but to focus on the job at hand, he knew, and most importantly, to stay calm despite the panic that was beginning to engulf him and despite the hurricane-force wind that tore at his body.

As G for George vanished into the distance and as Bloodstone began to fall faster and faster, he craned his neck as he scanned the sky around him in search of the wounded wireless operator. Sure enough, there he was, slightly to the south and several hundred feet lower, falling through the air with his legs and the remains of his arms flailing madly. He could just imagine the terror of the man, blind and no doubt in agony, falling, falling, falling and unable to do anything about the inevitable bone-crunching impact that would finish it all.

With that thought in his mind, Bloodstone twisted his body forward and forced his head downwards, tucked his arms into his sides and used his feet to direct himself towards Nobby as he rocketed through the air. The hills and forests of the ground below looked so far away, but he knew that they were coming up to meet him at a terrifying speed and that he only had seconds to make his move.

The distance between the two men closed as Bloodstone made himself as aerodynamic as possible, using his feet and hands to navigate across the sky in the direction of the still flailing Nobby. The force of the wind tore at his eyes and the freezing air battered his face, making it almost impossible to breathe, yet inch by inch, yard by yard, he closed on his crew mate.

And still the earth continued rushing ever closer, obviously so now as the features on the ground began to take shape. Bloodstone estimated that he had fifteen seconds left to get the parachute open, yet he was still a good twenty feet above and to the north of the falling Nobby.

The panic began to rise again and threatened to consume him, but he refused to give in and forced himself to concentrate. If he was going to die, he decided, he was going to do it on his terms; bravely and fighting to the very end, not filled with panic and crying like a little girl.

He was close enough to see Nobby clearly now and could see the mouth jabbering wildly while the gangly legs kicked out against the rushing sky. The destroyed eye was still attached by its string, bouncing crazily in the hurricane-like wind, while the stumps of his arms flailed about in sheer panic.

Bloodstone held out his left arm and generated enough drag to track himself across the sky until he was directly above the flailing figure. Ten feet to go. The ground continued hurtling closer and individual trees now started to take shape. Ten seconds left.

He tucked his arms back into his sides and forced his body as straight as an arrow, clenching every muscle as the wind ripped at his flying suit, threatening to tear the clothing from his body. Eight feet to go. Eight seconds left.

Nobby was almost within reach now, with every feature of his destroyed face visible as he plunged horizontally towards the earth. Bloodstone noticed for the first time that a boot was missing, leaving one foot bare and sockless. The ground was now worryingly close and tree-covered hills and valleys covered the landscape. Five feet. Five seconds.

The roar of the gale in his ears was deafening and the tears streamed from his eyes, yet Bloodstone barely noticed as he focused every fibre of his being on the man who tumbled to earth, now only a matter of inches away. He bellowed a warning, but his voice was whipped away by the wind and Nobby continued falling, unaware that help was just a heartbeat away.

Bloodstone angled his body so he was falling at the same speed as Nobby and glanced downwards, seeing that they were directly over a thick forest, the trees of which were already too close yet continued getting bigger every millisecond. Seeing the speed at which the trees were growing in size, he realised that time was up. It was now or never.

One last adjustment of his body brought Nobby into reach and Bloodstone dropped onto his prostrate form, crashing into him with the force of a truck and instantly wrapped his legs around the other man's hips. The wireless operator screamed out in terror, the sound vanishing away into the wind, and he lashed out with his arms and smashed the stump of his left hand into Bloodstone's face.

Despite the force of the blow that stung him clean across the still-tender nose, he managed to grab hold of the parachute harness strap that wound its way around Nobby's backside and hung on for dear life, while his other hand desperately searched for the metal release handle on the front of the pack.

The two men, now joined together in an ungainly lump, began to cartwheel through the air as they plummeted towards the earth at breakneck speed. Glancing downwards, Bloodstone spotted the rocks and trees below him and knew that it was too late. Even if he got the parachute open, they were well past the point of safety. Death was just seconds away now, but at least it was going to be instant, he reasoned, feeling strangely calm and almost ready to give up and accept his fate.

But a Bloodstone never gives up, he vowed, and with one last desperate scrabble at the parachute pack on Nobby's chest, he found the metal handle and tugged at it with his fingers, pulling with all his might. An instant later the pack burst open and vomited its silk contents skywards, jerking the two men upwards so violently that Bloodstone lost his grip on the harness and was left with just one gloved finger wedged under the strapping.

As if by a miracle, he managed to maintain a fingerhold on the harness and wrapped his other arm around Nobby's chest as he clung on with every last bit of strength in his body. He felt himself slipping but squeezed even tighter as he ignored the injured man's confused screams that were now clearly audible in his ears. Somehow he held firm and dared a quick glance down at the trees below, which were shooting up to meet them far too quickly.

The chute was now fully deployed into a white silk mushroom above them, but they were still travelling far too fast and, with no free hands to control the descent, Bloodstone had no way of reducing the speed or steering away from the trees that were now only seconds away.

They hit them with a horrible crunch, smashed into the green canopy and drove down through the branches at what felt like the speed of a falling meteor. They bounced from branch to branch and ricocheted through the foliage as razor sharp twigs scratched at their faces and clawed at their clothing, tearing flesh and stabbing at their bodies. As Bloodstone waited for a branch to impale him or the ground to shatter his body, he saw a leg flying inches past his face, with the bare foot twisted backwards at an impossible angle. A blood curdling scream assaulted his ears, but he knew not whether it had emanated from his own throat, such was his bewilderment as he tumbled through the trees, somehow still attached to Nobby.

Finally, with a thump that knocked the wind from his lungs and seemed to shatter every bone in his body, it was over. He found himself lying on his back and high above him, through a gap in the trees, he saw the tiny shape of a lone bomber making its way across the cloudless sky, with a thin trail of smoke in its wake. And then the world went black.

CHAPTER THIRTY-TWO

Bloodstone awoke with a start, the sweet sound of birdsong in his ears and an evil hammer thumping somewhere inside his skull. He opened his eyes and tried to focus on his surroundings, while his brain attempted to work out where he was and, secondly, why he was there.

His first thought was that it had all been a dream, but no dream had ever hurt this damned much. Apart from the mallet banging away inside his head, his nose felt the size of a melon, while his right arm felt as if it had been almost wrenched from its socket. His ribs felt as if they'd been crushed and he was sure that something akin to a red-hot poker had been shoved into the flesh of his right arse cheek.

And then there was the wetness. He seemed to be soaked from head to toe in something warm and sticky. Had he pissed himself? As the memory of his fall through the sky slowly seeped into his agony-filled brain, he thought it not unlikely. Which was rather unbecoming, he thought, especially as hadn't soiled himself since he was a small boy. Apart from a particularly alcohol-fuelled session on his last night at Eton, of course.

As his eyes finally cleared of blurry shadows, he looked down at his prostate body to see that it wasn't urine that coated him, but blood. Gallons of it, like someone had emptied a barrel of tomato soup over his flying suit, which also appeared to have been attacked by a man with a sword, such were the number of tears and slashes in the leather. His body hurt like the very devil, but he was pretty sure the blood wasn't his. Then, as his brain finally returned to something close to its usual capacity, he realised that left only one other option.

The pain in his head was excruciating as he swivelled his neck to the right, but the pain was nothing in comparison to the horror of the sight that greeted his eyes. Six inches away lay Nobby, his body a broken, twisted mess. Bloodstone had seen scores of men run over by tanks or shredded by grenades during his seven years in the military and the usual result wasn't much different to how Nobby looked now.

One gangly leg, bereft of boot and sock, was bent double at the thigh with the bone snapped like a lolly stick, while a branch as thick as a man's wrist protruded from his belly. Both hands had vanished, replaced instead by two ragged stumps, one of which was black and cauterised and the other a torn mass of veins, arteries and ligaments. The dangling eyeball had mercifully detached itself at last to leave one gaping eye socket and another with a mush of mangled flesh and splinters of metal. Completing the picture and entirely at odds with the mutilated body was Nobby's mouth, which was frozen in what appeared to be an idiotic grin of epic proportions.

Bloodstone stretched out his right arm, grimacing at the pain, and gently shook Nobby, whose body was coated in even more blood than his own. Not surprisingly, there was no response from the wireless operator, so he pulled off his glove and put his fingers to the unnaturally long neck. Again, nothing. Nobby had most definitely bought it, which, Bloodstone considered, was probably for the best considering his nightmarish condition.

With a deep breath and another grimace of pain, he pulled himself into a sitting position and looked around. He was sitting on a bed of needles on a slope in a small clearing in what appeared to be a forest of pine trees. Around him were broken branches, the telltale sign of their tumble through the canopy, and above him the trees stretched away towards the late afternoon sky. Tangled in the trees was the torn white silk of the parachute, still attached by its harness to Nobby's chest, while a single leather flying boot was wedged thirty foot up at a fork in the branches.

He took another deep breath, rolled onto all fours and pushed himself to his feet. As he stood up, the pain in his backside stabbed at him like fire and he probed at the area with his fingers and discovered a thick splinter of wood protruding from the leather trousers. Gritting his teeth, he grasped it and tugged it free from his muscle, ripping out a bloodstained piece of tree two inches long and as sharp as a razor. He tossed it into the undergrowth and knew that he needed to clean the wound, but that would have to wait for there were more pressing things on his mind.

Shaking his head to clear the fuzz, he forced himself to think. He knew that he was south-west of Freiburg, somewhere in France in the hilly forests near the Swiss, French and German borders, but that was all he knew. He'd work out his exact location later, but the most important thing right now was to get away from the landing site as quickly as possible. Despite what seemed to be a fairly remote location, he was in no doubt whatsoever that someone would have spotted the parachute crashing to earth and would, at this very moment, be heading in his direction. So it was time to move, and quickly.

He stooped down beside Nobby's battered body and checked the dead's man's pockets in search of anything that might come in handy.

"Sorry, old boy," he muttered as he rifled through the bloodstained trousers, finding nothing more than a stubby pencil, which he pocketed.

Next, he gently lifted aside the parachute pack, taking care to avoid the vicious looking branch that protruded from Nobby's stomach, and felt inside the pockets of the torn flying jacket. His fingers found the solid lump of a tobacco tin, which he extracted and opened, only to discover it contained a pack of pornographic playing cards and a US army issue condom.

"What the blazes are you flying with this for?" Bloodstone asked aloud as he shook his head in bewilderment and wondered, with some amusement, what had been going through Nobby's head when he had packed his sordid tin before today's mission.

Nevertheless, he slid the tin into his own pocket, zipped up Nobby's jacket and replaced the empty parachute pack, taking care to ensure that the body looked entirely undisturbed. With any luck, anyone stumbling across the scene would have no reason to think that there had been a second airman. After all, he thought, one parachute must mean one flier; who had ever heard of two men descending to earth on a single chute?

He hoped that this logic would buy him enough time to get a decent distance away, sort the hole in his backside and work out what his next steps were, which so far he'd barely dared to think about.

As he was zipping up his pockets in readiness to set off, a noise in the distance made him stand stock still. Was that the bark of a dog, he wondered, cocking his head and listening into the trees, noticing that the chatter of birds had stopped, leaving an eerie silence over the forest. There it was again, distant still but certainly the bark of a dog. Or maybe a wolf. Either way, he decided, it was time to get going. A quick glance at the sun peeking through the trees told him which way was south-east and, deciding that heading away from the barking animal and in the general direction of Switzerland was his best bet, he set off into the trees.

As he began to move, ducking under branches and weaving around the trunks of the pine trees, the hammering in his brain faded slightly but the throbbing in his nose, the ache in his shoulder and the crushing pain in his ribs refused to budge. As if that wasn't enough, he soon found that the flying boots he'd borrowed from Jimmy, who obviously had feet considerably smaller than his own size elevens, were wholly unsuitable for tramping around on solid ground and were chafing at his heels and biting at his toes. On top of that, the legs of his flying suit were so thick and bulky that he was forced to waddle like a duck as he pushed through the trees.

He quickly discovered that the forest was on the side of a steep hill, but the trees were so thick that it was impossible to see more of the landscape. He figured that he had two options; either get to the top of the hill, wherever that was, and spy out the surroundings, or continue down the slope and see what was at the bottom of the hill. He remembered catching glimpses of farm buildings as he fell and, not feeling ready to investigate the local populous just yet, decided that upwards, where there was less likely to be civilisation, was the best choice.

His decision made, he headed up the slope, half running, half waddling and trying to make as little noise as possible. The lack of a visible path made the going tough, but he also welcomed it as something of a blessing as he figured that no path meant no people.

That theory was shattered shortly after as another barking noise echoed through the trees from the direction that he'd just come. This time the barking was accompanied by shouts, too far away to hear the language or what was being said but shouts all the same. His aching brain filled with questions. Had they found Nobby? Did they know there was a second airman? Were they tracking him? Was he heading into a trap?

He didn't know the answer to the thousand what ifs that flooded through his head, but he did know that he had to keep moving and find somewhere safe to get himself together and sort the hole in his rear end before it started to rot. A glance at the Rolex on his wrist told him it was nearly 5pm and, guessing by the brief glimpses of the sky visible through the trees, that sunset wasn't too far away, he knew that time was of the essence. Any sort of light during the night was a big no-no and blundering about in a forest in the dark was asking for trouble, so it was time to start looking for somewhere to hole up before nightfall. He knew that staying put overnight was a gamble and if he was being tracked then the dogs would have a field day with his flying suit looking and smelling like a slaughterhouse. But, accepting that his options were somewhat limited at present, it was a gamble that he was more than willing to take.

After half an hour more of scrambling through the trees and slowly but surely climbing ever higher, he came across a crop of moss-covered rocks in the shadow of a thick and particularly ancient pine tree. Such was the size of the tree's branches that the rocks looked like they hadn't seen a glimpse of sunshine in years, while a nearby fallen pine formed a natural wall on the rocks' eastern side and made the little outcrop almost invisible to anyone ascending the hill.

"Perfect," he muttered under his breath as dropped to his haunches, paused and listened.

Apart from the twitter of birds and the sound of the trees rustling in the gentle October breeze, the forest was silent. He hadn't heard any shouting voices for a good twenty minutes and the noise of the dogs had faded too, leaving him feeling as if he was quite alone in this wooded corner of France. It was a strange sensation, he thought, considering that just an hour before he had been nearly twenty thousand feet up and blasting away at the Luftwaffe with a pair of Brownings. Now here he was, squatting on the ground, sweating in his thick leather outfit with his body feeling like it had been run over by a freight train.

How quickly life can change, he mused with an ironic smile as he dropped painfully to his backside and tugged off the calf high boots. He reckoned that he was only about three miles from the crash site, but those three miles had played havoc with his usually tough feet. With the boots now off, he wriggled his cramped toes deliciously and enjoyed the lack of chafing on his ankles.

Next, he pulled himself to his feet and unzipped the front of the flying suit, tugged free his arms and let the heavy leather drop around his waist. As he did so, a scrunched up and thoroughly bloodstained map fell to the floor. He bent down to pick it up and peered at the damp paper, trying to make sense of the markings that had been made almost illegible by Nobby's blood, but soon found that it was impossible. With the exception of what appeared to be the contours of north-west Italy, the map was too far gone to be of any use, which was entirely unhelpful he thought as he laid it on the ground with a stone on each corner. Perhaps it would dry overnight and prove to be of more use come morning, he hoped as he stood on one leg then another to pull down the legs of the flying suit.

He lay that on the ground too and emptied his pockets, piling his belongings on top of the folded flying suit. Sitting back down gently, his backside still painful, he glanced at the motley collection of what were now his worldly possessions. Some of them immediately sprang to mind as being useful, namely the twelve-inch combat knife, the Webley revolver loaded with its ten bullets, a box of matches and his whisky-filled hip flask. Others, however, seemed to be of much less use, especially the dirty playing cards that he'd looted from Nobby. In addition, his small pile contained a pencil, his tin of cigarettes, engraved with his name, and the rubber Johnny, the last of which he couldn't see being used for its intended purpose any time soon.

The sight of the prophylactic made him think of Bombshell Bell, who would no doubt be sprucing herself up right now in readiness for their date at the Fox and Hounds that very evening. That particularly delicious filly was going to have to wait, he thought with a sigh, before he reassured himself that some things were most definitely worth waiting for.

With his date now certainly on ice until further notice, he decided that he had an important issue to attend to instead, namely the mending of his punctured arse cheek. With that, he pulled down his woollen uniform trousers and tugged off his silk drawers, leaving his manhood swinging in the chilly early evening air and naked from the waist down except for two pairs of thick army issue socks.

He laughed to himself as he imagined the shock of any poor Frenchman who stumbled across him right now, before he grasped his backside and twisted around in an attempt to get a good view of the wound. Sure enough, there it was, a puckered, angry and swollen hole as big as his thumb, circled by a crust of freshly dried blood. He prodded at it with his finger and winced at the pain, then probed more gently, picking out splinters with his thumb and forefinger. When he was confident that he'd removed as much of the stray wood as possible, he unscrewed his hip flask and poured a generous measure of Scotch into the wound, hissing in agony as the spirit stung the torn flesh.

What a bloody waste of good whisky, he thought as he took a swig for himself, before he bent down and plucked some clumps of moss from the rocks at his feet. He scrunched them into a tight ball, took a deep breath, opened the wound with his left hand and shoved the vegetation deep into the hole with his right. Securing the plant with another prod of his finger, he exhaled heavily and straightened up, flexing the muscles of his backside as he did so.

Thank the Lord for crazy Great Aunt Gertrude, he mused as he remembered the long-dead and wizened old woman who was an ever-present during childhood ventures to his mother's homeland. When he was a small boy he'd laughed at her distrust of so-called modern medicines and had watched in horror as she made him eat nettles, rubbed various plants on his skin and pushed strange coloured leaves into his rectum. Fingers crossed there was some sense in the old lady's madness, he thought as he gave the moss one last prod and pulled up his bloodstained drawers and trousers.

His backside was now mended as well as possible, but there was nothing to be done about his various other bumps and bashes. The sore ribs and the aching shoulder would just need time and the nose could do with some ice, which he certainly didn't have. The throbbing head, however, needed a decent dose of sleep and, despite the Benzedrine that he'd necked a few hours earlier, he was more than ready to curl up for the night.

In spite of the sun that he'd been sweating under all day, he knew that an autumn night in the open air was going to be cold, so he took off his jumper, pulled back on his thick flying suit and crammed the fur-lined boots back onto his feet. He rolled the jumper into something resembling a pillow and lay down under the branches of the fallen pine tree, resting his tired head on the soft woolly material.

As he lay down, he felt his muscles relax for the first time in hours and enjoyed the sensation as the tension slowly drained from his limbs. He nestled his head into his homemade pillow and stared up into the trees above, watching as the last light of the day began to fade into darkness.

What a day, he thought as he mulled over the past twenty-four hours and wondered at the bizarre sequence of events that had brought him to this hillside forest deep in occupied Europe. Sure, the last four years had been an absolute apocalypse of action and adventure, but this topped it all, he decided. But what next? For the first time since he had taken the King's shilling seven years before, he was the master of his own destiny. There were no orders to follow, nobody to command and no mission to complete. But he couldn't sit on this hillside for the rest of the war, so what were the options?

As he lay staring into the darkness, he considered the possibilities. Firstly, wait until daybreak, wander down the hill and hand himself into the first Wehrmacht patrol that he found. He dismissed that one almost before it entered his head, not only for its pathetic levels of cowardice but also because he knew that Cousin Adolf had put a hefty price on his head after his summer escapares in Italy and the last thing he fancied was being paraded through the streets of Berlin in an iron cage.

Option two was to make a run for neutral territory and then work out a way back to Blighty. The obvious choice was Switzerland, which couldn't have been more than a day's trek to the south-east, but he knew that the Swiss border could be nigh on impossible to cross. And even if he made it through, then what? A land locked country didn't have a particularly large fleet of neutral merchant ships just waiting for him to hitch a ride home on. Most likely was a boring stretch of waiting out the war, which didn't tickle his fancy one bit. Spain was the other option. Far easier to cross into, but a hell of a journey away and, with winter on the horizon, it wasn't overly appealing.

But did he have to trek anywhere at all? Surely the SOE chaps were nipping in and out of occupied France all the time, dropping off agents and picking up their spies. But this far into France? He thought it unlikely and, anyway, that would mean breaking cover and sourcing a Resistance contact, which could well turn out to be undercover Jerry hunting out downed airmen. Not worth the risk, he decided.

Which, as far as he could tell, left only one real alternative and, as he lay on the forest floor watching the blackness descend, he knew in his heart of hearts that it had been the only thing on his mind since the moment he had hit the ground. Standartenführer Otto Heidler, the bastard who had murdered his mother and the man on whom he had sworn to exact a bloody revenge, was in France. And so was he.

"I'm coming to get you," he whispered, a wicked smile on his face.

As he closed his eyes, he felt for the knife at his side, enjoying the feel of the cold steel on his fingers and picturing the blade slicing into the German's flesh.

"I'm coming to get you," he said again.

Albert Bloodstone was going to Paris.

CHAPTER THIRTY-THREE

The high-pitched squawk of a nearby bird yanked Bloodstone from a dreamless sleep and he sat bolt upright and instantly alert. The animal screeched again from somewhere in the trees, and then was quiet, leaving a blanket of silence to descend over the hillside forest.

Cosy in his thick leather suit despite the chilly morning air, Bloodstone lay back on his homemade pillow and watched as a shaft of sunlight pierced through the thick canopy to brighten the murky shadows with its glow. A glance at his watch told him it was seven twenty, or at least it was back home in Blighty, and he grunted in satisfaction, glad to have had a decent night of sleep for the first time in what seemed like forever.

Nothing like a night in the open air to perk the old body up a tad or two, he thought as he pulled himself to his feet and stretched his limbs, noticing that he felt a damned sight less battered and bruised than the previous evening.

He was also excited, he admitted, feeling a little like a schoolboy on the first day of the summer holidays. Which, he reasoned, was ridiculous considering that he was hundreds of miles behind enemy lines, with no real idea of where he was and pockets full of not much more than prophylactics, filthy playing cards and a handful of bullets.

But if a spot of adventure didn't warm the cockles then nothing would, he thought. And an adventure was most certainly on the cards, unless of course Jerry nabbed him before it even started.

Before he set off, however, he was fully aware that he had to get his admin in order. The thick legs of the flying suit had been such a hinderance yesterday when trekking through the forest that he decided a quick spot of tailoring was necessary. Pulling the garment off, he took his knife to the battered leather and hacked at the waist, swiftly chopping away the legs to leave a frayed jacket. No more waddling like an oversized duck, he thought happily as he pulled on the homemade jacket.

Next to get the Savile Row treatment were the boots that had rubbed his feet almost raw the previous evening. Perfect for minus ten at twenty thousand feet but wholly inadequate for a yomp across a mountain, especially when at least two sizes too small, he sliced a hole in each heel and cut out two toe-sized spaces. He pulled them back over his stinking socks and wiggled his toes, finally enjoying the feeling of not having his feet scrunched up like some sort of elderly Chinese lady.

With his kit sorted as well as could be hoped for, he turned his attention to the map that he'd left out to dry the evening before. It was still there on the ground, still weighed down by the four stones and still covered in Nobby's blood, yet the night had not been kind. The thin paper was drenched with dew and even the north-west corner of Italy had now vanished beneath a sodden mix of blood and water. When Bloodstone attempted to pick the useless document up, it simply fell to pieces.

"Bugger," he said aloud as he bent down to retrieve the ruined scraps of paper and stuffed them into the pocket of his newly fashioned leather trousers.

As he straightened up, a stab of fire shot through his backside and he was reminded of the moss-filled hole in his arse.

"Bugger," he said again, dropping his battledress trousers and silk underpants and wrenching his head around to survey the wound, which was now leaking puss and looked considerably more swollen and certainly more angry than the night before.

So much for Great Aunt Gertrude's moss, he thought as he pulled the blood-soaked plant from the ragged hole and waddled across to a nearby rock. He scraped up another handful of the springy green vegetation and, with a grimace, shoved it into the wound, poking it in as far as possible with his forefinger.

With a new instalment of the seemingly useless medieval medicine in place, he pulled up his woollen trousers and glanced around to take in the surroundings of his makeshift camp. To all but the most eagle-eyed of trackers it would be impossible to tell that he'd passed this way, he decided, and used his foot to spread pine needles over what had been his bed for the night.

Satisfied with his handiwork, he tied the legs of his flying suit around his neck, patted his pockets to check his measly collection of belongings were in place and set off into the woods. He headed downhill, using the shards of sunlight that stabbed through the canopy of trees to guide him in what he presumed to be a northerly direction, but with no map, no compass and a thick forest to navigate through, he realised that he could be heading just about anywhere.

As he continued down the hill, the pine trees began to thin slightly, meaning he no longer had to force his way between the low branches, but could walk upright without risk of losing an eye to a rogue twig. It wasn't long before he started to sweat in his thick jacket and the first signs of thirst prickled at his tongue. His empty stomach soon followed suit with a rumble and he began to regret not thinking to stash an airman's escape pack into his flying suit back at Scampton. A bar of chocolate would be just the ticket right now, he mused, or a cigarette, of which he had plenty in his pocket but knew he couldn't risk lighting for fear of giving himself away.

On he trekked, heading ever downhill, yet still with nothing to see but trees, trees and more trees. The calf length flying boots were chafing his feet considerably less than the day before but were now beginning to suffer the ravages of the rocks and roots that he was forced to scramble over. The leather around the toe hole on his right foot was beginning to split and it wasn't long before it ripped completely and detached itself from the sole to leave a flapping piece of leather that threatened to trip him at every step.

Not long after, the left boot followed suit, tearing at the heel and rendering the piece of footwear entirely useless. With a curse, Bloodstone sank down onto a rock, careful not to put any pressure on his tender right arse cheek, and tugged off the battered boots. A quick inspection confirmed that it was indeed the end of the road for the fur-lined size eights and, not wanting to leave any trace of his passing, he shoved the broken boots inside the front of his jacket.

Next, he plucked off his two pairs of socks and pushed them into the pocket of his trousers. No point buggering up a decent set of socks too, he thought, praying that the thick leathery skin of his feet was tough enough to stand up to the forest floor. He knew he couldn't last for long like that, but options seemed to be rather limited at present, so he figured that he'd think of a solution as he walked.

Ten minutes later and with the soles of his feet starting to bleed, the gradient of the hill began to soften slightly and it wasn't long before he found himself walking on flat ground at last. A few minutes more and the trees thinned further, so much so that it seemed he was reaching the edge of the forest. He slowed his pace, cautious of what he'd find in the open space that he could now see beyond the trees. He dropped to his belly and edged forwards, slithering over the pine needles like an Apache until he reached the last few trees, where he lay stock still and glanced out into the open.

He appeared to have reached an empty flat valley a half-mile wide, the other side of which rose high and wooded, not dissimilar to the forested hills he had just descended. Meandering gently through the valley was a river, blue under the cloudless sky and the width of half a rugby field, with wide grass plains at each bank. Between him and the grassy expanse on his side of the river was a single-track tarmac road, not three foot from the edge of the forest where he now lay, silent and alert.

He shuffled forward another couple of feet until he reached the last tree and, keeping his body low to the ground, slowly and silently craned his neck to get a clear view along the road. First, he twisted his head to the right, his darting eyes taking in the view while his left cheek rested motionless on a patch of damp earth. The road appeared to stretch away into the distance, straight and narrow, before disappearing three quarters of a mile away around a right-hand bend, out of view from where he lay. Apart from the road and the river, there was nothing else to be seen in that direction; not a building, not of single sign of civilisation.

Gently he rotated his head, bringing his right cheek to the ground and peering out towards the left. Somewhat unhelpfully, the view in this direction was far more limited. Just two hundred yards away the road vanished behind the forest, seemingly following the path of the river that was flowing gently in that direction. Again, with the exception of the river, the road and the grass of the valley, there was nothing to be seen.

As far as he could gather from the position of the morning sun, the river flowed from north to south and, as he lay there on the edge of the forest, he cursed himself for not paying more attention to the ancient Master Bodkin during his achingly dull geography lessons at Eton. This river was big and should have given him a decent idea of where he was, yet the only two rivers he knew of in France were the Seine and the Somme. Old Bodders would certainly be useful right now, he thought, despite the fact that he'd probably be about four hundred years old by now.

Gathering his thoughts, Bloodstone decided that trying to cross the river would be fruitless until he knew exactly where he was, so the best plan of attack was to keep the water to his left and head north. He'd use the forest as cover, he concluded, and keep going while he kept an eye out for anything of interest, preferably a spot of grub and ideally, but unlikely he admitted, an abandoned pair of size eleven boots.

He was just about to creep backwards into the forest when a faint sound caught his ear, emanating from somewhere to the south. Was it another bird, he wondered? Funny sort of bird if it was. Then, there it was again, high pitched and louder this time, coming from beyond where the tarmac curved away to his left. He inched his head out further and glanced in the direction of the noise, peering along the length of the road and narrowing his eyes as a flash of movement caught his attention.

Another noise followed, now obvious as a human shriek, a female shriek, and the flash of movement turned into the form of a girl, running headlong along the road in his direction, hands clutching the bottom of her black ankle-length skirts as she looked behind her in what appeared to be complete panic.

As she got closer, Bloodstone could see a head of blonde locks atop a young woman he guessed to be about sixteen years of age, who was scurrying as fast as her skinny legs would carry her. As he watched, the figure of a man appeared from around the bend, twenty yards behind the girl and quite clearly in pursuit. If the sight of a petrified teenage girl wasn't enough to put a chill to his blood, the man that pursued her almost turned it to ice.

Even from two hundred yards away, it took Bloodstone less than a heartbeat to recognise the black knee-high boots, baggy trousers and drab green tunic as one of the most hated and most feared uniforms in all the world. A uniform that had spread misery across the length and breadth of Europe, had already left millions dead and now chased what seemed to be a helpless young woman along an empty road somewhere in south-east France. The uniform of the Wehrmacht.

CHAPTER THIRTY-FOUR

Bloodstone kept his eyes firmly on the pair of running figures as he pushed himself backwards with his elbows, using his bare feet to drag his body inch by inch away from the road. Half a yard behind him stood an ancient pine tree and he edged alongside it and nestled his right shoulder behind the thick trunk. With his left hand he scooped up a pile of damp mud and silently smeared it across his face, taking extra care to be gentle with his still-tender nose.

Through all of this he didn't take his eyes from the road, where the girl was now fifty yards away and slowly but surely being caught by the German infantryman. As the soldier grew closer, Bloodstone studied him through narrowed eyes, taking in every inch of him. In one hand was a Mauser rifle, on his head was a misshapen field cap and on the sleeve of his left arm were the double stripes of a corporal. The man himself appeared to be in his early forties, bulky beneath his uniform and with short cropped hair above a fleshy face. His mouth was fixed in a cruel snarl as he pounded along the road after the blonde-haired girl and the iron hobnails of his boots crashed on the tarmac as he closed on his quarry.

When she was yards from where Bloodstone lay hidden at the edge of the forest, the girl took another fearful glance over her shoulder and, as she did so, lost her footing, stumbled once and then tripped over her skirts, clattering to the ground with a scream. Within seconds the German was on her, his rifle abandoned to the floor as he grabbed a fistful of blonde hair and dragged the terrified teenager to her feet, the snarl on his face replaced with a sickening leer.

"Fucking bitch," he spat in guttural German, specks of phlegm spraying from his mouth as he twisted her hair with his left hand and unleashed a stinging slap across her cheek with the back of his right.

The girl let out a whimper and snot and tears smeared across her pretty face. The corporal slapped her again, harder this time, before he followed up with a vicious punch to the stomach. The youngster yelped out in pain and doubled up, trying desperately to catch her breath before the German dragged her upright again with a sharp tug of her hair. He had his back to the forest now, standing at the edge of the road and just feet from where Bloodstone lay silently against the tree, barely daring to breathe and with the fingers of his right hand resting on the combat knife that was tucked into his belt.

He could no longer see the soldier's face, but he could clearly hear the anger in his voice as the infantryman barked at the petrified girl in German tinged with a rough Saxon accent.

"When will you stupid French sluts learn your place?" he yelled as he yanked her head backwards by her hair, "Maybe it's time I taught you a lesson, ja?"

The girl, now facing towards the forest, whimpered pathetically as tears streamed down her red cheeks.

"No, monsieur, please, no," she begged in French, her face twisted with pain as the soldier tightened his grip on her hair.

"Shut up with that shitty peasant tongue," he ordered and followed up with another backhanded slap.

With the same hand he then grabbed hold of the front of the girl's dress and yanked once, ripping the material from neck to waist and leaving the poor creature shrieking in panic.

As slow as the night and without a sound, Bloodstone rose from the ground with his weight on the balls of his bare feet and his body crouched like a tiger ready to pounce. In his right hand he held the twelve inches of razor-sharp steel, the metal dull in the shadow of the ancient pine. He raised himself up another few inches, feeling the power in his muscles aching to be unleashed to the kill, and took a step towards the road, still as silent as the grave.

The German corporal still had his back to the trees and was too distracted to notice the black-faced and barefooted monster that emerged from the forest. He now had one hand inside the girl's torn dress and was pawing at her breasts, while the other hand held her around the throat. The girl was standing stock still, rigid with fear and staring wide-eyed over her attacker's shoulder as he groped and prodded at her near naked body.

Bloodstone took another silent step forward and straightened up to three-quarter height with the knife held backwards in his hand in readiness to slice into the corporal's throat. As he crept forward, now almost out from under the cover of the trees, the girl finally saw him and her eyes widened yet further, her mouth open and poised to scream.

Bloodstone paused and brought the forefinger of his left hand slowly up to his lips, motioning her to stay silent. Mercifully, the girl obeyed, but she couldn't tear her stare from the knife-wielding devil who was now just two feet behind the Nazi solider. Somehow, her attacker didn't notice the look on his victim's face, too distracted was he with trying to pull the tattered dress from her shoulders.

Bloodstone took one more step forward and shifted the weight of his body onto his right foot, finally ready to make his move. He raised the knife until the point was just inches from the back of the German's fleshy neck. He took a silent breath in, clenched the muscles of his right arm and slowly released the breath, ignoring the girl who now stared at him with abject fear and focusing instead on the flushed skin of the German. Three, two...

The man's head jerked upwards. Bloodstone froze, his aim distracted, and he held the knife exactly where it was, poised behind the dark cropped head, which was now looking along the road to the left.

In the half-second before the girl let out a shout and stepped away from her tormentor, Bloodstone heard the unmistakable sound of an engine, coming from the direction in which the German was looking. As the teenager shrieked and with the corporal preoccupied by the noise in front of him and by whatever was coming along the road, Bloodstone snatched his opportunity and dropped back onto his haunches, rolled backwards and fell silently to his belly in the shade of the old pine tree. Another quick slither backwards saw him sheltered firmly by the thick trunk and he pushed his body into the ground and only then dared a glance upwards in the direction of the road.

The girl had now retreated to the other side of the road and was miserably trying to cover herself with the remnants of her black dress. Her tormentor was still staring in the direction of the engine noise and had picked up his rifle and was straightening his uniform, giving his sweating brow a cuff with his forearm before he readjusted the skewwhiff field cap.

Seconds later, a black sedan sped past and, from Bloodstone's position behind the tree, he caught a fleeting glimpse of the occupants. One man was at the wheel and in the back seat appeared to be two officers dressed in green uniforms with peaked caps on their heads. The car was gone almost as quickly as it had come but, as the vehicle passed and the nearest man turned his head in the direction of his hiding place, Bloodstone could have sworn that their eyes locked.

Apparently unseen by the Nazi officer, the sedan sped on into the distance and its noise was replaced by another engine. Seconds later, a two-ton Opel truck skidded to a halt on the road with its brakes squeaking and the open rear filled with tightly packed soldiers. Sitting on benches, the men were dressed in the same drab green as the corporal, all sporting identical soft caps and all leering hungrily at the girl, who now stood at the side of the road with a broken look on her face.

One of the soldiers, a sergeant, stood up at the rear of the truck and shouted in the girl's direction.

"Having fun there, love?" he called in German and earned a bellow of approval from his comrades, "Fancy a ride?"

The girl clutched her torn dress, ignored the man and stared at the floor with fresh tears staining her swollen cheeks. The sergeant chuckled and turned away from her to look back at the corporal.

"Come on Schmidt, you old rogue," he said with a laugh as he leaned over the tailgate and offered the still-sweating soldier a hand, "Let's get you home."

The chubby corporal grabbed the hand and hauled himself up into the truck, where he received a slap on the back from the sergeant and some unintelligible words that Bloodstone couldn't catch. The grinning sergeant rapped once on side of the lorry and the driver ground the gears and the engine growled once before the truck moved off north to follow in the path of the now vanished black sedan.

As it moved away, Bloodstone could just hear the corporal's voice over the noise of the engine as he shouted back at the girl with an evil look on his face.

"You wait, you fucking French bitch, you just wait."

The girl, her cheeks red and her dress in tatters around her skinny body, glanced upwards, her face suddenly transformed from fear and terror to hatred and contempt.

"Fuck you Boche" she shouted in French at the retreating truck while sticking her middle finger up at the soldiers, "Fuck you!"

Bloodstone watched from the undergrowth and smiled at the obscenities coming from the young girl's mouth, admiring her show of undignified but fully justified rebellion. Then, when he was certain that the truck had disappeared around the distant bend, he sheathed his knife, raised himself up to his full height and stepped out from behind his tree with his hands raised in peace.

"Bonjour mademoiselle," he said with a gentle smile on his muddied face, "Ca va?"

CHAPTER THIRTY-FIVE

The sixteen-year-old girl had seen more than her fair share of horror during the last four war-torn years, but the creature that emerged from the forest was something else entirely. Six feet tall with bare feet and a tattered leather jacket, he had a face as black as the ace of spades and appeared to be coated from head to foot in dried blood. But, although he looked like something that had just stepped out of a nightmare, it was his smile, despite the obvious gap in his otherwise perfect row of snow-white teeth, that left her open-mouthed and speechless. It was a smile that cracked his filth-stained face in two and instantly left her feeling safe and secure, not to mention somewhat weak at the knees.

She continued staring, wide-eyed and mouth gaping like a fish, as he stepped out from under the trees and onto the roadside with his hands still raised above his head.

"My name's Bertie," he said in French, "It's a pleasure to meet you, mon cherie."

The girl kept staring.

"I'm not going to hurt you," he said as he lowered his hands and glanced quickly along the road in both directions, "I'm one of the good guys."

Finally, the girl stopped gaping and spoke, her eyes still wide and fearful.

"You're a Rosbif?"

Bloodstone laughed, a little disappointed that his perfect accentless French obviously wasn't as perfect and accentless as he thought.

"Indeed I am," he replied, flashing another smile, "I seem to be somewhat far from home."

He cuffed at a piece of mud that had become attached to an eyelash, before he continued.

"Would you be a dear and tell me exactly where I am? I'm a little lost you see."

The girl stared at him for a few seconds before she replied.

"You're in France," she said with a blank look on her face.

No shit Sherlock, Bloodstone thought to himself, wondering if the girl was a simpleton. "Whereabouts in France?" he asked gently.

"Guibert-le-Doubs," she said as she cocked her head and looked at him like he was the simpleton.

Old Bodders' achingly dull geography lessons came flooding back like a thunderbolt and he realised with a flash of pride that he actually knew three French rivers, not just a paltry two.

"That's the Doubs?" he asked as he nodded his head in the direction of the water that meandered its way gently through the valley and wondered how he remembered the river that snaked across southeastern France and dipped in and out of Switzerland.

Again, she looked at him like there was something wrong with him.

"Obviously."

Then, cocking her head to the other side, she looked him up and down.

"Where are your shoes, Monsieur Bertie?"

"Long story," he laughed, "Do you think you can find me some new ones? And something to eat would be tres bien too, if you know where I can find some food?"

"No," she responded sharply, taking Bloodstone aback with her curtness. Ungrateful little so-and-so he thought.

"But Papa could," she continued, bringing her head back to its natural position.

"Papa?"

"Oui, Monsieur Bertie. He hates the Boches even more than I do," she said, finally smiling a smile that contained nothing but pure malice.

"He *really* hates them," she continued as she looked Bloodstone in the eye and pulled her torn dress tighter around her.

If the rest of the occupying German troops were anything like Schmidt and his truckful of cronies, Bloodstone wasn't surprised, he thought, glancing along the road again and keen to be back out of view.

"If I wait here, do you think you can tell him where I am?" he asked as his stomach grumbled again with hunger, "Maybe he can send some food."

"And some shoes?" she asked with a grin.

"And some shoes," he agreed, thinking that maybe she wasn't so simple after all.

"I can do that," she nodded, "But first there's something I want from you."

"Go on," he said, somewhat tentatively.

"A cigarette," she demanded, surprising Bloodstone as she blew an invisible mouthful of smoke into the air.

He chuckled as he felt in his pocket for his gold tin. Finding it, he clicked it open and offered it to the blonde-haired teenager, who helped herself to three Woodbines and swiftly tucked them away somewhere in her torn dress.

"Smoking's bad for you, you know," Bloodstone said with a laugh, desperate for a hit of nicotine but still not wanting to betray his presence even more than he already had.

"Merde," she spat, picking up her skirts and turning towards the north.

"Now wait here," she ordered over her shoulder as she started marching along the road, "I'll send Papa."

"And don't worry," she almost shouted from a distance, "I won't tell the Boches that there's a Rosbif hiding in the woods."

I should hope not, Bloodstone thought, involuntarily ducking back under the trees and imagining that the Boches had probably overhead the loud-mouthed teen in Berlin.

"Au revoir Monsieur Bertie," she yelled again, this time with a wave in his direction, which made him duck once more.

"Au revoir," he murmured under his breath and realised that he hadn't asked the girl her name.

"Damned bad mannered of you, Bertie," he muttered as he strolled back into the forest and looked for somewhere to hide out until the girl's father turned up.

If he was going to turn up at all, he thought, knowing it was possible that the gobby girl would give him away and the lorry full of Jerries would be back to sniff him out. But not much he could do about that now, he pondered as he found a particularly thick pine tree and sat down, out of view of the road, to rest his back against the bark.

His stomach rumbled again and his brain was filled with thoughts of food. What he wouldn't do right now for a plate of steak and chips, he mused, closing his eyes and resting the back of his head on the bark of the tree, almost able to taste the juicy meat and crispy potatoes.

CHAPTER THIRTY-SIX

Albert Bloodstone had been shot, stabbed and blown up more times than he cared to remember, yet none of those less than joyful experiences could compare with the fire that now burned deep in the cheek of his arse. Like a small boy with an anus full of worms, he wriggled his backside around on the soft forest floor, desperate to find a position that didn't feel as if somebody was poking a red-hot poker into his very core.

Giving up, he probed uselessly at the afflicted buttock with a finger and pictured the shards of wood that were no doubt putrefying inside his flesh. His finger came away wet and smeared with a combination of watery blood and pus that resembled something akin to out-of-date cottage cheese. Dammit, he thought as his stomach grumbled again and a bolt of molten lava fired its way from arse to brain, where was the French bugger? A glance at his watch told him that he'd been shuffling around on his backside for nearly two hours and, almost midday, he dared a glance around the tree in the direction of the road.

The road was silent and deserted, just as it has been for the whole time he'd be sitting against the tree. Not a soul had passed since the incident with the blonde teenager and he was beginning to wonder if the man would come at all. He knew the Germans would exact a bloody revenge on anyone found helping a downed airman, so he figured it highly possible that the local populace wouldn't be overly keen in getting involved. No doubt there was a rich reward for those who handed over a captured flier, so it was also entirely plausible that he'd end the day in a cell.

Only one way to find out which way it would go, he thought with a sigh as he returned his head to its normal position against the tree. He decided that he'd wait until nightfall and, if the Frenchman hadn't come by then, he'd venture back into the woods on his bare feet, find somewhere to sleep and then head off north-west in the morning.

He glanced at his watch again and found that it was thirty-eight seconds after he'd previously looked. He groaned with boredom and watched as a large beetle wandered out from below a pile of fallen pine needles and ambled in his direction. It circumnavigated a twig and continued its journey, pausing when it reached the heel at the end of his outstretched right leg. It seemed to look up at Bloodstone and then waggled its antennas, no doubt protesting about the stench of his filthy feet, he thought.

"Well hello, little fellow," he said, fixing it with a stare, "Aren't you a chubby chappy?"

The black creature waved its antennas again and turned to go.

"Oh no you don't," Bloodstone muttered as, quick as a flash, he lifted his leg and brought the back of his heel crashing down on top of the critter.

With a brief apology he removed his foot from the helpless bug and surveyed his handiwork. The beetle was squashed entirely flat, with the exception of a single antenna that waggled pathetically for a second before falling still. He leant forward, grasped the dead bug between forefinger and thumb and in one swift movement deposited it onto his tongue. Not waiting to chew, he swallowed the creature whole, feeling its crunchy body slide down his gullet and leaving him with a distinctly unpleasant taste of beetle goo and burnt charcoal in his mouth.

A brief swig from his hip flask returned his mouth to its normal state and he looked at his watch once more. Still not even midday, he discovered miserably, feeling a tickle somewhere in his stomach that felt distinctly like the wiggling antenna of his latest snack. Another glance towards the road revealed yet more inactivity and, with nothing else to do, he reached into his pocket for Nobby's cigarette tin and extracted the pack of playing cards.

The cards were in perfect order and each one displayed a photograph of a different girl in various states of undress, posing in positions that the good Lord certainly hadn't intended for young females to pose in. Bloodstone whistled in appreciation as he leafed through the pack, admiring the rotund behind of the African beauty who adorned the queen of hearts, before peering intently at the excessively large nipples of the three of spades that reminded him somewhat of a beef burger that he'd eaten while on leave.

Dammit, food again, he cursed before he pushed the thought from his mind and continued his inspection of the cards. He wrinkled his nose as he reached the nine of spades, which displayed not only a deliciously nude and toe-touching stunner of an Oriental girl but was smeared with a crusty yellowy-white stain.

"Nobby, you filthy blighter," he said aloud with a laugh as he wiped his hands on his trousers before he continued his inspection of the playing cards.

He had just reached the four of clubs, which portrayed a pretty redhead complete with globe-like bosoms, a pert derrière and a face that bore a striking similarity to Corporal Bell, when the distant sound of a motor engine reached his ears. With no time to take a closer look to see if it actually *was* Bombshell Bell or maybe even her fabled twin sister, he shoved the cards into his pocket and rolled onto his belly, remaining behind the thick trunk of the pine tree as he glanced cautiously in the direction of the road.

As he lay and listened, the engine got louder and it was less than half a minute before the cab of a small truck appeared through the trees, revealing a rear piled high with what appeared to be some sort of fruit. The vehicle slowed but continued onwards and disappeared from view before grinding to a halt with a squeal of breaks somewhere away to Bloodstone's left.

He lay still as the engine idled and was then turned off, followed by the sound of somebody jumping down from the cab. He heard heavy footsteps on the road and, unable to see anything from his vantage point, grasped the handle of his knife with his right hand. The noise of the footsteps on the road stopped and twenty yards away to the left he saw a flicker of movement as someone, or something, pushed through the trees at the edge of the forest. He tightened his grip on the knife and pulled his body lower to the ground as he stared at the rustling trees.

Seconds later a figure emerged with an enormous belly leading the way and a short, middle-aged man attached to it. On his head was a black beret and around his gargantuan midriff strained a tatty waistcoat, with the single button ready to pop at any second. The man's fleshy face wobbled as he moved and on his top lip was a glorious moustache that put Bloodstone's own far-from-feeble efforts at facial hair to shame.

Bloodstone remained stock still as he watched the man crash though the undergrowth and wondered if this was indeed Papa or was actually just a random wandering local. Ten feet from his hiding place, the man paused, looked around and stroked his moustache.

"Tommy?" he called quietly, "Tommy?"

Still Bloodstone remained silent.

"Tommy?" he called again as he surveyed the forest, and then in French, "Are you here, my English friend?"

Taking a deep breath and keeping his knife clasped firmly in his hand, Bloodstone raised himself to his knees, drew himself up to his full height and stepped out from behind the tree.

"Tommy!" the man bellowed, his face suddenly split with a massive grin, "It is you!"

"Oui, Monsieur," Bloodstone replied and, before he could get another word in, the man covered the distance between them at a rate that defied his considerable bulk, flung his arms around Bloodstone's shoulders and planted an enormous kiss on each cheek.

"Tommy! Mon ami! Welcome to France! You have come to kill Hitler, yes?"

Bloodstone laughed, instantly warming to the jolly Frenchman who was now pumping his hand wildly and ignoring the twelve inches of steel that was protruding from his fist.

"I'm not sure about that," he replied in French with his hand still encased in the man's fleshy fingers, "But I'll see what I can do."

Finally, the man released his hand and stood back to inspect Bloodstone from grimy face to bare feet and then back up again.

"Mon ami, you have been in the wars, non? But worry not, we will have you mended and back home to England before you can say Adolf is a boudin."

Before Bloodstone could reply, the man grasped his hand again and continued.

"But forgive me, where are my manners? Cedric is my name and this is my little corner of belle France; welcome to Guibert-le-Doubs, the finest piece of land in all the world. Or at least it was until the stinking Boches arrived."

At mention of the Germans, he wrinkled his nose and spat contemptuously onto the ground, all humour instantly removed from his face.

It returned a split second later, however, as Bloodstone introduced himself.

"Bertie," he announced with his own pump of the hand, "It's a pleasure to meet you."

Releasing the hand, he continued.

"Cedric, I'm a little lost, as you can probably see. Could I trouble you for a spot of food and some boots? Then I'll be out of your way and on my way home."

"Nonsense," Cedric replied with a look of mock horror on his face, "You are our guest, Monsieur Bertie, and we will treat you as such.

"I have contacts, if you understand me," he continued with a wink and a tap of the nose, "So you will come with me, oui?"

"To where?" Bloodstone asked, still cautious despite the Frenchman's jolly demeanour.

"I told you, this is *my* corner of France." Another wink.

"You will have to trust me, my English airman, it is what friends do."

With his list of other options worryingly short, Bloodstone nodded.

"It would be a pleasure, Cedric, thank you."

"It is not a problem," the rotund Frenchman said as he waved away Bloodstone's thanks and gave him a friendly clap on the shoulder.

"Now, let's go," he continued as he turned towards the road and pushed his way back through the trees, Bloodstone following in his wake with his fingers hovering close to the knife that was now tucked back into his belt.

They emerged from the trees to find a small Renault truck parked on the grass verge at the side of the road, its brown cab scratched and dented and the flatbed of its rear filled to the brim with a mountain of onions. Cedric paused to wrench a wonky wing mirror back into position before he walked around to the rear of the truck. He looked at Bloodstone with a smile of amused embarrassment and then unhitched the tail gate and shoved some escaping onions back onto the flatbed as he did so.

"I'm sorry, mon ami, but you'll have to ride with the oignons. We shall hold the sausage eaters responsible for such an inconvenience, oui?"

Bloodstone smiled and pulled himself up into the rear of the truck, where he was quickly followed by the rotund Cedric, who mounted the vehicle with slightly less grace. The Frenchman then plucked up a shovel and set to work at the onions, digging a man-sized space in the middle of the pile of vegetables. Next, he grabbed a tattered blanket from the floor and shook it out, spraying bits of dirt and onion skin into the air.

"Now, you will hide, oui?", he said, gesturing at the gap in the mass of onions.

Bloodstone nodded and lay down on his stomach with his head facing the cab and his bare feet several inches from the rear of the truck.

"You must stay here until I return, Monsieur Bertie. Try to stay as still as possible, you understand?"

He nodded again and, with that, the Frenchman flapped the blanket once more and laid it across Bloodstone's prostate body, covering his face and plunging him into darkness. As the spade set to work again and the onions began to pile onto him, he grasped the hilt of his knife in his left hand and the grip of his revolver in his right.

It took several minutes for the shoveling to stop and, moments later, the engine coughed, spluttered and roared to life, sending a series of deep vibrations through the floor on which Bloodstone lay. A few more seconds and the truck jerked into life and started to bounce along the road.

Bloodstone, entombed in his onion world and with the stench of age-old musty blanket in his nostrils, closed his eyes and sighed.

No getting out of this now Monsieur Bertie, he said to himself, no getting out of this now.

CHAPTER THIRTY-SEVEN

The room was bare except for a small wooden chair and a single bed, on which lay a thin mattress and an even thinner pillow, both once white but now covered with grubby yellow stains. The room itself was square, a mere four paces from wall to wall, and the only light came from a tiny window high in the slanted roof. It was, Bloodstone thought, more of a cell than a bedroom, which was only enhanced by the fact that he'd heard the door locked from the other side just a few minutes before.

Immediately before that, he'd been excavated from his onion tomb by a silent youth with a shovel and had clambered down from the truck to find himself standing in a small courtyard, surrounded on three sides by two-storey buildings. On the fourth side was a rusty gate, which Cedric pulled closed before he scurried across the open space, grasped Bloodstone by the sleeve and led him quickly to an open door in one of the buildings.

"Quickly, Bertie," he hurried, looking around him before leading the major through the door and up a steep staircase, the walls of which were covered in a faded pink wallpaper decorated with dead-looking flowers.

When they reached the top of the stairs they took a turn to the right and Cedric opened a wooden door and ushered Bloodstone into the small room with the bed and chair. As the major surveyed the sparse surroundings, Cedric turned to go.

"I'll be back soon, please wait here Monsieur," the Frenchman said with a smile that set his enormous moustache twitching, before he retreated out of the door and closed it behind him.

Bloodstone heard the key turn in the lock and he slumped down on the bed, wincing as the now-familiar bolt of pain fired itself from arse cheek to brain and back again. The ancient bedsprings groaned in protest under his weight and, warm in the small room, he tugged off his battered leather jacket and lay it on the mattress bedside him.

He was ninety-nine point nine percent sure that the door would be unlocked soon and in would stroll Cedric with a big bowl of onion soup, but be knew there was still a very real chance that the next man through the door would be a German armed with a Luger and orders to whisk him off to the Gestapo. With that thought in mind, he pulled the revolver from the pocket of the jacket, checked its chambers and pushed it beneath the pillow to his right.

The minutes ticked by, during which time the grumbling in his stomach increased to apocalyptic proportions and a pigeon started to rap its beak tunelessly, and seemingly endlessly, against the window above Bloodstone's head. Tap-tap. Tap-tap. Tap-tap-tap. Tap.

He was just about to reach for his Webley and blast the creature from its perch when he heard the sound of hurried footsteps in the corridor and seconds later the lock grated and the door burst open. His hand instinctively shot to the gun but, with forefinger on the trigger, he kept the weapon hidden beneath the pillow.

First through the door was a short, bald-headed man with an angular jaw and a pointy nose, from which sprouted a forest of thick black hairs. Appearing to be in his late fifties, he possessed a set of beady eyes and some of the largest ears that Bloodstone had ever seen.

Squeezing himself through the door next was Cedric, his usual jolly face replaced with something halfway between apology and embarrassment, while behind the rotund Frenchman traipsed an

216

acne-cheeked youth, a Sten gun in his hands and a look of vacant doziness on his face.

Before Bloodstone could react, Big Ears pointed at the pillow and snapped his fingers twice.

"I would move your hand if I were you, Monsieur," he ordered in heavily accented English, "And slowly."

Bloodstone remained still with his eyes locked on the man's beady pupils.

"I won't ask again," he threatened with his right hand now inside his jacket and his left gesturing to the youngster behind him, who raised the muzzle of his machine gun in Bloodstone's direction.

Bloodstone thought it prudent to obey and brought his hand out from beneath the pillow, opening his palm to show that it was empty. Another click of the fingers brought the spotty youngster lumbering across the room to remove the revolver and yet another click instructed him to pat down the helpless Bloodstone. With a diligence that belied the youth's apparent dimness, his hands stripped Bloodstone of his possessions in seconds and he handed them one by one to the man who was quite clearly the boss.

As he was passed the pack of pornographic playing cards, a flash of what appeared to be disgust crossed the Frenchman's face, which was quickly replaced with a look of bafflement as he opened Nobby's tobacco tin to discover the condom. Bloodstone wriggled his bare toes and shrugged as Big Ears glared at him judgingly, although he was pleased to see that Cedric was trying and failing miserably to stifle a grin on the other side of the room.

His inspection of Bloodstone's goodies complete, the pointy nosed Frenchman grasped the chair from the corner of the room and dragged it across the floor, placing it in front of the bed before lowering himself onto it and smoothing down the creases of his trousers with his right hand.

"So," he began in English, "What are you doing here?"

Bloodstone thought that rather a strange question.

"Cedric," he pointed in the direction of his chubby rescuer, "Brought me here in his onion wagon."

"I know that, my friend," Big Ears replied coldly with not an ounce of friendliness, "I mean why are you here? In France?"

Considering his battered state and the flying jacket lying on the bed next to him, Bloodstone had assumed that was somewhat obvious.

"I think it's fairly clear why I'm here, *my friend*," he replied icily.

The Frenchman stiffened and straightened his trousers once more before he cocked his head slightly to one side.

"Now here's the situation," he said in his perfect but accented English, his eyes unblinking, "These two gentlemen don't speak a word of your language. If I tell them that you're a Boche spy then you'll be at the bottom of the Doubes with your throat slit before you can count to trois."

He wiped the back of his hand across his hairy nose and straightened his head.

"You're not a Boche spy, are you?"

"Of course I'm not a bloody spy, you damned fool," Bloodstone scoffed, feeling the anger begin to rise in his throat.

"Good," Big Ears responded as he cocked his head once more, "So shall we try again?"

The Frenchman paused and his eyes once again bored into Bloodstone.

"What are you doing here?"

Bloodstone wriggled his toes again, shifted his backside slightly on the bed and sighed. Time to 'fess up, he thought to himself, somewhat annoyed that he would have to explain himself to the ungrateful creature on the chair, but hoping that doing so would finally result in some boots, some grub and some medicine for his buttocks.

For the next ten minutes he recounted his adventures of the previous twenty-four hours, using a mixture of French and English as he told the full story of how he had ended up battered and bruised on a hillside in France. Well, not quite the full story.

He thought it prudent to remove the part about leaping from ten thousand feet without a parachute, conscious that a man should never paint himself as too heroic, or indeed too stupid. He also decided not to reveal the real reason why a Parachute Regiment major was on a Lancaster bombing mission and, when pressed by Big Ears about his uniform, he blathered something about being aboard as an observer. The name Bloodstone seemingly meant nothing to his interrogator and he was glad, although a little disappointed, that his supposed fame had failed to reach this small corner of Europe.

When Bloodstone's tale was complete and he had answered the numerous questions fired in his direction, Big Ears raised himself from the chair, apparently satisfied.

"I will now check if you tell the truth, Englishman," he said as he made for the door, looking over his shoulder at Bloodstone with a face that remained distinctly unfriendly.

"If you do, we will help you to return to the war. If it turns out that you have lied to me..."

His voice trailed off as he drew a finger across his throat in a gesture that needed no explanation.

He turned the door handle and made to leave, before he paused and spoke once more.

"You will wait here," he instructed, "Cedric will make sure you are attended to shortly. I will return."

With that, the three men left the room and the key was once again turned in the lock. As the sound of footsteps retreated along the hallway, he heard Big Ears instruct the youth with the Sten gun to remain on guard outside the door.

He pulled his legs up onto the bed, grimaced as the fire shot through his backside once more, and lay down with his head on the pillow. Within seconds the pigeon started up again, smashing its beak against the glass above his head.

Tap-tap-tap. Tap-tap-tap-tap. Tap-tap. Tap.

"Goddammit," Bloodstone cursed as he shoved his fingers into his ears and felt his empty stomach rumble yet again, "Goddammit it all to hell."

CHAPTER THIRTY-EIGHT

The sound of the door opening roused Bloodstone from sleep and he sat up to see Cedric enter the room with his mouth wide in the customary smile beneath his gigantic moustache. Following behind was a middle-aged woman in a striped dress with black curls upon her head and a round tummy of substantial proportions, which was topped by two excessively large bosoms that sagged and strained beneath the material of her outfit. Her chubby cheeks were rosy pink and an enormous smile split her face from ear to ear, while in her hands she carried a tray loaded with a steaming bowl.

"Monsieur Bertie, allow me to introduce Lillianna," Cedric announced as the rotund woman set the tray down on the bed, "My darling wife."

Before Bloodstone could rise to his feet, Lillianna grasped his face in her podgy hands and planted an enormous kiss on each cheek.

"It's a pleasure to meet you," he smiled as he stood up and smelt the delicious aroma of freshly baked bread emanating from her hair.

"The pleasure is all ours," she replied, her smile stretching even wider, "It is not every day that we welcome a brave Tommy to our home."

She rustled among her skirts and pulled out a brown bottle, which she uncapped, took a deep gulp and handed to Bloodstone.

"Salut, Monsieur Bertie," she grinned as he took a swig of his own, enjoying the taste as the beer sloshed deliciously down his throat.

"Salut," he replied and handed the bottle to Cedric, who knocked back a mouthful and unleashed an enormous burp before he passed the bottle back to Bloodstone.

The Frenchman wiped his mouth with the back of his hand and looked at the uniformed major who had returned to his perch, noticing the grimace of pain that shot across Bloodstone's face as his buttocks touched the bed.

"I must apologise for the manners of our large-eared friend, Monsieur Bertie," Cedric said with a grimace.

"He likes to do things properly and, although he is a good man, he should smile more often, I think.

"Right now, he will be making radio contact with your countrymen. When they confirm that you are indeed a British flyer he will make preparations for your escape. He is a man with connections, you see. Despite his unfortunate ears."

Lillianna giggled and Cedric continued.

"You are injured I see," he said as he nodded towards Bloodstone's backside.

"My wife is a good nurse, as well as a good cook. When you have finished your soup, she will tend to your wounds."

"Thank you," Bloodstone said between mouthfuls of the scrumptious onion soup that scalded his tongue but filled his aching belly.

Cedric waved away the thanks, dropped a small bag onto the bed and turned towards the door. As he departed, he gave his wife a playful slap on the bottom.

"Be good, my petite champignon," he grinned and received another giggle in response as he closed the door behind him.

While Bloodstone gobbled down the remainder of the soup, Lillianna opened the bag and emptied its contents onto the chair. A sewing pouch, a medical kit, a small green bottle and a metal dish were all lined up neatly, alongside another bottle of beer that she had fished from somewhere within her dress.

"So, Monsieur Bertie, where are you hurt?" she asked as she finished arranging her equipment.

"My, er, derrière, I'm afraid," he replied, slightly embarrassed that he'd have to brandish his stinking backside to the motherly Frenchwoman.

"Nonsense," she said, waving away his blushes, "I have seen the bottoms of many young men in my time. Now, remove your trousers and lie on the bed please."

As instructed, he tugged down his pantaloons and made to lie on the bed.

"And those," Lillianna ordered before he dropped to the mattress, pointing at his tattered silk boxer shorts, "Off with them too please, Monsieur."

Bloodstone nodded and removed his pants, noticing the brief look of shock on the woman's face as she caught a glimpse of his sizeable manhood. As she redirected her gaze to her own instruments, Bloodstone clambered onto the bed and lay face down with his bare rear end exposed to the world.

The woman bent forwards and let out as whistle as she peered at the festering wound puncturing his right buttock cheek.

"Ooh la la," she exclaimed, "That must sting a little, oui?"

Bloodstone nodded silently and watched over his shoulder as the lady's chubby hands grasped a pair of tweezers the size of garden shears and began prodding and poking at the ragged hole, unleashing a bolt of lightning somewhere inside his arse.

A second or two later the probing metal inside his flesh scraped against something solid, grasped whatever it was and then yanked roughly, tearing like fire against nerves and skin as the giant tweezers were withdrawn from his backside. He heard a tinkle as the object was dropped into the metal dish and then clenched his cheeks as a river of warm blood burst from the wound, cascaded into his arse crack, coated the underside of his testicles and spread across the already stained mattress.

"God in heaven," he whispered through clenched teeth as he let out the lungful of air that he'd been holding in during the operation, "What the hell was that?"

In answer, Lillianna offered the metal dish in his direction and he squinted at the bloody mess within.

"Jesus, there's one for the trophy cabinet," he laughed as he looked in horror at a short length of branch topped by a pine cone the size of baby's fist, "That was that all in there?"

"Indeed it was," the woman replied with a smile, "But what a brave soldier you are, oui?"

Bloodstone wasn't so sure about that but rested his head back on the pillow as Lillianna gently wiped the blood from his skin with a cloth, before she then picked up the small green bottle. She uncorked it with a plop and poured several drops of what felt like acid into the ragged hole. He gritted his teeth against the pain and could've sworn he heard a fizzing sound as the liquid scorched his innards.

As the pain ebbed from cataclysmic to only slightly volcanic, he watched as the woman plucked an enormous sewing needle from the chair and held it aloft, not dissimilar to a swordsman readying the coup-de-grace. Squinting towards the light of the small window, she fed a piece of thread through the eye of the rapier and then turned back towards the prostrate Bloodstone.

"You won't feel a thing," she said with a motherly smile that set her chins wobbling yet did nothing to assure Bloodstone that his already brutalised backside wasn't going to get yet another pummeling.

He closed his eyes as the woman leaned closer, surveying her patient, and clenched his fists in readiness for what was about to come. A millisecond later the needle plunged into the puckered flesh surrounding the wound, dragging its cotton behind it and, once again, filling Bloodstone's backside with the pain of a million white hot pokers.

"Holy fuuuuuuuuuuuuuck," he growled through his teeth as the needle was shoved through more skin, then in and out and in and out and in and out once more.

One last tug pulled the hole closed and a swift knot secured the thread and secured the injury once and for all. A sprinkle of some sort of powder and another few drops of acid followed, after which Lillianna gently wiped the last vestiges of blood from his buttocks and balls before taping a square of bandage over the still-throbbing wound.

"All done?" he asked, looking over his shoulder as the rotund woman slid the giant needle back into the sewing pouch.

"All done," she replied, gently slapping his good arse cheek with a fleshy hand and letting out a giggle.

"Try to keep off your bottom for a few days and make sure you keep the wound clean," she continued, picking up his filthy trousers and boxer shorts, "Which means these need a good wash."

She scooped up the rest of her belongings, leaving the bottle of beer on the chair, and waddled towards the door, leaving the homely waft of freshly baked bread in her wake. Bloodstone, still prostrate on the bed with his rear naked to the world, watched her go as he enjoyed the dull ache in his backside that had finally replaced the fiery pain of the last twelve hours.

"I'll send some fresh clothes for you, Monsieur Bertie," Lillianna announced as she squeezed her bulk through the doorway, "And no doubt our large-eared friend will return soon."

"Great," Bloodstone muttered under his breath, too quietly for the Frenchwoman to hear, "I can't wait."

"Au revoir," she said with a smile and pulled the door closed.

"Au revoir, the half-naked Bloodstone replied, scratching at an itch on his right testicle, "And merci."

225

CHAPTER THIRTY-NINE

Albert Bloodstone had never dealt well with boredom. As a boy, his father had scolded him constantly for his short attention span and his schoolmasters had often hinted at some sort of undiscovered syndrome that prevented him from being able to sit still for even the shortest length of time. Syndrome or not, it didn't stop any of them from whacking him endlessly for his fidgeting.

So, being locked in a near-empty room with only a bottle of beer and the occasional sniffs and snorts of the guard in the hallway was akin to torture for the major. Even the tap-tapping pigeon had vanished, leaving him with nothing to amuse himself but the bottle of booze and the aching of his freshly sewn bottom cheek. In addition to his lack of attention span, Bloodstone wasn't overly blessed with patience either, so in less than five minutes the beer had sloshed its way down into his belly. He span the empty bottle in a circle on the bare wooden floor and watched as it gradually slowed to a halt, finishing up pointing towards the door.

God, he was bored. How long did it take to radio back to Blighty, he wondered? Lord knows, he concluded, spinning the bottle once more, this time so ferociously that it careered off into the corner of the room, bounced against the skirting board and came to rest next to a pile of dead spiders.

He looked around for other entertainment but could find nothing to mollify his boredom. Thanks to the Sten-toting youth having smoothly liberated him of his Rolex, he couldn't even tell how long he had been waiting, although it felt like hours. He briefly considered a tug of the old pork sword; he was already half naked anyway, he reasoned, but assumed that Big Ears would think him even more of a deviant if he came in to find him mid-stroke with his tackle in his hand. And, anyway, where would he stash the resultant gentleman's relish, he wondered. He may have the patience and attention span of a caffeine-crazed three-year-old but, for all his sins, Bloodstone was always certainly one to think ahead.

He scratched at his ballbag again and rolled onto his back, taking care to keep the weight off his right buttock. He stared up at the tiny window in the roof and watched a cloud drift its way peacefully across the sky. Was it really only yesterday that he'd been up there blasting away at Jerry? It felt like an age ago. And what had happened to G for George? Had she made it safely to Switzerland? He hoped so, picturing Ashton, Bill and the Count happily munching chocolate on some Alpine mountainside, their war over.

No such luck for Buster, Nobby and Chalky, he mused as he remembered the sight of the tail gunner's brain slopping its way across the floor of the Lancaster. And poor Nobby, hands torn off and eye dangling by a string, more concerned about a gallop on the fictional Heidi than the state of his mangled face. Chalky had been much luckier, he admitted, dead before he knew it thanks to the Messerschmidt cannon ball that had drilled a neat hole into his forehead.

As he lay staring at the ceiling, Bloodstone wondered how he'd meet his maker. It didn't do well to think about such things, he knew, but in his line of work it was a very real possibility. If he didn't die of boredom first, of course. Hopefully quickly, he concluded, picturing the faces of the men he'd seen die slowly and in agonising pain over the last few years.

He thought about the first man he'd killed in what felt like a lifetime ago, but was barely five years before. A terrified nineteen-year-old second lieutenant in a dusty Chinese village, surrounding by marauding enemy troops, he'd shoved his bayonet into the guts of a screaming Japanese soldier, had forgotten his training and got the blade stuck in the sucking flesh. He remembered that no matter how much he kicked desperately at the dying boy, the blade wouldn't loosen itself and eventually snapped off, leaving the poor creature twisting and shrieking until eventually, mercifully, he bled out.

Every millisecond of that encounter was burnt into his memory and he knew that he'd never forget the desperate face of the youngster as the bayonet tore at him like a fishhook, ripping the life from him with every tug and twist. Bloodstone had lost count of the number of men that he'd slaughtered since that long-ago day on the other side of the world, but there was no doubt that the first would stick with him until his last breath.

Before he could think more on his grim subject, the key grated in the lock and the door swung open. Bloodstone swung himself into a sitting position with his hands clasped firmly over his manhood and watched as Big Ears stalked into the room, followed closely by Sten Boy and Cedric.

Big Ears scowled slightly at the sight of the trouserless Major before he composed himself and smiled for the first time that day. It wasn't a full smile, but a good effort all the same.

"Major Bloodstone, thank you for your patience," he said in English as he held out his right hand.

As Bloodstone released his genitals and raised his own right hand, Big Ears paused ever so slightly and quickly fought back another scowl before he gripped the Englishman in a soft but friendly handshake.

"I apologise for the inconvenience but these things are necessary, you understand, yes?" he continued, releasing Bloodstone's hand.

"Your countrymen have confirmed that you indeed who you say you are."

A sense of relief flooded through the major, who was pleased that he wouldn't be ending the night at the bottom of the local river with his throat slit. Despite the relief, he was a little disappointed that his name seemingly meant nothing to the Frenchman. So much for the claims of the maimed General Wilkins and good old Captain Jones that every Tom, Dick and Harry throughout Christendom knew who Bloodstone was. Maybe he needed to get back out on the rampage, he mused, win a few more medals and enrage a few more fascist dictators.

As he was silently brooding on his apparent lack of fame, the Frenchman continued.

"It is now my duty to get you home."

Before Bloodstone could announce that he had no intention of going home until his duties in Paris were complete, Big Ears spoke again.

"My name is Rene and you are our guest here in Guibert-le-Doubs. Tomorrow we will start the process, but tonight we will dine, drink wine and make plans. Is that acceptable, Major?"

Bloodstone nodded and his taste buds jumped at the thought of good wine and some decent grub.

"Very good," the Frenchman acknowledged, "But first you will need some new trousers."

He looked Bloodstone in the eye and, for the first time that day, finally grinned.

"Here in France it is bad manners to walk around with your pee-pee on show. This is not England, you understand, yes?"

CHAPTER FORTY

A t seven-thirty that evening Bloodstone pulled his chair into the table and wriggled his buttocks until they nestled nicely on a thick red cushion. Gone was his tattered uniform, replaced instead by a pair of dark woollen trousers, a freshly pressed shirt and, on his feet, a stout pair of leather brogues. His hair was combed into a perfect parting and the whiff of lavender in his nostrils reminded him of the hot tin bath that he'd stepped out of just half an hour before.

The steaming water had left him feeling like a new man and, if it wasn't for the dull ache in his backside, he could almost have forgotten that there was a war on. The large kitchen in which he sat was filled with the delicious aromas of whatever was bubbling and boiling on the hob, while the table in front of him was piled high with bread, cheese and a multitude of wine bottles.

There were five places set at the table and Bloodstone was positioned in the place of honour at the head of the feast. To his left sat the ever-jolly Cedric, his beret still lodged firmly on his head, while to his right sat Rene. The ears were as big as ever and the nose still sprouted a forest of whiskers, yet the man's cheeks were rosy and a hint of a smile hovered at the corner of his mouth as he smeared butter across a thick piece of bread.

Seated alongside Rene was Madame Rene, a pretty but slightly fragile looking woman with short dark hair and blue eyes that were far too large for her small face. A good ten years younger than her husband, she had uttered barely a word since the pair had arrived in the kitchen ten minutes earlier and now fingered the rim of her wine glass, occasionally daring a nervous glance in Bloodstone's direction.

The final place was set for Lillianna, who busied herself at the stove with a scarf tied around her hair and an apron over the striped dress that struggled to cover her ample bulk. After a last stir, she grasped an enormous pot with two hands and transported it to the table, where she deposited it atop a wooden trivet. As Bloodstone enjoyed the aroma of meaty stew that steamed from the pot, she scurried backward and forth to the stove an dumped an array of dishes filled with potatoes, vegetables and sauces onto the table.

At last, with the table ready to overflow, she lowered herself onto her chair and slapped her husband gently on the leg.

"Shall we, mon cherie?" she asked in French.

Cedric nodded and began to serve, loading the five plates with the multitude of steaming goodies. Bloodstone's plate was piled especially high with a precarious mountain of food that threatened to overflow onto the wooden tabletop, and he was forced to dam the tide with a well-placed fork.

With the food served, Cedric sat down and Rene pulled himself to his feet. Dammit, thought Bloodstone, will we ever get our nosh on, then immediately felt ungrateful as he realised that his hosts had been nothing but welcoming since his identity had been confirmed earlier that afternoon.

"I would like to raise a glass to our guest," announced Rene, holding aloft his wine glass and looking Bloodstone in the eye, "Thank you for honouring us with your presence, Major."

"Salut," he continued and, to Bloodstone's surprise, chugged down the wine in one.

"Salut," the three others repeated as they followed his lead, closely followed by Bloodstone who nearly choked as he knocked back the rough red wine in a single gulp.

The five talked as they ate or, more accurately, four of them talked and Madame Rene, who Bloodstone had discovered was called Josephine, quietly nibbled her food and sipped her wine. Through mouthfuls of meat and potatoes they mulled over the progress of the war, pondered when the invasion would come and bonded over their hatred of the Nazis.

Of course, Bloodstone kept the real reason for his loathing of the enemy a secret and neither did he reveal the lineage that tied him so dismally to the Fuhrer. In fact, talk of his escape didn't arise until after the fifth bottle of wine had been drained and Cedric had uncorked the next.

The consensus around the table was that Bloodstone should head for Switzerland where, Rene assured him, he had contacts that could get the major across the border. When safely on Swiss soil, the pointy nosed Frenchman confirmed, he had more contacts who would be able to smuggle him through Italy as far as the Allied forces.

Bloodstone thanked them but insisted that he had to north-east and onto Paris. Business to attend to, he told them as he tapped his nose and winked, almost as if he was part of a grand strategic plan and not some sort of half-cooked tomfoolery to track down a highly trained, and no doubt heavily protected, SS assassin.

"But, Monsieur," Lillianna protested with a slight slur, "The road to Paris is swarming with Boches."

"And the city itself is infested," Cedric chipped in, stifling a hiccup, "It is too dangerous. Non, I will not allow it Bertie."

"I'm sorry, my friend, but I have no choice," Bloodstone insisted with a smile, "I have to go to Paris."

"But, Bertie," Cedric slurred, drunkenly waving an arm in protest, before forgetting what he was going to say.

"Enough," Rene ordered with a lighthearted clap on the table, "Let us discuss this tomorrow. Tonight is for wine. And for forgetting the war."

"Amen to that," Bloodstone agreed, feeling distinctly light-headed but reaching for his newly filled glass all the same.

As he took a sip of the wine, the kitchen door opened with a creak, bringing with it a draft of chilly October evening air. First into the room was the spotty faced youth that had guarded his cell earlier that afternoon, although now the Sten gun had been replaced by a wine bottle that he clutched by the neck. Following behind and attached to his other hand was the delightfully foul-mouthed and somewhat ballsy blonde teenager that Bloodstone had almost rescued earlier in the day.

Her torn black dress had now been replaced by a pair of fashionable slacks and a polo-neck jumper that, to Bloodstone's surprise, hugged her not insignificant curves tightly. The tearstained face had been mended and the tangled hair had been brushed back into shape, leaving a picture of beauty that made Bloodstone wonder if she really was the daughter of his wonderful but not overly attractive hosts.

As the door closed behind the couple, Cedric jumped to his feet and grasped the girl in an enormous bear hug, kissing the top of her head and making the girl squirm and giggle.

"Monsieur Bertie, I believe you have met my precious Cristina," he said as he released her from his embrace.

"I have indeed," Bloodstone replied and rose to his feet to plant a kiss on each of the girl's cheeks.

"It's a pleasure to meet you in happier circumstances," he continued with a smile, before offering his hand to the gangly youth who could hardly tear his eyes from the blonde at his side. And I don't blame you, thought Bloodstone as he tried to avoid glancing at the girl's bosoms.

"Albert," he announced, focusing back on the bottle-wielding young man and smiling, "Although I think you know that already."

"Oui, monsieur," the youth replied, grinning and forgetting to offer his own name.

"Papa," Cristina announced, "Jacques and I will be in the salon."

"Playing cards," she added after a pause, to which Bloodstone stifled a snort.

"Very good, ma petite pomme," Cedric replied, "Be good."

Jacques blushed, Cristina giggled again and Bloodstone tried and failed to stifle a second snort.

"Ah, young love," Lillianna laughed as the couple opened a door on the other side of the kitchen and departed, hand in hand once more.

Bloodstone had just plonked himself down and was about to mop up the remnants of his plate with a chunk of bread when the kitchen door swung open again, this time far more forcefully than when opened by the skinny hand of Jacques just a few minutes before. The heavy wooden door nearly burst from its hinges and slammed back against the wall, causing Cedric to leap to his feet with a speed that, once again, belied his size, while the other four jerked their heads around.

A shrill scream came from Josephine's mouth and Lillianna paused with a forkful of potato an inch from her open mouth, staring at the doorway. Rene stiffened visibly, his eyes wide, while Bloodstone clenched his jaw and forced his face to remain expressionless, despite the icy chill that almost froze his blood.

Because barging into the room, forage cap still on his head, rifle on his shoulder and half-empty bottle of schnapps in his hand, was the ghastly figure of the German corporal, Schmidt, the man Bloodstone had very nearly decapitated on the road that afternoon.

"Where's the bitch?" the man snarled in French, his voice slurred with booze.

Nobody moved.

"I said," he repeated slowly, throwing the bottle to the floor and unslinging his rifle, "Where is that fucking French bitch?"

234

CHAPTER FORTY-ONE

The kitchen door swung shut of its own accord to leave the room silent save for the guttural breathing of the Wehrmacht soldier who stood amid the smashed remnants of his schnapps bottle, his rifle pointing ominously towards the head of the still-standing Cedric.

Lillianna's fork remained in mid-air as she stared wide-eyed at the greatcoat-clad corporal, who crunched forward across the broken glass with his rifle swinging to aim at Josephine. The woman whimpered, her face a mask of fear, and as the muzzle of the Mauser edged towards her, Rene scraped back his chair and made to stand.

The rifle instantly jerked towards the small Frenchman, stopping him mid-rise and leaving him frozen to the spot. A look of hatred was etched across his face as he stared at the snarling German, desperate to protect his wife but sensible enough to notice the drunken soldier's finger hovering over the trigger.

The snarl turned into a leer as Schmidt eyed Josephine, up and down, ogling her waif-like figure and the pretty face that, by now, looked as if it was about to burst into tears.

"Maybe I'll have you instead," he slurred, the rifle still aimed at her husband but his half-glazed eyes very much undressing the petrified woman sitting at the table.

"You want to watch?" he asked with a smirk as he glanced back at Rene, who was now gripping the edge of the table and visibly shaking with the effort of staying still.

Bloodstone, seemingly unnoticed by the marauding Nazi, watched it all with his face still entirely expressionless. The effects of the evening's wine had vanished as soon as the green uniform had burst through the door, leaving him instantly sober, and although his face gave nothing away, his mind was racing.

He cursed inwardly at how he'd managed to avoid the enemy for the twenty-four hours since his lunatic plunge from George, yet this particular cretin seemed determined to rumble him, albeit unknowingly. And the outlook was looking fairly bleak, he admitted, knowing that a blottoed and apparently rapacious Wehrmacht corporal stumbling around a Frenchman's kitchen was unlikely to end well. The Nazis generally got their own way as far as their unfortunate subjects were concerned and any sort of dissent was usually clamped down upon with ruthless efficiency.

So, what to do? He wasn't quite sure, but something needed to happen, and quickly, as it looked like Rene was about to explode any second, such was the look of ferocity on his face.

Schmidt took another step towards the table and Rene raised himself half an inch higher, his knuckles white with the force of gripping the wooden tabletop. The corporal saw the tiny movement and his eyes flared wide, the mouth creasing into a snarl. He jabbed the muzzle of his rifle roughly against the man's back, wiped his nose against the shoulder of his tunic and then spat onto the flagstone floor.

"Where do you think you're going, you big-eared fuck?" he growled as he eyed the man with a mixture of malice and amusement.

Rene didn't reply and the four other dinner guests remained silent, all frozen to the spot as they eyed the drunken intruder

"I asked you a question," he continued, jabbing the Frenchman with the Mauser, "You fucking French peasant."

Still silence, except for the quiet whimpering of Josephine, whose cheeks were spotted with tears as she watched her husband being

236

prodded by the Nazi. With no answer from Rene, Schmidt turned back to Josephine.

"Strip," he ordered curtly, "And vite, or I'll blow his ugly head off."

As the petrified woman blubbed and made to stand, Bloodstone decided that enough was enough. If there was one thing he couldn't stand, it was bullies.

In one swift movement he shoved his chair backwards and rose to his feet, drawing himself up to his full six foot. The rifle barely had time to move in his direction before he opened his mouth, a look of unadulterated fury on his face.

"Unteroffizier!" he roared, "What the hell do you think you're doing?"

The corporal froze, rooted to the spot, his brow creased with confusion and his rifle poised midway between Josephine and the now-standing Bloodstone. The other four occupants of the room stared on with similar looks of bewilderment plastered across their faces, staring wide-eyed at the moustached major. Because Bloodstone had spoken not in French, not in English but in fluent, unaccented and parade ground German.

Taking advantage of the shocked silence, he followed up in his best Prussian officer's tones.

"How dare you come in here and threaten these people?" he yelled, taking a step towards the flabbergasted Schmidt.

"How dare you?" he continued, taking another step closer and shoving his face just inches from the corporal.

"You, Unteroffizier, are a disgrace to the Fuhrer's uniform! What the hell are you doing disturbing my dinner? And why are you drunk on duty?"

As the four Frenchmen looked on in astonishment, Schmidt gaped like a fish, his Schnapps-sozzled mind trying to understand what was happening.

Bloodstone didn't give him a second.

"I asked you a question," he bellowed in German, "And you stand to attention when addressing an officer!"

The butt of the rifle crashed to the floor and Schmidt snapped to attention, his military training engrained deep enough to obey orders unflinchingly, despite his confusion and the copious amounts of booze in his system.

Again Bloodstone spoke, this time his voice quiet but as cold as ice.

"You still haven't answered me, Unteroffizier. I'm waiting."

The corporal's mouth moved but no words came and he swayed slightly on the spot, using the Mauser for balance.

"You disgust me," Bloodstone spat, taking a step back and glaring at the inebriated corporal in front of him.

As Bloodstone stepped backwards, Schmidt sniffed and cleared his throat, the look on his face changing slightly as he stared at what appeared to be an officer decked out in civilian clothes.

"Sir, what are you doing here?" he queried, now in German, cocking his head slightly, "I mean, here with these Franzmänner?"

"I beg your pardon?" Bloodstone asked icily, stepping forward again, "How dare you question me?"

"It's just that standing orders forbid fraternisation with the enemy, sir. And uniform must be worn at all times, with no exception. Isn't that the case, sir?

Bloodstone thought that this particular soldier was either exceptionally insubordinate or the drink had given him a decent dose of Dutch courage. Whichever it was, he wasn't going to stand for it.

He took another half a step forward, so close to the German now that he could smell the stink on his breath.

"What did you just say?" he whispered icily.

As the words left his mouth, he realised in horror that he had spoken them not in German, but in English. He saw something akin to realisation flash across the corporal's face and the eyes widened and the mouth gaped once more.

Before Bloodstone could speak again, the German beat him to it.

"I know who you are," he said quietly with a look of triumph on his face.

"I'd recognise that ugly gesicht and the stupid moustache anywhere. You're the Butcher of Italia, aren't you? The English mongrel bastard."

The next few moments seemed to go into slow motion as Bloodstone realised he had given himself away and the corporal realised he was standing toe to toe with one of the most wanted men in the Reich; a man who had a price on his head from the Führer himself.

Both men sprang into action as the four bystanders looked on in confusion, the time appearing to stand almost still. Schmidt went for his Mauser, twenty-five years of soldiering making the movement instinctive. In less than a heartbeat he'd hefted the butt from the ground, swung it into his right shoulder and planted his left hand under the barrel.

His right forefinger was millimetres from the trigger when Bloodstone let fly with his right fist, all his fourteen stone of bodyweight behind the punch. The knuckle connected with the corporal's throat with a sickening crunch, crushing the windpipe, destroying the larynx and driving the man's Adam's apple flat against his spine.

The force of the blow knocked him from his feet and sent him spinning to the floor, where he landed on his back with a crash. He clutched his hands to his broken throat, gasping for air, and his hobnailed boots kicked at the stone tiles as he choked. In a matter of seconds, the Nazi had been transformed from drunken thug to whimpering wreck, flapping like a landed fish as he desperately tried to force air into his wrecked gullet.

Bloodstone stepped back and looked down, feeling not a single ounce of pity as he watched the man jerk and writhe on a bed of smashed glass and spilled schnapps. It was a long time since he'd last used the deadly punch that his first drill instructor had taught him all those years ago, but he knew that there was no way back now for the corporal. With his airways destroyed and his mouth spraying out blood-specked spittle, Bloodstone gave him a minute at the most before his brain starved of oxygen and his heart stopped beating.

But it turned out that Schmidt didn't have a minute. In fact, he didn't even have thirty seconds. Because, as he lay kicking on the floor and as Bloodstone looked down upon him, the not inconsiderable figure of Lillianna pushed herself to her feet and, fork still in hand, strode across the kitchen until she reached the suffocating German. Without pause and in one single motion she leant forwards, lifted her right arm above her head and plunged it down into the man's face. The fork, complete with half-eaten piece of potato, punctured the eyeball and skewered the man's brain, cutting off his frenzied kicks and killing him instantly.

As the rest of the room watched on in shocked silence, Lillianna straightened up, wiped her hands on her apron and calmly returned to the table, leaving the fork protruding from the German's eye socket and a thin trail of potato-spotted blood dribbling down the side of his face.

"Jesus Christ," Bloodstone whispered, not quite believing what he'd just seen.

"Now," Lillianna said, seated once more, "Who's for dessert?"

CHAPTER FORTY-TWO

"I knew I recognised your name," Rene said through mouthfuls of apple tart, "You must forgive me for the interrogation."

Bloodstone waved away the apologies as he pushed a piece of pastry around his plate, not feeling overly hungry with the dead Schmidt lying two feet away with the fork still in place and traces of watery brain matter now leaking out of the ruptured eyeball and pooling on the floor underneath his head.

"I do think this changes things slightly, though," Cedric announced as he nodded in Bloodstone's direction, "Bertie is a hero and if he says he needs to go to Paris, who are we to stop him?"

"You're right," agreed Rene, his dessert now finished, "We must we do all we can to help."

He tugged at a hair protruding from his nostril before he continued.

"Paris is four hundred kilometres from here and, as Lillianna said earlier, the roads will be swarming with Boches."

"Cross-country then?" Bloodstone suggested.

"Non, Monsieur," Rene continued, "It'll take you weeks. And it's too risky. There are traitors everywhere and if the Boche find a man of your age without papers they'll put you against a wall and shoot you without a second thought."

"Are you thinking what I'm thinking?" Cedric chipped in again, looking at Rene with a raised eyebrow.

"I think I might be. Do you reckon it's possible?"

"Is what possible?" Bloodstone interrupted before Rene could reply.

Rene tugged at his nose hair once again before he cleared his throat and looked at Bloodstone.

"You go in full view of the Boches. Non, you become a Boche."

"I *become* a Boche?"

"Oui. If that little performance a minute ago was anything to go by, you're more of a German than most Germans. You'll have no trouble at all in blending in. No offence, of course."

"None taken," Bloodstone laughed, "But don't forget that there's a price on my head and my picture seems to have been all over the place."

"I mean, even that drunken idiot knew who I was," he concluded with a wave in the direction of the prone figure of Schmidt."

"Nothing a little barbery can't fix," Cedric offered.

"Barbery?"

"Yes, Bertie," he continued, "Lose that moustache and shave your head and you'll look just like one of our Wehrmacht friends."

"But papers? And a uniform?"

He looked down at his checked shirt and woollen trousers.

"I can't exactly go playing the Boche dressed like a Frenchman."

"Worry not my English friend, we are a resourceful people," Cedric smiled.

"Indeed," Rene continued, "And Josephine here is something of a maestro with a needle and thread. You just wait and see."

"But identification?" Bloodstone tried again, "Surely I'll need false papers?"

"Yes, Bertie, yes you will," Cedric agreed, glancing at Lillianna, "But it's lucky that my little champignon here is just as handy with a spot of forgery as it seems she is with a fork. The occasional dodgy document can be a good earner these days, and I'm sure that she can turn her hand to what you need too."

Lillianna nodded and smiled a rosy smile, apparently now returned to bubbly housewife after her brief stint as a cutlery-wielding killer.

"So, we are agreed?" Rene asked as he looked around the table.

Bloodstone, realising that his options were rather limited, nodded.

"Tres bien," Rene said, rising to his feet and picking at his nostrils one last time, "You will go with the two ladies now and they will begin the preparations. Tomorrow, you will leave for Paris, oui?"

"What about him?" Bloodstone asked as he looked at the dead corporal.

"Do not worry about that; Cedric and I will have him swimming with the fishes within the hour."

"I'll help you," Bloodstone insisted, standing up.

"No, Monsieur, it's too dangerous," the big eared Frenchman replied, motioning him to sit back down, "You must stay here and prepare for tomorrow."

He then turned to Cedric and instructed him to fetch a blanket.

"And bring Jacques," he ordered as he looked down at the stiffening corpse on the flagstone floor, "This is going to need three of us."

As Cedric departed through the kitchen door in search of a blanket, Rene cleared his throat, bent down and plucked the fork from Schmidt's eye with a sickly plop. He wiped the telltale signs of blood and brain on the German's greatcoat before he straightened up, deposited the now-clean fork on the kitchen table and followed Cedric out of the door.

"Right Monsieur Bertie," Lillianna said, gesturing to the door on the other side of the room, "Come with us please."

Not wanting to argue with what was quite obviously a woman who took no nonsense, Bloodstone obeyed and followed the waif-like

Josephine out of the door, pursued by Lillianna who clutched a freshly uncorked wine bottle in each hand. They traipsed up the stairs, along the corridor and back into the tiny room that had acted as Bloodstone's cell-cum-operating theatre earlier that day.

The small bed was now made up with a floral pillowcase and matching bed sheet, upon which Bloodstone was instructed to sit. As his buttocks sank into the thin mattress, the figure of the pretty Cristina appeared in the doorway, her blonde hair somewhat tousled and her cheeks flushed. In her hands was the same tray from earlier that day, although this time the bowl of soup had gone and in its place was a jug of steaming water, a pair of scissors the size of hedge trimmers and a brutal looking cut-throat razor.

With a grin she set the tray down on the floor and retreated from the room to leave Bloodstone alone with the two women. Lillianna dragged the chair across to the bed and lowered herself onto it.

"I'm sorry, Monsieur Bertie," she said with a smile as she plucked the scissors from the tray, "But I'm sure you'll still be a handsome devil by the time we've finished with you."

With that, she began to cut away at Bloodstone's curls, hacking off great clumps as she attacked his head with the ferocity of a demented gardener. He sighed with despair as lock after lock of black hair tumbled onto his lap and fell to the floor, watching as countless hours of careful coiffuring and styling was destroyed in seconds.

After a few minutes, Lillianna stopped and leaned back to observe her handiwork. Bloodstone was half pleased that he didn't have a mirror to admire what was undoubtedly a monstrosity of a hairstyle, but he rubbed his hand over his head anyway and felt the tufts and bumps of his newly sheared scalp. Grasping her scissors again, she inched in closer and went at his head again, this time with far more care as she expertly trimmed the remaining hair. She continued until his entire head was evenly covered with scarcely more than half an inch of hair, snipping away the last rogue strands with a satisfied grunt.

Next, she set to work with the razor, scraping at the sides of his skull, dipping the blade into the hot water and scraping again above his ears and around the back of his head until some semblance of style began to emerge. A brutal, parade ground style of epically Prussian proportions, but a hairstyle all the same.

With barely a pause, the blade went into the steaming water again and emerged, this time to attack Bloodstone's moustache. As the blade sliced through the whiskers, he closed his eyes and tried not to think about the manhours that he'd spent obsessively pruning and shaping what was, until a few seconds before, one of the greatest moustaches in all of Christendom.

It was all over a minute later and he stroked his face with his fingers, feeling, for the first time in years, the odd sensation of a cleanly shaven top lip. He wasn't impressed, not one little bit, but with a sigh he asked himself, yet again, what other option did he have.

With the evening's beautification seemingly complete, Lillianna folded away the razor and beckoned at Josephine, who had been watching in silence from the other side of the room. The small woman shuffled across the room, pulled a measuring tape from somewhere in her skirts and mumbled something incomprehensible in a tiny voice.

"Pardon?" Bloodstone asked politely.

"I need to take your measurements, Monsieur," she repeated, this time in a voice that was just about audible.

"My measurements?"

"Oui," Lillianna answered, "For your uniform."

"Rene wasn't lying when he said that Josephine here is a maestro with a needle," she continued, "You just wait and see what she brings you tomorrow."

Shrugging, Bloodstone, stood up and held his arms aloft as Josephine buzzed around him with her tape, whispering measurements to Lillianna who noted them down on a scrap of paper. As she bent down in front of him and ran her tape from ankle to groin, he looked up to see Lillianna's staring without any semblance of subtlety in the direction of his manhood. She caught his eye and, instead of looking away in embarrassment, she winked.

Bloodstone wasn't one to be easily unnerved but the look on the Frenchwoman's chubby face confused him somewhat; was she flirting with him? Surely not. Although, he thought, he'd been on the receiving end of more than his fair share of feminine advances and the glaring at his hidden tackle and the obvious eye action certainly looked like flirting to him.

He quickly recovered himself and, as Josephine fussed around him with her tape, he reached for one of the wine bottles and took a swig. The taste of the rough red wine hit the back of his throat and he realised that the effects of the evening's alcohol had worn off entirely. Not surprising, he thought to himself, considering the events of the past hour. He chugged down another swig and then handed the wine to Lillianna, who winked again and took the bottle.

Josephine finally finished her measuring, deposited the tape back into her skirts and headed for the door. As she left, she kissed Lillianna on both cheeks, dared a nervous smile in Bloodstone's direction and then vanished into the hallway, closing the door behind her.

"A creature of few words, our darling Josephine," Lillianna said with a laugh, "But she'll be back here tomorrow morning with a uniform fit for a king."

She brushed at the remnants of hair that had found their way onto her large bosoms and continued.

"When you have your uniform, we'll take your photograph too."

"For my papers?"

"Oui, Monsieur Bertie," she replied, "I will prepare them tonight, but we need the photograph to complete them."

"Thank you, Madame," he said, taking another gulp from the bottle, "I really am most grateful for your hospitality. This is a great risk you're taking."

"Nonsense," she replied, brushing again at her dress, "It is what friends are for, oui?"

Before he could answer, Lillianna spoke again.

"Bloody hair of yours," she said with a laugh, it's got everywhere."

"Apologies," he said with a smile that quickly vanished as he realised, appalled, that Lillianna had started to unbutton her dress.

Words failed him as he looked on, unable to tear his eyes from the terrifying sight that began to unfold not three feet away. He tried to speak, tried to tell her to stop, but no words came and he simply stared on in horror as the last button was undone and the dress was pulled over Lillianna's head.

The horror was magnified by the realisation that the Frenchwoman was wearing not a single stitch of underwear. Instead, two enormous breasts, not dissimilar to army socks each filled with a cricket ball, slumped on top of a gargantuan stomach that hung down like an old sack. Peering out below and half hidden by the drooping belly was a giant forest of thick black pubic hair, the sight of which made Bloodstone gag.

"That's better," she said as she looked at him with a glint that could be described as nothing other than predatory.

The major, entirely out of his comfort zone, thought that it most certainly wasn't better.

"Madame," he stuttered, "What, what are you doing?"

She took a step towards him and he found himself rooted to the spot, his feet refusing to move.

"Now I want something from you," she whispered as she took another step closer.

"But, but Cedric?" he blubbed, his feet still refusing to budge.

"Ha, you English are such prudes," she laughed, "My darling Cedric won't mind one single bit. In fact, he may even join us when he returns."

"Jesus Christ," Bloodstone blasphemed as he looked towards the door in horrified desperation.

"Now, do you want your papers or not?" Lillianna asked, her face half smiling and half serious.

For the umpteenth time that day, Bloodstone realised that he was all out of options. He simply nodded, his brain too befuddled to summon the words for an answer.

"Good, then come here," the podgy woman commanded as she lowered herself onto the bed in a sitting position with her short legs dangling in the air.

In some sort of daze, Bloodstone did as he was ordered and took a step towards the bed. As he did so, Lillianna leant back, lifted a belly riddled with the vestiges of childbirth and pointed at the overgrown thatch beneath.

"Here," she ordered, pushing Bloodstone to his knees.

What the blazes is going on, he said to himself as she guided his head towards her nether regions. The last thing he saw before he screwed up his eyes was the forest parting to display what could only be described as a pink trench haphazardly packed with soggy ham.

"God help me," he whimpered as his mouth was forced into the unruly gash and his voice was silenced by a faceful of damp pubic hair, "They better be bloody good papers."

CHAPTER FORTY-THREE

The kitchen floor had long since been scrubbed clean, the blood and brains washed from the stones and the body of Schmidt weighted down and thrown into the Doubs. The sun was shining in the sky and the first signs of winter were starting to appear in the French air.

It was the perfect morning to feel alive, yet Albert Bloodstone felt anything but. His body ached painfully and he was genuinely concerned that his private parts were about to fall off. He'd been ridden like a racehorse until the early hours, again and again and then again, crushed beneath the obese body of a woman with an appetite that he'd never seen before.

Only when he had been utterly drained of all bodily fluids and his rampant host had climaxed for what seemed like the twentieth time, was he finally allowed to rest. And only then, with a kiss on his cheek and a smack of his already-tender arse, did Lillianna depart into the night, with clothes over her arm and enormous backside swinging, leaving Bloodstone patently refusing to accept that he'd in any way enjoyed the past three hours.

As he sat at the kitchen table, miserably pushing his bacon around his plate, moustache gone, hair cropped and struggling to find the appetite to devour his breakfast, the whistling figure of Cedric appeared through the door.

"Bonjour, my English friend," he greeted with a large grin plastered across his face.

Bloodstone, unable to find the right words, simply nodded in return and smiled.

"I'm sorry I couldn't join you last night," he continued, "Our Boche corporal took rather longer to dispose of than expected."

Bloodstone waved away the strange apology with his fork, thanking his lucky stars that the beret-wearing Frenchman had been too busy to turn the sordid tryst into some sort of flesh-wobbling orgy.

"But," Cedric said as he stuffed a baguette into his mouth, "My darling Lillianna certainly enjoyed herself, so I must thank you."

Again, Bloodstone dismissed the bizarre gratitude with a wave and, just as it seemed that the bread-munching Frenchman was about to speak again, the door opened once more.

In came the diminutive figure of Josephine with a large paper-wrapped bundle in her hands and a bulging drawstring bag on her shoulder. Following in her footsteps was Lillianna, who had dark rings of tiredness under her eyes but a broad smile on her face. She bolted the kitchen door behind her as Josephine dumped her belongings on the table.

"Good morning Monsieur Bertie," Lillianna greeted as she loosened a piece of string tied around the paper bundle, "Josephine has a surprise for you, just as I promised."

Bloodstone craned his neck to watch as the paper was pulled off and dropped to the table to reveal a bolt of grey material. As the grey cloth was pulled free and shaken out, he whistled in surprise. Because there in front of him, held aloft by the rosy cheeked Frenchwoman, was the uniform of none other than the Waffen SS. And not just any uniform, but one boasting the epaulettes of an Obersturmbannfuhrer, the infamous unit's equivalent of a lieutenant-colonel.

"Where the hell did you get that?" he asked in astonishment as he admired the fine stitching on the uniform.

"Well," said Cedric, spitting out a mouthful of crumbs, "Back in '41, Rene and Josephine had the misfortune of being forced to billet a Boche bastard from the SS. Big horrible creature, what was his name?"

"Kunst," Josephine whispered.

"That's him," Cedric continued, a chunk of freshly torn baguette in his hand.

"One day this Kunst cretin packed up and left in the middle of the night. Terrible rush. Sent off to the Russian front apparently. Well, he was so fast leaving that he left half of his kit behind, stupid Boche."

As Cedric crammed the piece of bread into his mouth, Lillianna picked up the story.

"That's right, he never came back, killed hopefully, and it's been hidden away under lock and key in Josephine's attic ever since. You never know when these things might come in handy, oui?"

"Oui indeed," Bloodstone agreed, now realising what Rene had meant the night before by "You *become* a Boche".

There weren't many things more Boche-like than the Waffen SS and the thought of joining their ranks both petrified and excited him. He knew that he'd be shot as a spy if he was discovered, but, if the price on his head was anything to go by, it was likely that he'd be executed anyway if he was caught, SS impersonator or not.

And what better way to blend into occupied Europe, make his way to Paris and hunt down Heidler? Taking his present situation into account, there really wasn't one, he knew. But he also knew it was damned foolhardy but, again, what choice did he have?

While he was mulling over his lack of options, Lillianna had opened the drawstring bag and was emptying its contents onto the kitchen table. First came a pair of leather knee-high boots, polished almost to a mirror, followed by a black belt that had been equally buffed to perfection. Next was a grey officers' cap, rimmed with black and adorned with a menacing silver skull, after which came a leather holster complete with 9mm Luger. Bloodstone picked up the pistol, tested the weight in his hand and slid back the bolt to peer inside the chamber. Clean as a whistle.

After a few more items were dumped on the table, Bloodstone was ordered by Lillianna to change into his new uniform. Josephine left the room as he stripped off his shirt but his hostess remained in the kitchen, not even bothering to look away.

"Will it fit?" he asked, trousers around his ankles.

Lillianna tore her eyes away from the bulge in his borrowed underpants.

"Without a doubt, Monsieur Bertie. There's nobody finer with a needle and thread than dear old Josephine."

First on were the grey trousers, which hugged his thighs and backside as if they were made for him. Next followed an undershirt, over which he pulled the tunic and fastened its six silver buttons. Again, the uniform felt as if it was made to measure and he puffed out his chest and wriggled his arms, enjoying the sensation of being in a well-fitted uniform once again.

On went the boots and the belt, complete with its Luger, and then he pushed the cap onto his head and pulled the peak down over his forehead.

"Wait here," Lillianna ordered and left the room only to return a minute later hefting a full-length mirror, which she rested against the wall.

"God in heaven," Bloodstone whistled as he looked in the mirror, seeing not his own reflection in the glass but the devil itself. Everything that he hated stared back at him, from the shining Jackboots to the SS runes on his right collar and the eagle, swastika and skull pinned to his cap.

"It fits like a dream," Lillianna said from his side, "But I tell you something Monsieur Bertie, I'm not sure now if I want to kill you just a little bit more than I want to kiss you."

Not quite sure which option he preferred, Bloodstone had to agree that he did indeed look like a nasty piece of work. But his transformation wasn't finished quite yet as Lillianna laid a small leather box on the table. He opened the clasp and lifted the lid, revealing a red, white and black ribbon on which lay a glittering Knight's Cross. Turning back to the mirror, he tied the ribbon around his neck and straightened the collar of his tunic, leaving the small black and silver cross hanging at his throat. Now he looked even more of a monster, he thought with a shudder as he looked himself up and down in the mirror.

He was interrupted from his posing by the voice of Lillianna.

"Just one more thing now, Monsieur Bertie."

He turned from the mirror to find her setting an ancient camera atop a pair of wooden legs. The thing looked like something from the turn of the century, but Lillianna seemed to know what she was doing as she bolted it together before she stood back to admire her handiwork.

"Now stand against that wall," she ordered, pointing at the kitchen's off-white paintwork, "And no smiling."

He did as he was instructed, positioning himself in front of the wall and staring at the lens with his best arrogant-Nazi sneer. A second later the camera clicked and a puff of grey smoke emerged from somewhere within its box-like structure.

"Tres bien, tres bien," Lillianna mumbled as she removed a plate from the antique contraption and headed for the door.

"I will return shortly," she offered over her shoulder, business-like all of a sudden with not a trace of the previous night's miscreancy, "Please wait here."

Bloodstone did as he was ordered, turning back to the mirror and looking once more at his reflection. And once again he hated what stared back at him; a picture of pure evil.

CHAPTER FORTY-FOUR

"Wilhelm von Winkel?" Bloodstone asked as he peered at the handwritten letters scrawled inside the small book in his hands, "You couldn't get much more German than that."

"Austrian, actually," replied the large-eared Rene, who was sitting opposite him across the kitchen table.

"Indeed, very good," muttered Bloodstone as he flicked through the pages, "Born in Vienna, December 25th, 1919, apparently."

"A Christmas baby," chipped in Cedric, who had returned with Rene just a few minutes before and, after the initial shock of seeing the Englishman in full Nazi regalia, had pulled up a chair and handed Bloodstone the paper booklet.

After glancing at the brown cover, complete with SS logo, he had begun to leaf through the pages of the Soldbuch, the pay book that every German serviceman carried with him and that now displayed his photo on the inside cover. The thing was a piece of mastery, from the picture that had been taken just an hour before but now appeared faded and stamped, to the numerous lines of scrawl indicating everything from service history, medical record, decorations and next of kin, which was apparently a Frau Wilma von Winkel of 23 Gartengasse, Vienna.

"Wilma and Wilhelm von Winkel?" Bloodstone asked with a laugh, "Really?"

"My darling wife is nothing if not creative," smiled Cedric, "And not a bad forgery, oui, especially for a first effort?"

"It's incredible," Bloodstone, or von Winkel as he now was, agreed as he leafed through the pages.

"Poland, Holland, France, Russia, back to France again," he read aloud, "1st SS Infantry Brigade, Leibstandarte SS Adolf Hitler. I certainly have been around a bit, haven't I?"

"Exactly," Rene agreed, "And, with that medal around your neck, nobody's going to be asking you any questions."

"You'll be in Paris before you know it," Cedric added, "But just make sure you slit the throats of a few of your new comrades on the way, s'il vous plait."

"I'll see what I can do," Bloodstone answered, knowing that the jolly Frenchman wasn't joking.

"Anyway, talking of Paris," he continued, taking off his cap and laying it on the table, "What's the best way to get there?"

This time it was Lillianna who replied.

"It couldn't be easier Monsieur Bertie. Train from here in Guibert to Dijon, that's about two hours, then change and onto Paris, which will be another three hours. If you get the next train, which is supposed to be at 1.30pm train today, you'll be there this evening if all goes well."

If all goes well, thought Bloodstone, realising that was a big if. Here he was, a famous war hero with a price on his head, about to set out across enemy territory dressed in the stolen garb of an SS officer, carrying forged papers and no real idea of where he was going. What could possibly go wrong?

"So, the 1.30pm train?" he asked, pushing his doubts to the back of his head and glancing at his watch, "I probably should get going."

"Before you do, we have one more thing for you," Cedric announced as he hefted a faded leather briefcase onto the table and unbuckled its straps.

Bloodstone opened the case and peered inside, finding two neatly folded pairs of white underpants, a pair of green military issue socks and a bulging brown envelope. He pulled out the envelope and upturned it over the table, watching as two string-tied bundles of 50 Reichsmark notes dropped onto the wooden tabletop.

"Non, non, non," he protested as he picked up one of the wads of notes and waved it at Cedric, "There must be a thousand marks here."

"Two thousand, to be exact," the Frenchman smiled.

"Non," Bloodstone repeated, "I will not take your money, you've given me enough already."

"Don't be, what do you English say, daft?" he countered, still smiling, "How far do you think you'll get in Paris without a few francs in your pocket?"

"A few francs? This is a fortune. I'm sorry, but I won't take it," he insisted, waving the bundle once again.

"Bertie, do we look like poor people?" asked the Frenchman, looking at Bloodstone as if he were an imbecile.

Bloodstone thought about the sizeable house, the copious amounts of food that he'd devoured the previous night, not to mention the seemingly never-ending supply of beer and wine. Not bad for simple farmers living under the yoke of an occupying enemy, he admitted.

"I'm still not taking it," he concluded, laying the wad of notes back on the wooden tabletop, "But I will take the pants and socks if you don't mind."

"Bertie, Bertie, Bertie," Cedric soothed in a fatherly voice as he laid his enormous hand on Bloodstone's arm, "Do you really think that money is real?"

Bloodstone looked again at the two string-tied bundles.

"It's hookey?"

"It's who?"

"Hookey. Dodgy. Counterfeit."

"Of course it's counterfeit," Cedric guffawed, slapping the major on the shoulder, "One hundred percent, what do you say, hookey?"

"My darling Lillianna can't just knock you up a Soldbuch when you need it," he continued, "She does a particularly good trade in false notes. It's our little, how do you say, fuck you, to the Boche economy."

"So it seems," Bloodstone mumbled as he picked up the pile of notes again and inspected the greeny-brown paper, "I'm not overly familiar with Kraut currency, but it looks kosher to me."

"Kosher?"

"Genuine, the real thing."

"Of course it does," the Frenchman grinned, "My Lillianna is the best at whatever she does. But you already know that don't you?"

Bloodstone blushed, unable to think of a response.

"So, you'll take it?"

"It would be a pleasure, my friend, and thank you, truly."

"Nonsense," Cedric rebuffed, stuffing the bundles back into the envelope and placing it inside the briefcase, which he quickly buckled up and placed in Bloodstone's hand.

"Now, it really is time to leave," he continued, "The train departs in less than thirty minutes. It's only a short walk to the station but you'll have to go alone, I'm afraid we can't be seen mingling with the likes of an SS Obersturmbannfuhrer."

"Of course," Bloodstone agreed and picked up his new cap and pushed it down onto his freshly shorn head.

"But before I go, I must thank you from the bottom of my heart, both of you. I don't know what I would have done without you. And pass on my thanks to Rene and Josephine too, if you please."

As Lillianna and Cedric waved away his thanks, he stepped forward and planted a kiss on each of the Frenchwoman's cheeks.

"I think I should be the one thanking you," she winked as the wanton look of the previous night fleetingly appeared in her eyes once again.

Again lost for words, Bloodstone turned to Cedric and held out his hand, "Thank you, Monsieur, for everything."

Yet another smile spread across the man's chubby face and he ignored Bloodstone's hand, instead grasping him in an enormous bear hug.

"Just go and give those dirty Boches what they deserve," he said as he released the major and looked him square in the eyes, "I mean it."

"I know you do, Monsieur," Bloodstone smiled, "I know you do."

With his cap on his head and case in his hand, Bloodstone walked to the door and twisted the handle. He turned one last time to the couple who now stood, hand in hand, in the middle of the kitchen.

"I'll see you when this is all over," he smiled, "Au revoir, friends."

"Au revoir, Bertie," they replied in unison.

Bloodstone opened the door, stepped outside into the afternoon air and closed the door behind him. He took a deep breath and straightened his cap.

Major Albert Bloodstone was no more. Obersturmbannfuhrer Wilhelm von Winkel was on his way to Paris.

CHAPTER FORTY-FIVE

As Bloodstone ventured out of the courtyard, closed the gate behind him and took a left turn onto the road, he realised that, despite spending almost two days in Guibert-le-Doubs, he'd seen little more than the inside of a kitchen and his small cell-turned-bedroom.

He made his way towards the station, following the directions that Cedric had given him, and quickly discovered that the town that had been his home for the past forty-eight hours was barely a town at all. Instead, it seemed to be more of a collection of higgledy-piggledy houses, punctuated by the occasional boulangerie or charcuterie and nestling in the shadow of the pine-covered hills that towered away to the east.

During dinner the previous evening he'd learned that Guibert-le-Doubs had been around for nearly two millennia and had originally sprouted up to provide bread, wine and whores to a Roman fort that had long ago protected a bridge across the meandering river. The legionnaires were long gone, as were the vicious mountain tribes they opposed, but over the years a constant revolving door of new armies had taken their place.

And now it was the turn of the invading Germans to set up camp in the nineteenth century barracks that occupied the site of the ancient

Roman fort. The bread and wine were still sourced from the town in plentiful supply, providing the resentful populace with an unwelcome but much needed income, while the whores were much less common than in the days of Caesar, although apparently still available to those who knew where to look.

After a few minutes of walking and seeing not a single soul, Bloodstone took another left and found himself in what appeared to be the town square. A handful of market stalls were scattered across the small cobbled expanse, while a town hall stood at the far end, complete with red and black swastikas hanging from its frontage. Throughout the square was scattered a collection of locals who haggled for their wares beside the stalls that displayed the usual bareness of wartime.

Following the directions that he'd been given, Bloodstone headed across the cobbles towards the swastika-hung building, next to which appeared to be the entrance to the railway station. As he passed a vegetable stall, silence descended upon a pair of figures who had been negotiating the price of a bag of feeble looking carrots. With their conversation stalled, they stared at him with a look that he'd never quite seen before; not just hatred, which is what he would've expected from the French locals, but something more than that. Was it fear, he wondered, giving them a polite smile and a nod, at which their eyes widened and their faces hardened further.

As he left them in his midst, he realised it was terror that had been frozen on their faces, simultaneously realising that SS officers simply did not nod and smile at the occupied populace, not the ones that he'd heard about, anyway. Mistake number one, he admitted to himself, knowing that he simply could not afford to make mistakes if he wanted to live though the next few hours, let alone the coming days.

"Come on Wilhelm von Winkel, pull yourself together," he whispered under his breath as he decided that survival depended on adopting his new identity entirely. So, he thought, if the locals were expecting him to be a cruel, cold Nazi bastard, that is exactly what

260

he'd have to become. With that, he puffed out his chest, locked his face into a snarl and continued across the square.

Outside the town hall, a young Wehrmacht soldier stood sloppily at guard with his rifle hanging from his shoulder and a cigarette drooping from his lips. Upon seeing Bloodstone descending across the square, he slammed to attention, his back ramrod straight and his jaw clenched.

"Sieg Heil," he yelled as the SS officer neared, thrusting out his right arm in salute.

Bloodstone, the snarl still on his face, ignored the salute and crashed to a halt a foot from the youngster.

"Name?" he demanded harshly in German as he fixed the boy with a look that was enough to freeze the depths of hell.

The soldier stammered, his face a beetroot red.

Bloodstone leaned in closer until he was a matter of inches from the soldier's face. He reached up and plucked the cigarette from between trembling lips, tossed it to the ground and crushed it with his boot.

"I asked you a fucking question, Soldat," he growled as he stared into panicked eyes, "Are you going to answer me?"

"Um, eh, Bergmann, Obersturmbannfuhrer," he muttered quietly, his voice shaking.

"Louder!" Bloodstone bawled into the boy's face, forcing him to take a half-step back, before he recovered himself and crashed to attention once more.

"Jawohl, Obersturmbannfuhrer! Bergmann, Obersturmbannfuhrer!" yelled the terrified youngster as he stared with unblinking eyes over Bloodstone's left shoulder.

Bloodstone took a step back, still glaring at his shaking victim.

"If I ever see you smoking on guard duty again, Soldat Bergmann," he rasped, "I will rip off your balls with my bare hands and I will feed them to my dogs while you watch.

"Do you understand me?"

"Jawohl, Obersturmbannfuhrer!" the soldier repeated at a yell, his eyes still locked onto the distance and his jaw still trembling.

"Good," Bloodstone snapped, before he turned on his heel and strode off towards the railway station, leaving the petrified Bergmann in his wake and statue-still at attention.

It was good to give the Nazis a dose of their own medicine, he reasoned as he strolled the last few yards to the station and shamefully admitting to himself that he'd enjoyed dishing out Bergmann's rollicking. But more importantly, he knew, his little display of bullying would only have reinforced his identity to anybody passing by. He also knew that there was little love lost between the Wehrmacht and the SS, who often viewed each other with contempt and distrust, so he had no concerns about appearing to have stepped out of line.

Another Wehrmacht guard stood inside the entrance to the station building, this one without a cigarette, and offered Bloodstone a salute as he entered. He ignored it and headed towards a small ticket office window, in front of which was a queue of half a dozen civilians. Assuming that SS obersturmbannfuhrers didn't wait in queues, he barged to the front of the line, interrupting an elderly woman who was passing coins through the window, and growled in French at the uniformed official.

"Dijon," he demanded, "Which platform?"

"Platform two," the man replied nervously and once again Bloodstone saw that strange mix of loathing and terror spread across his face.

Without thanking the man and assuming that SS obersturmbannfuhrers didn't buy train tickets either, Bloodstone turned on his heel, stalked off across the small building and out onto the platform. The station was a small affair consisting of two short platforms linked by a footbridge, with the Dijon-bound train seemingly due to arrive on the opposite side of the tracks, so he crossed over and joined the handful of locals who were already waiting on the platform.

As he stood on the platform and waited for the train, a ragged poster pasted to the wall behind him caught his eye and he turned to take a closer look. The red and black ink was faded but the familiar image of Hitler, arm raised in a salute and standing before a swastika, was clear enough. He glared at the picture and, for the thousandth time in his life, wondered how it was possible that the same blood ran through their veins. The face, complete with its beady eyes and ridiculous moustache, was so malevolent yet so familiar. The similarity between the Fuhrer and his late mother was uncanny, yet where Cousin Adolf's face was cruel, Amelia Bloodstone's had been compassionate. Where his was hard and fierce, hers had been soft and beautiful. The anger rose as he stared at the poster and the rage reminded him why he was there, standing on a French platform waiting for a train to Paris and dressed in the uniform of his enemies, instead of taking the sensible, and far less risky, option of trying to get back to Blighty.

He was distracted from his brooding by the distant chug-chug-chug of a train in the distance and half a minute later an ancient steam engine towing a single carriage pulled into the station and squealed to a halt with a hiss of brakes and a burst of steam.

Bloodstone opened the rearmost door and climbed aboard. Conscious that he was unlikely to be the most popular man aboard and aware that the Resistance would love nothing more than to assassinate a lieutenant colonel of the SS, he selected a seat at the very back of the carriage that gave him a clear view of the entire compartment.

The carriage had been empty when the train pulled into Guibert-le-Doubs and the five passengers who boarded with Bloodstone all selected seats at the far end, no doubt keen to be as far away as possible from a hated Nazi.

He had already cast his soldiers' eye over the other passengers when he had been waiting on the platform and there was nobody in the group that had jumped out as a potential assassin. However, he knew that all sorts of innocuous looking characters were aligned to the Resistance, so he unbuckled his holster and slid the Luger under his right thigh. He would have much preferred to have his familiar Webley, but keeping it was too much of a risk, so he had left it with Cedric. It was the least he could give the Frenchman, he reasoned.

As the train let out a whistle and shunted into action, Bloodstone rested the back of his head against the seat and let out a deep breath, thinking once again about the bizarre chain of events that had brought him to this shabby French train, dressed in the uniform of his enemies and sitting atop a Luger.

No point thinking about the past, he mused as the train picked up speed, but better to be prepared for the future, whatever that was going to bring. With that thought in mind, he unbuttoned his tunic pocket and pulled out the Soldbuch, leafing through the pages and committing his imaginary history to memory.

As he tested himself on his newly created service record, his tongue brushed against something stuck firmly between two of his front teeth. It wouldn't budge so he tugged at it with his fingers until it finally came loose. Holding it up in front of him, he saw a thick black curly hair.

"Mein Gott," he said to himself as a realised with a shudder that it was one of Lillianna's pubic hairs. Just as he was beginning to forget it, the whole nightmarish previous evening came flooding back into his head.

"Mein Gott."

CHAPTER FORTY-SIX

The train rumbled on across the French countryside as hills and mountains gave way to rolling farmland and wooded copses. As Bloodstone watched the world roll by outside his window, it was almost easy to forget that there was a war on. In fact, if it wasn't for the occasional Wehrmacht soldier patrolling the rural stations that the train paused at, or for the shabby clothing of the few passengers that alighted each time, he could've imagined the country at peace.

But each time a new passenger did board the train, that peaceful illusion was shattered as soon as he saw their eyes upon him. The now familiar look of fear and hatred was all too clear to see and they continued to seat themselves in the far end of the carriage. It wasn't long before the forward half of the compartment was packed tight, while his half remained entirely empty.

The only person that acknowledged his presence was a uniformed train guard who passed through the carriage once to inspect tickets. Starting at the front and checking each passenger thoroughly, when he reached Bloodstone he chose not to request a ticket, instead offering a nod and a half smile before he turned on his heel and made his way back through the carriage.

The smile almost threw Bloodstone off-guard, but he maintained his cold face just in time and simply glared back at the Frenchman with a look bordering on disdain. His choice of facial expression wasn't entirely forced, he admitted as the guard disappeared from view, recognising that he was probably one of the numerous traitorous locals who were more than happy to work for their conquerors.

Just as the train passed what seemed like the hundredth farm of the journey and with his imaginary military service committed firmly to memory, Bloodstone was pleased to see the guard return to the carriage to shout, "Dijon, five minutes."

He slid the Luger back into its holster but chose to leave the leather pouch open in case of emergency and prepared himself for the next stage of his journey. He was in no doubt that he had been fortunate so far with nobody requesting his documents or engaging him in conversation, but he knew that wasn't likely to last long. Even the SS runes on his collar and the Knight's Cross at his throat wouldn't protect him forever, especially now he was firmly away from rural France and heading into a bustling and, no doubt, well-guarded city.

"Deutscher, Deutscher, Deutscher," he said in his head as he reminded himself that survival would depend on not only speaking in German but thinking and acting like a German too.

The speaking part of that shouldn't be a problem, he mused, knowing that his German was spotless thanks to the youthful pilgrimages to his mother's Austrian homeland, but the other elements would be trickier. Europe had changed dramatically over the past decade and with it so had its people, none more so than those who had lived under Hitler's twisted yoke.

That thought reminded him of something the monstrous General Wilkins has said to him just a week ago, although it seemed to Bloodstone to be a lifetime ago, "You evolve or you die."

The maimed man's words couldn't be truer, he admitted as the train slowed. If he wanted to survive this foolhardy escapade into enemy territory he was going to have to evolve. And stay evolving. So, forcing his newly acquired sneer back onto his face, he stood up, hefted his briefcase and stepped off the train.

The scene at Dijon couldn't have been any more different to the rural station he'd left at Guibert-le-Doubs. There seemed to be a dozen platforms, each packed with the flotsam and jetsam of war as groups of servicemen milled around, intermingled with nurses, labourers and civilians of all shapes and sizes. Steam and smoke lay thick in the chilly autumn air and the sounds of man and machine created a cacophony of noise familiar to any wartime city station across Europe. On the tracks sat everything from passenger trains to goods vehicles and in one case, a long series of flat beds loaded with Tiger tanks.

Bloodstone pushed his way through the crowds, elbowed a drunken sailor out of the way and headed for the sign marked *Sortie*. As he neared the end of his platform, he noticed a group of people, all civilians, waiting patiently in line. At the head of the queue were two greatcoat-clad Wehrmacht infantrymen, weapons slung across their shoulders as they inspected documents.

"Here goes," he said to himself and strolled purposefully to the front of the queue and pushed in front of a young woman who sported a faded red coat with several patches around the hem.

The woman tutted as Bloodstone stepped in front and he turned like a firecracker, staring at her with a face like thunder.

"Be careful," he snarled in French and noticed that not only was she was undeniably beautiful, but there was no fear on this face, just pure and unbridled hatred.

He wanted to tell her the truth, to explain that this was all a guise, but he knew that was madness, so, not wanting to make an unnecessary scene, he turned back to the two soldiers. The look on the face of the sergeant that held out his hand for Bloodstone's papers was equally appalled, no doubt disgusted with his attitude towards the red-coated girl. After all, good-looking women were good-looking women, whichever side of the conflict they happened to be on.

Bloodstone handed him his Soldbuch and waited as the man flicked onto the first page to look at his photograph. He looked back up at Bloodstone, his eyes quizzical, and then back at the small book in his hands. Bloodstone found himself blushing, feeling like a little boy who's been caught with his hand in the biscuit tin, and resisted the temptation to finger the handle of his Luger, which remained unbuttoned in the holster on his belt.

Another glance up and then back at the paper from the sergeant and Bloodstone realised that the Luger wouldn't do him much good anyway if he was rumbled. He could easily dispatch the two soldiers in front of him with a bullet each, but his chances of fleeing through a station filled with enemy soldiers, especially considering his not inconspicuous state of dress, would be challenging to say the least.

Nevertheless, he dared a quick glance over the sergeant's shoulder and out into the station concourse beyond. It too was packed with people and he was unable to see where the station's exits were located. He'd just have to chance it, he realised with a feeling of dread.

The sergeant's eyes came up again, flickering across Bloodstone's face. He shifted his briefcase into his left hand, his right edging slowly, ever so slowly, toward the Luger at his hip.

The soldier looked down again. This is it, Bloodstone said to himself, his fingers now a hair's breadth from the pistol and his body tensed, ready to leap into action. First the sergeant, he decided, bullet through the head. Then his comrade, the same way. Then off into the concourse for God knows whatever was next.

One final time the sergeant looked back up, casting his eyes across the SS runes and Knight's Cross. Bloodstone now had his hand on the handle of the Luger, feeling the cold metal as he began to slide the weapon gently up and out of the holster, millimetre by agonising millimetre.

"Danke, Obersturmbannfuhrer," the sergeant said, holding the small book out in front of him, "Proceed."

Bloodstone felt the tension drain out of him like a torrent and he somehow stifled a huge exhalation of breath. The Luger fell back into the holster unnoticed, he snatched the small book from the sergeant and pushed his way between the two soldiers, his face still masked with a snarl despite his red cheeks.

As he stormed away from the platform, the last few minutes reverberated around inside his head. He had been seconds away from blowing his cover, he realised, and likely only a few more seconds from ending up as a bullet-ridden corpse or, probably just as bad, captured. He had always lived by the mantra of act first, think later but he knew that was going to have to change if he was to see this thing through.

So, sucking in a deep breath of air, he composed himself and wandered into the station concourse. At the far end was a row of windows, each manned by a railway officer in a blue uniform, with a series of queues waiting at each one. With no obvious signage revealing the time of the next train to Paris, Bloodstone continued his newly discovered trend of queue-jumping and pushed his way to the window on the furthest left.

"Train to Paris," he demanded in French of the man behind the window, "When?"

"Non, Monsieur," the man replied, shrugging his shoulders unhelpfully.

"Oui" Bloodstone snapped as he fixed the man with a cruel glare and slammed his hand on the counter, "I asked you when the next train is. Well?"

The man blubbed something incomprehensible and Bloodstone saw that familiar look of fearful hatred spread across his face. He felt sorry for him, again wanting to explain that it was all just an act, but he knew he had to keep up the pretence.

As he smacked his hand on the counter once again, a voice interrupted from his right. A German voice.

"There are no trains to Paris," it said with a strange accent, "Fucking Resistance have blown up the tracks again."

Bloodstone turned and was met with a uniformed man who was smiling manically in his direction. In his early twenties and wrapped in a greatcoat, he sported an angular jaw, a snub nose and eyes so bizarrely red that they appeared to be swimming in blood. His hair was nearly the colour of fresh snow and on his head was an officer's peaked cap.

"I beg your pardon?" he asked, looking the man up and down and noticing instantly that the white-haired figure's cap bore the very same skull, eagle and swastika as his own. Waffen SS.

The man smiled that strange smile again, something between insanity and hilarity.

"Those Franzmänner fools have been at it again," he answered, "The line's down from Avallon to Auxerre; there'll be no more trains to Paris today, Obersturmbannfuhrer."

"Scheisser," Bloodstone swore, stepping away from the window and leaving the queue.

The man moved with him. "Are you trying to get to Paris?" he asked.

Bloodstone eyed him up and down again. There was something he didn't like about the man, something he couldn't quite place, and it wasn't just the fact that he was wearing the uniform of the SS. There was something about the strange grin that split his pale face from ear to ear that made Bloodstone distinctly uneasy.

"Apologies," the man said, noticing Bloodstone's less than friendly look, "Allow me to introduce myself.

"Sturmbannfuhrer Sven Helgeland," he continued, "Nordland Division."

"Obersturmbannfuhrer von Winkel," Bloodstone replied and inwardly squirmed as he shook the major's offered hand, "Liebstandarte SS Adolf Hitler."

"You're Norwegian?" he continued, finally placing the man's strange accent.

"Ja," Helgeland answered, "Joined Den Norske Legion back in '41. Someone's got to help you boys get rid of all those filthy Juden, eh Obersturmbannfuhrer?"

Again, that crazed smile.

Bloodstone forced a smile of his own, although he'd rather have garroted the man there and then. He knew of the Nordland Division, which was formed of Norwegians who had turned their backs on their own country when the Nazis invaded in 1941, and there was nothing he hated more than a traitor, especially a fascist Jew-hating traitor.

However, he knew that he couldn't allow his feelings to get in the way of the job at hand, especially as the SS major seemed willing to help him, so he softened his snarl ever so slightly.

"In answer to your question," he said, "Yes, I'm trying to get to Paris. I have important business to attend to."

"As do I," Helgeland replied, "So I have already sent for a car. It will arrive imminently. It would be an honour if you would join me, Obersturmbannfuhrer."

Bloodstone tried to smell a trap but failed. He had to assume that the man was simply keen to cosy up to a senior officer, especially one as highly decorated as von Winkel. From his own point of view, the thought of a comfortable car was certainly much more appealing, and probably a lot safer, than another jolting train journey, even if it was in the company of what was quite obviously a despicable human.

"I'll join you," he announced haughtily, following up quickly with, "Danke."

"Excellent, please come with me," Helgeland said as he pushed his way across the busy station and barged over an elderly lady in the process.

Bloodstone almost stopped to help her up before he realised who he was, so simply stepped over the poor creature and continued in the man's wake, forcing his face to stay frozen in its cruel sneer.

They reached the station exit and Helgeland paused at the empty taxi rank. Empty, Bloodstone, assumed, because of the rationing that resulted in virtually all fuel going into the tanks of the occupying Germans.

"Do you have baggage?" the Norwegian asked as he glanced curiously at Bloodstone's briefcase.

"No baggage," he replied, not feeling creative enough to manufacture a fictional tale, "It's a long story."

Helgeland didn't reply but simply smiled his crazed smile.

"My driver will be here in a second," he said, changing the subject, before he glanced admiringly at the medal at Bloodstone's throat.

"Von Winkel, did you say? Yes, Obersturmbannfuhrer, I am sure I've read of your heroism. You are a famous soldier, ja?"

Bloodstone was saved from replying by a black Mercedes-Benz saloon that screeched to a halt in front of them. The driver, a Scharfuhrer, the SS equivalent of a sergeant, leapt out and opened the rear door, simultaneously offering a punctilious salute with his right hand. He nodded in response, climbed into the car and settled his still-sore backside into the soft leather seat.

As he watched the red-eyed Helgeland take off his greatcoat and hand it to the driver, he mulled over the Norwegian's last comment. It seemed that the man was not only an SS officer, a traitor, a Jew-hater and a wannabe Aryan, but he was also a liar too. And a kiss-arse. Six things that Bloodstone despised immensely.

Yet Otto Heidler was in Paris. So, he mused as he tapped the Luger at his waist, he would have to endure just a few hours of this horrid man's company. Because Albert Bloodstone was going to Paris too. And Albert Bloodstone had some killing to do.

CHAPTER FORTY-SEVEN

The Mercedes sped its way through the Dijon streets and left the station in its wake as it headed out towards the suburbs. The driver, his SS runes glinting on his collar, obviously knew his stuff and took the city roads at breakneck speed, zigzagging in and out of what were barely more than alleyways and swerving past the few vehicles that occupied the streets.

As they headed north-west towards Paris, Helgeland chattered incessantly. By the time they'd reached the edge of the city, Bloodstone already knew that he had a sister called Maude and a brother called Alf, both of whom were apparently heavily involved with the Quisling administration. Having fought in the frozen snows of Scandinavia only a few years before, Bloodstone was well aware of the traitorous Quislings and the misery they were inflicting upon the staunchly anti-Nazi populace. One more reason to dislike the major seated to his right, he decided, but better to let the man rabbit on instead of getting involved in any potentially awkward conversations.

So he let Helgeland talk and, by the time that they'd passed through their first checkpoint a mile outside the city, Bloodstone had discovered that the Norwegian's favourite colour was black, he owned a poodle called Adolf and that he'd spent last night in the bed of an eighteen-year-old French girl called Audrey.

Sounds a lot more enjoyable than my night, Bloodstone thought as he closed his eyes and tilted the peak of his cap down over his eyes. Another mile further along the road and, with Helgeland still wittering in his ear, he drifted off into a dreamless and blissful sleep.

BANG! BANG! BANG! BANG again. Bloodstone lurched into consciousness, immediately wide awake and his hand at the pistol on his hip. He jerked his head towards the sound to his right and, as he did so, the stink of cordite hit his nostrils.

He blinked his eyes to wipe away the last vestiges of sleep and was confused to see the arse of Helgeland at eye level, with the top half of his body protruding out of the car window and one knee planted firmly on the seat.

"What the hell?" he shouted at the Norwegian's backside, realising at the same moment that the car was still moving.

"Cows!" came the excited response from the major, albeit barely comprehensible from outside the window of the speeding vehicle.

"Cows!" he yelled again, like some sort of giddy schoolboy, "Filthy French cows!"

"What?" Bloodstone asked, confused, leaning across the car and squeezing his head alongside Helgeland's rear end and out into the cold wind that howled past the vehicle.

As he did so, a burst of automatic gunfire crashed out, nearly deafening him, and he twisted his head upwards to see that his companion was brandishing an MP40 submachine gun, with the crazed grin plastered across his face once more.

Before he could say anything else, he watched as the head of a passing cow exploded in a fountain of blood and brain and, seconds later, a triumphant screech emerged from the throat of the Norwegian.

"Got one!"

"What the hell are you doing you damned idiot?" Bloodstone roared, his voice lost into the passing wind.

Before he could speak again, he heard a squeal of delight and the machine gun blasted off yet more rounds. He watched in horror as a small boy dived to the ground while the earth around him erupted as the bullets thudded into the mud.

"Enough!" bellowed the flabbergasted Bloodstone, yanking on the Sturmbannfuhrer's belt and tugging him back into the car, "What in God's name do you think you're doing?"

"Denying enemy soldiers of vital supplies, Obersturmbannfuhrer," he answered with a grin as he cleared the breech of his MP40, his face flushed and the red eyes sparkling.

"There are no enemy soldiers, you bloody fool," Bloodstone chastised, shocked, "There haven't been any since they all capitulated three years ago."

Helgeland laugher manically and Bloodstone wondered if he was sharing a car with an unhinged lunatic. He'd heard all the rumours of the questionable antics of the SS but shooting at passing small children was something else entirely.

It would be all too easy to put a bullet into Helgeland's skull and then deal with the driver, he thought, but what odds did a rogue SS Obersturmbannfuhrer stand in the middle of the French countryside, no idea where he was and with a car full of blood and brains? Not good odds at all, he admitted as he glanced at the man next to him who was now fingering the trigger of his weapon and staring straight ahead like a madman, the grin still there and the eyes still sparkling.

Much more sensible to get to Paris first and then deal this creature his comeuppance in his own time, he decided.

"I'm going to sleep," he announced, "Wake me when we reach Paris."

"And no more shooting," he added wearily, "That's an order."

CHAPTER FORTY-EIGHT

An hour later Bloodstone awoke, this time from a bump in the road and not the result of a gun-toting imbecile. He looked to his right and expected to be instantly bombarded with more inane drivel, but his traveling companion was fast asleep, his mouth wide open and the machine gun cradled in his arms like some sort of teddy bear.

"Thank the Lord," he muttered under his breath and reached into his pocket for a cigarette. He'd sensibly left his gold case, complete with its Woodbines, with Cedric so had to be content with a French Gauloises, which, he decided as he sucked in a lungful of smoke, tasted like manure.

With Helgeland asleep, he started to think about the next steps of his journey. What was he going to do when he got to Paris? How was he going to find Heidler? Unless he had a lead, and he had absolutely none, how was he going to find the man? Killing him would be tricky enough, he knew, but locating him in the first place was a whole different level entirely.

He considered trying to make contact with the Resistance, but where to start? It wasn't as if they'd be walking around with a Free French sign hanging around their neck and asking too many questions was only going to land him in trouble. He'd heard that Paris was filled with just as many collaborators as it was allies, so he couldn't risk trying that route unless things got really desperate.

Miserably, he realised that his best lead was sitting next to him, snoring gently. The Norwegian was obviously keen to please his newfound comrade and, as much as Bloodstone racked his brains, he couldn't see their meeting in Dijon as anything more than a coincidence. Of course, he accepted, it could be a trap, but it just seemed so very unlikely. It was just a risk that he would have to take. Anyway, it wasn't as if the last few days had been particularly short of risk-taking on his behalf, he mused, and he'd come through those reasonably intact.

So that was it, he decided. He'd stick with the noxious major for as long as he was useful and would suck as much intel as possible out of him, hopefully finding some sort of path to Heidler in the process. And when he'd exhausted his usefulness, he'd kill the man. Not just because Helgeland clearly deserved it but because he knew that anything he could do to disrupt the German war effort could bring the whole ghastly conflict one day closer to a conclusion.

As he glanced at his sleeping companion once again, he knew that he'd have to change his approach to the man. Helgeland had been more than friendly so far, despite Bloodstone's coldness, but even crazed Nazis had their limits. The last thing he wanted to do was drive the man away, which would leave him helplessly bereft of contacts and back at stage one. So, he decided on a change of tack, the thought of which made him feel almost sick.

"Sturmbannfuhrer," he said quietly, giving the man a gentle shake of the leg, "Sturmbannfuhrer."

Helgeland stirred, one eye opening and then the other, "Eh?"

"We're close to Paris," Bloodstone said, pointing out of the window.

Sure enough, the fields and trees of the past few hours had given way to the Parisian outskirts. Row upon row of buildings sped past the window, grey and murky in the early evening darkness, and the pavements thronged with people shuffling about their business.

"Ah, gay Paris," Helgeland sighed as he lay the MP40 on the seat next to him, "How I've missed you, you beautiful little bitch."

"Long since you've been here?" Bloodstone asked, forcing himself to make conversation.

"Too long, sir, too long," he replied with a wistful look in his red eyes, which quickly changed to something more malevolent as he continued.

"I've been in the damned Ostfront for most of the year, slaughtering those damned Bolsheviks. Bloody horrible place and, my God, the people, just like pigs."

"Tell me about it," Bloodstone agreed as he remembered that von Winkel had also recently served on the Eastern Front.

Without prompting, Helgeland continued, his eyes still glittering.

"But have you seen the camps, sir?" he asked as he turned to look at Bloodstone with his maniac smile.

"I haven't had the pleasure," he replied, feeling distinctly uneasy.

Like most British servicemen, Bloodstone had heard rumours of how the Nazis treated those who they considered unfit for their perfect Reich, shipping them to the East to work in labour camps, but war was full of rumours and, from his experience, most turned out to be nonsense.

"Oh you should see them," the Norwegian continued, the wistful look back in his eyes, "A thing of beauty."

"Really?"

"Oh yes. There aren't enough bullets on all of God's earth to kill them all, so they gas them. You should hear them scream. Then they burn the bodies and the ashes fall like snow. Oh, Obersturmbannfuhrer, it's beautiful."

Bloodstone felt sick and he turned away as the bile rose in his throat. His fingers caressed the grip of the Luger, but he swallowed and forced himself to stay calm, resisting the temptation to blow the brains out of the evil monster sitting beside him. Soon, he promised himself, as he took a deep breath and composed his senses.

"Where are you staying?" Helgeland asked, mercifully changing the subject.

Bloodstone thought quickly, remembering his last visit to the French capital almost a decade ago. This time, however, he had a briefcase stuffed with cash; it would be a shame not to use it.

"The Ritz," he announced and noticed a flash of admiration on the face of his companion, "Although this was something of a last-minute visit, so I have nothing booked yet."

"I'm sure they'll have rooms for someone as legendary as Obersturmbannfuhrer von Winkel."

"Exactly," replied Bloodstone as Helgeland leant forward and tapped the driver on the shoulder.

"The Ritz," he ordered and the Mercedes immediately swerved to the left, careered in front of an oncoming bus and took a side street.

Within minutes they were passing the Eiffel Tower and, as Bloodstone looked up, he recalled his very first visit to the city as a ten-year-old. He and little Algy Jones had thought it hilarious to lob ten-centime pieces from the uppermost viewing gallery of the enormous structure, he remembered, smiling at the innocent game that had no doubt caused a few sore heads down below. He also remembered the thick ear that his father had given them both.

"You blasted nincompoops," the General had scolded as he whacked at the giggling boys, before he fished a crumpled bag of ballseyes out of his pocket and offered them each a sweet, "Damned nitwits."

The tower vanished into the distance as the car veered to the right and crossed a bridge before it continued parallel with the dark waters of the Seine. A few minutes later it slowed to a halt and pulled up alongside the grandiose frontage of the Ritz.

"The Ritz, sir," the driver announced needlessly as he leapt from his seat and opened Bloodstone's door.

Helgeland looked across at Bloodstone and offered his hand.

"Obersturmbannfuhrer, it has been an honour to travel with you," he said in his heavily accented German, "I wish you well with your business in Paris."

"Thank you, Sturmbannfuhrer, likewise," he replied as he shook the man's hand.

Then, looking into the red eyes and trying not to choke on the words, he added, "It would be an honour if you would join me for dinner, Helgeland."

The Norwegian's face lit up, just like a child at Christmas.

"I would be delighted, thank you," he beamed, "And I know a perfect place. Pick you up at eight?"

"Eight o'clock," Bloodstone agreed, grasped his briefcase and climbed out of the car, glad to finally be away from the major.

As he made his way up the steps to the hotel's entrance, the Mercedes door slammed shut and the car revved into life and roared away, leaving in its wake the high-pitched yell of a Norwegian accent.

"Heil Hitler!"

CHAPTER FORTY-NINE

Bloodstone watched the steam rise from between his toes and lay back with a satisfying groan. Hot baths back in England seemed to be a rare commodity these days, but it appeared that Paris had no such problems.

In fact, he had been somewhat surprised with his Ritz experience so far. The moustached French receptionist, after a glance at the medal at Bloodstone's throat, had only been too welcoming. There was none of the hatred or fear that he had seen on other faces during the day. Instead, the man couldn't do enough and promised to give the Obersturmbannfuhrer the very best room available. He appeared pleasantly surprised when Bloodstone paid for his five-night stay in advance with fresh Reichsmarks and even offered a more than generous exchange rate as Bloodstone changed some of his currency for Francs.

He enquired whether the Obersturmbannfuhrer would require anything sent to his room? A bottle of Moët? A fine steak? Or some company perhaps? Did the Obersturmbannfuhrer know that Reichmarschall Göring had vacated the hotel's Imperial Suite only this morning?

Bloodstone found the Frenchman a little too proud of the hotel's celebrity guest for his liking but was pleased to discover that his stay wouldn't clash with that of Hitler's second-in-command. There were a decent number of recipients of the Knight's Cross, but it was likely that Göring would have a fair idea of some of them, particularly an SS lieutenant colonel. Certainly someone to avoid, Bloodstone thought, if he wanted to keep his disguise intact.

His bath complete, he lathered up his face and shaved with a complimentary Ritz razorblade, feeling a pang of regret as he scraped away at the now moustachless top lip. Next, he pulled on clean underpants but left his one and only fresh pair of socks for the following day. On went the uniform and boots, followed by the leather belt with its holster and pistol and then the Knight's Cross ribbon was tied around his neck. He momentarily searched the nightstand for a tin of hair pomade before a glance in the mirror reminded him that his newly shorn scalp required no such frivolity. Instead, he completed his routine with a splash of aftershave from a miniature bottle of Chanel, the creator of which, according to the receptionist, was apparently resident somewhere in the hotel.

A glance at the Rolex on his wrist told him that it was two minutes to eight, so he placed his cap firmly on his head, took one last look in the mirror and left his room. The same black Mercedes was already waiting at the hotel entrance and, upon Bloodstone's arrival, the driver leapt from the vehicle, offered a salute and opened the rear door.

Bloodstone climbed in to be met with a wall of perfume. As his eyes adjusted to the dim interior, he saw there were three people sitting in the back of the car, two of whom were young women in ballgowns.

"Obersturmbannführer," Helgeland greeted joyfully, "It's a pleasure to see you again."

"Likewise," Bloodstone lied as he squeezed himself onto the rear seat alongside one of the women.

"I hope you don't mind," the Norwegian announced, "But I thought I would provide us with some company for the evening."

Looking around the car, Bloodstone didn't mind one bit. The ladies certainly looked like good company, both in their early twenties, stunningly pretty and no doubt much less painful than a whole evening alone with Helgeland.

"Allow me to introduce Paris' finest Mademoiselle Sophie and Mademoiselle Claudette," the major said, indicating each of the women in turn.

"I know this one may look like a jewess," he laughed as he leant across to slap the lady sitting next to Bloodstone playfully on the leg, "But I can confirm that she most certainly is not."

The woman, Sophie, giggled and as she did so her enormous bust threatened to burst free from her low-cut dress. Bloodstone tore his eyes away her studied her face, noticing plump red lips, deep brown eyes and chestnut hair that rested on her bare shoulders. She certainly hadn't been affected by the rationing, he thought as he admired her buxom figure and tried desperately to avoid the sight of her jiggling bosoms.

Her companion was almost her complete opposite, with one exception. Tall, blonde and with a trim waist, she had a thin yet perfectly symmetrical face with misty blue eyes and high cheekbones. Her hair was wound tight above her head and her fingernails were painted grey to match her gown, the front of which was even lower cut than Sophie's. And just like the girl sat opposite her, Claudette appeared to be about to spill out of her attire, her bust equally enormous and equally alluring. For all his grotesque faults, Bloodstone admitted, Helgeland certainly had an eye for a good-looking female.

"It's a pleasure to meet you both," he announced in French, recovering his composure and offering one of his best smiles, "Wilhelm von Winkel."

"No need for French, sir," Helgeland corrected, "Both of these lovely ladies are lucky enough to have mastered the Fuhrer's tongue."

"Excellent," Bloodstone said, returning to German, "So, what's the plan for this evening?"

"I know a wonderful little place in Pigalle," the Norwegian replied, the grin returning to his face, "An establishment with the finest entertainment in all of the Reich."

The girls giggled in unison and Bloodstone saw a mischievous glint in the eye of Sophie as the Mercedes roared into life and set off. He forced himself to stare out of the window to avoid the four bouncing bosoms and realised that it would have been almost impossible not to look forward to the evening ahead were it not for the presence of the nauseating Helgeland.

After several minutes of high-speed careering through the blacked-out roads of Paris, the saloon reached a street that Bloodstone recognised from his teenage jaunts as the Boulevard de Clichy. He was surprised to see that very little had changed since those pre-war years and, despite the blackout, the garish lights of the various restaurants, bars and cabarets still flashed and flickered. Brightest of all was the unmistakable red windmill of the Moulin Rouge and, as the Mercedes sped past, he saw by the crowd of uniformed men at its entrance that it was very much still open for business.

Four hundred yards further on, the car skidded to a halt alongside a row of innocuous looking houses and Helgeland clapped his hands excitedly.

"My friends, we have arrived."

The door opened and Bloodstone waited for the other three passengers to exit before clambering out himself. In contrast to the bright lights of just a quarter of a mile along the road, this area of the street was in almost total darkness and Bloodstone looked around him.

"Here?" he asked, surprised.

"Ja," Helgeland replied, his red eyes shining with excitement, "Follow me, Obersturmbannfuhrer."

The Norwegian linked his arm through that of the blonde Claudette and strolled to the front door of what looked like a regular Parisian townhouse. He rapped three times with the heavy brass door knocker and stepped back. Sure enough, several seconds later, the thick door swung inwards and Bloodstone could just about make out the figure of a small beret-clad man, standing in the dark interior of the building.

The man bowed slightly and ushered them inside. Helgeland and Claudette went first, followed by Sophie and finally Bloodstone, who found himself following his companions along a featureless and gloomy hallway. At the end of the corridor was another door, which Helgeland pushed open to unveil a surprisingly large room, the size of a small theatre, from which a cacophony of noise and a flash of dazzling light emerged.

As the four of them entered the room and closed the door behind them, Bloodstone blinked twice to check that he was indeed seeing what he thought he was seeing. He glanced around, mouth wide open, his eyes adjusting to the light.

The first thing his brain made sense of was a small stage, on top of which perched a four-piece swing band, led by a blonde-haired trumpeter who seemed to have lost every stitch of clothing above her waist. The three other members of the band, all middle-aged Africans wearing top hats and bow ties, seemed oblivious to the topless woman that cavorted across the stage as she blasted away at the instrument clamped to her lips.

Still trying to make sense of his surroundings, Bloodstone next spotted four Wehrmacht officers seated around a table with knives and forks in hand and glasses of wine at their elbows. Laying elegantly across the table with her back arched and her head resting on her hands, almost as if she was soaking up the sun on a distant beach, was a dark-haired girl. Naked. Entirely naked, except for two half-strawberries that perched precariously upon each nipple and a fine selection of cold meats that were laid elegantly across her stomach. As Bloodstone looked closer, he noticed that her thighs were covered with slices of cheese, while an entire Camembert was balanced atop her nether regions.

A dozen other tables were spread throughout the room, none of them draped with nudes but all except one were occupied by groups

285

of men in military uniform along with a scattering of female guests. Very few of the guests seemed sober but none appeared to be as intoxicated as a Luftwaffe officer that Bloodstone spotted in the far corner of the room, on his knees and vomiting into a silver champagne cooler.

Within seconds of entering the room, Helgeland was approached by a yellow-suited dwarf, who bowed extravagantly in front of the Norwegian.

"Hauptsturmfuhrer," the little man smiled as a spoke with a French accent, "It has been too long."

"Sturmbannfuhrer now," Helgeland replied, tapping his collar and fixing the man with his red eyes.

"Ah yes, my apologies," the man responded uncomfortably, "Congratulations on the promotion, sir."

Helgeland nodded, seemingly satisfied, and followed the man to the last empty table in the establishment. Another dwarf, identically attired in a yellow suit, appeared from nowhere and joined his colleague as the pair seated Sophie and Claudette at opposite sides of the round table. Helgeland waited for Bloodstone to select a place and then also sat down, waving the dwarves away.

"I hate midgets," he declared abruptly, taking Bloodstone by surprise, who forced himself to smile.

"So, this is quite a place," Bloodstone commented, changing the subject as he looked around the room.

"Isn't it just," Helgeland grinned, his hatred of little people seemingly forgotten, "They call it Le Petite Escargot, although God knows why."

His eyes fixed on the topless trumpeter for a few seconds before he continued.

"It's something of a secret haunt. One must be a certain someone in the service to get a table. Not a damned Franzmänner in sight, thank God."

He clicked his fingers to summon yet another yellow-coated attendant before he turned to Claudette with a grin, "Present company excepted, of course."

The girl smiled back and, as Helgeland ordered schnapps and a bottle of champagne, Bloodstone watched the vomiting Luftwaffe office clamber to his feet, wipe his mouth with a sleeve and stagger to a nearby table, where he plonked himself down among a gaggle of equally inebriated flyers. As he did so, something at the airmen's table caught Bloodstone's attention and, once again, he peered closer to check that his eyes weren't deceiving him. Sure enough, perched on the back of a chair and kitted out in full Luftwaffe uniform was a tiny monkey, complete with a miniature officers' cap on its head and an oversized nut in its hand.

Bloodstone shook his head in bewilderment and averted his attention to the menu in his hand. He whistled under his breath as he surveyed the copious options, the choice of which he hadn't seen on a menu since before the outbreak of war. The French chef at his favourite London hotel had always been able to conjure up a feast that made a mockery of the ration book and dear old Barnaby was never short of an extra egg or two, but this was something else entirely.

He gave the waiter his order and leant back in his chair, eyeing his surroundings once more. If it wasn't for the array of Nazi uniforms that filled the room, he thought, one could be forgiven for almost forgetting that there was a war on. Almost.

He was distracted from his musings by the arrival of a waiter, complete with overloaded silver tray balanced precariously in his tiny hands. When the man had successfully deposited an unopened bottle of schnapps on the table and filled four glasses with champagne, he departed, leaving Helgeland to scrape back his chair and push himself to his feet.

"Obersturmbannfuhrer. Ladies. If you'll allow me the honour?"

The Norwegian didn't wait for a response from his guests but raised a glass to the air and, with a smirk of pride on his face, announced, "The Führer."

The girls raised their glasses too.

"The Führer," they announced in unison, before the dark-haired Sophie added, "May he live for a thousand years."

Bloodstone forced his face to mask the disgust that he felt coursing through his veins and, through clenched teeth, he mirrored the toast.

"The Führer," he forced, sipping the champagne and feeling sick inside.

As Helgeland lowered himself back into his chair he squeezed Sophie's arm.

"That's my girl," he grinned, looking at her proudly before he turned to Bloodstone.

"She may be French," he continued, nodding in the direction of the woman seated beside him, "But she speaks sense."

"She does?" Bloodstone asked, appearing vaguely interested but feeling entirely the opposite.

"Absolutely, my dear von Winkel," the SS major replied, the strange grin back on his face, "Rumour has it that the scientists have found a way to give him eternal life. For the great man to live forever."

"Can you imagine what that would be like?" he continued as the grin widened manically.

Bloodstone, who could well imagine what it would be like, cocked his head and looked questioningly at the creature sat opposite him, wondering if the man truly was insane.

He was saved from continuing the conversation by the arrival of their starters and it wasn't long before he was hungrily devouring a steak tartare, the like of which he hadn't enjoyed for years. As he finished the last sliver and washed it down with a mouthful of champagne, Helgeland piped up again.

"So, Obersturmbannführer," he asked, unconsciously spitting a globule of half-chewed mushroom onto the tablecloth, "Excuse my directness, but I didn't ask you what brings you to Paris. You said you had important business here?"

"I did, Sturmbannfuhrer," Bloodstone replied, forcing himself to smile as he tapped his nose, "Very important business indeed."

The Norwegian seemed to understand, nodding conspiratorially and, as he reached for his champagne, Bloodstone decided to take a risk.

"But first I want to catch up with an old comrade."

He paused.

"You may know him."

"Me?" Helgcland's face lit up at the prospect of finally being of some use to the moody but heavily decorated Obersturmbannfuhrer.

"What's the name?" the Norwegian asked, unable to keep the boyish excitement from his eyes.

"Heidler. Standartenführer Otto Heidler."

Helgeland cocked an eyebrow, thinking.

"Heidler?" he asked.

"Ja, Heidler," Bloodstone repeated, studying the man's face.

The red eyes looked at him quizzically as the excitement slowly disappeared, replaced instead by what appeared to be a vacant look.

"Never heard of him," the Norwegian replied disappointedly, "Where do you know him from, if I may ask?"

"Oh, we go a long way back," Bloodstone replied dismissively as he drained his champagne, "But not to worry, I'll keep looking."

CHAPTER FIFTY

For the next hour the conversation meandered backwards and forwards, mainly instigated by the increasingly inebriated Helgeland with the occasional offering from the pair of Frenchwomen who sat at either side of the table.

As he devoured a juicy steak, Bloodstone felt the effects of the champagne begin to tingle away inside his head and he had to constantly remind himself not to rise to the incessant stream of vitriolic nonsense that spewed forth from the Norwegian's mouth.

He nodded as the man fawned over Hitler, agreed as his dinner companion damned Churchill, Roosevelt and Stalin for their Jew-loving idiocy and smiled as he castigated his fellow Norwegians for their failure to accept the one true leader.

With the main course finished and a fourth bottle of champagne uncorked, Helgeland finally drew breath and leaned back in his chair.

"Sir, do you partake?" he asked, smiling.

"Partake? Partake in what?" Bloodstone queried as he wondered what madness the man was going to propose now.

"You know, Pervitin," he answered, reaching inside his tunic for a small metal tin, "The nectar of the Valkyries."

Sophie and Claudette giggled in unison as Helgeland set the tin on the tablecloth and opened the lid to reveal a number of white tablets, each the size of a man's fingernail.

"Ah, of course, Pervitin," Bloodstone repeated, recalling the German equivalent of the wakey-wakey pills that he'd gorged on aboard the Lancaster just a few days before.

He knew that the Wehrmacht issued the ephedrine tablets to men in the front line in an attempt to keep the brain focused and operating beyond its usual limits of tiredness, but he'd never heard of them being taken socially, which was what it appeared that the SS major was about to do.

"I had a sergeant who used to inject them," Helgeland explained as he crushed one of the pills underneath a spoon, "Stupid man charged a Russki machine gun post in broad daylight. Got his brains spread halfway across the Ukraine. Ha, good times!"

He laughed as he recalled the memory, the now familiarly manic look plastered across his face, and, seemingly satisfied with the small pile of white powder that he'd created, turned to Claudette.

"May I?"

"It would be my pleasure" the blonde replied as she leaned backwards in her chair, her bust taking the form of two great mountains half encased in grey silk.

With seemingly practised ease, Helgeland spread the white powder in a neat line across one of the hillocks, lowered his head and snorted.

"Woooo!" he exclaimed as he raised his head, his eyes unnaturally wide, and rubbed a smattering of rogue powder from underneath a nostril, "Das ist good, ja?"

"Ja," tittered the brunette Sophie from the other end of the table as her own mountainous mammeries jiggling with excitement, "May I?"

Without replying, Helgeland arranged another line of powder across Claudette's pale skin and beckoned the other woman towards him. Sophie pushed herself from her chair, glided around the table and lowered her head into her companion's cleavage.

"Mein Gott," Bloodstone muttered under his breath as he soaked in the glorious sight, his imagination going into overdrive.

Satisfied, Sophie straightened up and turned towards him with her cheeks and neck flushed red.

"Your turn, Obersturmbannfuhrer?" she asked with a cheeky grin.

Despite the champagne flowing in his blood and the copious amounts of flesh on view, Bloodstone forced himself to refrain. In normal circumstances he'd be more than happy to snort questionable substances from the bosoms of a pretty young Frenchwoman, but, he reasoned, these were far from normal circumstances. If he wanted to remain hidden in plain view, he knew that he had to retain at least some semblance of self-control among the chaos that was Le Petit Escargot and, he admitted miserably, that would be almost impossible with a nostrilful of Pervitin coursing through his veins.

"No," he replied with a smile, "But thank you."

As Sophie returned to her seat, Claudette picked up a dessert spoon and was about to sniff a heap of powder from its bowl when a yellow coated waiter appeared at the table.

"Can I tempt you with a desert?" he invited and lay a menu on the tablecloth.

Helgeland jumped to his feet, his red eyes wide.

"NO!" he roared, picking up an empty side plate, "Can't you see we're busy? Now fuck off!"

The dwarf bowed his head apologetically and shuffled away, followed closely by the plate, which sailed through the air, missed its intended target and instead landed plum on the head of the naked human dining table, who, main course now complete, was covered with an array of fancy-looking chocolates. The woman screamed as she leapt into the air, blood pouring from her scalp and confectionary flying in all directions.

The four army officers who, moments before, had been dining directly from the naked girl's body, jumped to their feet in shock and, enraged, appeared to be about to storm across the dining room towards Helgeland. They paused, however, as they noticed the Knight's Cross at the neck of Bloodstone who, seeing what was about to unfold, had pulled himself to his feet and was holding up a hand in apology.

"Apologies, kameraden," he shouted across the room at the angry Wehrmacht officers and then, clicking his fingers, summoned a new waiter and ordered a bottle of schnapps to be sent to the table.

Placated, the four men nodded their acceptance and returned to their seats, with the nude brunette nowhere to be seen and their table a mess of blood, smashed crockery and smeared chocolate.

Bloodstone sat back down and caught the eye of Helgeland who, far from appearing apologetic, was grinning like a lunatic.

"Are you sure you don't want some?" the Norwegian asked, crushing another tablet and snorting it directly from the tabletop.

"No, I'm fine," Bloodstone replied, "I have a big day tomorrow, need to keep my wits about me."

"Ha, so do I," Helgeland smiled, his nose looking like it had been dipped in snow, "I've got a batch of filthy Juden traitors to round up in the morning."

"You know, you're very welcome to join me if you like, Obersturmbannfuhrer," he continued merrily, "Nothing like killing a few rats to clear a hangover."

Clenching his teeth and forcing his face not to show the disgust he felt inside, Bloodstone smiled.

"We'll see," he replied unenthusiastically, "Let's see how tonight goes shall we?"

"Good idea," Helgeland agreed then, fingering another side plate, he shouted at a nearby waiter.

"Oi, bring us some desert. And quick about it, you filthy little goblin."

CHAPTER FIFTY-ONE

While Bloodstone and his three companions tucked into a particularly delicious chocolate mousse, the troupe of musicians departed the stage amid a cacophony of whoops and jeers from the other guests. A grand piano was wheeled on in their place and a tall, thin bespectacled man in a suit strolled onto the stage, bowed once and took his place at the keys.

"He looks like a Jude to me," Helgeland announced viciously through a mouthful of desert as the pianist began to belt out a jaunty melody, "We should shoot the bastard right now."

Bloodstone, knowing that the Norwegian probably wasn't joking, decided it a good time to press the man on the next day's mission that he'd alluded to earlier.

"So, talking of filthy Juden," he began, the words almost sticking in his throat, "Tell me about this round-up of yours tomorrow."

"Ah yes," Helgeland replied, the evil on his face instantly turning into a manic look of something akin to glee, "We've discovered a Jewish cell in the Seventeenth Arrondissement, women and old men mostly, but particularly repugnant all the same."

"And you'll be disposing of them, I imagine?" Bloodstone asked, already knowing the answer.

"Absolutely," laughed the Norwegian, licking the last remnants of chocolate from his spoon, "With pleasure."

His dish now empty, he took a swig of champagne and continued with the smile still plastered across his face.

"It'll be my usual method, which I personally find to be particularly efficient. My trusty assistant will first confirm the rats' nest and I'll pay them a simple visit. No need for a show of force. Mustn't waste the Führer's manpower, isn't that so, Obersturmbannfuhrer?"

"Indeed," Bloodstone replied and felt a chill run down his spine.

He took a small sip of his own champagne and looked Helgeland in the eyes.

"Mind if I join you?"

"My dear Obersturmbannfuhrer, it would be an honour," the blonde man answered excitedly, looking distinctly like a cat who had got the cream.

"Did you hear that?" he asked the dark-haired Sophie, tapping her on the arm and grinning like a schoolboy, "I will have some exalted company tomorrow."

The girl giggled and laid her hand on Bloodstone's thigh, "You are such a good man," she said, "Helping to rid the world of the untermenschen. The Führer would be so proud."

Not for the first time that evening, Bloodstone felt sick. But maybe, he mused, just maybe, he could save a few innocent lives tomorrow. Or maybe he'd lose his own. That thought wasn't particularly attractive, but he'd never been able to stand bullies and that's exactly what Helgeland was, he decided. A sick, twisted lunatic, but a bully all the same.

Raising his glass, he caught the Norwegian's eye once more.

"Prost," he announced, draining his glass and feeling Sophie's fingers glide their way across his thigh.

"Prost," the other three repeated and, as they did so, Helgeland pushed himself unsteadily to his feet, his Luger in his left hand.

"Oi, Pianoman," he shouted in the direction of the stage as he waved his pistol above his head, "Jazz it up a bit will you!"

The pianist shot a nervous glance at the drug-fuelled Sturmbannfuhrer, gulped once and launched into a fast-paced swing piece.

"That's more like it," Helgeland acknowledged excitedly as he slumped into his seat and threw the Luger onto the table, "Now, who wants to dance?"

He didn't wait for an answer but leapt up onto his chair and clambered onto the tabletop, crushing crockery under his boots and grinding remnants of chocolate mousse into the tablecloth.

"Yeha!" he yelled manically as he performed some sort of crazed jig in time with the crashing of the piano and the fists of the room's other guests, who were now pounding on their tables as they watched the SS major leap and jive like a mad thing.

"Yeha!" he screeched again and lent a well-aimed kick to a coffee cup that sailed through the air, narrowly missed the pianist's head and smashed to pieces against the far wall.

"Go on Sven!" cheered Claudette, who was looking up at the rampaging Norwegian with a face flushed with delight, "Go on!"

The dancing maniac looked down at her, booted another coffee cup through the air, and howled with glee.

"Watch this!" he yelled over the deafening racket of the piano and the thumping fists and the cheers, "Watch this!"

With that, Helgeland, reached down, unbuckled his belt and let his trousers fall to his ankles. Next, he grabbed hold of his underpants and yanked them down too, giving Bloodstone a full view of Norwegian anus as he bent over to wrestle the pants down his legs.

Then, with the cheers of the guests reaching deafening levels, Helgeland grasped his genitals in his right hand, tilted his head down and opened his mouth. As he did so, a thick stream of urine burst from the tip of his penis and fountained into the air, coming to land perfectly in his open mouth.

The crowd went wild, despite the pianist having ceased his playing as he looked on in amazement.

"What the..." Bloodstone gasped in utter befuddlement, having never seen anything like it in his entire life.

He couldn't work out whether he was outraged or impressed but decided that it should probably be the former.

"Ja!" clapped a delighted Claudette as she jumped up and down on the spot, patently enjoying the bizarre spectacle, "Ja, ja!"

As the man's bladder emptied, he struggled to find the required effort to fire the remaining piss all the way up into his mouth and, instead, the stream began to lose its battle with gravity and splattered first across his face and then his uniform shirt. Finally, with one last pathetic spurt, the liquid ceased completely.

With the crowd still cheering, Helgeland bowed and once again flashed the internals of his rear end to half of the room, before he reached down to pull up his urine-soaked undergarments.

As he did so, a tiny creature, clad in the uniform of a Luftwaffe officer, bounded onto the table, scampered up the man's naked leg and clamped its miniature claws around the Norwegian's testicles.

The piss-drenched man screeched in agony and writhed about wildly as the monkey held on for dear life. The diners were roaring again in delight and even the pianist struggled to keep a straight face as he watched the calamitous scene before him.

Finally, mercifully, Helgeland grasped the monkey, tore it from his balls and launched it into the air. As it sailed across the room, shrieking madly as it went, he reached down to the table, grasped his Luger and emptied bullet after bullet at the flying creature.

The petrified monkey landed on the floor and, unscathed by the projectiles, scampered to safety through an open door, while the diners, Bloodstone included, hit the ground with their hands covering their heads. Only the pianist, rooted to his seat in bewilderment, failed to move and it was into his forehead that the first bullet plunged, drilling a neat hole through his skull and spraying a gory fountain of flesh, bone and brain across the stage. A second bullet passed through the strings of the piano with a strange pinging noise and finished its journey lodged firmly in the already-dead man's chest.

Silence descended across the room and Helgeland, scratch marks festooning his genitals, bent down to finally retrieve his wet clothing.

As he straightened up, he buckled his belt and glanced across at the stage, where the pianist was now slumped across his instrument, globules of blood and brain dripping onto the keys.

Helgeland stooped once more, this time to retrieve a miraculously unbroken glass of schnapps, which he knocked back in a single gulp, before he looked across at the dead musician.

He studied the body for a moment before wiping a mixture of schnapps and urine from his top lip with the back of his hand.

"Filthy Jude," he uttered under his breath, "Filthy Jude".

CHAPTER FIFTY-TWO

B loodstone gulped back his third glass of water of the morning and rubbed at his eyes. His head thumped like the devil and he resisted the urge to scratch at the itching wound in his backside. Instead, he pulled himself from his bed and padded across the hotel room to peer into the small mirror above the sink.

"God in heaven, Bertie," he murmured as he inspected his reflection and grimaced at the haggard creature that stared back at him.

He still wasn't used to his new hairstyle and the sight of the shorn head thoroughly depressed him, almost as much, he mused, as the hairless top lip. In addition to the grim facial hair situation, he sported an enormous pair of grey bags under his eyes, which were the result of yet another night of severely diminished sleep.

As he splashed his face with cold water in an attempt to clear his hangover, he thought back to the night before and smiled at the memory of the uniformed monkey attaching itself firmly to Helgeland's scrotum.

The smile vanished almost as quickly as it had appeared, however, as he recalled the body of the pianist being carried from the stage and a pair of cleaners scrubbing miserably at the lumps of brain left smeared across the floor. No sooner had the gory mess been removed, than a set of fresh performers mounted the podium. This time it was a pair of dark-haired girls in grass skirts, complete with coconut bikinis and ukuleles, which they strummed in unison while singing a jolly ballad.

The crowd had mellowed slightly following the gunfire, yet Helgeland, still high on Pervitin, had continued to rant and ramble at his guests in his usual manic fashion. It wasn't until long after midnight that the Norwegian, his damp uniform now reeking like a urinal, decided to call it a night and invited Bloodstone to join him and the two ladies at his quarters.

The offer was made with a mischievous nod in the direction of Claudette that made it quite clear what was on the cards if Bloodstone choose to accept the invitation. As much as he knew he'd enjoy a gallop on the buxom blonde, he'd had more than his fill of his three companions and couldn't bear the thought of listening to even more of their vile drivel.

So, with excuses made, he was dropped back at the Ritz and, following Helgeland's seemingly customary yell of Heil Hitler from the departing Mercedes, made his way up to his room, pausing only to instruct the concierge to collect his uniform to be laundered.

Now, at just after six in the morning, he splashed another handful of water across his face and rubbed himself dry with a towel. His freshly laundered uniform arrived several minutes later and it wasn't long before he was fully dressed, his Luger in its holster and his knife secured to his belt. He took one more look in the mirror and, seeing the shaven-headed creature transformed once again into Obersturmbannfuhrer Wilhelm von Winkel, took a deep breath and headed downstairs to breakfast.

As he tucked into a particularly tasty omelette, Bloodstone wondered what the day ahead would bring. Except for killing Helgeland and rescuing a group of innocent women and old men, neither of which he yet had any idea how he was going to achieve, he had no clue how he was going to track down Heidler.

He figured that he had two options. Firstly, he could ingratiate himself in the military goings-on in Paris, hang around in the right places and ask the right questions, hopefully picking up a clue or two that would lead him to his nemeses. Or, secondly, he could try to make contact with the Resistance, get a line through to Algy and his Intelligence Corps pals and attempt to find Heidler that way. Both options, he admitted as he finished the omelette, were fraught with danger and likely to end with him being rumbled. And painfully so.

The third, option, he knew, was to forget about the whole damned thing and somehow get himself back to Blighty as quickly as possible. But, deep down, he knew that wasn't an option at all. He'd come too far to turn back now and, anyway, how could he allow his mother's murderer to go unpunished when he was so close? He simply couldn't.

He sipped his coffee and pushed thoughts of Heidler to the back of his mind, deciding instead to focus on the matter immediately at hand; Helgeland. Like many things over the past few days, he concluded that he'd simply have to let the situation unfold and wait for an opportune moment, as and when it arose, to kill the crazed Norwegian. As for saving the Jews, that would require an equally malleable approach. Finishing the coffee, he felt for the familiar bump of his lucky bullet, now tucked away in the pocket of his SS tunic, threw his serviette onto the table and pushed himself to his feet.

"Time to focus, Bertie, old boy," he said silently under his breath and strode out of the dining room.

The black Mercedes was parked outside the front of the hotel as arranged and Helgeland was leaning on the wing, sucking lazily on a cigarette. He immediately straightened up as he saw Bloodstone, threw his cigarette to the ground, clicked his heels and raised his right arm.

"Heil Hitler!" he bawled, loud enough to cause a passing cyclist to turn his head in alarm and almost crash into a lamppost.

"Heil Hitler," Bloodstone replied, far less enthusiastically and barely bothering to salute.

"How are you, Obersturmbannfuhrer? Are you well rested?" the Norwegian asked, ushering Bloodstone into the car.

"I am indeed, Sturmbannfuhrer," Bloodstone lied as he took his seat and noticed with surprise that Helgeland looked as fresh as a daisy.

"What a night, eh Obersturmbannfuhrer?" the blonde-haired major continued, "But such a shame you couldn't join us after. Claudette was most disappointed, I must tell you."

"I had business to attend to," Bloodstone replied vacantly as the car revved into life and swerved onto the quiet early morning Parisian streets.

"I completely understand," Helgeland responded, "You are a very busy man it seems."

Bloodstone glanced up, catching the man's eye and wondering if he sensed a trace of sarcasm in the youngster's tone. He raised an eyebrow, was met with the usual manic smile and decided that he was just being paranoid.

"So, what's the plan for this morning, Sturmbannfuhrer?" Bloodstone asked, changing the subject.

"It should be a nice and easy one. My trusty associate is already there and has confirmed the presence of the Juden cell. So, you and I will pay them a visit with just Baumer here for company."

At the mention of Baumer, Helgeland nodded in the direction of his sergeant driver.

"Just the three of us?" Bloodstone asked, "Is that wise?"

"Ja, Obersturmbannfuhrer," the Norwegian replied confidently, "When I've finished with the swine they'll be glad to accompany me."

Bloodstone felt a chill run down his spine as Helgeland continued.

"No need for a show of force, although of course there will be a cattle truck waiting in the vicinity, ready to cart the filth away when we're finished."

The white-haired youngster paused as he glanced out of the window with a wistful look on his face.

"Sometimes I think I have the best job in the world," he continued, "Don't you agree, Obersturmbannfuhrer?"

Bloodstone simply nodded, inwardly hating the man just a little bit more, and subtly stroked the hilt of the knife at his belt.

The journey continued in silence as the pair watched the streets rush past the window and Bloodstone found himself thinking back to the last time he was in Paris. A fresh-faced sixteen-year-old, recently graduated from Eton and on a last hurrah with his pals before taking the King's shilling, he'd been filled with the exuberance of youth and had drunk, gambled and fumbled his way through a glorious month of Parisian sunshine. Those elysian days seemed so long ago, he mused, finding it hard to believe that was a mere eight years before. So much had happened in that time, so much blood and chaos and misery, and he wondered if his teenage self would recognise the man he had become. As he glanced down at his SS issue breeches, he felt like those carefree days had happened to someone else entirely; someone who, at that moment, not an insignificant part of him wished he could be again.

He was jerked from his melancholy by the slowing of the Mercedes as it reached its destination. Following Helgeland's lead, he climbed out of the car and looked around, finding himself in a picturesque street of grand four-storey townhouses. On closer inspection he discovered that the road on which the car had stopped was actually one side of a square of nineteenth century houses, all of which faced onto a large central garden surrounded by a cast iron fence and a perfectly manicured hedge.

So well maintained were the park and the houses and such was the tranquility of the place that, once again, Bloodstone found it difficult to believe that this was a city at war.

"Hard to believe that even the most beautiful of places are infested with vermin, isn't it, Obersturmbannfuhrer?" Helgeland laughed, ruining Bloodstone's peaceful gazing and gesturing to a nearby house, "Shall we?"

Bloodstone nodded and followed the Norwegian as he strolled purposefully along the pavement, the driver Baumer alongside him with an MP40 submachine gun in his right hand. They reached a front door that was already opened inwards and Helgeland nodded at Baumer, who gripped his weapon in two hands and cautiously entered, with the muzzle of his gun leading the way.

As Bloodstone followed the pair into the building, his eyes snaking left and right and his breath held, he pulled the Luger from his pocket with his right hand and cocked it with his left, the familiar feel of a weapon in his palm calming his nerves slightly. They were met with nothing but a spacious but empty entrance hallway and Baumer continued for another seven or eight paces before he turned to his right and began to climb a narrow spiral stairway, the MP40 still prepped for action in his hands.

Helgeland followed and Bloodstone took up the rear, noticing that the stone steps were decorated with a mosaic of tiny red tiles and that a well-thumbed handrail snaked its way around the wall at waist height. They passed the closed doors of a first storey apartment and continued upwards, soon bypassing the second floor too.

As he climbed, always turning in a clockwise direction, he remembered a history lesson from his schooldays and recalled that the medieval lords of old would always build their castle stairways to favour the swords of their right-handed defenders. Looking down at the Luger in his right hand and feeling decidedly unprepared for whatever may be ahead beyond the stone central pillar, he shifted the pistol into his left hand and continued upwards.

Past one more closed door they went until finally they reached the fourth floor, on which stood a single green wooden door with a brass knocker. The door was already open a few inches and Baumer shoved the muzzle of his machine gun into the crack and slowly pushed the door open. Receiving no resistance from within, the sergeant opened the door fully and stepped inside, followed closely by Helgeland.

Two steps behind and with his pistol now back in his right hand, Bloodstone ducked as he passed through the doorway and found himself in a brightly lit room. His eyes adjusted from the relative darkness of the stairwell and he blinked as he looked around, his breath catching in his throat as he took in the scene that lay before him.

CHAPTER FIFTY-THREE

Bloodstone found himself in an expensively decorated parlour with walls of green and gold striped wallpaper, an elaborate carpet atop polished oak floorboards and two small chandeliers hanging from the ceiling. Several high-backed armchairs and a settee were arranged in front of an empty fireplace, above which a marble mantlepiece displayed an array of photo frames and, in its centre, the seven candlesticks of an impressively sized menorah.

Sitting on one of the chairs was an elderly man and squeezed onto the settee were four equally aged and decrepit women, between two of whom cowered a tear-stained and dark-haired boy of about twelve years of age. But it wasn't the sight of the petrified elderly folk that made Bloodstone catch his breath and nor was it the eerie silence in the room that was punctuated only by the miserable snivellings of the youngster. Instead, it was what lay on the floor in front of the sofa that had caused him to gasp, for face-down on the carpet was a body. A tiny lifeless body, not more than four or five years old, dressed in stockings and a checked dress, with chestnut hair pulled into two pigtails and a pair of pink slippers on its feet. The back of the child's head was a gory mess, the telltale sign of a bullet exit wound, and the carpet underneath was soaked with still-wet blood.

Bloodstone felt the morning's omelette rise in his throat and he forced himself not to vomit, unable to tear his eyes away from the corpse at his feet. It was Helgeland, standing to Bloodstone's left, who broke the silence.

"Had any problems, mein Liebling?"

The question jerked Bloodstone from his trance and, as Helgeland stepped forward to prod the lifeless body with his boot, causing one of the elderly women to whimper hysterically, he noticed that there was one more person present in the room. Seated to his left on another high-backed armchair, half obscured by the Norwegian major, was the figure of Sophie, her brunette locks resting on her shoulders and her hands folded neatly in her lap, a Luger visible beneath her small fingers.

"Hardly anything at all," the Frenchwoman replied in German with a dazzling smile.

"Although one of these Juden pigs tried to bribe me," she continued, nodding in the direction of the grey-haired man who sported a waistcoat and a silver watch chain, "So I had to let them know I was serious. Obviously."

"Obviously," agreed Helgeland, poking the body again with his toe and glaring at the man, who stared back with the desolate eyes of someone who had nothing left to live for.

"You've done well, my darling Sophie," he continued, before turning to Bloodstone, "Don't you agree, Obersturmbannfuhrer?"

Bloodstone, his icy fingers grasping the grip of his Luger and his brain struggling to fathom how someone so beautiful could be capable of such cruelty, simply nodded.

Oblivious to Bloodstone's disgust, Helgeland turned his attention back to his wretched group of captives.

"I hope you've learnt your lesson," he snarled in French as he took a step closer to the waistcoat-clad man and eyed him with malevolence.

The elderly man said nothing as he stared back at the Norwegian with clenched teeth and his face set in a look of unbridled hatred.

Helgeland simply smirked as he stared back.

"Worry not, you old Jewish fuck, they'll soon knock that look off your face where you're going to. If you make it that far. Isn't that so, Sophie?"

Sophie giggled and crossed her legs, smoothing her skirts. The boy snivelled once more and wiped his nose with the back of his sleeve. One of the old ladies hugged him a little tighter. Baumer absentmindedly scratched at his ear as he inspected the photographs on the mantlepiece.

The elderly man switched his glare from the Norwegian and cast his eyes upon Bloodstone, who found himself on the receiving end of a look of such withering disgust that he looked away immediately as the guilt stabbed his chest like a knife.

As he stood there in his SS uniform with the blood of the pigtailed girl soaking into the carpet, his mind raced. He knew that he couldn't allow six innocent people to be carted away to whatever fate the Nazis had in store for them, but he also knew that he had no chance against the two armed men and a woman who obviously had zero qualms about using the weapon in her lap.

He could make a go of it, he knew, maybe kill one or even two of them before he was filled with bullets, but the odds were exceedingly long and it certainly wouldn't do the prisoners on the chairs any good; their dreary fate would remain the same, if not worse. For once, Bloodstone was at a loss. Maybe there was nothing he could do, he mused. Maybe he had just to go along with the atrocity that was unfolding in front of his eyes. Maybe this was just war and he'd have to file it away in that deep, dark place in his head where he kept all the grotesque and unworldly things that he'd seen over the years.

"Any sign of that truck?"

He was brought back from his pondering by the voice of Helgeland, which had reverted to German and was aimed in the direction of Baumer.

The sergeant stepped over to a nearby window and glanced downward through the glass.

"Nothing, Sturmbannfuhrer," the man replied and Bloodstone realised that it was the first time he'd heard the driver's voice.

He couldn't help noticing that he had spoken with an Austrian accent, almost identical to that of his mother, and the all-too-familiar picture of the bloodstained body pinned with the Swastika calling card shot into his head.

Before he could brood on the image, Helgeland spoke again.

"Take a proper look, man," he ordered, pointing at the window.

Baumer laid his MP40 on the mantlepiece, knocking off one of the photo frames, and strolled over to the window to do as he was instructed. He grasped the sash with two hands and pushed up the glass, unleashing a blast of chilly October air that gushed into the room. With the window open, he leaned out and peered left and right, searching for the vehicle that would transport the six surviving Jews to their fate.

Now's your chance, Bloodstone realised as he stared at the protruding back of the driver. One bullet through the spine, then a lightning quick turn to the left to put one into Helgeland and another into the traitorous Sophie. There wouldn't be a better opportunity.

Readying himself, he shifted the grip of the Luger slightly in his palm and felt for the safety catch with his thumb. Finding it, he pushed upwards against the lever, preparing to aim the pistol in the direction of the sergeant and ready on his toes to spin in the direction of Helgeland as soon as the trigger was pulled.

But the safety wouldn't budge. He tried again. Nothing.

"Bugger," he cursed silently and at that very moment the driver pulled his torso back through the window frame and turned around.

"Nothing, Sturmbannfuhrer," Baumer repeated, oblivious to how close he'd come to a bullet in the back.

Bloodstone relaxed and let the tension flow from his muscles, the pistol falling loose in his palm.

"Fucking useless Wehrmacht," Helgeland cursed, "Always late."

"I haven't got all day to be hanging around here with these..." he failed to find an adjective insulting enough and, instead, waved dismissively at his captives.

Turning to Bloodstone, he continued, "Would you excuse me a for a moment, Obersturmbannfuhrer? I'll use the radio in the car to track down these transport fools. I shall be but a moment."

Bloodstone nodded, delighted to be about to reduce his foes by a third, but forced his face to stay in the emotionless mask that fitted so well with his SS uniform.

"Quickly," he ordered snappishly and turned away as he pretended to inspect the photographs that still remained on the mantlepiece.

Helgeland clicked his heels, opened the door and glanced back at the disconsolate prisoners one last time.

"I shall leave you in some very esteemed company," he leered at them, gesturing at Bloodstone in the process, "Obersturmbannfuhrer von Winkel here is a very famous soldier; you should feel honoured, oui?"

Met with silence, he cackled once and left the room, pulling the door closed behind him. Bloodstone, his mind making plans again, felt the waistcoated man's eyes burning into him and, not wishing to meet the old man's glare, he bent down to pick up the photo frame. The glass was shattered but he could still make out the image beneath, which showed a boy of about eight with his hand proudly on the leg of a seated and well-groomed elderly gentleman. Cradled in the man's arms was a baby wrapped in a blanket and, as Bloodstone looked closer, he noticed that stretched across the man's belly was a silver watch chain.

Realising that the baby was the young girl now sprawled lifeless on the floor, Bloodstone's breakfast threatened once again to regurgitate itself and he quickly placed the cracked photo frame back on the mantlepiece and forced himself to focus on the job at hand.

With the departure of Helgeland, his odds had shortened considerably but he knew he had to act fast if he wanted to clear up the whole messy situation before the Norwegian returned. He ran through the plan once more in his head, subtly fingering the safety catch again and this time finding that it slid into the off position with no trouble at all. He said a silent prayer of thanks and, once again, gripped the Luger tightly in his palm.

The first bullet would be for Sophie, he decided, who still sat on her chair, with her legs crossed and her own pistol in her lap. Next would be a half-turn to the right and a bullet in the back of Baumer, who had returned to the window and was peering down into the street. It couldn't be simpler, Bloodstone thought, taking a deep breath, tensing his muscles and silently counting down. Three. Two. One.

CHAPTER FIFTY-FOUR

The shoulder hit him thigh-high, crashing into his left side like a rugby tackle, albeit a particularly weak and feeble rugby tackle. Instinctively and without thinking, he grabbed his assailant's neck in a one-armed headlock and dropped to the ground, rolling like a crocodile while desperately trying to keep hold of the Luger with his other hand.

As he rolled, a tousled brown head of hair wedged in the crock of his elbow, the pistol fell from his grip and dropped onto the stone fireplace, where it bounced upwards, cartwheeled madly and let off a deafening crack as it sent a bullet spinning across the room.

In a heartbeat Bloodstone was up, with a knee on his assailant's chest and a hand firmly around his windpipe. He had acted entirely without though as the years of military training kicked in instinctively and it was only now that he realised that the figure squirming underneath him wasn't the elderly man but was in fact the boy who, only seconds before, had been sobbing on the sofa.

He took a moment to catch his breath and looked around, assessing the situation that only a heartbeat before was entirely under control and had been about to end in the quick end of the two Nazis. Instead, he was now kneeling on the floor with a twelve-year-old boy wriggling beneath him and the Luger seemingly nowhere to be seen.

The elderly women on the settee were sitting like statues, their mouths open in shock, while the waistcoated man had sprung to his feet and was now frozen, stock still, halfway between the chair and the fireplace. Also standing, her right arm extended, her pistol pointed directly at the old man and her face fixed in a cruel glare, was Sophie.

No longer on his feet, however, was Baumer, who, thanks to the single rogue Luger bullet, was now slumped in a sitting position with his back against the windowsill and his eyes unnaturally wide. His hands were clutched to his throat and from between his fingers pumped a torrent of bright red blood, which cascaded down his uniform shirt and soaked his breeches. The gurgling noise that came from his bullet-mangled throat and the drumming of his boots on the oak floorboards were the only sounds in the small parlour and Bloodstone only needed one glance at the sergeant to know that he had barely a minute to live.

As he watched Baumer's lifeblood flow from his body, Bloodstone stood up, placed his boot firmly on the squirming youngster's throat and unsheathed his combat knife with his left hand. As he did so, the elderly man made a half step towards him, but a slight jerk of Sophie's pistol stopped him dead in his tracks.

"Keep still," she ordered coldly in French, "Or I'll kill you all."

One of the women on the settee let out a whimper and Sophie whipped the Luger in her direction.

"Silent, you Jewish bitch."

The woman blubbed once more and was silent, her hand clasped tightly in that of the elderly lady seated next to her.

Bloodstone, his boot still forcing the boy to the ground, turned to Sophie.

"Your pistol," he ordered, "Give it to me, quickly."

As she took a step towards Bloodstone, the woman whimpered again.

"Please, Monsieur, non," she begged through a faceful of tears.

"Shut it!" Bloodstone yelled in French, pointing his wickedly sharp knife in her direction and, again, the woman fell silent.

313

Sophie reached Bloodstone and passed him the Luger, grip first. "Thank you, mein Liebling," he smiled as he took the gun.

He was still smiling as he raised his arm and, with not so much as a half-second pause, squeezed the trigger once. The bullet plunged into Sophie's surprised face from less than a foot away, drilling a small neat hole into the top of her nose and blowing a gruesome jet of blood and brain from the back of her skull.

She crumpled to the floor and Bloodstone, feeling not an ounce of emotion at murdering the traitorous beauty, turned to the window with his arm still raised. He found that Baumler was already motionless, however, with his eyes staring blankly and his mouth fixed in a monstrous grimace.

Bloodstone turned back to the elderly man, who was still frozen to the spot but now had a look of utter confusion plastered across his face, lifted his boot from the neck of the youngster, sheathed his knife and held both hands in the air.

"Je suis Anglais," he said, confusing the man even more.

Silence fell once more across the room and nobody moved, except for the boy who scrambled to his feet and ran to the settee to wedge himself back between two of the old ladies.

The waistcoated man broke the silence.

"Eh?"

"I said I'm English," Bloodstone repeated in French, trying to hide his impatience but failing miserably.

"English?"

"Oui, Goddammit, English. Now do you want to get out of here before it's too late?"

"But the uniform?" the old man mumbled, his face still a picture of befuddlement.

"It's a long story. Now, let's go, vite!"

Bloodstone clapped and the old man sprang into action, turned to the rest of the group and urged them to their feet. The elderly women rose from the settee and began to spread throughout the room, picking up an assortment of small bags, ornaments and picture frames as they went.

As they did so, Bloodstone crossed to the window and stood astride the blood-soaked corpse of Baumer to look down into the square below. The street was empty except for the parked Mercedes, which now had its trunk open to reveal a radio unit, while stood behind the car with a set of headphones over his ears and speaking animatedly into a handset, was Helgeland.

It was clear that, miraculously, Helgeland hadn't heard the two gunshots but what was also clear was that it wouldn't be long before the absent truck arrived to pick-up the prisoners. As Bloodstone pulled his head back into the room and stepped over the body of Baumer, he saw that the elderly group were still scooping up belongings.

"No time," he urged loudly, "We have to go, now, or else that Norwegian bastard will bring the whole bloody German army up here."

The elderly man pointed at the blood-spattered body of the child.

"But my granddaughter," he pleaded with desperate eyes, "We can't leave her here."

"I'm sorry," Bloodstone replied, seeing the heartbreak on the man's face, "But we've got no choice. We have to leave, right now."

Understanding, the man nodded and corralled the rest of the group together so that they huddled by the door with the young boy in their centre.

Feeling a lot more confident than he felt and having no idea what he was going to do with the motley band if and when he got them out of the building, Bloodstone grabbed the MP40 from the mantlepiece and glanced around for the Luger that he'd dropped when he wrestled the boy to the ground. He spotted it underneath the settee and picked it up, making sure to flick the safety catch back on.

"I don't suppose anybody knows how to use one of these?" he asked, waving the pistol.

"Of course," the old man replied, holding out a wrinkled hand.

"Verdun," he explained as he noticed Bloodstone's questioning look, "I thought I'd seen the last of war."

Bloodstone said nothing but handed over the gun, holstered Sophie's Luger, hung the MP40 strap on his shoulder and headed towards the door. As an afterthought he ran back to the body of Baumer, plucked two magazines from a bloodstained pocket and shoved them into his jacket.

"Right, let's go," he said as he opened the door and peered out into the stairwell, "Follow me."

CHAPTER FIFTY-FIVE

Bloodstone led the way as he hurried down the stairs with the MP40 now firmly in his grasp and the index finger of his right hand hovering over the trigger. He was followed closely by the elderly gentleman, who clasped the Luger in a bony hand, and behind him hobbled the four old women. The boy brought up the rear with a cloth holdall slung over his shoulder and a suitcase in each hand.

He paused briefly to gesture to the shuffling group to hurry, before he continued down the spiralling stairway as silently as his hobnailed boots would allow. Once again, he thought of the medieval fortress designers of years gone by and realised how much more of a commanding view of the stairway ahead he now had than when he'd ventured upwards just ten minutes before.

Down past the third floor they went, then the second and then the first. Bloodstone's heart began to beat faster as they descended and he readjusted his grip on the machine pistol as they neared the bottom of the stairs. With two more steps to go, he paused, signalled the man behind him to do the same, took a deep breath and raised himself up onto the balls of his feet. He tiptoed down to the final step, exhaled, raised the barrel of the MP40 and stepped out into the hallway.

As he emerged from the safety of the stairway, he immediately swung the muzzle of his weapon to his left towards the door through which he had entered with Helgeland and Baumer. Seeing the hallway in front of him empty, he swung back to his right to scan the far end of the lobby, which, mercifully, was empty too. Still raised up on the balls of his feet, he hurried towards the doorway, beckoning his followers to stay close behind him. Once again, he paused when he reached the door and slowly craned his neck around the wooden doorframe to peer out into the street.

The square remained deserted except for the black Mercedes, which was parked against the kerb forty yards away to Bloodstone's left. Helgeland was still standing at the open trunk and was facing away from the doorway of the house with the headphones no longer at his ears. He appeared preoccupied, fiddling with something in the boot of the car, but Bloodstone was fully aware that the Norwegian could turn around at any second.

He summoned the captives closer with a wave of his gun and, with a finger at his lips, pointed out into the street.

"Stay here and do not move," he whispered into the old man's ear, "And keep silent."

"I'll finish off that SS swine and then I'll come back and get you out of here, so just wait," he continued, suddenly amazed, and not just a bit relieved, at how easy it was going to be to free the Jewish prisoners.

He checked that his MP40 was cocked and ran through a hastily assembled plan in his mind. Fill the unsuspecting Helgeland with some much-deserved 9mm lead, he decided, throw his body into the trunk of the Mercedes, bundle the prisoners into the car too and then get the hell out of there before the truck arrived. He'd drop them off somewhere in the city, wherever they thought was safe, and then dump the car and its bullet-ridden passenger on a quiet backstreet. With any luck it would be a day or so before the grisly cargo was discovered and assumed to be the work of the Resistance, by which time Bloodstone would have been back to the Ritz to collect his briefcase of Reichsmarks, checked out of the hotel and vanished into the city to resume his search for Heidler. Where exactly he would start that hunt again was something that he hadn't yet thought of but, he decided, there was plenty of time for scheming after Helgeland had met his maker.

He pressed his forefinger to his lips once more, held the MP40 behind his back and stepped out into the street. He turned left out of the doorway and began walking towards the Mercedes, where Helgeland still stood, facing away from him but now with a lit cigarette visible in his right hand. He tried to keep his footsteps as quiet as possible as he closed on the car, tempted to snatch up the machine gun and open fire immediately, but such was his unfamiliarity with the German weapon that he knew he had to be as close as possible to guarantee the kill with a single squeeze of the trigger.

When he was thirty yards from the car, the Norwegian turned, the cigarette between his lips. He looked surprised to see Bloodstone and quickly plucked the tobacco from his mouth and blew out a waft of smoke, before his face broke into its lunatic grin.

"How is everything going up there, Obersturmbannfuhrer?" he asked, nodding upwards towards the open fourth storey window.

"All under control," Bloodstone replied as he continued to close the distance between the two men, "But how is that truck getting on?"

"Not long at all now," the Norwegian answered, "I just spoke to..."

CRACK!

Bloodstone instinctively threw himself to the ground as the sound of a bullet whizzed past his right ear and missed his head by a matter of inches. As he hit the pavement, the taillight of the Mercedes shattered and he saw Helgeland scamper around beside the car, shock plastered across his face. Bloodstone rolled towards the safety of a doorway on his left and grasped the MP40 in front of him in both hands, his finger on the trigger.

CRACK!

Another bullet crashed out and smashed into the wing mirror of the car, sending a shower of broken glass over the kerb. As it did so,

Bloodstone swivelled his head to see where the gunfire was coming from and was amazed to see the elderly figure of the waistcoated man, Luger in hand and striding purposefully along the pavement towards him.

"Come out you coward," he shouted in the direction of the car, his face of mask of hatred, "Come and face me like a man!"

"You damned fool," Bloodstone yelled in English, momentarily forgetting who and where he was, "Get out of here!"

But the man ignored him and continued towards the car, marching past his prone body as he let off yet another bullet. Bloodstone watched the car's offside rear tyre burst as the bullet struck it and he saw Helgeland's head momentarily pop out from behind the shelter of their vehicle.

Their eyes met for a second and the look on the Norwegian's face went from shock to disgust to rage as his confused brain realised that he'd been betrayed by von Winkel. Bloodstone twitched the muzzle of his MP40 towards the protruding head but, before he could line up his sights, Helgeland vanished back behind the car.

Five seconds later and with the old man now just twenty yards from the vehicle, Bloodstone heard a cry from behind and craned his neck to gawp back along the pavement. He was met with the sight of the old women who were hurriedly shuffling away in the opposite direction as fast as their aged legs would carry them, bent over and cowering close to the brickwork of the houses as they retreated along the street. Only the boy remained, frozen to the spot outside the open door, with his hands grasping the suitcases and his mouth wide open as he watched his grandfather storming towards the black sedan.

"Go!" yelled Bloodstone, waving the boy towards the retreating pensioners, "Vite!"

The youngster looked towards the four women, glanced helplessly back again at the old man and, finally snapping out of his trance, turned and sprinted after them. As he did so, three pistol shots rang out in lightning quick succession from the direction of the Mercedes.

The first bullet missed the boy's head by a hair's breadth and shattered the ground floor window of the house past which he was running. He cried out in alarm but didn't miss a step as he released his grip on the bags in his hands, dropped them to floor and continued to run after the rapidly retreating women.

The second whizzed past Bloodstone's face and thudded into the door behind him, driving out a thick wooden splinter that narrowly missed his left eye.

The third bullet thumped into the leg of the old man, blasting out his kneecap and sending him crashing to the ground with a grunt. The Luger fell from his hand and skidded off the pavement onto the road, while his silver pocket watch detached itself from its chain and rolled away to tumble down a nearby drain grating.

As the old man squirmed towards the lost gun, dragging his crippled leg behind him, Bloodstone squinted down the barrel of his MP40 and squeezed off five rounds towards Helgeland, whose head was once again visible behind the Mercedes. The bullets riddled the bodywork of the car but missed the Norwegian, who ducked back behind the front of the vehicle just in time.

As soon as he'd pulled the trigger, Bloodstone was on his feet, his years of military training kicking in as he sprinted towards the car and closed the distance on his enemy. Ten yards further on he threw himself down into the next doorway and squeezed the trigger again, blasting another series of 9mm shells in the direction of Helgeland.

As he watched his bullets pummel the car and confident that he was keeping the man's head down, he dared a quick glance along the road behind him and was delighted to see the gaggle of prisoners disappear to safety around a corner at the far end of the street. He turned back towards the riddled Mercedes and, as he did so, another pistol shot echoed out from behind the vehicle.

The bullet smacked into the wriggling figure of the old man, hitting him under the armpit and puncturing his lungs. He let out an agonising gasp and ceased his crawling, his shoes drumming on the road as he struggled desperately for air.

"Ha ha, have that you filthy Juden pig," yelled Helgeland from behind the car, his voice dancing with glee.

"You're next von Winkel, you traitorous scum," he continued, "I'm going to fuck you up!"

Bloodstone ignored the taunts and collected his thoughts as he kept the sedan in the sights of his MP40. The wheezing coming from the prostrate figure on the road told him that the elderly man was all but finished and, with the rest of the prisoners now seemingly vanished, there was nothing left to do but kill Helgeland and flee the scene before back-up arrived.

Easier said than done, Bloodstone admitted as he silently cursed the old man for ruining an almost perfect situation. He knew that he couldn't take the car now, even if it would start, for a black Mercedes riddled with bullet holes would attract instant attention on the quiet Sunday streets of Paris. Instead, he'd have to make his getaway on foot, find a taxi and get back to the Ritz as quickly and as possible. But that was after. First, he needed to finish off the abominable Norwegian who was sheltering behind the solid structure of the car while he, Bloodstone, was cowering in the scant cover of a doorway.

His best bet, he decided, was the large garden that lay twenty paces away on the other side of the road in the centre of the square. It was surrounded by a waist-high cast iron fence, inside of which ran a thick ornamental hedge of the same height. A much better hiding spot than his current doorway, he thought, knowing that he could hide behind the bushes and pick Helgeland off at pleasure. The gate to the square was further along the road, past the Mercedes, so he'd have to vault over the fence to get himself to safety.

With his mind made up, he tensed, ready to leap up and run towards the square. Just as he was about to lift himself from the ground, he saw a booted foot appear alongside the front tyre on the opposite side of the car, only just visible underneath the bodywork. He didn't hesitate but squeezed the trigger and saw the foot jerk backwards as a bullet smashed into the ankle. A scream was still forming in Helgeland's throat as Bloodstone leapt to his feet and sprinted towards the square, firing from the hip as he ran. Across the road he went at full sprint, still spraying bullets towards the car, and took the fence and the bushes in a single leap. He landed perfectly on his feet, threw himself to the ground and crawled on his belly parallel with the hedge until he estimated he was ten yards past the car.

He paused to change the magazine on his MP40 and, as he did so, a pistol shot rang out from the direction of the car. The bullet crashed through the hedge close to where Bloodstone had landed just thirty seconds before and zinged across and out of the other side of the garden square.

"You think I can't see you?" screeched Helgeland, his voice tinged with pain but manically excited all the same, "You're a dead man von Winkel, you Jew lover!"

Bloodstone ignored the Norwegian's goading, checked that his new magazine was securely inserted into the weapon and, as quietly as he could, pulled back the cocking handle. Still on his belly, he gently pushed the muzzle of the gun into the hedge and silently parted the leaves, giving himself the tiniest of peepholes. The first thing he saw through his leafy spy hole was the old man, lying in the middle of the road in a pool of blood and, from the sight of the unmoving eyes and ashen face, quite clearly dead.

Bloodstone manoeuvred the barrel of his weapon ever so slightly to the right and forced the leaves apart to give himself a view of the Mercedes. The road beside the car was scattered with broken glass, while the bodywork was pitted with bullet holes and a steady stream of oil dripped from under the engine. He could see by a shadow from the early morning sun that Helgeland was sheltering on the far side of the vehicle, crouching and invisible behind the front wheel.

Bloodstone reckoned that if he was five yards further along the hedge he'd be able to get a clean shot on the Norwegian and was just about to slide his weapon back out of the foliage when an engine spluttered away somewhere to the right. The shadow moved as Helgeland glanced towards the sound and, as he did so, his good foot momentarily appeared alongside the tyre. Again, Bloodstone didn't hesitate but squeezed the trigger and watched as the 9mm bullet punched through the man's boot, snapped his ankle clean in half and sent a mist of blood, leather and bone fragments spraying into the air.

"Aaaaaaaarrrgggghhh!" he screeched and collapsed to the ground, falling behind and in front of the car, just out of view from Bloodstone's leafy hole but surely visible from above the hedge.

"Bingo," he exclaimed as he ripped his MP40 out of the hedge and pushed himself to his feet in a single movement, preparing to empty his magazine on the Nazi who now writhed on the road in clear view.

As he lifted the machine gun to his shoulder, something to his right caught his eye and he glanced along the road in that direction. What he saw made his blood run cold and he instinctively dropped back down onto the grass to conceal himself behind the hedge.

Because, fifty yards away and heading along the road towards him was a truck, drab green, a Balkenkreuz cross painted on its cab door and, much to Bloodstone's horror, a squad of soldiers standing aboard its rear bed.

"Haha!" cackled Helgeland gleefully from the other side of the hedge, his bullet-riddled limbs seemingly forgotten, "You're fucked now, von Winkel."

And Bloodstone, his belly pressed into the damp grass and his hand wrapped around the stock of his stolen MP40, reluctantly admitted that he was.

CHAPTER FIFTY-SIX

Bloodstone listened as the truck approached and hastily ran through his options in his head. It took him barely a moment as he quickly realised that there weren't many options at all. In fact, there were only two that he could think of. And neither was particularly attractive.

One, stay low, crawl along the hedge line, get to the far end of the square, vault the bushes and the fence and make a run for it. But, if he even made it that far unscathed, which he knew would be unlikely, where would he go? The Ritz, along with his briefcase of cash, would be a no-go once Helgeland revealed that Obersturmbannfuhrer von Winkel had released the captured Jews and had tried to kill his own comrade. Instead, he'd have to take his chances on the streets of Paris, and how long would a fugitive lieutenant-colonel of the SS last doing that? Not long at all, he admitted.

Which brought him to option two. Fight it out, kill the Boche, flee the scene, get to his money before the enemy knew to start hunting for von Winkel, shed the uniform and find somewhere to lie low while he worked out the next steps of his self-appointed mission. Not a particularly attractive option either, he admitted as he heard the truck rumble closer, but one that he reckoned gave him slightly better odds than the other choice. Anyway, he reasoned, a Bloodstone never runs. So fight he would.

With his mind made up, he leapt into action and began crawling as quickly as he could along the hedge line in the direction from which the truck was coming. He knew that his survival over the next few minutes would depend on lightning-quick movement and unparalleled levels of aggression, so he began to do his calculations in his head as he moved silently across the grass.

From the split-second view that he'd had of the truck, he'd spied two men in the cab and six standing in the rear, although he knew it possible that there were others that he hadn't seen. So at least eight men that he needed to eliminate, not including the crippled Helgeland, and he had how many bullets? Assuming that his magazines had been full when he'd liberated them and that Sophie's Luger had fired just two shots, he had sixty-three rounds left for the MP40 and six in the Luger at his hip. Sixty-nine bullets to kill nine men. Not impossible, he decided, but of course it all depended on the quality of his enemies. It was unlikely that a truckful of soldiers sent to round up a group of elderly Jews were battle-hardened veterans and even less likely that they'd be heavily armed. At least no grenades, he assumed, wishing at that moment that he had a few potato mashers of his own that he could lob towards the truck.

He crawled another fifteen feet and, as he did so, the truck passed him and ground to a halt alongside and just in front of the Mercedes, now twenty yards behind him on the opposite side of the hedge. He paused and listened as he heard Helgeland haranguing the troops, who, seconds later were on their feet and rushing towards the rear of the truck in readiness to jump down to the road.

Bloodstone took a deep breath, counted to three and leapt up. The machine gun was in front of his face by the time he'd cleared the height of the hedge and he took a millisecond to glance along the barrel before he squeezed the trigger. He held his finger down and the weapon jerked in his hands as he pumped round after round into the troops preparing to leave the truck.

The men screamed as they were hit and Bloodstone had a brief glimpse of one soldier's jaw being shot clean away as a bullet struck him in the face. The man next to him collapsed like a sack as he was hit plum in the heart, while a third received a bullet directly through the eye and proceeded to topple over the side of the truck to land in a twisted heap on the road. Two more green-clad soldiers were knocked from their feet and the remainder leapt to safety over the far side of the vehicle, with one landing on the legs of the wounded Helgeland, who screamed out in a hysterical mix of rage and agony.

As the remaining men poured from the truck in an effort to escape the carnage, Bloodstone realised that he had grossly underestimated the number of troops he was up against. He'd hit five as far as he could tell but had seen at least another five flee his deadly assault and seek shelter behind the Mercedes.

Too late now, he admitted, knowing that the only way to win this battle was to crank up the violence and not give his enemies a single second to organise themselves. With that in mind, he sprinted twenty yards back along the hedge, firing from the hip towards the sheltering troops as he ran, until he was level with the truck's cab. The driver, still in a state of shock at seeing his vehicle under such unexpected attack, had his door half open when Bloodstone drew level. The man, a portly hatless figure with red hair, looked up in surprise as he saw the gun-toting Obersturmbannfuhrer raise his weapon. His mouth was still open as a bullet passed straight through it and blew out the back of his head. His passenger was halfway out of the door on the other side of the vehicle when Bloodstone squeezed his trigger again and shot him twice through the spine, leaving him to slide down to the road in a bullet-ridden mess.

He knew that he had to keep the pressure on and that to pause now would give his opponents time to think and to retaliate. So, with a single leap he was over the fence, letting the now-empty magazine in his MP40 drop to the ground as he rammed his final mag into place. He bolted into the road, expecting a hail of bullets to come flying his way, and ducked down beside the front wheel of the truck.

The red-haired driver had toppled out of the brain-spattered cab and was sprawled on the road next to him, but Bloodstone barely gave the man a glance as he took another deep breath and crept around to the front of the vehicle.

The Mercedes, complete with its gaggle of sheltering Wehrmacht, was now just ten feet away around the other side of the truck and Bloodstone could clearly hear a frantic argument taking place among the confused soldiers.

"Move!" yelled a voice which he recognised as that of Helgeland, "Get out there and get the bastard, now!"

"Nein!" came a desperate response, "We need back-up, we don't know how many there are."

"There's just one of him, you fucking coward, now move!"

Bloodstone didn't wait to hear anymore but burst out from his hiding place and rounded the rear of the Mercedes, where he came face to face with four kneeling Germans, huddled together alongside the recumbent figure of the wounded Helgeland. The men looked up in horror as Bloodstone appeared and not one of them was able to let off a shot before the MP40 thundered into life and peppered them with bullets. The carnage was terrible as the 9mm shells struck home from just a few feet away, ripping into flesh, marmalising organs and turning human beings into so many chunks of twitching, bleeding offal.

The only one who was somehow spared from the spraying bullets was Helgeland, who lay helpless on his back and watched in horror as the men around him were slaughtered. The Norwegian's side arm, the pistol that had killed the old man, was nowhere to be seen and he made a desperate attempt to reach for a Mauser that had been dropped by one of the dying soldiers, but Bloodstone stepped forward and kicked the rifle away.

The Norwegian looked up at his assailant and Bloodstone could see the terror in the red eyes. The mouth moved but no words came and Bloodstone saw a circle appear at the man's groin.

"Pissed yourself again?" he asked in English, kicking one of the Norwegian's shattered ankles and producing a scream.

"You're pathetic," Bloodstone continued as he pointed the smoking barrel of his weapon at the man's face, "You make me sick."

The eyes widened as Helgeland saw his own death coming and the mouth moved once more.

"Heil Hitler," he whimpered and Bloodstone pulled the trigger.

The bullet that took him between the eyes shattered his skull, mangled his brain and drilled its way down into the pavement below. The snow-white hair was instantly sprayed red and the lifeless mouth somehow set in its usual and unnerving manic grin.

"Damned coward," cursed Bloodstone as he looked down at the dead Norwegian and spat a globule of phlegm onto the Norwegian's ruptured face, "Go to hell."

As Bloodstone tore his glare from the mangled Sturmbannfuhrer, he looked around at the other corpses littering the pavement. Four men lay dead around him, their bodies riddled with bullets and their blood pooling on the ground below them.

"Four?" he said under his breath, "Four?"

"Damn," he muttered, sure that he'd seen five men leap from the rear of the truck in search of safety behind the Mercedes.

Maybe he'd been seeing things, he thought, maybe there had only been four. Or perhaps the fifth had been hit in his first assault on the men in the back of the truck and was already lying dead on the other side of the Mercedes.

The crack of a rifle and the zing of a bullet flying past his cheek solved that conundrum and he dropped to his knees and nestled in against the door of the car. Gathering his senses, he realised that the shot had come from further along the street, somewhere in the direction from which the truck had come only a few minutes before. He squeezed as close to the bodywork of the Mercedes as he could and scanned the street beyond the car, peering over the sights of his MP40 as he hunted for the elusive gunman.

Another shot rang out and the bullet smashed into the already-mangled wing mirror just three inches above his head. He ducked involuntary and cursed as he peered along the pavement.

"Where are you, you damned bastard?" he muttered.

A slight movement in a doorway forty yards along the street caught his eye and he pulled the trigger in an instant. The machine gun kicked in his hands and he watched as his two shots smashed into the stonework of the house, driving out a cloud of dust and narrowly missing a Wehrmacht soldier that he could now see cowering in the narrow cover of the doorway. The man raised his rifle once more and, before he could get a shot away, Bloodstone squeezed his finger and sent a volley of bullets careering down the street and thumping into the man's chest, knocking him to the ground.

He lined his weapon up on the writhing figure and pulled the trigger again, just to make sure that the man wouldn't get off another shot before he died, but the MP40 in his hands clicked as the firing pin came down on an empty chamber.

"Balls," he cursed, realising that he'd emptied his last magazine, and threw the useless gun to the ground.

The fingers of his right hand went to his hip and in one movement he unbuckled the holster, pulled out the Luger and aimed the pistol on the green-uniformed soldier, who was now pawing the pavement as he desperately tried to force air into his ruined lungs. Bloodstone squeezed once and watched his bullet puncture the man's helmet, killing him instantly.

With the final enemy now eliminated, he straightened up and let out a lungful of air, somewhat amazed that he'd managed to single-handedly wipe out the entire truckful of soldiers, not to mention the vile Helgeland, who now lay at his feet, still grinning crazily. As the adrenaline of battle began to fade and his heartbeat returned to almost normal, he collected his thoughts, knowing that he needed to flee the scene as quickly as possible. He was tempted to take one of the Mausers that now littered the pavement, but knew that an Obersturmbannfuhrer armed with a rifle was likely to cause unwanted attention, so decided to stick with just the Luger that was now safely back in its holster.

He turned to the front nearside window of the Mercedes that was somehow undamaged and looked at his reflection in the glass. Apart from his flushed cheeks, a few grass stains on his elbows and a slightly ruffled uniform, there was little to show that he'd spent the morning unleashing bloody chaos on his Nazi comrades. He straightened his cap, brushed at some mud on his sleeve and readjusted the Knight's Cross at his neck.

"Come on von Winkel, time to go," he said to the reflection and turned to leave.

As he turned his back on the car, a sudden movement caught his eye and he instinctively flicked his head around, just in time to see something cartwheeling through the air towards him.

A grenade.

"Shit!" he exclaimed, momentarily rooted to the spot and watching as the missile spun in his direction, launched from somewhere on the other side of the truck.

As the potato masher grew closer, his instincts kicked in and he jerked into life. His right foot thrashed out and he caught the grenade cleanly, booting it back into the air just as cleanly as if he was on the rugger field at Eton. The projectile arced back into the air, its stick spinning wildly, and it exploded with a deafening thump above the truck.

The force of the explosion shattered the last intact window of the Mercedes and showered Bloodstone, who was now hunched down beside the car, with thousands of tiny fragments of glass. He reached out to grab one of the discarded Mausers and pulled back its bolt as he peered through the wrecked vehicle in search of his unexpected assailant.

"Where the blazes are you?" he whispered as he scanned the area, listening out for his enemy as he did so.

As he searched, another grenade came spinning through the sky, again lobbed from somewhere behind the truck. This one's trajectory was much higher than the previous and he didn't rate his chances of being able to propel it safely away before it burst, so made the lightning quick decision to flee his current hiding spot and get around to the rear of the car, from where he could hunt down his attacker.

So, with the newly acquired rifle in his hands and his right finger hovering on the trigger, he tensed his leg muscles and burst into life, leaping to his feet as he prepared to flee the incoming grenade and sprint to safety. But as he pushed himself to his feet, his hobnailed boots slipped on the broken glass and first one leg, then the other, gave way. He sprawled to the ground, desperately scrabbled to get back to his feet but fell again as his boots failed to find purchase. He tried again, shards of glass tearing into his palms as he struggled to push himself upright, and panic began to engulf him. Finally, he was up on his feet, hunched over, head down and the Mauser forgotten as his whole world became a desperate attempt to get away before the grenade exploded and blew him to bloody ruin.

Three feet behind Bloodstone, the grenade hit the body of Helgeland, bounced once on the corpse's chest and exploded. It tore the Norwegian's corpse to pieces and sent scraps of torn uniform and mangled flesh twenty yards in all directions. The force of the explosion blew Bloodstone from his feet and sent him flying through the air to crash headfirst against the brick wall of the closest house. Somehow, miraculously, his limbs were left undamaged by the blast and his torso remained intact, although the shock wave of the explosion left blood pouring from his ears and cascading from his nostrils.

Battered, befuddled and bloodied, he tried to stand but found that his legs refused to obey his aching brain. He slumped down onto his backside, his back against the brickwork and tried to make sense of where he was, but all he could hear was a dull ringing noise clanging through his head and in front of his eyes was a clouded grey fog. He blinked and shook his head as he tried to force himself back into some sort of consciousness, but the sense wouldn't come and the fog wouldn't clear.

He leaned his head back against the wall and closed his eyes, enjoying the feeling of calmness that came over him as the thumping in his brain began to fade. He wanted to sleep but something, somewhere in the very depths of his mind, told him that he needed to stay awake, but exactly why he couldn't quite fathom. He opened his eyes again and the grey fog began to dissipate ever so slightly, replaced instead with a blurry mist that thickened at the edges of his vision.

He tried to focus, tried to make sense of his surroundings, but all he could see was what seemed to be something burning in the distance. Where was he? What was on fire? Why couldn't he smell it? As he stared at the dancing flames, another image formed in front of him, slowly getting bigger as it came closer. He squinted, trying to make out what it was and smiled when his brain finally realised that it was a figure. A figure dressed in blue.

"Bell? he mumbled, "Corporal Bell, is that you?"

He reached out an arm towards the approaching figure and laughed as she came closer.

"Damn fine filly you are, Rosie Bell," he smiled, "Fancying seeing you here."

He blinked once more as he tried to get rid of the greyness and get a better look at the WAAF corporal. She took a few steps closer and Bloodstone saw that she wasn't alone. In fact, at her side was another version of herself, marching in perfect unison towards him. He laughed again. So, she was a twin after all. What damned good luck.

The two continued walking towards him and Bloodstone scrunched up his eyes and shook his head in another attempt to clear the greyness that still fogged up his vision. As he opened them again the two girls merged into one single body and the blue uniform slowly began to fade to green. A dark green. A green that Bloodstone had seen somewhere before. But where?

"Rosie?" he asked again, confused as the figure in front of him stopped and seemed to raise something into the air.

"Rosie?"

"Shut it, Tommy," Rosie ordered in a strange voice, still holding a blurry object above high above him.

Bloodstone's vision finally cleared, just in time to see the upturned butt of a rifle, gripped by the bleeding hands of a green-jacketed Wehrmacht sergeant.

The butt swung down and slammed once into his forehead. And the world went black.

CHAPTER FIFTY-SEVEN

"**W**ake up, you swine."

Bloodstone blinked and the tiny movement sent a bolt of white-hot fire zinging from the back of his eyes to the very core of his brain.

"Egh?"

"I said, wake up, pig," this time accompanied by a stinging slap across the cheek.

He blinked again and tried to open his eyes but the burning inside his skull was just too much and he clenched his eyelids tightly shut.

Another murmur was half out of his mouth when a bucket of ice-cold water landed full in his face, waking him with a jolt and forcing his eyes wide open.

"What the blazes?" he exclaimed as he struggled to adjust to the light and tried to force his addled mind to work out where he was.

"Talking English again are we?" growled a gruff voice in German and suddenly everything came falling into place in Bloodstone's confused brain. Heidler, the Lancaster, Cedric, von Winkel, Helgeland, the Jews, the shootout in the square and the incoming grenades.

"The bloody grenades," he murmured as he closed his eyes again and remembered the stench of burnt cordite and fried flesh.

Another slap, this time across the other cheek, brought him crashing back to the present.

"Wakey wakey, pig."

Bloodstone forced his eyes to focus and came face to face with what could only be described as a monster, inches in front of him and leering disgustingly. The creature possessed a squashed nose on a wide fleshy head and a shiny scalp that boasted not one single hair. The man's ears stuck out like two handles of a trophy and beneath his thick lips was a mouth filled with two rows of broken, yellow teeth. The face reminded him of an ogre that he recalled from a childhood picture book and he noticed with some despair that, just like the images in the book, the huge head sat atop an equally huge body that rippled and wobbled with fat and muscle underneath a stained white singlet.

"Like what you see, eh?" the ogre mocked as he saw Bloodstone studying him.

Bloodstone ignored the man and instead switched his inspection to his surroundings. He discovered that he was seated barefoot on a metal chair inside a damp stone-walled room no bigger than a large scullery. The ancient bricks on the wall were covered with green slime and the occasional rusty stain that looked suspiciously like dried blood. A hefty meat hook, suspended from the ceiling by a chain, hung in one corner and the floor beneath it was splattered red with what, he realised with a shiver, was most definitely blood. The cell was windowless and the only light came from a flickering electric lightbulb that hung on a wire just above his head.

"I asked you a question, pig," the monster snarled and swatted out a giant palm that caught Bloodstone across the left ear.

He reacted instinctively, balled his fists and made to leap from the chair and let fly at the beast. His efforts were in vain, however, as he found that his wrists and ankles were bound tight to the chair, rendering him unable to move. The only thing that he was able to flex was his head and he tried, but failed, to duck out of the way of the next enormous hand that came flying his way, this time cracking him across the right ear.

The giant laughed and took a step back to watch as Bloodstone shook his head in an attempt to clear the stars that were dancing in front of his eyes. As he did so, a droplet of blood fell from his scalp and trickled down his cheek. For the first time since he came to in the cell, he remembered the Wehrmacht sergeant and the almighty whack that the butt of the rifle had given him. It didn't take a genius to work out that he'd been scooped up from the pavement and deposited here, wherever here was.

As he wriggled his hands and feet and looked around the small room once more, the gravity of his situation finally began to dawn on him. He was in trouble, he knew, big trouble. Not only was he tied to a chair in a slimy cell somewhere, he assumed, in occupied Paris, but his jailor was one of the biggest and ugliest men he'd ever seen. And Bloodstone had come across some brutes in his time. But, if that wasn't enough, he realised, he was wearing the stolen uniform of an Obersturmbannfuhrer of the SS and carrying the papers of an imaginary Wilhelm von Winkel.

"Bugger," he said under his breath, realising that his odds weren't good at all.

In fact, they were positively terrible. He knew that the Nazis didn't mess around when it came to extracting information and he was fully aware that they'd have no qualms at all about putting a spy up against the wall and filling him with bullets. And a Brit running around Paris in the garb of an SS lieutenant-colonel certainly fell within the realms of spying.

The alternative, he realised, didn't bear thinking about. If his interrogators discovered who he really was then it was likely to be a much worse end. The news footage of little over a month before had seen Hitler publicly ripping up Bloodstone's picture and the German newspapers had gone to town with their ridiculous castigation of the so-called Italian Butcher, so it was clear that the Führer's cousin-once-removed would be a much sought-after addition to the Nazi trophy cabinet. The end result was likely to be the same, a blindfold and a bellyful of lead, but it would no doubt be a far more painful road to get there.

He also knew that it wasn't just him that was involved in all this now. The last thing he wanted to do was lead the enemy to Cedric, Lillianna and the rest of the Guibert-le-Doubs gang but he was fully aware that he was likely to have little choice in the matter when the Gestapo's finest starting turning the screws. No, he decided, he'd keep quiet for as long as possible and, when they eventually forced him to talk, which he knew that eventually they would, he'd spin the spy tale and make up something about being sent to Paris by the Allies. There'd be no mention whatsoever of Albert Bloodstone, he promised himself, no matter how much they went to town on him.

Of course, he hoped that it wouldn't get that far and that an opportunity to make a run for it would arise but, as he surveyed the cell once again, he knew that the chances of that happening weren't good at all. Revenge on Heidler would have to wait; now it was all about his own survival.

"Bugger," he muttered again, feeling somewhat desperate at the futility of his situation and not just a little frightened at what might lie ahead.

"What was that, pig?"

Bloodstone ignored the man and closed his eyes as, once again, he tried to numb the gigantic hammer that seemed to be banging away inside his head. What he wouldn't do for a soft bed and a decent night's sleep, he thought, or even just a regular army issue cot with a rock-hard mattress. Anything but this stinking cell and the hulking beast that was leering down at him with a look that made his stomach churn.

A grating noise behind Bloodstone brought him back to full attention and he opened his eyes as what sounded like a door being opened behind him. He craned his neck towards the sound, but a hefty slap brought his head back around and he listened with trepidation as footsteps approached him from behind. Fully expecting something to hit him across the back of the head, he closed his eyes again, tensed his neck muscles and waited for the blow to come. But as the footsteps kept moving and as his tender head stayed unassailed, he relaxed his body slightly and opened his eyes to find a uniformed figure standing in front of him. The figure, who was dressed in green, sported blonde hair beneath a peaked cap and possessed a set of high cheekbones on a cruel face, glared down at him with a pair of the bluest eyes that he'd ever seen.

"Vell vell vell, vot do ve have here?"

CHAPTER FIFTY-EIGHT

Bloodstone stared at the women who stood before him. He'd always had a thing for a lady in a uniform, but there was something about this particular individual that definitely didn't exactly float his boat. Granted, her olive-green tunic and skirt were cut tantalisingly tight around her well-formed figure and her blonde hair and blue eyes would certainly turn heads, but the look on her face sent a chill down his spine.

She bore no rank insignia that he could see yet the way that the singlet-clad brute had taken a step back and was now standing deferentially against the wall told Bloodstone that she was an officer. She certainly gave off an aura of authority, he thought as he stared back at the eyes that bore into him, but it was a type of authority that made him distinctly uncomfortable.

She unclasped her hands from behind her back and Bloodstone saw that she wearing black leather gloves, in which she held his Soldbuch. She cracked her knuckles and spoke again in English.

"Vilhelm von Vinkel, yes?"

Bloodstone ignored her and looked away. She stepped back and the giant took a pace forward and let fly with a clenched fist that crunched into the side of his head and sent stars spinning across his vision. He shook the twinkles from his head and fixed his eyes on a green patch of slime on the wall.

"I vill ask you vun more time. You are Vilhelm von Vinkel?"

Again Bloodstone ignored her and again the fist thumped into him, this time directly into his gut, knocking the wind out of him and leaving him choking for breath. The giant returned to his position by the wall and the women stepped forward once more.

She glared down at him as she waited for Bloodstone to regain his breath and, as he finally forced some air into his lungs, she spoke again.

"You like to play games, yes?"

She smiled but there was not a single iota of warmth in the expression.

"Ve can play games too," she continued before turning to the hulking monster.

"Ziegler, go and round up our little friends," she ordered in German, to which the man nodded, walked to the door behind Bloodstone and disappeared.

"So, it is just me and you now," she sneered, once again in English, "Do you vant to cooperate before our friend returns?"

Bloodstone took a deep breath and looked at her with a face that he attempted to force into his best impression of an enraged Prussian officer.

"I have no idea what you're saying," he snapped in German, "But I suggest you release me this instant."

The blonde laughed a humourless laugh.

"If you insist," she offered, now in German and strong with the accent of Berlin, "We'll try again, shall we? You are Wilhelm von Winkel?"

"Obersturmbannfuhrer Wilhelm von Winkel," he corrected harshly, "And I highly recommend that you untie me right now, otherwise I can assure that you'll be on a train to the Ostfront before you can say Heil Hitler."

He spoke with a confidence that he didn't feel and the woman simply smiled back at him. A cold, cruel smile that, once again, sent a chill through Bloodstone's body.

"I find it very odd that an SS Obersturmbannfuhrer is gunning down innocent German boys on the streets of Paris. Do you find that odd, Obersturmbannfuhrer?"

She added a mocking emphasis to the last word and Bloodstone simply glared at her as she continued.

"But what I find even more odd is that you get knocked unconscious and apparently start rambling away in English. Do you also find that odd, Obersturmbannfuhrer?"

Again the withering emphasis on the rank.

Bloodstone continued to glare. "There are things in this war that are way beyond your comprehension, *Fraulein*, now I will give you..."

A leather-clad hand whipped out and landed a stinging slap on his cheek, cutting him off mid-threat.

"Do not underestimate me," she warned as she pulled off a black glove, "There's a reason that I'm here today, which is because I'm very good at what I do."

She took a step back and smiled cruelly.

"But you'll find that out for yourself very soon, *Obersturmbannfuhrer*. And I can assure you that you'll find it far from enjoyable. Now, I'll admit that I have no idea who you are, although I do know that you're not who you claim to be. But, like I say, I'll find that out very soon. So, for one last time, would you like to tell me who you really are?"

Bloodstone glanced at the meat hook, looked back at the smirking woman and spoke, again with a forced and entirely unfelt confidence.

"For the last time, my name is Obersturmbannfuhrer Wilhelm von Winkel. And you will soon be in serious trouble, *Fraulein.*"

She laughed and stepped back, just as the door behind Bloodstone scraped open. Heavy footsteps came closer and he watched as the bulk of the giant Ziegler walked past him and set down a wooden crate in the corner of the cell. He peered at the box and the panic started to bubble as he tried to guess at the horrors that lay concealed within.

The woman muttered something that Bloodstone couldn't catch and Ziegler nodded in obedience, stepped closer until he was standing over the chair and leered down with a toothy grin. A string of spittle fell from the yellow mouth and hung in the air for a moment before it plopped onto Bloodstone's thigh. As he glared up at the man's ugly face, Ziegler fished in a pocket and pulled out a scrunched-up dark cloth. He shook it out and Bloodstone just had chance to see that it was a piece of brown sacking before it was forced onto his head and yanked down over his face.

He bucked his head as he fought against the hood, but his efforts were fruitless and a vicious thump on the back of the skull and a fist in the stomach stilled him and left him gasping for air. With his world now plunged into near darkness, he forced his mind to stay calm as he reminded himself that he couldn't allow his two captors to see his fear, no matter how much they went to town on him.

He slowed his breath and peered through the sacking but could see nothing more than dark shadows. He subtly wriggled his wrists, testing the bonds that tied him to the chair, but the rope wouldn't budge and he gave up, having achieved nothing more than badly chafed wrists.

From across the cell the woman snapped out an order. "Take them off."

Bloodstone could just about make out a shadow coming closer and he tensed as he sensed the presence of the hulking Ziegler looming over him once again. The man grabbed a fistful of his wet shirt and he squirmed as he felt a knife slash down through the material, cutting from collar to waist and leaving his torso open to the damp air. He was helpless to resist as, next, his belt was torn from its loops and the knife went to work again, slicing through the cloth of his trousers and underpants. The shredded clothing was ripped away from his body and tossed to the floor, leaving Bloodstone strapped to the chair in nothing more than a torn shirt. His backside and testicles were cold on the bare metal of the chair and he clenched his jaw underneath the hood, forcing his body to stop shivering as his mind went into overdrive thinking about what was coming next.

He didn't have to wait long to find out as something zipped through the air, slashed against his bare thigh like a firecracker and sent a bolt of pain searing through his body. He barely had time to comprehend that he'd been hit with a whip when the leather snapped through the air again and sliced into his belly, leaving a thick stinging welt across the skin.

Bloodstone tensed as he sensed the whip being lifted into the air again and he desperately tried to force his thighs together to shield his manhood, which felt more exposed than ever before. With his ankles strapped to the chair, however, his efforts were in vain and the leather cracked down to land perfectly on the tip of his unprotected penis, tearing into the skin and causing him to screech in agony. As his manhood shrivelled to the size of a walnut, he gritted his teeth and inwardly cursed himself for showing any sign of weakness to his captors.

The damage was already done, however, and a shrill command of "Again!" brought the whip crashing down onto his already-shrunken nether regions for a second time, then a third, then a fourth. The temptation to scream out was enormous yet, somehow, he managed to suffer the agony with nothing more than a hiss emanating from between his clenched jaws. The pain was horrific, however, and it was something of a relief when Ziegler changed his aim and starting slashing at the flesh of his stomach instead.

Each tortuous cut knocked the wind from Bloodstone and he gagged under the hood as he desperately tried to force air into his lungs, at the same time determined not to cry out as the whip continued to tear at his flesh. Once again Ziegler readjusted his aim and the whip went to work on Bloodstone's thighs, crisscrossing bloody stripes into the soft skin before finishing with an almighty and well-aimed slash of his already-brutalised genitals.

344

As he forced himself not to yell out from the fire-like pain that riddled his legs, groin and torso, the sack was snatched from his head and he found himself blinking in the blinding whiteness of the single bulb. His eyes adjusted to the light and he saw that his belly and legs were a mess of flayed skin and dripping blood, while his penis was barely visible between his bloodied legs.

The green-uniformed woman was standing in the corner of the small room with her arms crossed and, as he looked up and caught her eye, she stepped forward and held out her hand for the whip. Ziegler dutifully passed her the implement and retreated to stand behind Bloodstone, while the blonde took another step closer.

Now just a foot in front of him, she looked down with a mocking sneer and prodded Bloodstone's manhood with the handle of the whip, causing him to shudder involuntarily.

"I've never seen anything so small," she mocked in German as she poked at the offending member once more, "It's pathetic."

"In fact, you're pathetic," she continued, taking a step back.

"Now, before we carry on, would you like to tell me who you really are, Wilhelm von Winkel?"

Bloodstone inhaled, filled his lungs with damp air and looked down at the bleeding wounds that covered his body. He knew that this was only the start and that it would continue until the evil witch had forced him to talk. Soon, he knew, the whip would be replaced by something far worse, yet he was also fully aware that as soon as he did start to talk, all was lost. One little crack and they'd have him, he admitted, and when it started it wouldn't finish until they'd sucked every last piece of information out of him. Not just about who he was and what he was doing on the streets of Paris, but about Cedric and Lillianna and Rene and Josephine and Algy and Wilkins and the regiment and every other goddamn thing he knew. There was no option, he decided, and, although the realisation utterly terrified him, he knew that he had to stay silent no matter what. Even if the what was a slow and hideously painful death.

He looked up and caught her eye once again.

"Fuck you," he spat.

The words were barely out of his mouth when the whip snaked out and caught him viciously across the face, missing his left eye by a hair's breadth but driving a stinging welt from forehead to chin.

As she coiled the whip in her hands, she inspected the cut across Bloodstone's face, just like a painter would survey his handiwork. Seemingly satisfied, she brushed a curl of blonde hair from her forehead and glared at her victim.

"Do you want to speak to me like that again?"

Bloodstone, probing his swollen lip with the tip of his tongue, looked away towards the far wall and chose not to answer. There was little point antagonising the bitch, he decided, especially when he knew he was going to be beaten to a pulp sooner or later anyway. No need to make it any worse than it had to be.

She appeared to have read his mind and nodded towards Ziegler, who lumbered across the cell to the wooden crate that he'd set down earlier. As he bent over and began fiddling with it, she stroked the whip and looked down at Bloodstone.

"So, here's what's going to happen," she said in her hard Berlin accent, "Ziegler and I will now leave you to have a little time on your own. When we return later today, if you still choose not to cooperate, we will hang you from that hook..."

She paused briefly to give Bloodstone chance to glance at the meat hook that she indicated with a slight tilt of her head.

"...and we will whip you until your flesh is hanging from your bones like a rag doll. Then, if you still choose to be stubborn, we will tear out every fingernail and every toenail, which I can tell you right now, hurts more than you can conceive."

Bloodstone swallowed as she continued.

"And then, if you still choose not to talk, which is highly unlikely, Ziegler here will bring out his sledgehammer and will break every bone in your body, starting with your feet and working his way up. All the way up."

She paused to let her words sink in and Bloodstone forced his face not to show the fear that was churning away inside him.

"But don't worry," she continued, "We won't let you die. You should know that we're experts at what we do and you'll talk eventually. Everyone does. So, my suggestion is that you tell us everything we want to know when we return and save yourself a lot of pain."

"Although of course that would disappoint Ziegler terribly," she laughed and the bald head in the corner turned towards Bloodstone and leered grotesquely.

The woman, her speech over, looked at the monster. "Ready?"

He grunted in response and straightened up. As he did so, Bloodstone was horrified to see that the beast held a rat in each hand, gripped firmly by the tail and wriggling wildly as they tried to escape the man's grip. The creatures were bigger than any rodent Bloodstone had ever seen and he could make out huge yellow teeth protruding from their snapping mouths.

"Jesus," he cursed silently as he clenched his jaws together and tried to control the trembles that wracked his body.

Ziegler came closer, holding the rats high in the air as he walked, and the blonde spoke again.

"Our little friends here have had the misfortune of not being fed for a week. Poor things. I think it's fair to say that they're somewhat hungry. I do hope that they don't decide to have a nibble on your, what shall we call them, tender parts?"

She poked at Bloodstone's bloodstained genitals once again with the handle of the whip before turning to Ziegler.

"It is lunch time, ja?"

The giant nodded and waited for her to make her way to the door, which she swung open before leaving the room. As her footsteps faded into the distance, he too stepped towards the doorway, now out of view behind Bloodstone. The lightbulb clicked off, leaving the room in near darkness, with the only light coming from beyond the open door.

"Have fun, pig," Ziegler laughed and launched the rats towards Bloodstone with an almighty throw.

As the first creature landed claws-first on the back of Bloodstone's neck, the door slammed shut, plunging the cell into pitch-black darkness.

CHAPTER FIFTY-NINE

Bloodstone let out an almighty roar as the rat sunk its yellow teeth into the soft flesh of his neck. With his captors gone, he allowed the terror and the rage and the fear to pour out of him in a torrent and he bucked and kicked and screamed at the rodent that had embedded its talons firmly into the skin of his shoulders.

The thing hung on for dear life as Bloodstone threw his head from side to side and backwards and forwards as he tried desperately to dislodge the creature that had now withdrawn its teeth from his flesh and was viciously snapping its jaws just millimetres from his right ear.

He knew that there was a second one out there somewhere in the blackness but all of his efforts were focused on the vile critter that had now worked its way up the back of his neck and was clamped firmly to the top of his skull. He continued to throw his head around like a mad thing but somehow the rat clung on and Bloodstone almost sobbed as he felt it sniff at the open wound on his scalp. A second later it plunged its teeth into the torn skin and he howled again, tossing his head forward so violently that he nearly broke his own neck. This time, however, the rodent was unable to hold on and was thrown from its perch and cartwheeled through the air to land with a thump against the wall.

Just as Bloodstone heard it hit the brickwork, he felt the whiskers of the second rat tickling the toes of his right foot. With a grunt of horror, he tried to wrench his foot away but the rope around his ankle prevented him from doing anything more than lift the ball of his foot several inches from the ground to leave his toes pointing skywards. The creature, surprised by the movement, jumped on top of Bloodstone's foot and scurried up his bare leg. He shuddered as he felt its thick tail slide across his shin and tried desperately to force the top of his legs together to shield his tortured genitals. So shrunken were his crown jewels that, mercifully, he was somehow able to force his thighs close enough together to give himself some semblance of protection, just as the rat arrived on his lap.

He forced himself not to move as the creature sniffed at the bloody welts that crisscrossed his skin and he winced at the stabbing sensation of its claws digging into the wounds as it skulked across his thighs. He told himself that if he remained as still as a statue then the animal would simply sniff its way across his body and then disappear in search of tastier prey, so willed himself into stillness despite every part of his brain screaming at him to throw the thing off.

It took two seconds for his theory to crumble as the rat reared up on its back legs and dropped forwards to spear its teeth into the already-lacerated flesh of his belly. While its jaws went to work on his stomach, the rodent's snout went into his belly button and Bloodstone shrieked in a mix of pain and horror, throwing his hips forward in a pathetic attempt to free himself from the animal that felt like it was burrowing its way inside his body. His struggles proved fruitless and the creature continued its frenzied nibbling, its yellow teeth jabbing away as it tore chunks of skin from his torso.

As if that wasn't enough, Bloodstone felt the first rat scamper across his left foot and, half a second later, it too had scaled his leg and arrived on his lap. All attempts at his strategy of staying immobile had by now been long abandoned and he flailed about as wildly as his rope bonds would allow as he desperately tried to force the creatures from his body. The rodents refused to budge, however, and Bloodstone squirmed as he felt the newcomer push its nose between the skin of his thighs to sniff at what lay half-concealed beneath.

Before it had chance to investigate further it appeared to be distracted by its companion and it leapt from thigh to stomach to add its jaws to the feeding frenzy that was going on around Bloodstone's belly button. The feasting rat was none too impressed with the intrusion and gnashed its jaws at the interloper who, far from being put off, snapped back angrily. Not willing to share its meal of torn belly skin, the second rat abandoned its feast and set upon the new arrival, unleashing a high-pitched screech as it launched itself at its opponent.

Bloodstone, blind in the darkness, could only listen on in disgusted horror as the two rodents went to war on his bloodied thighs, scratching and biting as they fought for possession of his body. He tried again to jerk his hips forward to throw off the fighting creatures but somehow they clung on, their claws embedded in his legs as they tore and screeched at each other.

After half a minute of ferocious battling, the beasts seemed to tire and first one, then another, fell from Bloodstone's lap. The first landed with a thump on the stone floor, lay still for a second and then dragged itself away into a corner of the cell, squeaking pathetically as it moved. As Bloodstone listened to its broken body shuffle across the stone floor, the second rat dropped from his thighs and landed on the ground, its bleeding head resting on top of his foot. It too lay still for a moment, seemingly disorientated, and Bloodstone, as quick as a flash, lifted his toes and forced the ball of his foot down onto the creature's skull. The animal struggled as Bloodstone pushed with all his might, but he had it pinned and the fight had exhausted its strength. He felt the bone crunch under his skin and something plopped and soaked the sole of his foot as its head split open. Certain that it was dead, he lifted his foot and kicked the bloodied corpse as far away as his tied ankle would allow.

"Have that you filthy little blighter," he muttered as he felt his body relax slightly and his pulse return to something close to normal after the hellish ordeal of the last few minutes.

As he attempted to scrape a small piece of squashed rodent brain from under his foot, he mused that it had been nice to have a little victory for the first time that day, despite the fact that he knew it was likely to be his last for a long time, if ever.

"Damn" he growled, "Damn, damn, damn."

Here he was, potentially in the same city as his mother's murderer, yet tied to a chair in a stinking cell and seemingly unable to save his own skin, let alone even begin to entertain any thoughts of revenge. So close but so, so far, he thought miserably and tried to ignore the fact that at some point later that day his already battered and torn body would be brutalised beyond anything that he could imagine. A wave of self-pity flooded through him but he forced it away, refusing to give into the terror that he knew would engulf him if he allowed it.

"KBO, Bertie," he said out loud, "KBO."

And keep buggering on he would, he promised himself, for as long as he had breath left in his body and a functioning brain in his head.

CHAPTER SIXTY

He must have dozed off in the darkness and the scraping of the cell door brought him back to his senses. The bulb was flicked back on and the room was flooded with light. As Bloodstone's eyes adjusted, he saw the mutilated corpse of a rat, complete with grotesquely squashed head, on the floor just a few feet in front of him. The second creature lay dead in the corner next to its wooden crate and a thin trail of blood betrayed its final journey from the chair.

The heavy footsteps of Ziegler approached until the monster was standing in front of Bloodstone, staring down with amusement at the torn flesh of his abdomen. A look of surprise flashed momentarily across the German's face as he caught sight of the two dead rodents but the emotion vanished as quickly as it had arrived as he punted the closest corpse into the corner with a kick of his hobnailed boot. As the rat slammed into the brickwork, Bloodstone noticed that the singlet-clad man clenched a sledgehammer in his right hand, holding the heavy tool as if it were nothing more than a child's toy. He gulped, trying not to picture the weapon smashing into his bones, and forced his face not to show the terror that he felt inside.

The slamming of the cell door interrupted his thoughts and the voice of the woman spoke from behind him.

"I see that you've been enjoying yourself," she mocked, "Although you've all made a bit of a mess of each other, ja?"

Bloodstone assumed that the question was rhetorical and he looked away in the direction of the mangled rats as he listened to her heels tapping on the floor as she came closer. Ziegler made a step backwards and the blonde took his place, leering down at Bloodstone as she stood a foot in front of him with the whip still in her hand.

"Have you thought about what I said?" she asked with a glare as she caressed the handle of the whip with her fingers, "I presume you're ready to cooperate now?"

He ignored her and continued looking at the dead rats, noticing that the headless one was also missing a leg. Serves you right, you filthy bugger, he thought.

"The lady is asking you a question, pig," Ziegler grunted, moving closer.

Bloodstone averted his eyes from the maimed rats, looked into the monster's eyes and cleared his throat.

"Kiss my Austrian arse."

A flash of rage shot across Ziegler's face and he lunged forward with an enormous fist raised in readiness to strike down. A small leather-gloved hand snapped upwards just in time, however, stopping the man in his tracks.

"No, no, no," cackled the blonde cruelly, "Patience, Ziegler, there's plenty of time for fun, don't worry about that."

"Isn't that so?" she continued, smiling at Bloodstone as Ziegler stepped back again.

"So, where were we?" she mused as she fingered the whip once again, "Was it the flensing first, then the nails and then the bones? Or was it the bones first?"

Bloodstone glared into the cold blue eyes for a heartbeat and then looked away to stare back at the mangled rodents, trying desperately to hide his terror at what was about to come.

"No, it was definitely the flensing first," she concluded with a touch of glee in her voice, "Now, Ziegler, string him up."

The beast nodded obediently and lumbered towards Bloodstone, who realised that he would have to be untied from the chair before his adversaries would be able to attach him to the meat hook that swung gently from the ceiling. For the first time since he'd woken in the cell, a tiny flame of hope flickered in his chest. If he was going to have one chance to escape, this was it.

He clenched his fists behind the chair, impatient now for the man to cut his wrists from their bonds. Even a second of freedom would be enough to throw his battered body into action, he decided. A head butt followed by a few choice blows learnt from a kung fu master during his time in China and the two Nazis would be out for the count. After that, God knows what, but he had to cross the first hurdle before he could even think about how to flee from whatever prison he was being held in.

Ziegler took another step closer and Bloodstone wriggled his toes, willing him to hurry up. He disappeared behind the chair and Bloodstone caught the eye of the woman and held her glare as she leisurely fingered the whip.

"You just wait, you bitch," he said silently, imagining snapping her neck like a twig.

He was still staring into the blue eyes when something smashed into his stomach with the force of a freight train, driving the air from his body and causing him to vomit the remains of his breakfast across his bleeding thighs. As he gagged, desperate to force some oxygen into his gasping lungs, the thump came again, even harder this time and sent another bellyful of omelette spurting from his mouth. Through tear stained eyes he caught a brief glimpse of the sledgehammer and realised that Ziegler had laid into him from behind with the heavy wooden handle.

As he choked, unable to breathe, he felt his wrists being untied and his arms flopped limp and helpless behind him. No matter how much he tried to regain control of his limbs and clench his fists, his attempts were fruitless. His body was entirely devoid of any strength as his every effort was absorbed by a desperate need to fill his lungs

355

with even a thimbleful of air. He was helpless to resist as Ziegler forced his hands onto his lap and roped them together with a nimbleness belying his size.

Bloodstone could've sobbed as he felt his wrists tied once again and, finally able to force some oxygen into his burning lungs, he gulped down mouthful after mouthful of damp air. Seconds later a giant hand lifted him under the armpit and picked him up, still attached to the chair by his ankles. Powerless to resist, he was half carried and half dragged across the small cell, the legs of the chair scraping on the stone floor, until he found himself directly underneath the sinister-looking hook. Before he had chance to resist, Ziegler lifted him up and hung him from the hook by the rope around his wrists, his body dangling in the air and still firmly attached to the chair.

The Nazi cut the bonds at his ankles with his knife and the chair fell to the ground, leaving Bloodstone suspended in mid-air with his feet several inches above the floor. The ropes cut agonisingly into the skin of his wrists and his shoulders felt as if they would pop at any moment as his entire body weight hung from the hook. One more slash of the knife stripped away the remnants of his ripped shirt and he was left entirely naked, swinging by his wrists as his captors looked on with amusement. He heard the whip being unfurled behind him and the giant Ziegler pushed his sweating face an inch in front of Bloodstone's.

"Ready, pig?" he laughed and sprayed a mouthful of rancid spittle across Bloodstone's cheek in the process.

Bloodstone slammed his head forwards in reply, driving his forehead into the man's podgy face with all his might. He felt the bones of Ziegler's nose crunch under the impact and the giant recoiled with a pained howl. As he clenched his hands to his broken nose, a female shout of anger came from behind and Bloodstone heard the whip crack through the air before it slashed into his back in burning agony.

His body shook from the impact, driving the breath from his lungs, and he tensed, fully aware that Ziegler had straightened up and was coming at him, his ugly face plastered with rage. Blood poured from the man's nose and Bloodstone saw the knife, still clenched in a giant paw. The hand rose into the air and plunged towards his face, the blade glinting in the dim light of the bulb as it sliced towards his right eye.

Bloodstone could do nothing but shut his eyes and desperately twist his head away from the incoming blow, hoping beyond hope that it would smash into the bones of his skull instead of spearing through his eyeball and on into his brain. He yelled in fear and anger and helplessness as the razor-sharp blade flew closer, now just a millisecond from tearing his head to bloody ruin.

"STOP!" yelled a voice from somewhere behind.

The knife stopped with the blade a quarter of an inch away from puncturing into Bloodstone's ear, and Ziegler turned towards the sound with a look of fury on his bloodied face.

"Danke," said the voice calmly and, as Bloodstone's body twisted slowly towards the sound, he saw that the cell door had been thrown open and a man was standing in the doorway.

The figure wore the uniform of the SS, complete with colonel's leaves on his collar and a Knight's Cross at his neck. But it was the face that sent a shiver through Bloodstone's battered body, for it was a face that he would recognise anywhere. A face that he'd only seen once, on a photograph. A face that, nevertheless, had burned its way into his memory and a face that he would never forget. The face of the man he'd come to Paris to find. The face of the man who had murdered his mother. It was the face of Otto Heidler.

CHAPTER SIXTY-ONE

Bloodstone swayed gently from the hook and watched as Heidler crossed the cell towards him, seeing a man who, with short blonde hair, piercing eyes and a hard face framed by an angular jaw, was the very epitome of the Aryan race. He'd hated him from the moment that he'd first seen Algy's photo, but now that Heidler was here in the flesh, that hatred was like nothing he'd ever felt before.

But despite the anger that raged through his body and made him want to scream out loud, he forced himself to stay silent and keep his face rigid and emotionless. It would have been all too easy to curse Heidler and to threaten him with all the damnation in hell, but he knew that would get him nowhere. Maybe the man didn't know who he was or, if he did, maybe he was unaware that Bloodstone knew that he'd killed his mother. So many maybes, he thought, and with every ounce of his willpower taken up with keeping his rage from bubbling over, he simply didn't have enough brain capacity to figure them all out.

As Heidler reached Bloodstone, he stretched out a hand and, grasping a shoulder, twisted the naked man towards him. Bloodstone's body swung around as the hook swivelled on its chain and he found himself face-to-face with the German. The two men studied each other for a moment and Bloodstone found himself staring into the eyes of a man of about his own age, an inch shorter than his own six feet and with a mouth pursed in interested study. The Knight's Cross at his neck glittered with oak leaves and swords and a jagged scar ran vertically from underneath one ear, disappearing beneath the collar of his tunic. The man's eyes sparkled with life and, apart from the scar, his skin was clear and tinged with the remnants of a suntan. His strong jaw and high cheekbones framed a handsome face that was topped with a crop of short blonde hair, while his body appeared lean and muscular beneath the grey SS uniform.

A waft of cologne reached Bloodstone's nose and he glared at the man, who was now inspecting the old bullet scar on his bloodied chest. The colonel looked back up at his face and nodded to himself, seemingly satisfied.

"You are Albert Bloodstone, yes?"

A strange feeling, half surprise and half relief, shot through Bloodstone's veins but he forced his face to remain still as he continued to glower at the colonel.

"I will ask you once more, before I leave you to Fräulein Brandt here and her deranged assistant," he said again in well-spoken German tinged with an aristocratic accent, "You are Albert Bloodstone?"

Bloodstone looked at his two torturers, who were now standing to one side, almost at attention, and knew it was pointless to resist. Whatever Heidler had in store for him couldn't be worse than slowly being flayed to death in this stinking cell, he decided.

He cleared his throat and stared back into the blue eyes of the colonel.

"Yes," he grunted morosely, nodding his head slightly and, again, feeling something akin to relief.

Heidler smiled briefly and turned to Brandt and Ziegler.

"Do you know who this man is?"

Before they could respond, he continued.

359

"This is Major Albert Bloodstone, or the Italian Butcher as he prefers to be known."

The woman's eyes widened in shock while Ziegler's bloody face remained dumbly impassive.

"The Italian Butcher?" she asked, surprised, "But, Herr Standartenführer, how do you know?"

Heidler turned back to inspect Bloodstone and spoke to Brandt over his shoulder as he did so.

"There aren't too many Tommies as handy with a weapon and with such perfect German as our friend here. And you see that scar?"

He paused as Brandt peered at the old gunshot wound on his chest.

"That was picked up when he was scurrying away from Dunkirk back in '40, am I correct, Major?"

Bloodstone, somewhat perturbed by the man's knowledge, simply glared into the blue eyes.

"You see, we have a file as thick as my arm on this man. He is, how shall we say, of particular interest to the Fuhrer."

He took a step back, still inspecting Bloodstone as a man might survey a particularly interesting piece of art.

"So, when I heard that a bilingual gentleman had been picked up in Paris after ambushing a troop of our own Wehrmacht in broad daylight, I thought I'd come to take a look. After all, I hear that you were asking after me, isn't that so, Major?"

Bloodstone closed his eyes as he remembered yesterday's drunken antics at Le Petit Escargot and his brief enquiry to Helgeland.

"Sturmbannfuhrer Helgeland may have been a nasty piece of work, but he wasn't as stupid as he looked," Heidler continued, "So when I received a telegram early this morning to tell me that an Obersturmbannfuhrer von Winkel with the Knight's Cross was enquiring about me, I must admit that I was rather intrigued.

"Putting two and two together is my job, you see. And this time it seems that two and two have most definitely made four, wouldn't you say?"

Bloodstone could think of lots of things to say, but miserably concluded that silence was the best approach. Before he could continue his brooding, Heidler spoke again.

"It seems that there's little point introducing myself. You know who I am, don't you, Major?"

Bloodstone ignored the colonel, who simply smiled.

"Anyway, where are my manners?" he continued, "You must think we are animals, ja?"

He didn't wait for a response but turned to Ziegler.

"Cut this man down. And be gentle about it."

Knife in hand, the hulking monster strode across to Bloodstone, reached up and slashed once at the ropes around his wrists. No longer attached to the vicious hook, he dropped the three inches to the floor and landed on the balls of his feet. His legs refused to carry his weight, however, and he slumped to the ground in an ungainly pile of limbs.

"Pick him up," Heidler ordered and Ziegler grasped Bloodstone's armpit and hauled him to his feet with a grip that threatened to tear his arm from its already-tender socket.

"Gently!" snapped Heidler and Ziegler softened his hold ever so slightly as he forced Bloodstone upright, still with a giant paw digging painfully into his arm.

Bloodstone's legs felt like jelly and his head was swimming from the loss of blood, but he forced himself not to show any of this to the Nazi murderer so straightened his back and locked his face into a defiant scowl. He was helpless to resist, however, as Heidler grasped his wrists and slipped them into a pair of handcuffs behind his back.

"Apologies, Major, but we must take precautions, you understand. It would do neither of us any good if you were to be so foolish as to try to escape."

He paused as he turned to Brandt.

"Fräulein, bring this man something to wear, quickly."

Brandt left the cell and returned a minute later with a grey Wehrmacht blanket, into the centre of which a square hole had been cut. Ziegler unceremoniously tossed the blanket around Bloodstone and manoeuvred the hole over his head, leaving him wearing something akin to an Indian poncho. He hissed as the wool grated against his torn skin but felt decidedly less vulnerable now that he was no longer stark naked.

Heidler picked up the chair, set it back on its four legs and motioned for Bloodstone to sit. As he did so, Heidler turned to Brandt.

"You may leave us now. And take him with you," he continued, nodding in the direction of Ziegler.

"Jawohl, Herr Standartenführer, we will be outside," the blonde replied.

"Nein, you will not be needed anymore, this man is now in my charge."

Bloodstone noticed a brief flash of concern cross her face and Heidler laughed.

"Worry not Fräulein, my men are stationed just along the corridor. Our friend here will most certainly not be escaping today."

She nodded obediently, clicked her heels and marched towards the door with Ziegler lumbering in her wake. She pulled the door open and departed with not so much as a glance behind her. Ziegler, however, fixed Bloodstone with a deathly stare as he left, to which Bloodstone simply glared back and mouthed a farewell obscenity.

A second after the two had left the cell, a square-faced sergeant in the uniform of the Waffen-SS entered the room and closed the door behind him. Bloodstone surveyed the man, noticing the MP40 machine gun in his right hand and a set of short legs beneath a stocky but powerful-looking body. Heidler didn't acknowledge the man's presence and the sergeant said not a word as he stood at ease in front of the door, staring away into nothingness as he assumed the role of sentry.

Bloodstone realised that any attempt at escape was futile. He knew that Heidler was a trained killer and the guard looked fairly handy too, even without the weapon in his hand. When he added into the mix the fact that his wrists were chained together, his body was torn and battered like a piece of raw meat and there were undoubtedly more men outside the cell door, he knew that his chances of getting away were zero. Better to wait for a less suicidal opportunity, he concluded, whenever that may be.

As he was convincing himself of the virtues of patience, Heidler spoke again.

"I must apologise for the behaviour of my colleagues, they are a disgrace."

Bloodstone's head jerked up in shock as he heard the words. Not because of the unexpected apology, but because Heidler had spoken in faultless and unaccented King's English.

CHAPTER SIXTY-TWO

Heidler laughed as Bloodstone gawped at him agog, his weary brain trying to make sense of this latest development. "You seem surprised, Major," he said, once again in English, "You see, you're not the only one who has a gift for languages."

As Bloodstone stared, Heidler continued.

"Just like you, Major, I am the result of, what shall we call it, an international alliance. My father was German and my mother was British. Well, Scottish if we're being particular. I even schooled at Harrow for a term or two; I'd be surprised if we didn't meet on the rugger field once or twice. Funny how life turns out it isn't?"

Bloodstone thought that life was anything but funny at that moment but kept his mouth shut as Heidler continued.

"But we all have to make choices, don't we? So, you chose your side and I chose mine. And here we are."

"Here we are," Bloodstone repeated through gritted teeth, desperately trying to keep his anger from erupting.

Heidler cocked his head and smiled as he looked down at the battered Bloodstone.

"It seems that we're not so different, you and me. I have wondered many a time if we wouldn't be friends if things were different. Do you..."

Bloodstone snapped and the rage and the hatred and the frustration poured out of him.

"We are nothing alike!" he roared as he strained against the handcuffs that held him to the chair, "You're a filthy murdering Nazi bastard and I'm going to fucking kill you!"

Heidler appeared genuinely taken aback by the outburst and took a step backwards as Bloodstone continued, his voice now a whisper.

"You just wait," he hissed between clenched teeth, "One day I'll gut you like a fish and I'll burn you alive, you fucking coward."

The guard at the door took a step forwards but Heidler, still looking down at Bloodstone, waved him back into position with a flick of his hand.

"Ah yes, your mother," the German said remorsefully as his face took on a look of sadness, "Please accept my apologies for that whole regrettable incident."

Bloodstone glared, wide-eyed, as Heidler continued.

"I can assure you it was nothing personal. I was simply following orders. I took not one ounce of pleasure in doing what I had to do. We both have masters, yes? And when those masters give us orders, we have no option but to obey. Am I correct?"

"Not if that order's from an evil bloody maniac. And not if it's to murder an innocent woman," Bloodstone spat back, the rage still pumping through his blood but feeling ever so slightly more under control now that he'd unleashed his wrath.

"Interesting," Heidler mused, "I had a dear aunt in Hamburg, killed recently in her bed by a bomb dropped by your brave terror fliers, who would've had something to say to you about that.

"You see, Major, it is all a question of perspective. Now, we could sit here all day discussing the principles of jus in bello and rights and wrongs, but I don't think that's going to get us anywhere, do you?"

When Bloodstone didn't reply, Heidler continued.

"So, I would ask your forgiveness for my part in your mother's death and request that you see my involvement for exactly what it was, just business. So, Major, no hard feelings?"

Bloodstone could've laughed if the topic had been anything else. Was Heidler for real, he wondered, or was he simply goading him? Either way, he still utterly despised the man who stood in front of him, even more so now that he'd finally met him in the flesh. He also realised that he'd been a fool for allowing himself to lose control and lash out. He'd shown weakness, he knew, and there was no doubt that a professional like Heidler could smell weakness a mile away and could exploit it expertly. From now on, Bloodstone decided, it would be Geneva Convention all the way. Name, rank and number only.

Heidler seemed disappointed that his captive hadn't responded to his offer of forgiveness and shrugged sadly. He smoothed a stray strand of blonde hair, cleared his throat and spoke again.

"I'm sure you're not surprised to hear that there will be someone who will be very pleased to see you. As far as I'm aware, you've not met your Cousin Adolf before, is that correct?"

Again, Bloodstone chose not to reply and Heidler continued.

"That talk of a price on your head wasn't fiction, you know. The Führer would be genuinely interested to meet with you. Family is family, after all, is it not?"

Bloodstone snorted derisively and Heidler smiled kindly.

"You mustn't be afraid, dear Major. The Führer is, what do you English say, a thoroughly decent chap, despite what your ridiculous newspapers would have you believe."

Bloodstone snorted again.

"Now, I will leave to make a telephone call and you will wait here. I won't be long and Hauptscharführer Gunther here..."

Heidler nodded in the direction of the SS sergeant.

"...will take good care of you. I highly recommended that you don't make any foolish attempts to escape. Gunther is one of the toughest men I have ever met, and I can tell you that I've met a few.

Several of his comrades are also waiting outside the door and they are equally ferocious. In summary, Major, you have nowhere to go."

As Bloodstone watched Heidler leave the cell, he had to admit that his options were somewhat limited. The door was slammed shut behind the colonel, but not before Bloodstone caught a glimpse of several uniformed men, decked out in SS grey, standing at ease in the corridor beyond. He sighed to himself, tilted back his head and closed his eyes, determined not to show Gunther the fear that swilled around inside his torn belly. His future was very much in his enemies' hands, he admitted miserably, and there was nothing right now that he could do about it. It would have to be a case of wait and see and, if the opportunity did arise to escape or to exact bloody revenge on Heidler, he'd snatch it then.

He sat in silence for several minutes, listening to the drip-drip-drip of a leaking pipe somewhere behind him and pretended to be asleep. He wished real sleep would come but his tattered skin stung like the devil and his fear of what the future held refused to allow his mind to rest.

It wasn't long before the door swung open again and Heidler returned. He beamed at Bloodstone as if he was returning to a long-lost friend.

"It is good news, Major," he smiled, "The Führer's staff have confirmed that we should attend him post-haste. He knows not of your capture yet, but I have no doubt that he will be delighted to hear the news."

He continued to beam as he spoke, seemingly unable to hide his glee at the summons to see his leader.

"It seems that we have a journey to make, Major, so we will depart as soon as possible. Of course, we still have lots to discuss and you have much to tell me about how you landed in Paris and precisely what you're doing here, but there will be plenty of time for that after. I can assure you that my methods are far more refined than those of Fraülein Brandt and her monster, but they are guaranteed to be successful.

"Anyway, I digress," he smiled, "We have an appointment to get to so we must hurry, you wouldn't want to keep your cousin waiting, would you?"

For the first time since he'd met Heidler, Bloodstone saw a glint of something flash across the man's eyes. It was gone almost before it had arrived and it distinctly unnerved him. It wasn't quite the Helgeland madness, he reasoned, but was something else. Something colder, crueler. Whatever it was, it sent a shiver down his spine and he forced his face to stay emotionless, despite the unease that flooded through him.

His grim thoughts were distracted as Heidler spoke again, still in English.

"Of course, we'll need to get you cleaned up before we leave. Those thugs have made quite a mess of you it seems. But be assured that we have the very best medical care available; you will be well looked after, Major."

Bloodstone was still trying to decide if Heidler was being serious or was mocking him when the German retreated behind Bloodstone and unlocked the cuffs that bound him to the chair. At the same time, he saw Gunther heft his MP40 and point the muzzle in Bloodstone's direction.

"Let's go," Heidler ordered and headed for the door, beckoning for Bloodstone to follow.

He rubbed at the skin of his wrists that had been chafed raw by the rope and the cuffs and pushed himself wearily to his feet. He swayed slightly as his battered body protested at being forced to support itself and he reached out to the back of the chair to steady himself.

As the door swung open, Gunther motioned menacingly with his weapon and Bloodstone, understanding the message, tottered after the colonel with the MP40 following just inches from his spine. Four SS troopers crashed to attention as the trio emerged into the corridor and Heidler motioned for them to stand at ease. They eyed Bloodstone coldly and he returned their glares as he passed, following closely behind Heidler who strolled purposefully along the corridor, which consisted of whitewashed brickwork interspaced with a series or metal doors every few paces. The soldiers, all armed with machine pistols, dropped into step behind Gunther and the six men continued onwards in Heidler's wake.

The motley procession followed the corridor as it took a left turn and passed a small doorless room that Bloodstone saw contained a tattered wooden desk of the type that he'd used at school. Slumped with his head on the desk and his backside on a low stool was a wrinkled old man, entirely naked except for a set of chains that bound his skinny ankles to the legs of the table.

Bloodstone heard a titter from behind him and he glanced backwards to see one of the SS troopers smirking in his direction.

"Juden," the soldier laughed as he winked at Bloodstone.

Another of the soldiers laughed and Bloodstone turned back to his front, utterly disgusted. Before he could look again at the helpless creature sprawled on the desk, they had passed the room and were ascending a narrow staircase, which brought them out into another immaculately whitewashed corridor. A few paces further and Heidler paused outside a steel door. He turned a handle and the door opened inwards, at which he gestured for Bloodstone to enter.

Bloodstone did as he was instructed and found himself inside a windowless room measuring five paces by five paces and, once again, painted brilliantly white. A bed, not dissimilar to the type found in a hospital, stood in the centre of the room, while a metal sink and a small matching toilet were set against the far wall. In one corner and more suited to an officers' mess than this bleak white chamber was a brown leather armchair and it was to this that Heidler pointed.

"Wait here," he ordered and closed the door, leaving Bloodstone alone.

As he heard the door lock behind him, Bloodstone glanced around in search of a potential escape route. He wasn't surprised to find the effort wasted, however, as he discovered the room entirely devoid of any features that would enable him to flee his current situation. The low ceiling, also painted white, contained no air vents or grates or anything else of interest, while the lack of windows made the recently bolted door the only way in and out.

Disappointed, he shuffled across to the armchair and sank down onto the leather, grimacing as the rough blanket snagged against a piece of torn skin. He had barely settled his aching backside into the chair when he heard the sound of the door being unlocked and, seconds later, it swung open to reveal Gunther, still with the MP40 in his hands. The

hauptscharführer strode into the room and Bloodstone, not bothering to stand, watched as he was tailed by two female nurses decked out in the blue and white uniform of the DRK, Germany's own Red Cross. One of the women was pushing a metal trolley and Bloodstone eyed it suspiciously as he wondered at the contents of the boxes and bottles piled upon it.

Gunther gestured for Bloodstone to stand and he reluctantly did so as the trolley was parked alongside the bed and a brake applied to one of its wheels. His eyes wandered from the trolley to the two nurses and he studied them closely, taking in their matching grey stockings, blue and white pinstriped dresses and the white starched aprons that seemed very much at home in the small sterile room. Both women were around five feet tall and in their mid-twenties with dark hair pinned beneath their white caps, with one thin and wiry and the other well-built and busty. Neither of them could be described as pretty, but they weren't unattractive either. They looked simply functional, Bloodstone thought as he watched them fiddle with the contents of their trolley.

Gunther pushed passed him and dropped his backside onto the chair, the MP40 on his lap and the muzzle pointing in Bloodstone's direction. The bustier nurse, who appeared to be the senior of the two, beckoned him silently towards the bed and, doing as instructed, he made his way towards her. Without a word and with a blank expression, she reached out and lifted the blanket over his head. As the wool was removed to reveal his bleeding nakedness, the second nurse let out a gasp, which caused the first to whip her head around and fix her with a scolding glare. Rebuked, she stared nervously at the floor as her superior perused Bloodstone's cuts and welts with a professional eye.

Seemingly satisfied with her inspection, she tapped the bed with a firm hand, indicating for him to lie down. He did as ordered and lifted himself onto the crisp white sheets and lay back with his hands covering his battered genitals. With her face still entirely expressionless, she swatted his hands away and surveyed the formerly magnificent example of a penis that was now a bruised and shrivelled wreck punctuated with tiny teeth marks.

She rapped something unintelligible to her colleague, who reached to the bottom shelf of the trolley and came up with a small steaming bucket, which she held aloft. The supervisor then dipped a cloth into the liquid, squeezed out the excess moisture and proceeded to dab at the wounds on Bloodstone's stomach. He hissed as the cloth made contact with his torn flesh but the hands were surprisingly gentle and, despite the pain, he rested the back of his head on the pillow in the knowledge that, finally, here was a German who wasn't trying to do him some harm.

The nurse continued to clean his wounds, moving from his belly to the shredded skin of his thighs and then onto his lacerated privates, all the while her face a picture of rigid professionalism. The pain was terrific as she swabbed at the cuts on his nether regions and he gritted his teeth, determined not to show weakness in front of the onlooking Gunther. The bucket-holding nurse caught his eye, however, and he saw a look of sympathy flash across her face before, once again, she glanced nervously away.

When all the wounds were clean, including the lash on his back, the throbbing welt across his face and the hole in his scalp, the bucket was replaced with a tub of thick white salve that gave off a minty aroma. Bloodstone tensed as the senior nurse scooped up a liberal handful and smeared it across his wounded stomach but, instead of the expected sting, he found the cream to be delightfully soothing. He let out a groan of satisfaction as she smothered his skin, replacing the fiery agony with a refreshing tingling feeling. Next, layers of soft white bandages were wrapped around each thigh and he was instructed to sit up to allow another to be swathed around his torso, leaving him somewhat mummified from knees to nipples.

Only when the final bandage had been secured with a series of wicked-looking safety pins did the nurse step back to assess her handiwork. Seemingly satisfied, she nodded to herself and clicked her fingers at her colleague, who produced a pint-sized tin flask from the trolley and uncorked it. A metal tumbler followed, into which she poured a generous measure of milky liquid and handed the cup to Bloodstone. Gathering that he was meant to drink and assuming it unlikely that they would try to poison him after going to the trouble of bandaging his wounds, he raised it to his lips and took a sip. He nearly choked on the bitter medicine that tasted like a mix of sweat and battery acid, but the head nurse eyed him sternly.

"Trinken," she commanded and Bloodstone obeyed, forcing the rancid mixture down his throat and somehow resisting an overwhelming urge to gag.

"Now, rest," the nurse ordered in German as she busied herself with repacking her trolley.

Her job complete and with her face still emotionless, she nodded once at Gunther and then motioned toward the door with a tilt of her head. Her colleague, understanding the instruction, pushed the trolley toward the exit and rapped once on the steel door. A second later the door swung open and the pair departed. As Bloodstone watched them go, he noticed a final glance from the thinner of the two nurses and a nervous half-smile in his direction that vanished almost before it had appeared.

He tried to return the smile but found that the muscles of his face refused to work. Instead, his cheeks and his jaw seemed to have been engulfed by some sort of paralysing pins and needles. He attempted to pinch the skin of his cheeks to bring them back to life, but his fingers wouldn't move and his arms remained limp and useless at his sides. A strange sensation tingled at his toes and began to move slowly up his body, flowing through his legs like a warm wave and continuing onwards and upwards until his entire being felt as if it was wrapped in a deliciously cosy cocoon. His eyelids drooped and he fought to keep his eyes open but the overwhelming desire to drift away into blissful unconsciousness was just too much.

His sluggish brain still had just enough sense to know that whatever he'd been forced to drink was casting him off to sleep, but he didn't care. For the first time in what seemed like forever, there was no pain. None at all. Instead, his skin and his limbs and his bones and every part of his body felt glorious and the thought of the impending sleep that careered towards him was delightfully welcome. He finally allowed his eyes to close and sighed as the cocoon hugged him even tighter, like an enormous piece of cotton wool. The last thing he heard was a dull and faraway thump as the door was bolted shut once again, but he didn't care. He felt good.

CHAPTER SIXTY-THREE

"Wakey wakey."

Bloodstone groaned.

"Eh?"

"Wakey wakey, Major," he heard again and hesitantly opened one eye.

He was met with a dazzling whiteness that was punctuated with a blurry pink blob and he blinked several times as he attempted to adjust his sleepy eyes to the light. After a few more blinks the pink blob slowly defuzzed to reveal a set of blue pupils beneath blonde hair topped by a death head-adorned cap.

"Did you have sweet dreams, Major?" Heidler asked with a smile.

Bloodstone scowled at the smiling face and looked down at his prone body to see that he was tucked in beneath cotton bedsheets with just his arms, shoulders and head protruding. He was still in the same room where the nurses had bandaged him up and he looked around to see that the gun-toting Gunther had vanished, leaving the room empty except for the beaming Heidler. The windowless room meant he had no idea what time of day it was and he had no clue how long he'd been asleep for, although he was surprised to find that, for the first time in what felt like forever, he felt fully rejuvenated. Strange, he thought, considering that he'd quite obviously been drugged by whatever the grim-faced nurse had fed him.

He was snapped out of his musings by Heidler, who was holding up a coat hanger, the contents of which were hidden inside a black suit cover.

"This is for you, Major," the Nazi announced and walked to the armchair, over which he draped the bag.

"Be ready in twenty minutes," he ordered as he walked towards the door, "We have an appointment to get to."

With a final smile he left the room and the door was locked behind him.

Intrigued, Bloodstone pulled himself upright on the bed and pushed back the sheets. He found that he was naked except for the bandages that covered half of his body but was somewhat surprised to discover that his wounds didn't hurt like he'd expected them to. Sure, they throbbed a little under the bandages but, for a body that had been beaten and flogged and gnawed at, he didn't feel too ropey.

He swung his legs over the side of the bed and stood up, stretched his arms skywards and cracked his knuckles. He padded across to the chair and lifted the coat hanger, which he carried back and laid upon the bed. The suit cover had a zip on the front and he pulled it down.

He let out a whistle as he saw what was inside and pulled the contents out and laid them on the bed. First came a pair of khaki trousers, complete with perfectly pressed creases down the front. Next was a matching blouse, followed by a battledress shirt with the badge of the Parachute Regiment on the sleeve and epaulettes boasting the twin pips of a British major. A tie, belt and Army issue socks and underpants completed the collection, along with a red beret that, once again, was decorated with the livery of the Paras. Bloodstone fingered the familiar metal badge and stroked the soft red material, feeling a pang of nostalgia for the regiment that had been his home for the past two years and, right now, felt further away than ever.

As he looked down at the clothes spread out on the bed, he had to admire the Nazis' logistical abilities. The uniform looked as if it had been weaved yesterday in the mills of Manchester and the label inside the collar of the blouse proudly boasted the War Office mark that he had seen a thousand times since taking the King's shilling. His enemies were either excellent copycats, he thought, or they had a handy source inside the warehouses of His Majesty's stores.

With a final stroke of the red headpiece, he tossed the beret onto the bed and started to dress. He had little doubt that his next destination was Berlin for a date with the Führer and by now he had accepted that was unlikely to conclude with anything other than a grisly end. However, he was determined to show his enemies how a British officer faced his maker and he could think of nothing better to do it in than the uniform of the best damned regiment in the world.

As he dressed, he wasn't the least bit surprised to find that the uniform fitted him perfectly. The only thing missing, he realised, was the glorious row of medal ribbons that should've been stitched above his left breast pocket. That and a pair of boots, he thought as he sat on the bed and pulled on the familiar woollen socks. Fully dressed at last, he padded across the room and brushed his teeth with a toothbrush that had been left, complete with blob of minty toothpaste, on the small metal sink.

He had just washed out his mouth with a handful of cold water when the door creaked open and Gunther appeared, the MP40 in one hand and a pair of black leather boots in the other.

"Put them on, now," the sergeant ordered in German and threw the boots onto the bed.

Bloodstone turned from the sink and glanced nonchalantly at the boots, then at Gunther, then back at the boots. Instead of obeying the squat man's order, he casually turned back to the sink, picked up the toothbrush, now devoid of toothpaste, and started to brush his teeth all over again.

"Quickly," Gunther commanded and Bloodstone ignored him, choosing instead to scrub lazily at his teeth.

"I said quickly," he snapped and Bloodstone turned to give him a toothy grin.

"Can't you see I'm cleaning my teeth?" he replied in German through a mouthful of toothbrush, before adding, in English, "You damned fool."

Whether or not the sergeant understood, Bloodstone didn't know, but the condescending tone of his words were clear and the man took a step forwards and cocked his weapon. Bloodstone smirked, spat out a mouthful of water and carefully placed the toothbrush back on the sink. He turned casually back to Gunther and spoke in German once again.

"What did you want me to do?"

"The boots. Now," the sergeant hissed and waved the barrel of his machine pistol menacingly at the bed.

"These ones?" Bloodstone asked dumbly as he pointed at the boots that lay atop the clean white sheets.

Gunther growled and took another step closer.

"Alright, alright," Bloodstone laughed in English, "Don't get your knickers in a twist."

As he spoke, he strolled over to the bed and plucked up the offending footwear, which he saw were British standard issue paratrooper boots, buffed so brightly that he could almost see his face in them. He plonked his backside onto the bed and pulled the boots, one by one, onto his stockinged feet. Again, it was no surprise that they fitted like a glove.

"You know something, Hauptscharführer?" he said in German as he tucked the hems of his trousers into the boots, not deigning to look back in the sergeant's direction and not waiting for an answer, "I don't think you'd make a very good Para, do you?"

He continued as he felt Gunther's eyes burning into his back.

"I mean, these boots look like they've been polished by a sailor," he lied, "If you were in my company, I'd have you up on a charge. You should be ashamed of yourself."

He looked over his shoulder to give the SS man a broad grin before he returned his attention to his laces, which he tied with a flourish. Next, he straightened the bottom of his trousers and stood up, turning to face Gunther.

"Oh, and another thing, Hauptscharführer," he said with the most condescending smile that he could muster, "When I'm in the uniform of a British major, you will address me accordingly, do you understand?"

Gunther glared at him with a look of thunder, which Bloodstone took a moment to enjoy before he continued.

"That means you'll reply *Jawohl, Major.* And you really should salute too," he gloated gleefully as he pointed to the badge on his beret.

The Nazi growled once more, took a step forward and Bloodstone could see that it was taking every ounce of the man's self-control to stop himself from lashing out. He was just about to continue with his mockery when a second uniformed figure entered the room. It was Heidler, still dressed in the full grey garb of his SS uniform.

All the joy of the last few minutes' teasing immediately drained from Bloodstone and was replaced by an ice-cold loathing and a deep desire to strangle the man who was now smiling warmly at him. Now it was his own turn to practice some self-control, he thought.

"Well, well, well, Major," Heidler exclaimed in perfect English as he looked Bloodstone up and down, "Just like new."

"Are you impressed with the uniform?" he continued, "You see, you Brits aren't the only ones who can turn their hand to a spot of forgery when required."

That last statement was something of a comfort to Bloodstone, who realised that his enemy assumed that his Wilhelm von Winkel attire had come directly from the Allies, which hopefully meant that Rene and the rest of the Guibert-le-Doubs gang were in the clear. Nevertheless, he knew, he'd have to get his story straight for when the inevitable interrogation began again.

He was snapped out of his daydreaming by the muzzle of Gunther's MP40 prodding him in the small of the back.

"It is time for us to leave," Heidler continued, the Führer is waiting."

Once again, the glint of icy cruelty flashed across the man's eyes and Bloodstone swallowed. It vanished within a heartbeat and the smile returned.

"I must apologise once again, Major, but I'm sure you understand that precautions are necessary."

As Heidler spoke, Bloodstone's arms were grasped behind him and, before he had chance to react, a pair of handcuffs were slipped onto his wrists. Next, his beret was snatched from his head and a hood took its place, plunging his world into near darkness. It all happened so quickly that Bloodstone could do little to react and his efforts to shake the hood free proved fruitless. The muzzle of a gun poked him in the back again as a signal to move and he did so, walking blindly forwards and directed by a hand that grasped his upper arm.

The sounds that penetrated the hood and the occasional glimpse of the ground beneath his boots were the only clues to his surroundings as he was marched away from his room. He tried to count his footsteps and memorise whenever he went left and right, but he soon found it hopeless and lost his bearings entirely as his blind stumbling turned first one way then the other. It wasn't long before the concrete floor gave way to wooden floorboards and the sound of typing and muted office chit-chat reached his straining ears. Several paces further on and a chilly blast of air told Bloodstone that he was outside, although so little light penetrated the hood that he found it impossible to tell whether it was day or night.

A warning of "Steps!" rang out from beside him and he faltered as he was led down a short flight of stairs, still guided by the hand around his bicep. He continued forwards until the hand pulled him to a stop and he could just about make out the sound of idling engines intermingled with low voices chuntering in the distance.

The voices came closer but still he was unable to comprehend any words and he resisted as the barrel of the gun prodded him hard in the spine, instructing him to move once again. The prod came again and he tensed, completely bewildered in the darkness and unwilling to move forwards into the unknown.

"Relax," came a voice in English from beside him, which he could just about make out to be that of Heidler.

"You're about to get into a car. Please, I suggest that you don't struggle."

There was something almost reassuring about the voice and Bloodstone would've felt calmed if he hadn't have known that it came from the mouth of a cold-blooded and thoroughly dangerous killer. Nevertheless, he allowed himself to be guided downwards as he clambered blindly into the seat of a car. His head whacked the metalwork as did so and he winced as the impact fell exactly on the point of the recent rifle butt to his skull.

Finally seated, he felt fingers fiddling with the handcuffs and seconds later they were released. He was tempted to take advantage of this moment of freedom and rip the hood from his head but the muzzle of the MP40 that was now pushed against his chest made him think again. A few more seconds and his right wrist was back in the cuffs and a metallic clicking sound told him that he'd been chained to the car. He shook his wrist, which seemed to be locked to something to the side of his right thigh, but the attempt was useless and he gave up, unable to move his arm more than in inch in any direction. He satisfied himself with the scant consolation that his other wrist had been left unrestrained but another prod from the gun when he reached up to the hood, this time against his forehead, once again persuaded him otherwise.

He felt the car rock as other bodies climbed silently inside and seconds later the engine roared and the vehicle took off. The occasional flash of artificial light visible beneath the hood told Bloodstone that it was darkness outside and he assumed that it must be late into the night as the car seemed to speed along the Parisian roads unhindered.

As the vehicle accelerated along the city streets and swerved around unseen obstacles, Bloodstone began to feel distinctly car sick underneath his hood and he felt an overwhelming urge to vomit. He forced himself to keep control of his gut, however, determined not to soil himself in front of his captors. The thought that surely it couldn't be long until they reached Le Bourget airfield, or wherever it was that they'd board a flight to Berlin, helped to strengthen his resolve.

Half an hour after departing, or what felt like half an hour but could well have been five minutes, the hood was suddenly pulled from Bloodstone's head. The car was still travelling at breakneck speed and he glanced about him as he tried to make sense of his surroundings while simultaneously gasping in mouthfuls of fresh air. The interior of the car was bathed in moonlight and he saw that he was sitting in the forward-facing backseat of a top-of-the-range six-seat Mercedes, not dissimilar to the car that he'd shared with Helgeland yesterday. Or was it yesterday, he wondered as he realised that he had no idea how long he'd been asleep. Directly in front of him and separated by a glass screen was the driver, of whom Bloodstone could see only the back of a black-haired head topped with a green field cap. To Bloodstone's left sat Gunther, with the MP40 on his lap and, as ever, the muzzle pointed in his direction. Opposite Gunther and sitting in the rearward-facing seat was Heidler, who twirled the hood in his hands as he smiled at Bloodstone.

"I'm sorry about that," he said in German as he wagged it in Bloodstone's direction, "But I think you would do the same, ja?"

Bloodstone scowled and turned his head to look out of the window, watching as the moonlit-clad landscape sped past. He saw that they had left the streets of Paris far behind and were cruising through flat, open countryside, punctuated by shadowy trees and the occasional farmhouse. His confusion must've showed on his face as Heidler spoke again, seemingly reading his mind.

"You thought we were flying to Berlin, yes?"

Bloodstone scowled again and ignored the colonel who, unperturbed, carried on.

"No, no, no, Major, the Führer is not in Berlin. We will be meeting him somewhere else entirely. We don't need an aircraft for this journey, so just settle in and enjoy the drive."

Bloodstone refused to let the surprise show on his face but a small part of him was relieved that he wasn't destined for the very centre of his enemies' lair. However, another part of him knew that the end result was likely to be the same, wherever it happened.

Before he could wonder about the likely destination of the nighttime journey, Heidler spoke again.

"This is yours?" he asked and reached out a clenched hand in the darkness.

Bloodstone eyed him warily and Heidler laughed.

"You shouldn't be so suspicious, I really have no wish to do you harm you, surely you believe me?"

Again, the briefest look of cold steel appeared and was gone almost immediately.

"Go on, take it," he insisted and opened his fist to reveal a small piece of metal.

Bloodstone squinted in the darkness and saw that the Nazi was holding a bullet. His bullet, the lucky Mauser round that had been gouged out of his flesh after the Dunkirk evacuation three years before and that he'd last seen in the breast pocket of von Winkel's SS uniform. He held out his left hand and Heidler dropped the dented piece of brass into his palm. He eyed it briefly before he unbuttoned the pocket of his khaki battledress and tucked the lucky charm safely away.

He looked up to see Heidler watching him with his head cocked and a look of studious interest plastered across his face. As the blue eyes of his mother's killer bored into him, Bloodstone touched the bulge in his pocket. He was going to need more than just good luck when the speeding Mercedes reached its destination, he knew, wherever that was going to be.

CHAPTER SIXTY-FOUR

"You know, Major, I do miss London tremendously. What's it like nowadays? I imagine the war has somewhat taken the shine off it, am I correct?"

Heidler had been trying to make conversation for the last hour but Bloodstone had refused to respond and chose instead to stare out of the window and watch the shadows of the passing countryside. He had noticed a while ago that the car was travelling in the wake of two motorcycle outriders and occasionally the dimmed headlights of the Mercedes would illuminate the riders to reveal their coal scuttle helmets and the machine guns strapped across their backs.

"I was tempted to spend a few days there last time I was in England," Heidler continued, unabated, "Christmas '41, I think it was, but unfortunately there just wasn't the time. Such a shame."

Bloodstone stiffened, knowing full well why the Nazi had visited England two Christmases ago and an image of his mother's bloodstained body flashed through his mind. He clenched his fists in silent rage and, for the umpteenth time since the journey began, he wriggled his right wrist against the handcuffs that chained him to a reinforced metal ring beside the seat.

"Does the Dorchester still serve that wonderful foie gras? Oh I miss it so! And did you ever visit Miss Nora's in Pimlico? What girls, Major, what girls!"

Bloodstone had indeed tasted the pâté and he'd also enjoyed the questionable wares of London's finest knocking shop, but he was damned if he was going to humour Heidler by joining in the conversation.

He was saved from further conversation when, a few minutes later, the car slowed and pulled to a halt at the side of the road. Bloodstone's door was opened and he was met with a torch shining in his eyes, held by one of the motorcycle outriders. In the man's other hand was an MP40, which was aimed directly at Bloodstone's face. Thoughts of a bullet in the back of his head in some dark and distant French backwater flashed into his mind but vanished as Heidler spoke.

"Comfort break, Major?" the colonel asked as he unlocked the cuff from its metal ring.

Without response, Bloodstone, climbed out of the car and walked to a nearby hedge, where he unbuttoned his flies and urinated into the dark foliage. Any notion of escape was impossible thanks to the twin weapons of Gunther and the motorcyclist, both of which were trained on his back from a few paces away. His business finished, he tucked his still-tender manhood back into his trousers and followed the gesticulating guns back to the car.

Heidler reattached the cuffs to the metal ring and then took a Thermos flask from the driver, from which he a poured a steaming coffee into a tin mug. He offered the cup to Bloodstone, who took it without thanks and sipped at the hot liquid. The coffee tasted good but he screwed up his face anyway, feigning disgust. Despite the mock revulsion, he downed the drink and handed the cup back to Heidler, who slammed the door and returned to his side of the car, where he clambered in and resumed his seat diagonally opposite Bloodstone. He rapped once on the glass partition behind him and the driver gunned the engine and the car roared into life, returning to the tarmac in a shower of gravel.

"I presume you're a tea man, Major?" Heidler asked as the car resumed its journey, to which, for the countless time that night, Bloodstone simply stared away into the distance.

"I'm surprised your Austrian genes allow you such tastes," he continued, unperturbed, "My Scottish mother tried her best, but it was coffee all day long for me. Tea is just so weak. Don't you think it tastes just like drinking a puddle?"

Get me out of these cuffs and I'll give you weak, thought Bloodstone as he continued to watch the world go by outside his window. The bright light of the moon had begun to fade and the beginnings of dawn were visible far away on the distant horizon to his right. He realised that if the sun was rising to the right of the car, they were travelling north. He tried to visualise a map of the land north of Paris and, for the second time that week, found himself wishing that he'd paid more attention to ancient Master Bodkin's geography lessons. Could it be Lille, he wondered, or Brussels? Or maybe they'd turn north-east at some point and head across to Holland. Amsterdam? He knew that it didn't really matter where Hitler was waiting for him; the experience was going to be grim and fairly final wherever it was, but he had never liked not knowing where he was going. It always left him feeling out of control and, as he wriggled the handcuff again, he realised that things couldn't be any more out of his control if he tried.

The sun continued to creep over the horizon as the car proceeded northwards, bathing the world in a faint orange glow. Mid-October mornings were slow to begin in this part of the world and the farms, forests and villages that they passed were still cast in murky shadows. Bloodstone looked up at the sky that still twinkled with a last few stars and marvelled that it was just four days since he'd passed through these very skies en-route to Freiburg. What had become of Ashton, Bill and the Count, he wondered, praying that they'd made it safely to Switzerland but knowing that the reality was probably very different.

Heidler carried on chatting away but Bloodstone was paying no attention as he gazed out of the window. Despite his fairly rudimentary geography, he did know that many of the Great War battlefields were to the north of Paris and he wondered if they'd already driven through the fields of the Somme, where his father had fought all those years ago and where Uncle Cecil had been transformed into a broken, twitching wreck. As he remembered the wartime tales that his father had told him as a boy, his eyes settled on one of the motorcycle outriders who zoomed along twenty yards ahead of the car with his body wrapped tight in a leather greatcoat and his MP40 strapped to his back.

Out of nowhere, the motorcyclist's head burst open, exploding in an unexpected bolt of blood and brain and broken steel that sprayed into the dawn light. The noise came next, a tremendous roaring sound punctuated by the ear-piercing rat-tat-tat of heavy machine gun fire. The rider's body, minus its head, was still upright on the bike as the road in front of him erupted in a crescendo of bullet-spattered tarmac and, half a heartbeat later, an enormous bird-like shadow zoomed over the car and roared away into the murky sky beyond.

Heidler was the first to react.

"Dive bomber!" he yelled as twisted in his seat to stare through the windscreen after the aircraft that had now vanished from view but could still be heard over the sound of the Mercedes engine.

The driver swerved to avoid the tumbling headless motorcyclist, but the man's body smashed into the front of the car and went under the wheels. The car bucked as the tyres crushed the corpse and the driver fought to keep control of the vehicle.

"Don't stop!" roared Heidler at the driver, "Keep going!"

As he shouted, Gunther yanked down his window and forced the top half of his body out into the open air, leaning out of the car with his machine gun in his hand as he searched for the attacking aircraft.

"There it is!" he roared from outside and gestured away to the west, where the dark shape of an aircraft could be seen skimming towards them over a copse of trees.

Bloodstone saw the aircraft, recognising it immediately as a Typhoon, and frantically shook the handcuff on his wrist, knowing that the action was useless but desperate not to be blown apart by his own side. Gunther began to fire his weapon, firing bullet after bullet at the incoming fighter, and the sound of the outgoing rounds reverberated through the car. Heidler clutched his door as he glowered at the aircraft with a look of pure rage on his face.

"Bastard Tommy!" yelled Gunther from outside the car as he squeezed the trigger and sent yet more rounds spinning toward the plane, which was now close enough for Bloodstone to see the RAF roundels painted on its fuselage.

Bloodstone took a deep intake of breath, leant across the car and stretched out his left leg, the boot at the end of which he lined up with the centre of Gunther's backside, and pushed once, channeling all his strength into the kick. The SS sergeant stumbled and lost his grip on the MP40 as he desperately tried to grasp hold of the doorframe, but his efforts were in vain and he toppled headfirst out of the open window and screamed as he landed face-first on the road at 70mph, snapping his neck instantly.

Heidler whipped around to stare at Bloodstone with a look of unadulterated anger plastered across his face.

"You stupid idiot!" he yelled in enraged German and went for the Luger at his hip.

He had half drawn the pistol when the world exploded in a nightmarish cacophony of white lightning and roaring thunder. The car reared like a whipped stallion and appeared to take off into the morning sky, with its windows shattering as it left the tarmac road far below. A sheet of blinding whiteness ripped across Bloodstone's vision and the last thing he saw before the world went black was a green field cap, tumbling through the air with half of a dark-haired head still inside.

He awoke half a minute later with a mouthful of mud and his ears thumping like a steam drill. He opened his eyes to find himself lying face-down in a ditch at the side of the road, with his left hand in a pile of thistles and, somehow, his beret still on his head. He tried to push himself to his knees, but his right arm wouldn't move and he tenderly turned his head to investigate the cause. What he saw sent of wave of despair through his already-addled brain. His right wrist was still encircled by the handcuff, the other end of which was still attached to the car. Or what was left of the car.

A pile of twisted metal had replaced what, less than a minute before, had been an expensive Mercedes sedan. Torn seats and battered panels lay in a higgledy-piggledy pile, while shredded tyres and a smashed engine were intermingled with what appeared to be the mangled body of the driver. And to all of it, Bloodstone was still attached by the cursed ring that had somehow survived the explosion intact and was still bolted firmly to the now-dented chassis. If that wasn't enough, an overwhelming odour of petrol assaulted his nostrils and he knew it wouldn't be long before the wreckage burst into flames and cremated him in a fiery incendiary.

He looked around in search of Heidler but there was no sign of the colonel. Surely the German had been turned to mincemeat as the car was torn to pieces, but Bloodstone knew that, by some miracle, he himself had survived so it was entirely possible that the Nazi had too.

He tugged his wrist against the ruined vehicle, but he was stuck fast. He rattled the ring with his free hand, trying to unscrew it, but it simply turned and turned and turned and refused to come loose. He found a small piece of loose wreckage that resembled a twisted tent peg and attempted to crowbar the metal ring from its holding, but the peg simply snapped under the pressure.

The smell of petrol grew stronger and a sense of panic began to engulf Bloodstone. He rattled his wrist, more vigorously this time, and beat against the metal ring with the broken peg. As he did so, a low rumbling noise reached his ears, getting slowly louder as he listened. The Typhoon was coming back.

"Shit, shit, shit!" he shouted, now almost hysterical with fear.

He knew that the RAF fighter would make one final swoop to unload its guns on the wreckage, just to make sure that its quarry was entirely destroyed and that there were no survivors. Now immobile, the remains of the car were a sitting duck and even the worst pilot would have no problem riddling the target with his cannons. Firmly attached to that target was Bloodstone, who estimated that he had about thirty seconds before he was turned into offal. He shook his wrist once more and looked at the ring, begging it to break from its fixtures. He looked at the handcuff, attached firmly to his arm and willed it to somehow, miraculously, unlock. He looked at his hand, wishing that he had been born with tiny hands and thin, ladylike fingers that could have simply slipped out of the cuffs.

He looked again at his hand, hairy and grimy and large, and an idea flashed into his mind. A horrible idea that he almost dismissed as soon as it entered his head. Would it work? Could he even do it? His stomach churned at the thought and the sound of the Typhoon's engine grew louder.

He made up his mind. What choice did he have anyway? It was either this or flaming bloody death from a bellyful of 20mm bullets.

As the noise of the aero engines came ever closer, he growled and grabbed his right thumb with the fingers of his left hand. He tugged as hard as he could and heard the bone grate as he attempted to tear his own thumb from its socket. His hand slipped and the thumb stayed intact as the Typhoon's roar inched closer, unseen somewhere over the lip of the ditch. The panic and the fear and the desperation boiled up inside him and he grasped the thumb again.

"AAAAAARRRRRGGGGGHHHH!" he screamed and wrenched the bone with every last ounce of his strength.

The tendon snapped and the socket popped as the bone was ripped from its housing, turning one hundred and eighty degrees in the process to leave the thumb twisted backwards and dangling limp.

Bloodstone howled in anguish as he looked at his ruined hand, but the Typhoon was almost upon him and he knew he had no time for self-pity. His ears filled with the sound of the fighter's roar and he wrenched one last time at the cuff that bound his wrist, dragging the metal bracelet up over the twisted hand and past the flopping thumb. The nerves of his ruined digit screamed out in tortured agony as the handcuff crushed his broken joint but, somehow, unbelievably, he was free.

Released at last from the wreckage of the car, he vaulted to his feet and ran from the ear-splitting screech of the Typhoon, which was now lashing the ruined Mercedes with its cannons. Bullets pinged off the metal and tore up the muddy ground and Bloodstone continued sprinting, tearing down the ditch as he fled the onslaught, before finally throwing himself prostrate onto the dirt. He landed on his thumb, bending the flapping bone yet further backwards and yelled out again as the pain ripped through his body.

He lifted his head just in time to see the belly of the fighter disappear overhead and, on one hand and two knees, he scrambled up the side of the ditch and lay at the lip, watching as the Typhoon banked to port and sped away northwards. He waited until it was a mere speck in the distance before he ducked back down into the ditch and crawled across to the opposite side. Using the leaves as cover and staying as still as he could, he peered through a clump of thistles and surveyed the road beyond.

The carriageway was littered with bits of shattered Mercedes and in the centre of the road was a crater two feet deep and around ten feet in diameter. Putting two and two together, Bloodstone realised that, in its second attack, the Typhoon had dropped a bomb that had blown the car into the air, depositing half of it in the ditch and spreading the other half across the tarmac.

The car's bumper lay intact at the edge of the crater and alongside it was a twisted bundle of leather that Bloodstone recognised as one of the motorcycle outriders. Despite his body being a broken mess, the man's head was intact, which told him that both bikers had been killed in the attack.

"Good," he muttered under his breath as he continued surveying the road.

Far away to the left he spotted the prone figure of Gunther and, despite the distance, it was clear from the unnatural angle of the man's neck that he would offer no more threat. That left just one more enemy to be accounted for. Heidler.

It took Bloodstone only a few more seconds to spot the colonel, thirty feet to his right and lying face down on the surface of the road. The force of the bomb appeared to have blown Heidler out of the car and it was clear that his legs had taken the full force of his return to earth. His left leg was bent at right angles away from his knee, while his right thigh had snapped clean in half, resulting in his foot coming to rest just inches from his own face. Despite the horrific state of his limbs, the colonel was very much alive and was attempting to drag his broken body across the tarmac in the direction of the crater.

Bloodstone watched from behind the clump of thistles and saw what Heidler was trying to reach. A Luger, silver and glistening in the early morning light, lay at the edge of the crater, just twenty feet from the shuffling Nazi.

"Oh no you don't," Bloodstone whispered as he pushed himself to his feet and stepped out into the road.

Heidler's head jerked up as he saw Bloodstone emerge from the ditch and a look of rage spread across his features. With his eyes locked firmly on Bloodstone, the German scrabbled to drag himself even more quickly towards the pistol, pulling his shattered legs behind him. The effort that it took to move even a couple of inches was terrific and Bloodstone watched as the angry features were clouded with pain, but not once did Heidler take his eyes off Bloodstone.

If it was anybody else, Bloodstone would have felt some sort of respect for a man who ignored a pair of disgustingly smashed legs to haul himself across a piece of tarmac, but the only emotion he felt as he watched the pitiful sight was anger. He let Heidler pull himself another six inches forwards and then made his way towards the Luger. As he stepped through the scattered wreckage, he spotted a discarded cigarette lighter close to the body of the motorcyclist and he stooped to retrieve it, depositing it in his trouser pocket. He was now standing over the Luger and bent to pick it up, after which he strode the last few feet to Heidler and stared down at the man, who looked back up at him with a mix of fury and despair.

"It seems that the tables have turned, Colonel," he said in English as he glared down at the shattered creature and noticed that the man's right femur had snapped like a twig and was protruding, jagged and bloody, through the skin of his thigh.

"It was business, dammit, just business," Heidler half spat and half pleaded, "Surely you understand that?"

Bloodstone ignored him and rested his booted foot on the German's shattered thigh, pushing down until he heard the bone grate and a guttural howl emanated from the man's throat.

"Do you remember what I told you I was going to do to you, Colonel?" he asked as he watched Heidler's face distort in agony, "Well, I always keep my promises."

He saw a flash of fear on his enemy's face, but it vanished in an instant as the colonel somehow gathered his resolve and fought back against the unbearable pain in his legs.

"We're the same, you and I, Major, the same," he hissed, "We just serve different masters."

"Shut it," ordered Bloodstone and pushed down even harder with his boot.

As the Nazi howled again, Bloodstone pocketed the Luger and bent down to grab Heidler's collar. With a fistful of material in his left hand, he proceeded to drag the man across the tarmac towards the ditch. His victim screeched and growled and begged as his shattered legs bumped and grated on the road, but Bloodstone ignored him, summoning every ounce of his strength as he hauled on the German's shirt.

392

Finally at the edge of the road, he kicked Heidler down into the ditch and watched as he rolled down the embankment and came to rest against the dented wing of the Mercedes, his legs now twisted even more horribly than before. As the man struggled to pull himself into a sitting position, Bloodstone jogged down into the mud and grasped the tunic again. With his boot back on the colonel's shattered thigh and his right forearm blocking Heidler's pathetic attempts to fend him off, he tore open the uniform's top buttons and fumbled beneath. It took seconds to find what he was looking for and he tugged once to rip a thin silver chain, complete with matching identity disks, from the man's neck. Still with his boot on the German's broken femur, he thrust the chain into his pocket and took out the Luger, which he held by the barrel in his left hand.

He looked Heidler in the eyes and let fly with the butt of the pistol, catching him full across the face. The blow crushed the man's right cheekbone and snapped off two teeth, which dribbled from his mouth in a ghastly river of blood, spittle and broken bone.

"That's what happens when you murder an innocent woman, you Nazi bastard," Bloodstone spat as he raised the Luger again, ignored the incoherent ramblings coming from Heidler's broken mouth and brought the weapon crashing down once more.

Two more teeth were smashed from their gums and came tumbling out between bloody lips to land in the mud. Bloodstone looked down at the man at his feet, seeing the once proud colonel reduced to a pawing mess of twisted limbs and shattered bones and felt not one bit of pity. The mewing noises coming from the frothing mouth made no sense and, once again, Bloodstone grabbed a fistful of the German's shirt, dragged him along the side of the battered Mercedes and dumped him against the shredded rear tyre. The tyre was half submersed in a pool of muddy liquid and Bloodstone saw Heidler's eyes widen as he realised that he was lying in puddle of petrol.

He took three steps back, pulled the lighter from his pocket and pushed open the lid. Heidler's arm came up in a final desperate plea but Bloodstone ignored him, flicked the lighter's tiny wheel and watched as the flame ignited. He caught Heidler's eye once more and saw pure panic on the man's battered face.

"See you in hell, Heidler," he said calmly and launched the burning lighter towards the car.

The lighter landed in the pool of muddy fuel and Heidler screamed as the liquid ignited immediately, roaring skywards in a burning crescendo of white-hot heat and dancing flame. The Nazi was engulfed in seconds and he screamed in agony and thrashed his arms as the fire clung to his skin, melted his flesh and vaporised his uniform.

Bloodstone lifted the Luger, took aim and squeezed the trigger. The bullet caught the thrashing colonel in the left eye, punching through his burning brain and killing him instantly.

"That's for Mother," Bloodstone spat as he watched the Nazi's corpse get consumed by the inferno, before he turned away in disgust.

He plucked the beret, complete with its winged badge, from his head, glanced at it once and tossed it back in the direction of the burning car. His aim was perfect and the red piece of cloth landed in the mud, just outside the puddle of burning fuel that was rapidly cremating the body of Heidler. Satisfied that anyone who stumbled across the burnt-out wreck would assume the charred remains to be those of a British Para, Bloodstone took one last look at the flaming body of his nemesis and clambered out of the ditch.

CHAPTER SIXTY-FIVE

The sun had now fully risen over the horizon and the land was bathed in the glorious gold of a chilly autumn morning. Bloodstone knew it wouldn't be long until the burning car attracted attention and he had no desire to be around when it did, so he paused for a moment to survey his surroundings. The road on which he stood appeared to be in the depths of the countryside and the only visible buildings were a smattering of barns way out towards the eastern horizon. The Typhoon had made its attack as the Mercedes had been passing through a shallow valley, which meant that Bloodstone's view of the land to the north and south was restricted to a quarter of a mile in each direction, both made up of recently ploughed fields. Away to the west, however, the farmland sloped very gently upwards to a ridge two hundred yards away, upon which sat a small copse of trees.

He decided immediately that the trees would be his best bet, not only to provide some cover while he figured out his next move, but because the high ground on which they grew would give him a much better view of his surroundings. He looked down at his thumb, which was now dangling like a swollen pink sausage, and he knew that he was going to have to try to force it back into its socket, but the priority right now was to get away from the wreckage as quickly as possible.

So, he decided, the flopping digit would have to wait until he reached the cover of the trees before he attempted any sort of corrective surgery.

With a final glance back at the burning body of Heidler, he set off at a jog across the road, pausing only to stoop down to retrieve the MP40 from the battered corpse of the motorcycle outrider. He slung it over his back, crossed the ditch on the far side of the road and climbed between the bars of a wooden fence. He was now in a grassy meadow, punctuated by clumps of thistle, that sloped away westwards towards the trees on the ridge. To his right and running up to the ridge from the road was a chest-high hedge and he ran towards it and ducked down. He took a quick glance around to check that he wasn't being watched and then he was on his way, running uphill at a stoop as he kept as close to the hedge as possible. After a hundred yards he paused and dropped to his haunches once again as he scanned his surroundings for any sign of life. With the exception of a lone cow happily munching at the ground on the far side of the meadow, he appeared to be entirely alone so jumped back to his feet and continued up the gentle slope.

When he was ten yards from the crest of the ridge, he dropped to his belly and began to crawl. With his right hand virtually useless, it took some effort to drag himself forwards while clutching the Luger in his left hand, just in case there was a nasty surprise waiting for him in the woods. He was a yard from the edge of the small copse when the distant sound of an engine stopped him in his tracks. He slowly twisted his head around and stared in the direction of the noise, which was coming from somewhere to the north. It took him a few seconds to find the source of the sound, which appeared to be a truck a mile or so away, heading south along the road in the direction of the burning Mercedes.

He shuffled forward into the edge of the copse and manoeuvred his body until he was concealed behind a thick beech tree, lying flat on his stomach with a clear view down the slope towards the scene of the wreckage. He watched the distant truck rumble closer and it wasn't long before he saw that it was a green-painted troop carrier, similar to the one that he'd ambushed in Paris and, just like that one, its rear was crowded with helmeted troops. Moving slowly, he unstrapped the MP40, checked the magazine and laid the weapon on the ground by his side. Next, he scooped up a handful of mud and rubbed it expertly into his face, stinging the still-sore welt but breaking up the contours of his features so that he would appear almost invisible to anybody who happened to glance in his direction.

The truck ground to a halt a hundred yards from the crater and the troops dismounted and dropped to their knees on both sides of the road to form a defensive perimeter around the stationary vehicle. From his vantage point Bloodstone could see that they were Wehrmacht infantrymen and he watched as the squad of ten men cautiously approached the crater with their weapons in their hands, clearly prepared for contact. They shuffled towards the body of the motorcyclist and the soldier on point bent down to check the condition of the man. Finding him very much dead, they continued onwards and split into two groups. One group skirted the crater and proceeded along the road in the direction of Gunther's broken body, while the other paused at the side of the road and stared down at the Mercedes.

By now the inferno had died down slightly but flames still flickered in the wreckage and black smoke still plumed skywards. Two of the infantrymen clambered down into the ditch and ventured closer to the burning car, shielding their faces from the heat as they peered into the debris. From his vantage point Bloodstone could just about make out the remains of Heidler and could see that the heat of the fire had been so great that all distinguishing features, including the uniform, had melted away to leave a blackened lump in the vague form of a human being. He watched as one of the soldiers spotted the red beret at the edge of the wreckage and bent down to pick it up. The man and his colleague spent a moment inspecting the headgear before one clapped the other on the back in apparent celebration and threw the beret towards the three infantrymen waiting on the road.

The man who caught it had a quick glance before handing it to another comrade and Bloodstone could see the men visibly relax, confident in the knowledge that the cremated body was that of an enemy paratrooper.

Bloodstone watched the men shoulder their weapons to break out a packet of cigarettes and he switched his gaze to the other group of infantrymen who had continued further along the road. They had already passed Gunther's body and were now investigating the headless corpse of the first motorcycle outrider, which lay in a squashed heap in the centre of the carriageway two hundred yards further on. Finding that there was little they could do for the man, the five soldiers turned their backs on the gory mess and ambled back towards their colleagues. After more cigarettes and a pause for several of the infantrymen to relieve themselves into a hedge, eight of the Wehrmacht strolled over to the truck and climbed into the rear. The vehicle started its engine, performed a neat three-point turn and rumbled back in the direction from which it had come.

Two infantrymen were left behind and the pair chatted briefly before one headed back along the road in the direction of the headless biker, swigging from his canteen as he went. The remaining man watched his colleague depart and sauntered across to the crater, next to which lay the body of the other motorcyclist. He knelt down beside the corpse and began rifling through the man's clothing, finding several items of apparent interest, which he pocketed. His looting complete, the soldier stood up and tramped across to a lone tyre at the side of the road that had seemingly detached itself from the Mercedes and survived the explosion intact. The man dropped his backside onto the tyre, rested his rifle on his knees and relaxed as he stared back along the road in the direction of the recently departed truck. Bloodstone switched his view to the other infantryman and saw that the man was similarly positioned, twenty feet away from the headless biker and sitting on a log on the verge, facing towards the south.

Bloodstone assumed by the soldiers' failure to clear up any of the wreckage that a mopping-up party would be along sometime soon and the two men left at the scene were simply there to act as guards and to redirect any traffic that happened to pass along the quiet country road. He was fairly confident that the recent enemy patrol would report finding the charred body of a British soldier in the wreckage of the Mercedes so was satisfied that there'd be no immediate manhunt for an escaped Albert Bloodstone. However, he was sure that someone at some point would work out that there was a body missing from the scene of the accident, which would mean a closer investigation of the cremated corpse and, potentially, the realisation that the body wasn't that of the enemy but of a highly decorated SS colonel. After all, Heidler was apparently due to report to the Führer at some point in the next twenty-four hours and his absence would undoubtedly be noticed, again resulting in a thorough search of this part of France. Or wherever this actually was, he thought.

Either way, Bloodstone had no intention of being in the vicinity when questions started to be asked or when people started poking around the crash site. He needed to get moving quickly, he decided, establish where he was and then figure out what his next steps would be. But, looking down at the flopping thumb, he knew that there was something he needed to do first. The thought filled him with dread, but he knew that he had no other choice unless he wanted the hand of a cripple for the rest of his days.

He slithered backwards and sat with his back against the tree, hidden from the road by the thick trunk. On the ground was a small branch and he picked it up and wedged it between his teeth. Next, he grasped the dangling thumb with the fingers of his left hand, took a deep breath, bit down onto the stick and yanked. With the exception of a bolt of bone-shuddering agony shooting through his body, nothing happened.

"Bugger," he cursed through the piece of wood in his mouth and clamped his fist once more around the brutalised thumb.

"Three, two, one..."

He tugged again, harder this time, and he heard the bone grate as it was forced back into the socket, popping horribly as it slid into place. Once again, the pain was obscene and he felt tears on his cheeks as he spat out the branch that he'd gnawed nearly clean through. He looked down at the thumb and saw that it was swollen almost beyond recognition, yet it was finally back in its socket, albeit at something of a jaunty angle. Hesitantly, he flexed his hand and watched as the thumb sluggishly obeyed his command, sending yet another bolt of agony through his body.

With his latest round of homemade surgery complete, Bloodstone decided that it was time to be on the move and to get as far away from the burning wreckage as possible. He swung the MP40 onto his back, dropped once again onto his belly and began to crawl deeper into the small woods. He was still going slightly uphill and as he moved through the undergrowth his nose picked up a scent that seemed so very familiar but, for the life of him, he just couldn't place. His nostrils twitched as he moved over the old leaves and damp mud and his brain battled to identify the smell that, for some reason, reminded him of his childhood.

A sudden rustling noise ahead brought him to a dead stop and he pushed his body entirely flat and felt for the Luger in his pocket as he peered into the trees. The sound came again, this time closer, and he drew the pistol out as slowly and silently as he could and held it in his left hand, ready for whoever it was that was coming through the trees towards him. The leaves rustled again, a twig snapped and Bloodstone cocked the Luger, just in time to see a giant seagull descend from the canopy, drop through the air and land three feet in front of him. He let out a pent-up lungful of air and the tension drained from his body as the bird tilted its head and fixed him with an enormous yellow eye. The creature stared at him for several more seconds, let out a mighty squawk, flapped its wings once and was off again, crashing through the copse as it disappeared from view.

Bloodstone smiled to himself, slipped the Luger back into his pocket and began to crawl through the undergrowth once again. He stopped.

"A seagull?" he muttered, "A bloody seagull?"

Suddenly the connection between his nose and his brain clicked into gear and the familiar smell was even more familiar, but now he knew exactly what it was. The sea.

"The bloody sea!" he said almost out loud, now hurrying on his belly as he dragged himself through the small patch of woods.

And then there it was, visible between the gaps in the trees and stretching off to the horizon in an endless sheet of twinkling bluey green. But not quite endless, he realised with a start as he continued forwards, creeping closer to the edge of the copse.

Was it? Could it be? No, it wasn't possible. His eyes must be playing tricks. He was hallucinating. He blinked and looked again, scrunching up his eyes as he stared across the blueness towards the very edge of the world, where, so far away that it appeared as little more than a scratch at the bottom of the sky, was a tiny smear of white. White cliffs.

The White Cliffs.

Blighty.

CHAPTER SIXTY-SIX

Bloodstone could've wept as he lay in the mud and the leaves and stared at the most beautiful thing he'd ever seen. There was home, so near that he could almost reach out and touch it, yet so impossibly far away. He thought back over the past five days and marvelled at the journey he'd taken since he'd lifted off aboard G for George, waved off by Bombshell Bell and the rest of the RAF Scampton crew. Once across France, almost as far as Switzerland, and then back again via Paris to here, somewhere on the French north-east coast.

Despite his questionable geography, he knew enough to realise that he must be somewhere close to Calais, which was where Heidler must've been taking him for his rendezvous with the Führer. He realised that if it wasn't for the Typhoon swooping in on their early morning journey, no doubt he would have been paraded like a monkey in front of his mother's cousin by now and God only knew what would have followed that uncomfortable family reunion.

Instead, here he was, flat on his stomach and staring out at his homeland across a stretch of twenty-something miles of water. But not just any water, he knew, one of the most heavily defended stretches of water on the entire planet. He'd seen the newspaper photos of the Atlantic Wall and had no doubts that this particular piece of coastline on which he now lay would be a military mastermind of defensive kickassery.

But what did it really matter anyway, he wondered? It wasn't as if he could simply wade into the Channel and swim home. He might be within sight of the British coast, but he felt just as far from home as when he'd been in Paris. His best option at the moment, he decided, was to get as far away from the crash site as possible and try to somehow link up with the Resistance. Maybe then he could be smuggled aboard a neutral ship and finally escape from the Reich that way. Lots of ifs and buts and it didn't help that he was decked out in an enemy uniform and had no possessions whatsoever except for his lucky bullet, a Luger and an MP40. He had no food, no water and, worst of all, no cigarettes. What he wouldn't do for a fag, he thought, sniffing the air in the vague hope of picking up a scent of tobacco smoke. As if the nicotine shortage wasn't bad enough, his torso and thighs were starting to throb beneath the bandages and he had no doubt that it wouldn't be long before whatever magic the nurses had worked would wear off.

Although he had a fantastic view of the ocean stretching away into the distance, Bloodstone's sight of the actual coastline was still hidden. All he could see from his position in the trees was a bumpy grassy field that stretched away for twenty yards before sloping out of view, beyond which was the distant sea. He assumed that he was close to the top of a cliff and wriggled forward until he was at the edge of the copse, half hidden behind a spindly beech.

His view of whatever was beyond the field was still hidden so he rubbed another handful of mud across his face and slowly emerged from the cover of the trees. Keeping as low as he could, he slithered through the grass, creeping an inch at a time and constantly peering left and right as he moved. As he inched forward over the lumpy ground, he saw that the grass on which he crawled came to an abrupt stop several yards ahead. There was no doubt now that he was on top of a cliff and he squirmed forward the last few feet and slowly craned his neck to peer over the edge.

His view was almost like something from a picture postcard, with a golden sandy beach stretching away to a blue sea that appeared as calm as a mill pond. The beach upon which he looked was in a small cove, maybe three hundred yards in width, with tall chalky cliffs sealing off each side of the bay. Rock pools, slimy with seaweed, stood between the sand and the cliffs, while pieces of driftwood peppered the sand. It would have been the perfect spot for a family day at the seaside or a lovers' picnic, but for one thing.

War had come to this beautiful piece of France and it had been brutal. The beach was a tangled mass of barbed wire, set out in rows across the sand and held in place by thick concrete posts, and between the lines of wire were enormous tank traps, vicious iron caltrop-like monstrosities that threw their numerous spikes skywards. To complete the destruction of the once-idyllic beach was a concrete pillbox, half built into the bottom of the cliff at the left-hand end of the cove. The size of a large garden shed, the square structure had small gun slits, a searchlight on the roof and a narrow doorway, at which a thick steel door stood open above a small flight of stairs.

Standing on a step beside the door and with a finger burrowing away inside his nostril was an infantryman, decked out in the drab green uniform of the Wehrmacht and complete with rifle slung over his shoulder and coal scuttle helmet perched on his head. A pair of binoculars hung around the man's neck and he stared disinterestedly out to sea as prodded and poked at his nose. Finally freeing the offending lump of snot, the soldier sucked it from his forefinger and retreated inside the pillbox, leaving the door open behind him.

Bloodstone tore his gaze from the concrete structure and swivelled his head to the right to survey the rest of the bay. His eyes settled on another German solider, who was identically attired and was sitting on a rock close to the bottom of the cliff at the other end of the cove. The man's rifle was propped against his leg and he had a handful of small pebbles, which he was launching one by one at pile of wood on the other side of a stretch of barbed wire. After a couple of minutes, the infantryman's pebbly ammunition had been exhausted and he picked up his rifle, pushed himself to his feet and began to amble across the sand in the direction of the pillbox. He wandered effortlessly through gaps in the wire that Bloodstone hadn't previously noticed and several minutes later arrived at the opposite end of the cove, where he climbed the small flight of stairs and disappeared into the interior of the pillbox.

Bloodstone assumed that the two soldiers were guards posted to protect the small cove and knew it was likely that there would be similar set-ups along the rest of the coastline. No doubt there would also be heavy gun emplacements on top of the cliffs and, although he couldn't see any from his current grassy lookout, he knew that where there were gun emplacements there would always be soldiers. And lots of them. Despite the view of the British coastline that lay tantalisingly close across the narrow stretch of water, he realised that he had to get moving, head inland and find somewhere safe to lie low while he worked out his next steps. Now that Heidler was dead, there was no reason for him to stay on enemy territory for a minute longer than he had to, so the priority had to be staying hidden and working out how to make it home in one piece.

As he pondered the difficulty of that task and prepared to slip back into the small copse of trees, he took one last sweeping look across the cove. He saw a fishing rod propped up against the front of the pillbox, a piece of old sacking caught on a stretch of barbed wire and a broken lobster pot half buried in the sand at the water's edge. His gaze swung right and he spied two seagulls squabbling over the remains of a crab, half of a bicycle tyre protruding from between two rocks and, finally, way up at the far right end of the beach and half hidden behind a coil of barbed wire, the pile of wood that the guard had been bombarding with pebbles.

His gaze paused. There was something about the pieces of timber that wasn't quite right. He scrunched up his eyes and peered through the barbed wire and his heart skipped a beat, because it wasn't a pile of wood at all. It was a boat. A tiny rowing boat, no bigger than a bath and it certainly looked like it had seen better days, but it was a boat all the same. The thing sat half on its side on the sand and an old rope protruded from the bow and was tied to the top of a nearby iron caltrop.

Bloodstone whistled silently and looked at the boat, looked at the distant white cliffs and looked again at the boat. Could it be done? Although it was only twenty-something miles, that was a bloody long way in little more than a bathtub, he thought, eyeing the boat once more. Despite spending much of his youth just a stone's throw from the Solent and despite the DCM ribbon that was ordinarily stitched to his chest, he was the first to admit that he knew next to nothing about the sea. Tides and currents meant little to him and he sighed and peered again at the expanse of water that stretched away into the distance. Where was Grandpa Horatio when you needed him, he mused as he remembered the white-haired old admiral who had been so appalled at the young Bloodstone's insistence on forsaking the senior service for a career in the Army.

"Bugger it," he cursed under his breath, his mind made up.

Deciding he was going to do it was one thing but working out exactly how was something else entirely. At least the boat was outside the stretch of barbed wire, meaning that after he'd freed it from its mooring he only had to push it out to sea, hop aboard and paddle for home. Easy, he thought, if it wasn't for the fact that the beach was patrolled by at least two Wehrmacht guards and no doubt the water beyond the cove was under constant surveillance too. He also had to hope that there were oars stowed inside the boat, otherwise he'd be paddling to England with little more than one and a half hands and an MP40.

As if all of that wasn't enough, he still needed to make it across the beach undetected. Nighttime was the only option for that, he knew, but if tonight was anything like the last, the moon would play havoc with any attempt to stay undetected. But before he could worry about that, first he needed to get to the beach. He pulled himself forward another few inches and risked poking his head above the grass to peer further over the edge of the cliff. In front of him was a sheer fifty-foot drop to the rocks below. No way he could descend that silently, especially with a busted-up thumb. He peered left along the cove and saw that the cliff was the same all the way around, past the pillbox and as far as the edge of the bay a hundred and fifty yards away. No way down anywhere, unless he could somehow source an extraordinarily long rope.

The view to his right was similar, with the exception of close to where the pebble-throwing infantryman had been sitting just a few minutes before. Here, a pile of rocks sat at the bottom of the cliff and Bloodstone could see that they were the result of a rockfall, where the sheer surface had collapsed to create a higgledy-piggledy slope that stretched thirty feet up against the cliff wall. The uppermost part of the cliff remained in place to leave a frail-looking overhang that appeared as if it could give way at any moment. He looked closer and realised that if he could descend the top twenty feet of the vertical cliff face and somehow wriggle underneath the overhang, he'd be able to drop onto the top of the rocks and carefully navigate his way down the craggy pile to the beach below. It would take some doing, he knew, and relied not only on the fragile overhang staying in place while he clambered down it, but also on the pile of rocks remaining steady as he picked his way down them. And all in silence, he thought gloomily as he looked back towards the concrete stronghouse, from which one of the guards had now emerged and was staring out to sea.

He knew that his odds of getting to the beach undetected were long to say the least, let alone boarding the rowing boat and paddling out of the cove. Even if he managed to do that, next was the not insignificant task of crossing the Channel without being blasted out of the water by an enemy patrol boat.

"Bugger it," he said again, knowing this was the best chance he was likely to come across for the foreseeable future and fully aware that the longer he stayed in occupied territory the harder it would be to stay undetected.

Tonight, he decided as he looked up at the sun and guessed that it was probably about 10am, which meant he had at least eight hours until darkness. It also meant that he had a long day ahead and a day seemingly without anything to eat or drink. If he was going to spend the night battling the seas, he'd need some energy and the thought of dining on beetles again churned his stomach. Oh for a pint and a plate of chips, he thought as he looked once more at the white cliffs that teased him from across the shimmering expanse of water.

Soon, he promised himself, before he banished all thoughts of food from his head and slid silently back from the cliff edge. He knew that he'd have to watch the cove to discover the guards' patrol patterns to make sure that he didn't unwittingly blunder into the enemy in the darkness, but he could do that later in the day. There was little point poking his head over the side of the cliff and risking discovery for longer than he needed to, so he wriggled his way across the grass and back into the relative cover of the copse of beech trees.

As he reached the shade of the trees, he heard the rumble of engines from down in the valley and crawled back through the small wood until he reached his original vantage point behind the thick trunk. He unslung the MP40, laid it on the ground next to him and peered down towards the site of the wreckage. The two infantrymen who had been left behind were still in their spots and a small convoy of vehicles could be seen heading in their direction from the north.

Bloodstone watched as they came closer and soon saw that the convoy consisted of three vehicles. The first was a lorry with an empty flatbed, the second was a truck with a small crane mounted on its rear and the third appeared to be some sort of ambulance. The leading vehicle slowed as it neared the crash site and came to a halt next to the crater. The guard, now back on his feet, chatted briefly to the occupants of the lorry's cab and then strolled to the back of the ambulance, which had parked nearby. The man swung open the rear doors and then seemed to gesture menacingly into the interior with his rifle. A few seconds later a dozen skeletal figures wrapped in brown rags stumbled from the vehicle and hastily assembled in a line at the side of the road. Bloodstone squinted to get a better look and saw that each of the twelve men had short cropped hair and a yellow star pinned to their chests.

"Jews," he whispered angrily, remembering the poor creatures that he'd rescued yesterday morning and recalling Helgeland's vile ramblings about camps in the east.

The sorry-looking gang parading at the side of the road certainly didn't look to be in a good condition and, once again, Bloodstone despaired at the lengths that the Nazis were willing to go to stamp their evil doctrine on Europe's populace.

The guard, now joined by several other uniformed men who had spilled from the cabs of the three vehicles, began to harangue the line of captives. Seemingly following instructions, the work detail broke ranks and began to scuttle around the wreckage that was strewn across the road, picking up pieces here and there and depositing them on the bed of the truck. The infantrymen, rifles in hand, watched their prisoners closely and barked out the occasional order that left the emaciated group scurrying across the tarmac towards whatever piece of tangled debris they'd been told to retrieve.

The crane was brought into action to lift the motorcycle, which was unceremoniously dumped onto the truck alongside numerous other pieces of twisted metal. Finally, three of the ragged work gang were ordered to collect the body of the biker and the trio struggled under the corpse's weight as they lifted him onto the rear of the lorry, where he was covered with a blanket.

With the carriageway around the crater cleared of debris, the crane manoeuvred across to the opposite side of the road and the twelve prisoners were ordered down into the ditch to start working on clearing the bulk of the Mercedes, around which the charred bodies of Heidler and the driver were still scattered. Under the instructions of a guard and with some difficulty, the prisoners extricated the blackened bodies and, with four men carrying each corpse, ferried them towards the truck. As they attempted to climb out of the ditch, the man carrying Heidler's right leg slipped on the mud and fell to his knees. As he did so, Heidler's blackened and twisted limb snapped at the thigh and detached itself from the body, leaving the shocked man clutching what resembled an oversized joint of burnt ham.

Within seconds, the nearest guard raised his rifle and cracked the unfortunate captive around the side of the head with the weapon's butt. A second infantryman joined in with a boot to the stomach and the man dropped the blackened leg and curled up in a ball on the muddy ground. The guards dealt out several more blows with boots and rifles before they stood aside and screamed at the cowering creature to get up. Bloodied and on shaky legs, he stood, grasped the stump of Heidler's thigh and the sorry contingent staggered towards the truck with their grisly cargo. Another prisoner was ordered to collect the discarded leg, which he scooped up and deposited on the flatbed alongside the corpse of its owner.

Bloodstone's blood boiled as he watched the miserable scene unfold below him and he silently cursed at the bullying Nazis, who were recovering from their exertions by breaking out a new pack of cigarettes. One of the slave labourers took advantage of the guards' distraction and darted up the opposite side of the ditch and dropped flat onto the ploughed field beyond. He lay silently for a second before he began to drag himself, inch by inch, away from the ditch and further into the furrows of the muddy field.

"Go on, chap," Bloodstone willed as he watched the man slowly creep away from the site of the wreck, half camouflaged by his dirty rags and entirely unnoticed by the guards who were busy with their cigarettes.

There was a slight dip in the field ten yards ahead of the crawling figure and he angled towards it, dragging his bony body over the ploughed earth as his colleagues continued clearing the wreckage in the ditch behind him. One of the guards blew an impressive smoke ring into the air and his colleague turned to watch it as it blew eastwards on the morning breeze. As he did so, the escaping prisoner chose that exact moment to drag himself over a clump of mud. The guard saw the man's backside rise from the earth and he let out a yell as he pointed at the crawling Jew.

"Halt!" he boomed and brought his rifle to his shoulder.

The escapee heard the shout, leapt to his feet and began running across the muddy field, desperately trying to flee as fast as his skinny legs would carry him. He half slipped, regained his balance and set off again, a giant clod of earth stuck to his right boot. The guard let out another shout, trained his rifle on the man's back and pulled the trigger. The crack of the weapon reverberated around the small valley, but the bullet missed by a hair's breadth and sailed over the prisoner's shoulder as it zipped away into the field beyond. Another bullet followed and zinged narrowly past the left ear of the man who had now adopted a frenzied zig-zagging tack as he sprinted across the empty field, while his fellow captives watched wide-eyed and silent from the ditch.

A third bullet passed an inch from his other ear and Bloodstone watched with despair as a second guard threw down his cigarette, dropped to his knee on the lip of the ditch, raised his rifle to his shoulder and squeezed the trigger. The bullet covered the fifty yards in half a millisecond and punched into the back of the fleeing man's neck, slicing through flesh, bone and spinal cord as it killed him instantly. He collapsed to the ground, twitched once and was still.

Bloodstone's hand went involuntarily to the machine gun at his side, but his brain kicked in just in time, stopping him before he snatched up the weapon and sprayed a hail of bullets in the direction of the Nazi bullies in the valley below. He took a deep breath and composed himself. As tempting as it was to storm across the meadow and gun down every single last German, he knew that was far from the sensible course of action. He'd probably last two minutes before he joined the blood-soaked pile of rags that now lay in the mud on the other side of the ditch but, if by some miracle he did survive, he'd have every enemy soldier in a fifty mile radius hunting him down.

Far better to stay silent, he knew, get back home to fight another day and then give the goddamned Hun a thoroughly good bashing. He wanted nothing more than to play his part in bringing an end to the evil regime that seemed hell bent on wiping anyone from the face

411

of the earth who didn't share their warped ideas, but he knew that wasn't for today.

He growled in frustration, released the MP40 and watched as two of the prisoners were dispatched to collect the bloodied body. The corpse was laid on the back of the truck and the clear-up continued, culminating in the mangled chassis of the Mercedes being hooked onto the crane and dumped on the truck alongside the pieces of twisted metal, burnt tyres and broken bodies. The small convey then moved further down the road to collect the bodies of Gunther and the headless motorcyclist and his bike, after which the surviving eleven Jews were prodded and poked into the back of the ambulance-cum-prison-van. The three vehicles performed a series of neat U-turns and drove back towards the crater, where the two original guards deposited a series of red and white bollards around the hole in the tarmac and climbed into the cab of the mobile crane. The convey then departed northwards, leaving the crater and the burnt grass of the ditch as the only signs of the morning's attack.

As Bloodstone watched the vehicles vanish into the distance, silence descended once more on the small valley. He presumed from the lack of any search parties that the enemy still believed him to have perished in the Typhoon attack, but he knew that assumption could come crumbling down at any point in the not-too-distant future. As long as it happened after he'd freed the rowing boat and was well on his way back to Blighty, he couldn't care less.

The sun was now directly above him and the sky remained blue and cloudless, except for a thin strip of white cloud away on the eastern horizon. His stomach rumbled and, once again, he dismissed all thoughts of food and instead busied himself with exploring the small clump of trees that had been his sanctuary for the last few hours. The copse was the shape of a rough circle and he estimated it to measure a hundred feet from edge to edge, perched atop the hill and no doubt battered by the sea winds in winter. He traversed the leafy undergrowth but discovered nothing more exciting than a rusty old paint tin and the scattered bones of a long-dead fox.

Close to the edge of the wood was a tree that had been blown half over to leave a muddy hole where the roots had been ripped from the earth. The hollow, sheltered on one side by the base of the fallen tree, was filled with leaves and Bloodstone thought it the perfect place to settle in for a couple of hours of sleep and build up some strength for what was undoubtedly going to be a long night. He took off his battledress shirt and rolled it into a pillow before he clambered down into the hole and lay down on the bed of leaves. He shoved the homemade pillow under his head, placed the MP40 next to him and closed his eyes. The scent of the sea filled his nostrils and it wasn't long before he was fast asleep, dreaming of white cliffs and fish and chips as the beech leaves rustled gently above him.

CHAPTER SIXTY-SEVEN

A large splodge of rain landed square on Bloodstone's nose and woke him from his slumbers. A second plopped into his ear and he sat up, rubbing his eyes. He could see through the canopy above that the blue sky had been replaced by thick grey clouds and he smiled, hopeful that tonight's escape would no longer be illuminated by the moon.

He picked up his pillow and shoved it into a gap between the tree roots where it would stay remotely dry in readiness for the evening's journey. He then rolled onto his knees and crawled out of his leafy hole. As he did so, something dug into his kneecap and he looked down to see a small brown furry shell, half of the size of a conker and covered in soft spikes.

"Beech nuts," he muttered and picked up the shell, which he pulled apart to reveal a tiny brown nut.

He popped it into his mouth, chomped down and grimaced slightly as his mouth was filled with an irony tannin taste. Not quite the cod and chips that he'd been dreaming about, he admitted, but he knew that the tiny nuts were packed full of energy. He was also aware that if he ate too many then he'd likely get a dose of the runs, which was something he certainly didn't fancy mid-channel. Nevertheless, he scooped up a handful from the ground around him and poured them into his breast pocket. He paused to munch down a few more and then continued towards the edge of the wood, taking the small paint tin with him. He crawled out of the cover of the wood and set out across the grass towards his vantage point at the top of the cliff. The rain was now starting to bucket down and he set the tin upright against a tuft of grass and watched with satisfaction as big globules of water dropped into it.

He reached the edge of the cliff just in time to see one of the guards sprint across the last ten yards of the beach as he sought the shelter of the pillbox. The man ducked inside and vanished, just as a crack of thunder rang out from the heavens and, a heartbeat later, a flash of lightning lit up the sky. Bloodstone looked out across the sands and saw that the cove was empty, except for the boat that was still moored to the iron spike away to his right. He was tempted to take advantage of the storm by scaling the cliff now and making out to sea while the guards hid inside their concrete bunker, but he could see that the tide was coming in and he knew he'd have no chance of escaping the cove if he had to paddle against an incoming tide.

Instead, he watched. And he watched and he watched, cold, wet and miserable as the rain cascaded down onto him and soaked him to the skin. He reckoned it to be about an hour before one of the guards finally ventured out from the pillbox and, wrapped in a waterproof poncho, plodded miserably across the sand as he set out on his patrol. The man skirted through the gaps in the wire and seemed to be barely looking around him as a hurried across the beach, his head tucked into his collar as the water dripped from the rim of his coal scuttle helmet. He reached the far end of the cove, took a perfunctory look out to sea and then turned on his heel and headed back the way he'd come. As he made his return journey, Bloodstone peered through the rain at the pillbox, but the man's comrade was nowhere to be seen, clearly preferring the dry shelter of the bunker.

As the guard climbed back up the steps and vanished inside the concrete structure, Bloodstone had timed the patrol at just shy of nine minutes. He made a mental note of the time and then settled back down to continue his surveillance of the bay. A few minutes after the infantryman had finished his recce, the rain slowed and then stopped completely. Bloodstone was pleased to see that the sky remained filled with a blanket of grey clouds and he celebrated by nibbling on a beech nut before he returned to his bored scrutiny of the cove.

Three patrols later and with dusk nearing, Bloodstone had established that the guards reconnoitered the beach every hour and took between nine and fifteen minutes to do so. It was always only one man who tramped the sand, while, weather dependent, the second watched from steps of the pillbox. Occasionally the patrolling guard would pause to rest his backside on the rocks near the rowing boat, but apart from that the routine appeared to be fairly regular.

He looked up at the sky and saw that the clouds were starting to thin. He didn't want to be caught in the open should the moon reappear so, knowing that he needed to get going as soon as possible, he decided to begin his climb down the cliff immediately after the next patrol was over. By then, the tide would be fully on the ebb and darkness would have set in, meaning he'd have at least ten hours at to get as far as he could across the Channel before sunrise.

With his mind made up, he shuffled away from the edge of the cliff, turned around and crawled back towards the cover of the trees, pausing only to retrieve the paint tin, which he was delighted to see had been half filled with rain. He picked a fleck of rust from the surface of the water and put the tin to his lips, enjoying the sensation of finally slaking his thirst despite the strange taste of the water. He then made his way to the hollow beneath the fallen beech, retrieved his battledress shirt and put it on.

Next, he unlaced his boots and pulled them off, followed by his socks. With one hand only half working, he knew that he'd need all the grip that he could muster if he was going to descend the twenty feet of sheer cliff face without plummeting to the pile of rocks below, and ten toes would be much more use than two heavy boots. He tied the boots together and then attached the handle of the paint can to the laces, which he secured firmly to his belt, so the load dangled down over his backside. He was fully aware that his little boat was likely to ship a fair amount of seawater on the coming voyage so the tin might come in handy if he needed to do a spot of bailing. Finally, he slung the MP40 across his back, checked that the Luger was safely in his pocket and touched the lump of the lucky bullet that was nestled among the beech nuts.

"Let's do this Bertie," he said under his breath and made his way to the edge of the copse.

He dropped to his belly once again and crawled through the grass, this time angling right in the direction of where the cliff had collapsed at the far end of the cove. The daylight had now almost entirely faded and he used the last slithers of light to guide him as he dragged his body along the clifftop, keeping low as he moved. After ten minutes he reached his destination, poked his head out from the grass and peered down onto the beach below. Sure enough, he was in the right spot and he could just about make out the shape of the boat in the fading light, lying on the sand behind a roll of barbed wire and less than fifty feet from the foot of the cliff.

Five minutes later the daylight had vanished entirely and, with the moon hidden behind the clouds, the cove was plunged into almost complete darkness. A light blinked from the pillbox at the far end of the bay as the steel door was opened and an infantryman emerged, torch in hand and rifle on his shoulder. The door closed behind him and he descended the stairs and began his walk along the beach. His flashlight swung from side to side as he ambled across the sand, lighting up the ground in front of him and occasionally flashing across the cliffs and illuminating the iron caltrops around which the seawater swirled. Bloodstone willed himself even flatter as the man padded closer and he held his breath as the guard passed directly underneath him. He continued for another twenty paces before he turned on his heel and wandered back along the beach in the direction from which he'd come, his torch lighting the way.

Bloodstone exhaled as the swinging light got further away and eventually the German reached the pillbox at the far end of the beach, opened the door and vanished inside. With the exception of twin chinks of light that seeped from the concrete structure's two gun slits, the cove was almost pitch black.

"It's now or never," he muttered and, taking another deep breath, shuffled onto the overhang.

He half expected the cliff to give way underneath him at any moment, but he pushed the thought from his head as he forced his brain to concentrate on the job at hand. He turned his body around so that the soles of his bare feet were facing towards the sea and, inch by inch and with his belly on the ground, he wriggled backwards. His toes were now dangling into thin air and, a second later, his lower legs, then his knees followed suit. One more shuffle and his hips reached the edge of the cliff. He dug his hands into the soft earth, counted to three and pushed backwards another inch, letting his legs swing downwards and over the side of the cliff.

Panic bubbled up but he forced it away as his feet scraped against the rock, searching for purchase. They found it and, like a monkey, he gripped the cold stone with his toes and shifted his bodyweight onto his legs. Tentatively and fighting against every instinct, he released his grip with his left hand and scrabbled at chest height for a handhold. As the pain in his battered right hand mounted, the fingers of his left discovered a minute fissure in the rock and he grasped it, adjusting his weight and fractionally reducing the agony in the hand that was still gripping the earth atop the cliff. He then released his aching fingers from the mud and felt in the darkness for a second handhold on the rock, which he found and grasped as tightly as his throbbing hand would allow.

He dared a quick glance to his right towards the pillbox, but all was still and quiet, which he thought was something of a miracle considering he felt so conspicuous, clinging to the cliff face like some sort of deranged limpet. He looked down but was unable to see the rocks below him in the darkness, so shifted his left leg and felt below him for somewhere to clamp his toes. With his digits successfully wedged, he shifted his other leg, then one hand and then the other, slowly inching down the face of the cliff as he did so.

He began to build up some momentum and was starting to feel fairly pleased with himself when a flash of light to his right brought his head snapping around. The light came from the open door of the pillbox and he watched with horror as a rifle-carrying figure emerged from the bunker and strolled down the steps, flashlight in hand. He told himself that the man was merely stepping out for a breath of fresh air or maybe an evening cigarette, but his blood turned to ice as he saw the figure switch on the torch and begin wandering along the beach in his direction.

The man seemed to be in no rush, so Bloodstone assumed that he wasn't the target of the unexpected foray, yet still he knew that there was still a high possibility that he'd be spotted. He considering scrambling back up the cliff to safety but knew that he couldn't do that in time and the approaching guard would be onto him before he made it to the grassy top. He thought about continuing downwards but he had no idea how much further he had to go and, anyway, he was bound to make a racket whenever he did reach the pile of rocks below. He concluded that his best bet was to stay exactly where he was and hope that the patrolling infantryman passed by without flashing the torch in his direction. The thought made him distinctly uncomfortable, and not just a little terrified, but he was all out of options, so he gripped the cliff face even tighter and watched from the corner of his eye as the soldier neared.

The cone of light from the man's torch swung across the sand and Bloodstone could hear the sound of jackboots crunching on the pebbles. His heart seemed to be thumping so loudly in his ears that he was convinced that the approaching German would be able to hear. He held his breath and shut one eye, squinting his right almost closed as he watched the man get closer. Thirty feet away then twenty feet and still the torch swung from side to side, lighting up the sand. Ten feet further and the soldier raised his light and flashed it across the cliff face, illuminating the rock with a ring of white light that seemed to be about to land on Bloodstone but dropped away at the last moment, swinging back to the sand and out to sea.

Five more feet and the man paused, now almost directly underneath Bloodstone at the edge of the pile of fallen rocks. His heart was now booming in his chest and he twisted his neck half an inch to see what was happening on the sand below him. As he did so, the big toe of his right foot slipped from its place in a tiny gulley and he gasped as he fought to maintain his balance. The other toes went into panicked overdrive and dug against the cold rock, straining to keep him upright until the big toe miraculously found another crack and somehow managed to hold on tight.

He heard the sound of whistling coming from the lips of the infantryman and recognised the Nazi anthem of Die Fahne Hoch. He dared a glimpse downwards and saw that the infantryman was facing away from him and looking out to sea, with one hand fumbling somewhere at his waist as the torch dangled from the other. Several seconds later the pattering of liquid told Bloodstone that the man below was relieving himself on the sand and he used the distraction to flex the fingers of his right hand in an attempt to alleviate the agony that was building up around his battered thumb.

The movement gave him a brief moment of relief but was almost immediately replaced by a burning in his left calf as the muscle began to cramp. He gritted his teeth and tried to blank out the agony for just long enough for the German to finish his bathroom break and move on down the beach, at which point Bloodstone could shift his leg and eradicate the torturous fire in his muscle. He heard the man zip up his flies and he held as breath once more as he waited for the footsteps to start again. Silence.

Now shaking from the pain that was threatening to consume him, he looked down again and was dismayed to see that the soldier had dropped to his backside and was now sitting on a rock ten feet from the bottom of the cliff. The torch was propped against his thigh and his hands were busy with a packet of cigarettes.

Bloodstone clenched his jaw and tried to ignore the muscle that felt like it was about to tear itself apart. His leg began to twitch and he could feel sweat prickling at his forehead. Slowly, ever so slowly, he flexed the toes of his left foot and moved them half an inch across the rock in a last desperate attempt to stop himself tumbling from the cliff face. It failed as the tiny movement sent an electrifying bolt of pain through his calf, which caused his toes to lock and involuntarily kick out against the face of the rock. The movement sent him flying backwards and he yelled in panic as tried hopelessly to hold on with his fingers. It was to no avail, however, and his hands and feet flailed wildly as he plunged downwards into the darkness.

CHAPTER SIXTY-EIGHT

Bloodstone landed with a thump that knocked the wind from his body. The boots and the paint tin took the full force of the landing, but the impact with the rock smashed through him like a freight train.

The sentry let out a startled shout and was on his feet in a heartbeat, the torch in his hand as he plunged the beam in Bloodstone's direction. Despite the force of the landing and the light that half blinded him, Bloodstone knew he had seconds to act. He leapt from the rock on which he'd landed, onto the sand and closed the ten feet between them before the astonished German could unsling the Mauser from his shoulder.

He hit the man high in the chest with the full force of his shoulder and the two went over in a pile of scrabbling limbs. The torch was knocked from the infantryman's grasp and fell to the ground, the light extinguished, and Bloodstone was on his man like a rabid beast. Before his victim could rise, he grabbed the throat with his left hand and his right rained blow after blow into the shocked face. He ignored the agony in his thumb as he punched down again and again and again, feeling teeth and bone crunch under his fist. White fear-filled eyes stared up at him from a young freckled face and the man's fists flailed at his face, but Bloodstone attacked with the ferocity of a demon and the soldier below him was no match for the instant and enormous violence.

Still holding the throat and with his head tucked in to avoid the wild blows that came at him, Bloodstone dropped his hand to the man's waist and felt for the bayonet that he knew must be attached to the belt. His fingers found it and he pulled it from its sheath and, in a single movement, he lifted it above his head and plunged it down between his clenched fingers into his victim's throat. Blood spurted up in a rancid geyser of red, spraying Bloodstone's face, as the blade tore through the man's Adam's apple and into the jugular. He ripped it free and stabbed downwards once more, tearing a hole the size of a fist in the tattered flesh. The German gurgled horribly and his legs kicked pathetically as Bloodstone watched the life blood drain from the man in the light of the fallen torch. He made one last desperate choking sound, twitched and then was still.

The whole incident had taken no more than thirty seconds and, looking down at the mangled face below him, Bloodstone breathed out for the first time since he'd launched his ferocious assault. His right hand was a mass of shooting agony and his lower back throbbed like the devil from his landing on the rocks, but now was no time for self-pity. He tore the rifle strap from the corpse's shoulder and slung it over his own, plucked up he fallen torch in his left hand and, with the bayonet clutched in his right, ran doubled up towards the gap in the barbed wire that he knew was just five yards ahead. He found the thin gap, slipped through and headed for the boat that was still tied to the iron caltrop, just another five yards further on.

He splashed through the ankle-deep water, barely noticing the chill on his feet, and slashed once at the mooring rope with his bayonet. The blade cut through the frayed old rope like a knife through butter and he tossed the bayonet into the rowing boat without looking down. He glanced back across the cove towards the pillbox and, seeing nothing awry, he grasped the breasthook at the bow and prepared to drag the boat out into the bay. It was then that he looked down at the small boat.

"Shit!" he exclaimed, "Shit, shit, shit, shit, shit!"

Because the boat wasn't really a boat at all. To be fair to the thing, it had been a boat once upon a time but was now just a hull with no bottom. The boards had long ago rotted away, leaving a useless shell of a craft that sat on the sand, half filled with water and a miracle that it hadn't yet been taken by the ocean.

As this realisation hit Bloodstone, the searchlight kicked into life from the roof of the pillbox and snaked its dazzling light across the beach, flooding the sand with whiteness and coming to rest on the blood-spattered body lying close to the rocks. Seconds later, the door of the structure was flung open and not one, but three rifle-carrying figures poured from the building and vaulted down the steps.

Bloodstone dropped to his belly in the water, pulled the rifle from his shoulder and lay stock still. His brain was still trying to catch up with the frenetic action of the last few minutes and he forced himself to compose his thoughts. He saw the figure of a fourth man beside the searchlight and, moments later, the giant bulb swung on its pedestal again and proceeded to vomit its stabbing light across the bay as it swung from side to side, searching for whatever or whoever had killed the freckled infantryman.

Thinking quickly, Bloodstone estimated that it would be forty seconds before the three running soldiers, the rearmost of which was carrying a torch, reached the body of their comrade and half of that time before the searchlight lit up his paltry hiding place beside the ruined boat. Instinct kicked in and he raised the Mauser to his shoulder, worked the bolt and squinted along the barrel as he stared straight into the blinding light of the searchlight. He squeezed the trigger and felt the rifle kick into this shoulder as the weapon let out a crack that reverberated around the bay. His aim was true and the bullet smashed into the glass of the searchlight bulb, shattering it and extinguishing the light instantly.

At the sound of the gunshot, the three soldiers threw themselves to the ground and thrust their weapons in Bloodstone's direction. The man at the rear had left his torch alight, however, and his illuminated comrades now paid in blood for his mistake as Bloodstone fired twice more, each time sending a bullet spinning into the bodies of the prostrate men. He cycled the bolt and lined up the third man in his sights, just as the soldier realised his error and flicked out his light. It was too late, however, and Bloodstone's finger had already squeezed the trigger, pumping out a bullet that caught the man full in the face, puncturing him above the nose and blowing out the back of his skull.

Bloodstone worked the bolt again and heard the final bullet drop into the chamber. As he did so, he saw a speck of light appear on top of the cliff high above the pillbox. Another joined it and then he heard unintelligible yells as someone barked out orders. He looked to his left and his right, glancing the full length of the cove, and knew that there was still at least one enemy soldier alive somewhere near the searchlight. Looking again at the twinkling lights on top of the cliff, there was no doubt that the alarm had been raised and the beach would soon be awash with Wehrmacht troops, hunting for whoever had dared to gun down their comrades in the darkness.

There was no escape inland from the beach now, he realised. In desperation, he looked over his shoulder and stared out into the blackness beyond the bay. Somewhere out there in the darkness, a long way away, was Blighty. Home.

It was almost suicide, he knew, but what choice did he have? He could stay here and fight against whatever was about to be unleashed at him, or he could stick two fingers up to the Boche, dive into the Channel and swim for home.

"Bugger it," he exclaimed for the twentieth time that day and threw down the rifle then tore off his belt and let his boots and the rusty paint can drop into the shallows.

Then, half crawling and half swimming, he turned his back on the lights and began to drag himself through the shallow water. He skirted the base of an iron tank trap and felt the sand beneath him drop away, leaving him choking for a moment beneath the salty water. His head re-emerged above the surface and he gulped in a lungful of air before he threw himself forward and began to power through the water with his arms. He scissored his legs up and down and his bare feet kicked against the surf, driving him onwards into the night. He felt the tide take him and he was dragged forwards, away from the beach and the cliff and the slain Germans and out into ever deeper water.

He chanced a glimpse back towards the land and saw that the lights on top of the cliff had multiplied and were swinging their beams to and fro across the beach below. Seconds later, the searchlight on the pillbox kicked back into life and threw its blinding cone of light out into the night sky. It shot across the length of the sand, paused briefly on the three dead infantrymen who lay like a trio of toppled dominos before it flashed across the white cliff face. It then shifted its angle and began to sweep the waters of the bay.

Bloodstone could see the light zipping across the surface towards him and he kicked his legs into the air and catapulted himself downwards. His feet vanished below the waterline just as the beam shot over him and he kept his eyes open as he plunged down into the murky depths. The light moved on and he pushed himself back up, gulped down a mouthful of oxygen and saw that the light had reached the edge of the cove and was coming back for another sweep of the water. Once again, he forced himself down towards the seabed and stayed beneath the surface until the beam skimmed over the water above him and vanished across the bay.

As he emerged, the current caught him once more and he was sucked further out towards the open sea. He let the water carry him along and rolled onto his back so he could look back at the beach, which was now two hundred yards away and disappearing quickly. The cove was a dazzling display of light as the searchlight methodically worked its way backwards and forwards across the sand and up against the walls of the cliffs. More pinpricks of light were visible on the beach itself as armed men shone torches among the rocks and lit up the sea defenses along the shoreline in search of a fugitive. The top of the cliffs seemed to be a hive of activity as lights flickered and flashed and

Bloodstone could just imagine the confusion as officers and NCOs no doubt bellowed angry orders as they tried to work out what had happened and how many enemy troops they were up against.

He smiled smugly at the thought and a wave crashed over his head and filled his mouth with seawater, wiping the grin from his face. As he spat out a mouthful of salt water, he rolled back onto his stomach and began to work his arms and legs, adding his own body power to the tug of the tide that continued to pull him away from the land. The searchlight danced across the water again and again and each time it neared he dived downwards, fearing that he would be caught in the probing finger of light. But somehow, miraculously, his progress went unnoticed and he continued to add distance between himself and the bay.

Before long he was out of the cove and in open water and the swell of the waves increased, battering his face and sending gallon after endless gallon of stinging seawater into his nose and mouth. The waves and the darkness meant that he could see no more than six feet in front of him, so he screwed up his eyes and swam blindly. The current was still pulling him away from the shore and he saw little point in trying to navigate in any particular direction so chose to simply let the water take him where it wanted.

He looked back towards the land, which was fast disappearing in his wake, and saw that the torches continued to flicker on the beach and above the cliffs. The searchlight also continued its probing, but he was out of its range now and the white light danced across an empty sea.

He tried to peer ahead of him but here was nothing out there except a giant expanse of darkness. As another wave crashed over his head, he was hit with the blunt reality of his situation. He was cold, he was drenched and his body was already battered and bruised, yet here he was being washed out to sea in the pitch blackness with absolutely nothing to keep him afloat except the strength of his own aching limbs. He had no possible way of navigating, with the exception of keeping the coast behind him and swimming in the opposite direction, and, to top it off, all he'd had to eat and drink in the past day and a half was a mug of coffee, a handful of scabby nuts and a bucketful of rusty rainwater.

Yet, he'd made his bed and now he must lie in it, albeit it a decidedly soggy bed. So, with no other choice, he banished the aches and pains from his head and focused on his stroke, striking out with his arms and kicking with his legs. To take his mind off the pain and the cold and the water assaulting his nostrils and throat, he began counting in his head.

"One, two, three, four, five..."

At eight hundred he paused his front crawl and allowed himself to roll over and look back towards the coast while he rested his muscles. With the exception of a tiny pinprick that he assumed was the distant searchlight, there was nothing to see except a faint orange glow further along the coast to the north. Calais, he guessed, assuming that the French weren't doing too well with following their blackout regulations. He decided he was far enough from shore to ditch the MP40 and unslung it from his back and let it fall away into the depths of the Channel. The release of the weight made him feel lighter and he noticed the difference as he began to swim again, this time adopting a slow methodical stroke instead of the previous powerful efforts that had helped get him away from the cove but had done nothing for his sapping energy.

At one thousand nine hundred and eighty-two the waistband of his trousers slipped down over his backside and became twisted around his thighs. He paused to attempt to extricate himself from the tangled mess and nearly drowned as he ended up upside down with his legs, complete with pantaloons around his ankles, waggling in the air like an upended duck. He eventually freed himself and kicked away the trousers, which, weighed down by the Luger in the pocket, drifted down to the seabed far below.

At two thousand seven hundred he looked back towards land to find that the coast had vanished entirely and there was nothing to be seen in any direction. Now he really was up against it and entirely alone. He had no idea whatsoever where he was or in which direction he was swimming and he realised that he could just as easily be heading towards the North Sea or even in the direction of the Atlantic.

"Bugger," he said out loud and was instantly rewarded with a mouthful of wave.

At three thousand one hundred and nine he was stung across the face by what he could only assume was a jellyfish. The sting, which had zapped him over the bridge of his nose and across both cheeks hurt like hell and he would've laughed out loud at the battering his body had taken over the last forty eight hours if he wasn't so bloody miserable.

At six thousand, eight hundred and sixty-eight the moon emerged from behind the clouds and bathed the ocean in an eerie white glow. The sea was calmer now, almost like a giant endless lake and Bloodstone celebrated the arrival of the moon by rolling onto his back and allowing himself to float face-up for a minute, letting his tortured limbs have sixty seconds of blissful rest.

As he lay staring up at the sky, the twinkle of stars began to emerge from between the dark clouds. He gave himself permission for another sixty seconds of lying on his back and, by the time he was ready to get moving again, the moonlit sky was a dazzling display of thousands of glittering stars. Among them was the Big Dipper and Bloodstone smiled as he recalled the booming words of his Grandpa Horatio, so long ago that it seemed another lifetime.

"If you're ever dimwitted enough to get lost at sea, boy, find the North Star and you'll be home before you can say shiver my timbers."

Remembering the lesson, he traced an imaginary line from the ladle of the Big Dipper and spotted what he assumed was the North Star, shining bright and proud high in the sky. He then pictured a map of the Dover-to-Calais strait and reckoned that heading north-west from where he had entered the water should bring him to somewhere in the vicinity of the British coast. So, as long as he continued to keep the North Star above him to the right, he couldn't go wrong. Unless of course he already had gone wrong, in which case he'd probably find himself washed up on the coast of Holland.

He gave himself one last blissful sixty seconds of floating and then rolled back onto his stomach and began to swim once more, peering out of the corner of a bloodshot and salt-caked eye to make sure that the glinting star stayed high above his right shoulder, just where it should be.

CHAPTER SIXTY-NINE

At nine thousand nine hundred and three, Bloodstone vomited. There was nothing in his stomach except for a bellyful of saltwater and a few beech nuts and the rancid concoction jettisoned from his gullet mid-stroke. It stuck to his face for a second before it was washed away and drifted astern to be food for the fishes. His stomach contracted again and tried to heave but there was nothing to bring up and he simply gagged, just in time for a mouthful of seawater to wash into his spew-filled mouth and nearly choke him.

Somewhere after fifteen thousand he lost count and his befuddled mind had no desire to start again from zero. Instead, he began to think about Rosie Bell and tried to picture every last detail of the buxom redhead. He remembered Bill had claimed that the pretty WAAF had a twin sister and, although he highly doubted that it was true, he enjoyed himself for a few hundred yards by picturing every imaginable detail of her too.

He was halfway down the sister's sumptuous legs when the sound of an engine tore him from his daydreams. He stopped swimming and let his feet drop below him as he trod water and glanced around for the source of the noise. Despite the moonlight that still threw its white light across the surface, there was nothing to be seen. The noise increased and he twisted his neck around, first one way then the other, but to no avail. Was he imagining things, he wondered, as he forced his stinging ears to listen out over the lapping of the water? The sound increased, growing to a throaty roar, yet still there was nothing to be seen.

A second later the roar magnified to ear-splitting proportions and a dark shadow zoomed towards him, making him involuntarily duck his head under the water. He emerged just in time to see the silhouette of a pair of wings pass over him, not fifty feet above the surface, and as he peered at the vanishing shadow he saw that they were round wings. A Spitfire! He shouted and he hollered and he waved his aching arms above his head but it was to no avail and the aircraft disappeared into the night, taking its growling Merlins with it and leaving the ocean once again silent, empty and enormous.

The envy he felt for the pilot, warm and dry and seemingly heading for home, was immense but he refused to feel sorry for himself and, instead, floated back onto his belly and struck out again with his arms and legs with a renewed vigour. He had no idea how far he'd come or how far he still had to go, but he'd be damned if he was going to give up now. After all, he had a belated date with a beautiful redhead to get to and no amount of seawater, jellyfish or burning muscles was going to get in the way of that.

His powerful strokes couldn't last forever, however, and it wasn't long before his limbs began to tire and niggles of cramp began to seep into his muscles. His arms and legs felt as if they were weighed down with lead and his right hand had swollen to almost double its usual size. The army issue woollen underpants chafed at his groin with every kick and his lacerated thighs and stomach had long ago shed their bandages and were a burning, stinging, fizzing agony.

He kicked himself over onto his back and let his arms rest as he paddled with his feet. For the first time he noticed that one of his big toes was missing its nail and realised it must have been ripped off on the cliff face, yet he found it somewhat odd that he was only just noticing now. As he stared at the offending toe something beyond, far

432

away in the distance, caught his eye. It was a faint orange glow, tiny and way down on the horizon and he cursed as he remembered the lights of Calais. Had he spent all this effort just to swim around in circles off the coast of France?

He laid his head back in the water in exhausted resignation and stared up at the sky, almost tempted to give in and let himself be swallowed up by the ocean. But something in the sky wasn't right. Where were the stars? Why was the moon fading? And why was the world changing from an eerie white to a rust-tinged darkness? The answer hit him like a shot in the arm, for it wasn't the blackout-breaking lights of Calais that were bobbing up and down behind his feet at all; it was the first awakenings of dawn.

As he watched, the tiny orange glow stretched its way across the horizon and began to climb upwards, transforming the dark of the night sky into a rich deep blue that dimmed the moon and replaced it with the warm glowing sun of a perfect autumn morning. The sea, still as calm as a mountain lake, took on a new hue yet Bloodstone, still floating on his back and watching the sun inch into the sky, felt terribly small and a long way from home.

Sighing miserably, he twisted back onto his stomach and forced his throbbing arms and legs to start working again. Slowly, he began moving through the water and looked backwards to make sure he had the sunrise behind and just to the right of his kicking feet. Satisfied with the direction in which he was heading, he turned back to the fore and closed his eyes as his exhausted stroke submerged his stinging face for what felt like the millionth time. He came up for air and glanced ahead over the glass-like surface of the water, expecting to see the ever-depressing sight of nothing but sea stretching out for as far as the eye could see.

But this time there was something else, something other than endless water all the way to the edge of the world. That something was white and it was rocky and it was glorious and, despite the fact that it was little more than a blob on the horizon, Bloodstone yelled out in triumph. Because it was the same white cliffs that he'd seen from France yesterday morning. *The* White Cliffs, yet this time they were bigger and whiter and a whole lot closer.

He shouted out again and got a bellyful of seawater, but he didn't care. He'd done it, he was almost there, so very nearly home. Finding strength that he didn't know he had, he thrashed his arms forwards and kicked his legs, driving himself onwards towards Blighty as fast as his battered body would allow.

A bolt of cramp tore through his right leg but he ignored it and kicked harder as he powered towards the cliffs that rose out of the sea no more than two miles distant. The muscle of his left bicep pulled and threatened to snap, but he banished the pain from his brain and drove his arms even faster. A bucketful of saltwater forced its way into his mouth and down into his lungs and he choked and spat as he tried to force it from his body. Another dose of seawater followed, filling his nose and clogging his throat, yet still he ignored it as the cliffs came closer.

They were so close now and he ignored the voice in his head that was telling him to slow down. Why should he? Why would he stop now? A few more strokes and he'd almost be able to touch them. He threw his arms forward again, but they refused to work and flopped onto the surface of the water. He kicked his legs frantically, but they too refused to obey and dangled down towards the seabed, limp and useless and pathetic. His mouth took in another draught of choking, stinging seawater and he sank below the surface as his exhausted brain tried to force his failing body into action.

He thrust his head out of the water, desperately trying to gulp down a lungful of air, and he caught another glimpse of the distant cliffs. So close, he thought, before his head went under again. He summoned every last ounce of strength to keep his body from sinking but it was no good, there was just nothing left. His vision blurred, cleared for a second and then blurred again. Somewhere in his head were voices. German voices, he thought. He flapped at his thigh for the Luger in his pocket and then remembered that the weapon, along with the trousers, had gone a long time ago.

Somehow, he forced his head above the surface one last time and a great grey shadow filled his clouded vision. He blinked, trying to clear the blurriness from his eyes, but his brain was starting to shut down. He blinked again and this time the vision cleared, yet the shadow was still there. He squinted upwards and the shadow faded, replaced by a face.

A bearded face with rosy wind-bashed cheeks and a mouthful of crooked teeth. The mouth smiled a cheery smile.

"Allo guvnor. Need a ride?"

EPILOGUE

A flurry of snow fell against the windowpane and the distant
sound of Christmas carols could be heard on the chilly
evening air. A log crackled in the fire and a flurry of sparks
leapt out onto the hearth rug, narrowly missing a crumpled khaki shirt
and a pair of impressively shiny black boots that lay strewn in front of
the fireplace. A quarter-full bottle of Scotch stood on the mantelpiece,
alongside two empty Christmas stockings and a half-eaten mince pie.

"Bertie, may I read this to you one more time?"

Bloodstone smiled and blew a smoke ring towards the ceiling.

"If you must, darling."

She giggled, sat up against the headboard and folded the
newspaper onto her lap. As she did so, the blanket slipped down to
reveal a pair of the most wonderful bosoms that Bloodstone had ever
seen. She giggled again, tucked a strand of hair behind her ear and
cleared her throat.

"On October 10th, 1943, Major Albert Beaumont Fortescue
Bloodstone, DSO, DSC and MC with bar, was aboard an RAF
Lancaster in an observational capacity..."

Bloodstone guffawed. "Observational capacity, ha!"

"Shhh," she admonished, "I'm reading."

She straightened the newspaper and continued.

"...was aboard an RAF Lancaster in an *observational capacity* during a mission to attack the railway yards in the German town of Freiburg, deep in the enemy Reich.

"The aircraft had suffered severe damage, including the loss of three engines, and had already lost two crew members killed when it came under sustained attack from anti-aircraft fire. The assault caused significant further damage to the Lancaster and severely wounded the radio operator, who was blown from the aircraft at a height of fifteen thousand feet.

"Major Bloodstone recognised that the wireless operator was too badly injured to open a parachute and, with no concern for his own well-being and displaying extraordinary bravery of the highest level, leapt from the aircraft without a parachute in pursuit of his wounded crew-mate."

She turned to look at him, shook her head in mock astonishment and carried on reading.

"Falling through the sky at tremendous speed, Major Bloodstone was able to reach the wounded airman mid-air and activate the parachute, which brought them both safely to earth. Unfortunately, despite the Major's best efforts, the wireless operator subsequently died from his wounds."

Bloodstone grimaced as he recalled Nobby's mangled body lying on the pine needles and, not for the first time, he marvelled that Przybylowski had apparently spotted the whole crazy exit from his seat in the cockpit. He glanced up at the stockings on the mantlepiece and smiled in the knowledge that the Count, Ashton and Bill were safely out of harm's way and no doubt preparing for a very different type of Christmas in their Swiss internment camp.

He was snapped out of his daydreaming by a gentle slap on his scarred thigh.

"Are you listening to me?"

"Sorry, darling."

She tutted, pushed the rogue strand of hair behind her ear once again and resumed her reading.

"Major Bloodstone then made contact with the French Resistance and proceeded to journey undercover through occupied France, dressed in the uniform of an enemy colonel. Again, showing little regard for his own well-being and acting entirely independently, he undertook numerous attacks on enemy troops and was able to cause significant casualties, including the elimination of two senior Nazi officers.

"Finally, leaving a trail of destruction in his wake and monopolising considerable enemy resources, Major Bloodstone proceeded to swim unaided and at night across the English Channel and was picked up just two miles from the English coast by a Royal Navy patrol boat."

Bloodstone shook his own head this time, remembering the utterly miserable night that he'd spent in the water and still astonished that he'd made it as far as he did. He shivered and pushed the thought from his head as she continued.

"In recognition of Major Bloodstone's complete disregard for his own safety, an extraordinary devotion to duty and unprecedented valour in the face of the enemy, His Majesty the King has been graciously pleased to approve the award of the Victoria Cross."

She whistled, threw down the newspaper and picked up a black leather box that lay on the bedsheet beside her. She opened the lid and lifted a crimson ribbon into the air, under which hung a small bronze cross.

"Look at it, Bertie," she insisted, "That's yours, the bloody Victoria Cross!"

He grudgingly tore his gaze from her glorious bosoms and looked at the medal that she dangled between her fingers. She was right, it was his and nobody could take that away from him, but what a damned painful experience it had been to win it. But, he admitted as he recalled the final panicked look on Otto Heidler's face, it had all been more than worthwhile.

She laid the medal back in the box, handed Bloodstone a glass of Scotch and turned to face him.

"I know you've had a long day, Bertie, what with the visit to the palace and tea with His Majesty, and I know it's Christmas Day tomorrow, but would you be awfully offended if I gave you your Christmas present a day early?"

Bloodstone looked at her with a raised eyebrow and took a sip of his whisky. He might be able to leap from aircraft without parachutes, take on half of the German army single-handedly and swim the Channel in his underpants, but he was powerless to refuse a request from the half-naked bombshellian creature at his side.

"If you insist," he said wearily, putting the glass on the bedside table.

She giggled, coughed once and the door opened.

"Bertie," Rosie smiled, "I'd like you to meet my sister."